A
Mark
on
my Soul

JORDON GREENE

FRANKLIN/KERR

CONCORD, NORTH CAROLINA

Published by Franklin/Kerr Press, LLC
349-L Copperfield Boulevard #502 | Concord, North Carolina 28025
1.704.659.3915 | info@franklinkerr.com
www.FranklinKerr.com

For information about special discounts available for bulk purchases, sales pro-motions, fund-raising and educational needs, contact Franklin/Kerr Press Sales at 704-659-3915 or sales@franklinkerr.com.

Edited by Christie Stratos
Cover Image © 2019 Robert Webb
Cover Art & Interior design by Jordon Greene

Printed in the United States of America

FIRST EDITION

ISBN-13: 978-0-9983913-8-0
ISBN-10: 0-9983913-8-7

Library of Congress Control Number: 2018915130

Fiction: Young Adult Contemporary
Fiction: Coming-of-Age
Fiction: LGBT/Gay

To Melanie Rowe
for helping me finally be me.

And to those who feel like giving up
We're here for you. We need you. We love you.

ACKNOWLEDGMENTS

There are so many who have helped bring this book to fruition. It's truly impossible for me to thank everyone, but I'm at least going to give it a try.

Thanks so much to my friends Sandra Farley, LeAnn Dupree, Haley Greer, David Kummer, Ali Smith and Heather Lovins for helping me put the idea into a understandable story, find quotes and let me run ideas past them. Thanks to Tatum Atwood, Alexandria Sexton, Kevin Hagan and Austen Workman for taking the first looks into the finished manuscript and helping sculpt the story into something more refined. Thanks to Michael Edwards for some of the jokes. Unfortunately I'm not that funny, so that helped a lot.

I can't thank my editor, Christie Stratos, enough. Everyone thinks writers just write well (or decent) on their own, but it's really the keen eye of an editor that makes it readable, we just have the idea. Also, I am so thrilled to have had Robert Webb do a custom painting for the book's cover. I love it!

But most of all, I have to thank my Editions family for all your constant support! Thanks to Dawn, Tina, Elana, Leigh, Abigail, Lauryn, Grace, Beryl and Gavin. Each of you had a hand in literally every aspect of writing this story, but especially in providing me with moral support along the way. You all are the MVPs in my book.

Friday
August 31, 2018

I'm gay.

No, that's too blunt. I hit Delete and groan. The cursor blinks at me like a ticking bomb. I reposition my head on my pillow and stare at my phone. This shouldn't be so hard.

I try again.

I have a secret…

No. I stop before finishing the thought. That's way too typical. It sounds like a line from some cheesy movie.

I have a huge fucking secret. I'm gay.

Not that different, but dammit, is that too much? Maybe. I don't know. This is crazy. I shouldn't even have to do this. I mean, if I'm gay, I'm gay, right? It shouldn't be a big deal. But of course it is, otherwise I'd have done this years ago.

I let the words hang under the Facebook logo for a solid minute with my finger hovering over the Share button. My pulse is racing. I swear it pumps twice between each cursor blink. My fingers are shaking; hell, my whole body is.

I want to post it so bad. I need to post it. I need to kill this secret and be done with it.

Hold on a second. Maybe I should post a picture with it? Supposedly posts with pictures do better anyway, and that's the point, right? I want everyone to know so I only have to say it once. I don't want to have to say it again. I know it sounds bad, maybe a little weak, but it's not easy.

But I know that's not how it's going to work. Plastering it on Facebook isn't going to save me from having to say those dreaded words again and again.

Then there'll be people asking about the girls I dated. But it's what boys are "supposed" to do, it's "normal," and according to my mom, apparently it was cute when I hugged Amanda in first grade and she slapped me. Maybe that's why I'm gay—getting bitch slapped in first grade must do something to a boy's psyche, right?

I'm being stupid, of course not.

It's just who I am.

It wasn't until seventh grade that I realized it. I just wasn't interested in the same things my guy friends were. All the "hot" female pop stars and actresses, and yeah, the porn. I was more interested in watching anything with Chris Hemsworth in it, from his all-too brief appearance in *Star Trek* to *Thor*, definitely *Thor*, or scrolling through Andy Black's Instagram feed. Oh, and don't forget Spider-Man and that skin-tight suit.

For the longest time I wrote it off as a totally normal puberty thing, just a little confusion. The problem was that the "confusion" never ended. I guess I really knew when I developed a crush on my best friend, Parker. That lasted for years, but he's straight, like every other boy I know. Well, not every boy. I do have a gay cousin, and there are the two guys at school, but I don't know them. I've made a habit of avoiding them. I don't need people putting two and two together, and hanging with them would be a sure-fire way of making that happen. I also think there might be a few lesbians, but that's not the same. Somehow it's *hot* if two girls kiss, just not two guys. Yeah, it's messed up.

Dammit, it should be easy to come out. I mean, Mom and Dad aren't a problem. I'm not worried they'll disown me or tell me some crap like I'm going to hell or take away my stuff. I'm just afraid they'll look at me differently. I don't know, like I'll be their gay son Noah instead of just Noah. I just want to be Noah Andrews, the simple, slightly nerdy, socially awkward guy, minus the big-ass secret.

Sitting here with the status blaring on my screen, I know inside that I should tell my parents before I blurt it out to the whole world. They deserve to hear it first, but that seems harder, especially my dad. He's not a homophobe, I just feel like he expects me to be "normal." I mean, my older brother, Zach, is. I feel like telling him I'm gay would be a blow, a loss somehow.

I shift my finger to the left and discard the status. Yeah, I can't do it—again. I force the air from my lungs and cave my chest in defeat. I grind my teeth, but my heartbeat slows. That's at least the tenth time this week I've *almost* come out to the world, not even counting the times I've tried over the past two months.

Honestly, though, I bet a lot of people wouldn't believe me anyway. I might have taken Lemony Snicket's advice a little too seriously. The whole "To keep a secret, tell it to everyone you know, but pretend you are kidding" line. Yeah, that's me.

It's worked well. The upside is that I could admit I was gay without actually admitting it. I can't even remember all the gay jokes Parker, my brother, *and* my dad have told over the last few years. What they don't realize is that I'm the unintended butt end of each one. I just go along with it nowadays, and it's always best with Parker. He squirms so bad when I do it. It's probably why he doesn't tell them anymore.

The sad part is they don't realize I'm crying out, admitting a dark secret, begging to be free under a veil of thinly masked humor. It works, but it sucks.

I'm so ready to finally be out. I'm really ready, like really. But I'm so fucking nervous about *actually* being out. I'm afraid I'll only trade the burden I know how to bear with another I don't.

On one hand I'm tired of watching all the girls hold their boyfriends' hands or kiss in the halls at school and thinking I'm never going to have that. And on the other hand, I'm scared to admit who I am to the world.

But if I don't do something I'm going to grow up to be that lonely, bald, and nerdy, closeted thirty-year-old who's still too scared and pathetic to be himself. I don't want to be that guy. I don't want to look back with regrets, not for what I did, but what I didn't do.

Maybe I can tell Camila first instead. We've been inseparable since kindergarten. She's my partner in crime, my hard rock diva (with a little R&B thrown in for good measure), my confidante. I tell her everything. Everything except this. At least, I haven't yet.

Maybe that should be the plan.

I check the time on my phone. It's 6:57 a.m. That gives me eighteen minutes to get ready and out the door for school. I drop my phone on the bed and throw my feet over the side. My room is simple and small. It's barely big enough to house the bed set in the corner, the television propped up on a runt of a table that holds my PlayStation and a few Blu-rays, and the messy, cramped metal desk next to the closet.

There's just enough room to walk between it all.

I pick a shirt off the floor and sniff it. It's clean—a little wrinkled but clean. I slip it on and choose a pair of tan shorts from my dresser, then head off to the hallway with my backpack slung over my shoulder.

In the kitchen my mom is hovering over the sink, cleaning last night's dishes. We had her homemade lasagna last night. She doesn't cook often, but she does lasagna right. She hears me enter as I find Dad sitting at our small, four-person dining room table, a half-eaten waffle covered generously in silky brown syrup on his plate.

"Morning, sleepy head," Mom says without turning.

"Morning," I say and head for the island counter in the middle of the kitchen where a plate of fresh waffles sits. "These for me?"

"Yes." She turns around and gives me a smile. I have the prettiest mom. Her long dark-brown hair is up in a ball and her bangs hang above bright-green eyes. "Are you actually going to have breakfast with us?"

I squint and pluck one of the waffles from the plate.

"Not really," I say.

"Come on, Noah," Dad says.

I step back and look at him. My friends say he looks like Vince Vaughn, the actor, but I don't see it. Sure, he's sort of tall. I think he's like an inch over six feet. But even with his receding hairline and brown eyes, I still don't get it. Just like I don't see how I'm ever going to admit to him that I'm a faggot. Okay, I probably won't phrase it like that, but yeah.

"Can't be late," I tell him.

"You mean you want to be early?" Dad smiles. "You do realize the girls will still be there all day, right?"

"Haha," I laugh with as much sarcasm as I can muster. "I'll keep that in mind."

That's my cue to leave. I turn and make for the door.

"Don't forget to bring me home a latte tonight," Mom yells after me as my feet touch our tiny front deck.

"Got it!" I yell back.

* * *

Ten minutes later I'm sitting in the school parking lot, leaning back in the driver's seat of my car and discreetly bobbing my head to a tune from Imminence. I check my watch. It's 7:34 a.m. Parker's running behind, or early, depending on how you look at it; sure we still have another twenty minutes before classes start, but I hate being late. I'm sticking with late.

The lot is filling up. It's one of those places that's a nightmare to navigate if you don't arrive early. Yet another reason to get here well before school starts.

I ignore most of the kids walking past my car, except the few I actually know, like Cam's friend, Macy, who walked by a few minutes ago with Stephanie, and of course I couldn't help but notice Jacob Walters' stark white hair. It's dyed and looks like something from the fifties, but damn it if doesn't look good on him. I even like the small gauges in his ears and his pale skin, though that's not normally my thing. And inevitably I fail at not noticing his tight black pants, part of his rocker vibe.

Most of the remaining spaces are at the end of the lot, and they're filling up fast. Parker is going to have fun finding a decent spot if he doesn't hurry.

He doesn't know it, but he was my first real crush. He was the new kid, a transfer during seventh grade. He was so cute — still is actually — but that's not the point. I really wanted to be around him. Something inside me was obsessed with him, so I did everything I could to talk to him, and I'm not the talking type.

It didn't take long to realize he'd never feel the same, so I buried it, but by then we were already friends. He'd become the third point in Cam and my friendship triangle, and you just don't break those things, so I pushed through. It sucked at first, like really sucked, but I did it and I'm glad. He's a great friend, the best. Of course, I'll never tell Cam that.

I'm about to check the time again when Park's massive gunmetal gray pickup barges into the parking lot. He drives down two aisles before finding a spot about fifty yards farther from the school than where I sit. I let him park and give him a head start before taking off across the lot to intercept him.

"Park," I yell.

He finds me and stops to let me catch up just before we cross the road and pass the school's billboard announcing *A.L. BROWN HIGH SCHOOL*.

"You're a little behind," I tell him.

"Just a little," he says. He knows better than to claim otherwise, even if it would technically be true. "How you doing?"

"Good," I lie as usual. Well, it's a lie if you count my secret, otherwise it's not. "We're supposed to discuss *Lord of the Flies* in English today, and of course I haven't read any of it yet."

"What the hell, man?" Parker squints. "You love to read.

Why do you not read the shit you're supposed to for class? I mean, I at least have a reason."

"I don't know." I shrug as we walk through a set of double metal doors. I put on a sly grin. "I just don't. It's not as fun if it's not my own choice, I guess. Plus, I did read a chapter-by-chapter synopsis of the book online, so I'm ready."

He laughs and punches me playfully on the shoulder.

"You're something else, man, you know that, right?"

I don't answer.

* * *

I don't think Camila's lips have stopped moving since she ran me down in the hallway after weight class. Yeah, I'm taking weight class.

It was interesting trying to sell that decision to Parker and Cam when we were debating our senior year class schedules. It's not exactly a typical Noah move to make. I'm not a twig, but I can't claim bodybuilder status either. If I'm honest, I'm not even what anyone might call fit. Maybe athletic...maybe. I don't have any of the cool chiseled lines in my chest, and flexing my biceps is more embarrassing than impressive. Slim is perfectly fine with me though.

I remember Camila telling me it was a waste of a perfectly good credit. She asked why I'd want to get all sweaty and worn out with a bunch of guys in the middle of school. Internally I beamed at that very thought. Parker was content at taking the gay joke route. It was another one of those times I took Lemony Snicket's advice to heart and just went with it. I even told them how I just wanted to "spend more quality time with Mateo." The funny part is that the joke was really on Parker because it was true.

"Did you see Macy's new car?" Cam asks as we grab a place in the lunch line.

"No," I say and swivel back to catch her eyes. I know Macy, but we're not that close. "She got a new car?"

I try to sound interested, and I guess I am, but my mind is going in circles. I'm drowning in how I could manage to come out to Cam before Parker gets down here. I don't want him here when I do it.

"Yeah, her parents told her if she saved up enough to pay half the down payment they'd put down the other half."

Damn. It must be nice having rich parents.

I hand a few dollars to the tiny old lunch lady at the register and grab my change before turning and waiting on Camila.

"What'd she get?" I ask. I bet it's something crazy.

"A new Camaro," Cam says. She looks at me oddly. "Are you okay, Noah?"

"Huh? Yeah, I'm good." I stumble at first, but I rebound. I keep my mouth moving, saying the next stupid thing that comes to mind. "That's it? She didn't get a Beemer or something?"

"Really? She still has to help make half the payment." Camila drops her tray on our table, the same table we claimed two weeks ago when school started.

"Okay, yeah, that makes sense." It really does, but being able to breathe normally and tell Cam I'm gay should make sense too, but it's not reality.

My lungs are growing heavy and my voice is shaking, and I haven't even spoken the words yet. There are so many people in here. What if one of them hears me? What if they decide the whole school needs to know? No, I can't have that. Not yet.

"I finished my application for Stanford last night," Camila says. Her brown eyes are beaming, and her chocolate skin is radiant. I'm surprised she's held back telling me this long, honestly, and for a moment my nerves don't seem to rattle my brain.

I want all three of us to go to the same college, but that's just a pipe dream. All of our top picks are different. Cam wants to go to Stanford, Park wants to go to Michigan, and I want to go to Illinois. We each have our compromise school, but who really wants to go to their compromise school?

"That's great!" I tell her and take a quick glance around for Parker. If I hurry I might still be able to tell her. "Did you do the early action app or the regular app?"

I kick myself mentally. All I had to say was, *Hey, Cam, I need to tell you something. I'm gay.* Then it would be over and done with, but no, I keep her talking about college applications instead.

"Early action," she says. "I want so bad to go to Stanford. Their astrophysics program is top notch. But that application, damn was it long! And it cost ninety bucks just to apply, just for a chance to get in. Did I tell you about my essay?"

Yeah, she's a geek. Well, we're all geeks really, but she's the geekiest. Geek of geeks. I mean, really, astrophysics?

"Cam," I start, intentionally and unintentionally at the same time ignoring her question. I take a quick breath to brace myself. I'm about to do this. My hands tense up and it's suddenly hot in here. I swear everyone is looking at me. I shake my head and open my mouth anyway. "I—"

"Hey, guys!" Parker slaps his tray on the table.

Fuck! My whole body seizes up. Really? You couldn't have been two minutes later? Just two fucking minutes, that's all I needed. Not to mention quieter. I sigh and let the pressure in my chest subside. That's a good thing, right? I'm definitely not getting my secret off my chest now. *Just calm down, Noah.*

"Hey, Parker." I throw my fist up and he gives it a bump. We're nerds, we have to do something that looks remotely cool, so a fist bump it is.

"You nearly scared the shit out of Noah." Camila grins at Parker.

I don't know why, but it always seems weird hearing her cuss. It's like hearing the little sister I never had say a dirty word. It shouldn't matter, it doesn't. It's not like she's a stranger to the potty mouth.

"What are you hiding, Noah?" Parker grins and stuffs a spoonful of below par applesauce in his mouth.

"Hiding? Huh?" I can imagine the guilt on my face, but I don't want to.

"Yeah, you've been awful quiet and nervous all day." Cam leans over the table, setting her elbows parallel with her tray.

"No," I say. Am I really that obvious? I search for something to say, anything. Hell will have to freeze over before *this* is how I come out of the closet. It's not happening. "I was just mesmerized by all the details of your college app."

"Oh burn," Parker hisses.

I want to crawl inside myself. It was stupid, and it sounded a lot worse than I'd intended, not to mention stupid.

"That came off a lot meaner than I meant it to," I say and

give Camila my best puppy dog eyes. "I promise I wasn't trying to be mean."

"How could you?" she asks. Her eyes are hurt, but I can see the mischief hiding behind them.

I raise my brow and smile. She's bluffing.

"You know I love you, Cam," I say.

"You're still a douchebag." She smirks and shakes her head. "But you're my douchebag, and no one else's. So I forgive you."

"I'm pretty sure he's my douchebag too," Parker says.

"Well first, I'm not a douchebag, and two, Parker? Really?" I laugh.

"What? What's wrong with that?" Park asks.

"It does sound a little odd." Camila winks at me.

I shake my head and decide I should have just kept my mouth shut, but no, that wouldn't have been like me. I never know what to say, and when I do speak, half the time it becomes a foot-in-mouth moment.

"So, did I miss anything else?" Parker moves on.

"Not really, just that Cam's trying to leave us and run off to Stanford after graduation while we're stuck in Charlotte probably."

I'm hoping for the best. I doubt I'll have much trouble getting into State, and I know I can make it into UNC Charlotte. Illinois and Boston are not as certain. Parker will probably get acceptance letters in March or April to every school he applies to, and he's planning to apply to Yale, UC Berkley, the University of Michigan at Ann Arbor, NC State, and UNC, both Chapel Hill and Charlotte.

"Speaking of traitors, I hope you two enjoy the Comicon on Sunday without me." Park's cuter than normal when he's aggravated. He tends to purse his lips like he's doing now. "I'll be stuck at home. Thank God there are no football games on, otherwise I'd probably be forced to watch that. I had to watch the Cowboys and Texans game last night with Dad. Ugh!"

"Don't blame us. We didn't tell you to scream *fuck* in front of your parents," Cam reminds him.

It wasn't his best moment. From what Parker admitted to, he's grounded for two weeks, effective this past Tuesday, for yelling fuck in earshot of his dad and then trying to claim he didn't. It happened because he stubbed his toe on the big wooden coffee table in their family room. I know the exact one, and yes, I've stubbed my toe on it more than a few times. Of course, I didn't blurt one of their least favorite words though. I doubt I would've been invited back if I had.

"I didn't scream it," Parker tries. "Well, okay, sort of. I still can't believe I did that. I'm usually so careful."

"It was bound to happen eventually," I tell him. It was inevitable, but it's worse when it happens in Parker's house. His family is so strict, very religious. He's not even allowed to read certain "bad" books at school technically. Technically.

"You still sticking to the plan?" Park asks.

"Yeah," I tell him. We'd agreed weeks ago on our costumes. Yes, we cosplay. I usually like to go as some comic character or someone from a movie, but this time we decided to go as video game characters. Parker *was* going to be dressing up as the kick-ass Altaïr Ibn-La'Ahad from Assassin's Creed. I'm *still* dressing up as Commander Shepard from Mass Effect. "Still going as Shepard."

"Good," Parker says. "I wouldn't want you pussying out on me just 'cause I can't make it. What about you, Cam? You never said what you're going as."

"Not telling yet," she says, still stalwart in not joining our little cosplay deal. "You'll have to wait and find out Sunday. I'll send you a pic, Park."

"Oh, the suspense," he jabs at her.

We've been trying to get it out of her for the past two weeks. It's not going well, obviously. I guess we'll see this weekend though. Of course, I'll see in person, and Parker in digital.

Speaking of secrets, it looks like I'll be holding on to mine a little longer.

* * *

"Why is it so damn hard?" I ask the steering wheel. There's no one else to ask. It's just me, a dangerously close to full parking lot behind Editions, and my self-loathing.

I let my forehead fall to the wheel and a faint groan slips between my lips. Why *is* it so hard? It's just two simple words. All I had to do was say two little words to Cam and it would have been over. That's it.

But it feels more complicated than that. After I say it, like some unforgivable insult I can't take back, I know there will be questions. But would they be good ones? Maybe she'd ask how long I've known and if I like to wear girl clothes. I could answer those easily, and the answer to numero dos, by the way, is a resounding *no*. I'm not *that* gay, no offense meant to anyone who is—it's just not me. Or maybe she'd ask who I like? That's an easy one too. Mateo Portillo.

It might sound like he's a character out of some poorly acted short film, but I promise he isn't. He goes to A.L.

Brown too, he's in my grade, and we both have weight class, the last of which is not exactly a coincidence. Oh, and he's one of the local pizza delivery boys. I tend to order pizza a lot. I can't count the number of times I've given my dad hell for giving Mateo, and only Mateo, a tip I didn't deem enough. It's hard rationalizing that one.

He's gorgeous. His skin is this creamy light brown, like a perfect tan, and his eyes are a deep mesmerizing brown. How was it that Camila described them our freshman year? Cognac, that's it, cognac brown. And his hair—he's got the softest looking black hair. Yes, softest *looking*, I've never touched it, I promise. Plus, he's just enough athlete, just enough nerd to balance out his looks and personality. And when he speaks in Spanish it makes my day. Sure, I don't have a clue what he's saying, but that doesn't really matter.

But what if Cam asks something harder, like why I didn't come out earlier? *Well, you see, Cam, I'm a pathetic loser and it took me over six years to say two little words.* I feel utterly stupid every time I think about it. I know they'll change everything, but they're still just words, and it is the twenty-first century, not the dark ages. That doesn't seem to matter though. I'm still afraid that Cam and every other person in the world will start seeing me differently even though I'm still just me.

I lift my head from the steering wheel and peer past the windshield at the coffee shop—well, bookstore and coffee shop, to be exact. It's one of the old mill-houses left over from when Kannapolis and the surrounding areas were dominated by a textile mill. It's a simple but cozy little white house with a covered burnt-orange ramp leading up to the entrance, and it's only like a mile from school. It's also my favorite place. It's one of those few spots I can get away to and simply relax. Plus, there are books and coffee. It doesn't get much better than that.

I take a deep breath and inspect my face for stray tears. Yes, I was crying. I'm *that* pathetic. But I'm going to relax now, which means I'm going to do what I always do at the shop: pick up a good thriller and have some coffee.

Satisfied I don't look like a little bitch, I get out of the car and head inside. The moment I walk through the door and the tiny bell gently announces my entry I feel refreshed. The aroma of coffee beans blending with the scent of old books acts like an opiate for my on-edge nerves.

"Hey, Noah!" L.A.'s tiny voice is excited, and I can see the same in her green eyes.

"Hey, L.A." I say. Well, I'm nervous again.

I think L.A. goes to Concord High, which is why I don't know her that well. Actually, I don't even know her real name. I think I might have heard Sandra call her Leigh or Lisa. I don't remember though. What I do know, or at least I'm pretty sure about, is that she has a crush on me.

At least that's what it feels like. It's uncomfortable. I'm not saying she's pushy or weird or anything, but it's obvious and well, I think it's equally obvious I don't exactly have a thing for her. I was really hoping Camila's friend, Macy, was working today so I could avoid this, but that hope was dashed the moment I drove into the parking lot and a new Camaro wasn't sitting out back.

"What can I get you?" she asks, but I'm already turning left down the hall and bypassing the bar.

I have to get a new book first. There's no sense in paying for coffee and a book separately.

"I'll be right back," I tell her, glad to at least dodge talking to her for a few minutes.

I'm about to reach the thriller section when Sandra pops into the hallway and greets me, which I wasn't expecting. My feet leave the wooden floor and a stilted scream shoots from my mouth.

"It never gets old," Sandra laughs, one hand grasping the doorframe.

I shake my head and grin. It's one of those little joys that Sandra takes full advantage of. I'm easy to scare. I actually don't mind it either, it's something I'm used to after this long, plus she's awesome, so it sort of balances itself out.

Sandra Farley is the shop owner. She's a pretty lady with greenish-brown eyes, olive skin, and almost black curly hair that does whatever the hell it wants instead of what I *think* she tries to make it do. I believe she's in her early forties, maybe late thirties, but I've never made the mistake of asking. I don't think she'd mind, but I'm not risking it.

Once my heart stops racing and I resume my previous level of tension, I finally manage to put words together.

"How you doing?" I ask.

"Well," she says. She tips the left edge of her lip upward and squints. I'm not sure what that means, but she keeps talking. "How about you?"

"Good." That's when it all comes flooding back. I almost wish she'd scare me again. For a brief moment I wasn't worried about all the drama going on in my head. I was focused on being here and looking for a book. I was thinking about the frappe I'm planning to get and avoiding L.A. It was simple and peaceful, unlike my real life.

"That's good," she says when I don't elaborate. "So, are we looking for something new to read?"

"Yep," I tell her, but I already know what I want. "I'm looking for James Rollins's *The 6th Extinction*. I finished *The Eye of God* last night."

It's taken me a solid five months, but I've finished the first nine Sigma Force books. I like to finish series once I start them—it's a thing. I would have finished it quicker, but I've been a lot more anxious lately and it's made it hard to concentrate.

"Well..." Sandra chews on her lip and looks past me at the shelves. "I bet I have that one. I've got most of Rollins's books."

I follow her a few feet down the hall and she starts running her fingers across a row of books along the top ledge. It doesn't take her long to grab one and hold it out to me.

"Ta-da."

"Thanks." I take the paperback. I'd usually talk a little, but right now I just want to get lost in this book so I don't have to think about anything else. "That's the one."

I turn around and head for the counter. I forget that L.A.'s behind the bar until the register comes into view past the clear pastry box and the little swivel stand holding the cup lids and straws. Oh, here we go. I drop the book on the counter and give her an obligatory smile.

"New book?" she asks.

I want to say something sarcastic. Maybe she wouldn't like me if I did, but I can't do it. It would hurt her, and I'm not that person. Don't get me wrong, she's cute. I can still say that, right? I mean, she is, but I'm just not into it, any of it.

"Yeah, finished the one before it in the series last night. Gotta love James Rollins." I'm waiting for her to ask what I want to drink, but it doesn't seem to be working.

"I've never read him. I'm not really a big reader, actually. I know, I work in a bookstore." She does this little thing where she throws her hands up in the air like it's a big deal and giggles nervously.

Oh my God, why me?

"Not everyone likes to read, that's okay," I tell her, trying to fill the space, hoping that eventually I'll get to order a coffee.

L.A.'s about to open her mouth again when Sandra walks behind me.

"Would you like to just take a picture?" Sandra asks and makes her way behind the counter. "It'd be less awkward, *and* you can at least take that home with you."

I'm sure my face is an equal match to the lack of color in L.A.'s. I don't know what to say. It's funny and surprising at the same time. My mouth hangs open, but nothing comes out, and I'm not sure I should even say anything.

"Sandra!" L.A. yelps. I grin now that the focus isn't on me. She blinks nervously at me and then the register. "Uh... What can I get you to drink?"

"A Frosty's Favorite Frappe with almond milk," I tell her once I unfreeze. It's this amazing hazelnut and cinnamon drink that Sandra put together last Christmas, and I haven't been able to stop ordering it since.

"I'll ring him up." Sandra steps behind the register to let L.A. distract herself with putting together my drink.

I hand her my money, and a few minutes later L.A. hands me the frappe. I smile awkwardly at her and escape to the enclosed front porch around the corner, just out of sight. I take a seat between a set of wide windows. Cars speed, literally speed, down Main Street. A massive pin oak occupies the space just next to my window, its thin leaves too high up to see from my vantage. Besides the construction across the street, it's really nice.

I take a sip from my cup and open my new book. No matter how much I try, I struggle to focus. Every time I get more than a paragraph in my thoughts retrace back to how pathetic I am. I failed to come out today, and yesterday, and the day before, and so on. The more I read, the more down I get. After a little bit I'm just looking at the same page without end and letting the scenarios roll through my head.

What if I come out and my parents don't go along with it? What if by some twist of fate they can't accept it and throw me out of the house, take my car, disown me? No, that's stupid. They won't care that I'm gay. Hell, they've marched for gay rights. But what if they can't stand that *their* son is gay? Will they think they made a mistake, that they did something wrong?

I squeeze my eyes shut and pinch the page between my fingers. *Stop it, Noah, you're being stupid. They'll take it well. You don't have anything to be worried about. You're making a big deal out of nothing.*

But what about everyone else? *No, Noah. Just stop, just fucking stop right there.*

The front door to the shop chimes and I let my eyes stray from the page. I need a distraction, so I wait for whoever just entered to pass by the porch's open doorway.

It's a little girl in white capris and a bedazzled top. The tiny pigtails scream that she's no more than ten years old, and I think the woman with her is her mom. She looks old enough, but she looks young enough to be the big sister too.

I notice Sandra standing at the discount bookrack on the

porch a few tables down, looking at me through squinted eyelids. I grin, and she goes back to whatever she was doing.

Before I have a chance to go back to "reading" the bell chimes again and someone I know walks it. It's Gabriel Ellis. He's *so* cute. I lean back in my seat and lift my book up a little higher. Okay, it's really high technically, but it's the only way I can look at him without it being super obvious. Well, this is probably obvious too, but it feels better than just staring.

He goes to A.L. Brown too. I met him last year in Art II. I'd only known him from distant stare sessions before that. He's fine. His mouth is small, but he has those generous kissing lips, and his dirty-blonde hair is neatly kept.

He's talking to L.A. I can't tell what's being said, but it looks like he's flirting with her. Oddly, she's not flirting back, and inside I'm angry she's missing the opportunity, but at the same time I'm angry that he's flirting with *her*. It makes no sense. Even if he was gay, which he's not, it doesn't mean I'd have any right to him, or a chance in hell.

He looks my way and I throw my eyes back to my book. I catch "Pierce says" and "James Rollins" at the top of the page, but my mind is racing with whether Gabriel saw I was looking him over.

Is he still looking?

"Hey, man." The voice melts my insides. It's all right that I swoon over more than one guy, right?

I peel my eyes from the page. It's amazing how in one instant I want to look at him and in the other I'm horrified that doing so might blind me.

"Hey," I say, stopping short of actual conversation. We also have first period English together. He sits two rows ahead of me and three to the left.

"You really *do* like to read, don't you?" Gabriel asks.

"Yeah, I guess I do," I tell him. I don't know what else to say.

There's a long pause, and Gabriel just stands there. I don't know what to say. Finally he nods.

"Well, I'll see you in class next week," he says and heads out the door.

I slump back in my chair once he's gone. I didn't even think to say goodbye. Nope. I just grinned and nodded back. I'm so pathetic. When you like someone you should be able to talk to them, right? I mean, I'm not saying I like Gabriel, but still. He's cute, and he's nice, but I can't even manage a "Bye, Gabriel."

"Noah, I know I asked this already," Sandra starts. I look up. I didn't hear her walk up, and the sound of her voice tells me this can't be good. "But are you sure you're okay?"

Sandra's perceptive. If I can say anything about her, that's it. Maybe it's a good trait for a business owner — or shrink — but right now I'm not real excited about it. I mentally prepare myself to lie.

"Of course."

She turns a book in her hand. I can't tell what it is. She keeps her eyes on me. They're kind and understanding, but I feel like they're searching my soul, trying to root out my lie and out me right here on the spot.

"You do know you can talk to me if you need to, right?" she asks.

I'm glad she cares, but right now I just need a distraction. I don't need to think about it more. Internalizing is what I've done best for the last six years, and I think I can do it a few more days.

"Yeah, sure." I tell her. It comes out more high-pitched and nervous than I'd intended, but it's out, unlike other things.

"All right. Well, I'm not going to push you. Just know that if you ever need to talk, I'm here." She turns and goes back to sorting her books but does a double take. "You like quotes, right?"

I don't have to answer, she knows I do.

"In James Joyce's *Ulysses* one of his characters said, and I quote, 'Secrets, silent, stony sit in the dark palaces of both our hearts: secrets weary of their tyranny: tyrants willing to be dethroned.' Keep that in mind."

I haven't heard that one before, but I like it. Not to mention she hit the nail on the head. I do have a secret, and hell, does it want to be dethroned, but I can't do it. It only takes me a second to come back with a quote of my own.

"The great White Wizard Gandalf once said, and *I* quote, 'Keep it secret, keep it safe.'" I even throw in a poorly done Ian McKellen accent.

"Touché, *Lord of the Rings*."

I smile at her, proud of myself, but I'm actually hiding how much I both love that quote and hate it at the same time.

Sunday
September 2, 2018

This costume isn't meant for driving.

I'm on my second pass through the parking lot and I still don't see Camila's car. She's supposed to meet me here, because hell if I'm going in alone dressed like this. Actually, on second thought, I wouldn't go in by myself even if I wasn't dressed like this.

I shift in my seat. The fake plastic panel hiding my shorts-clad bottom doesn't bend, so it's pushing up my back. Dressing up like Superman, or maybe more like Superboy, would have been more comfortable. But no, I'm dressed up as Commander Shepard as promised, and Parker isn't even here to see. Plus, I wouldn't go as Superboy. I firmly believe if you dress up in a skin-tight onesie, you ought to have the body to make it look good. That rules me out.

I continue my search, passing a couple cosplaying the Joker and his Harley Quinn, and then a guy dressed up as Captain Jack Sparrow, I think.

Camila's not here. I would have spotted her little Scion by now if she was. On queue, my phone dings. I pluck it from the cupholder and pray a quick apology to my mom for texting while driving as I open up a message from Camila.

Sry Im late. Parents made me go to lunch with our Pastor.

I sigh, but before I have a chance to type out my displeasure, the little bubbles flicker at the bottom of the screen and a new message comes up.

Have to change first. Be there soon. Go on without me.

Hell to the no. Forget it. I'll wait in the parking lot all day before that happens.

It's an anxiety thing, social anxiety according to the internet. Yes, I self-diagnosed myself, and no, I'm not a doctor, so I could have something else. I just know this can't be normal.

It's stupid, but I get really nervous when I'm around big crowds by myself. It feels like everyone is looking at me, even though I know they couldn't care less if I'm there or not. It's one of those things I feel so stupid about after the fact, but I can't seem to do anything about it in the moment.

Charlotte Comicon is no exception. Not only are there a bunch of people here, but half of them are dressed up as imaginary characters. I feel like that should help, but it doesn't, somehow it makes it worse. Just the thought of going in alone makes my heart rate increase.

Fun fact. Charlotte Comicon doesn't take place in Charlotte. Nope, it's right here in Concord, North Carolina, over in the Concord Mills area by the mall. Why? Don't ask me. I'm sure there's a good reason to call it Charlotte Comicon when it's not in Charlotte, but I don't know the answer. Come to think of it, the Charlotte Motor Speedway is literally a minute down the road and it, too, sits in Concord.

Nope. I'll wait in the car. I'm not going in alone.

I shoot back my reply and look up just in time to hit the brakes and avoid flattening Goku and some random dude. Goku throws up his hands and the other guy flips me off. I grin stupidly and let them pass while I drop my phone back into the cupholder.

After a quick search I grab a parking space. There's a new text from Camila when I put it in park.

U rly should go on. Be there by 2.

I laugh at that. She knows me too well, she knows I'm going nowhere right now, and on top of that I've got nearly an hour to wait. I maneuver my ass around to get comfortable, but this suit isn't having it. It's *almost* enough reason to get out of the car.

I leave Camila's text unanswered.

Even if I did go in, I'd just be bored without her. I love these things, but Camila is the one who makes it fun. She's the one who stops other cosplayers to get pictures, buys a bunch of paintings she doesn't have room for, and talks to the vendors. I'm the one who just looks and runs when someone tries to sell me something. Without Camila, I'm not stopping anyone to get a picture, even if it *is* Spider-Man, Jason, or the poorly played Loki that just passed my car.

I watch Loki enter the hotel. *Noah, it's really not that difficult. I mean, just get out of the car and put one foot in front of the other. You'll get there. Just don't make eye contact and stick to the edges.* I purse my lips and eye the door handle. Maybe I *can* do it.

My heartbeat quickens and my pulse shoots down my wrist. I brush my fingertips along the door handle but pull back. Why is this so fucking hard? Why does *everything* have to be so fucking hard?

After a two-minute stare off with the door handle, *it* wins and I'm left tossing my eyes between the hotel entry and my dashboard. I catch a family jogging across the parking lot. Mom and Dad are not cosplaying, but their kids are dressed up like the Ninja Turtles, complete with orange, blue, and red bandanas. They're all smiles as they disappear inside.

I wish I could do that.

I glance at my phone. Only another twenty-three minutes before Camila gets here.

Monday
September 3, 2018

Camila better be glad I love her. She better be damn glad I love her.

I'm going on three hours sitting around waiting for her now. First, yesterday at the Comicon where she finally arrived dressed up as Michael Burnham, Sonequa Martin-Green's character in the new *Star Trek* series. And now for the past two hours.

I'm on the top row of the small set of bleachers in the auxiliary gym. I always go to Cam's games, and today wasn't going to be an exception, even if my car does hate me.

It's in the shop. The brakes started squealing yesterday, but as I'm discovering, you apparently can't take your car to the shop without them finding another problem. Something about a seal and one of the engine mounts.

So I'm without a car today and probably tomorrow, which sucks. Parker picked me up this morning, which meant I was left panicking on my front porch until he finally pulled up. I hate not being early. Mom had planned on picking me up after class, but I opted to stay at school instead.

It's okay though, I have a book to entertain me, and Rollins never disappoints. Actually, give me a book and I'll be happy just about anywhere.

The bleachers are barely half full, and the game is in full

swing. Camila's on the sidelines while her teammates, Macy included, form up for the next serve. I think that's the right way to say it. I don't know much about the game except what Cam's told me, and if I'm honest with myself, I don't remember half of that. The way I see it, I'm here for moral support, win or lose, not the technicalities.

Beyond parents and family there are a few groupings of boys from both my school and Cox Mill, the school we're playing, settled in huddles. I imagine they're ogling the girls' thighs in their high-cut shorts. That's what Parker and Mateo always talk about at least. I just go along.

I purse my lips and instead of watching the girls on the court, I take quick side glances at them. It's not fair, really. With the lone exception of baseball, and maybe soccer, the outfits in boys' sports aren't as nice as the girls' teams. I mean, the short shorts, tight tops, all of that. Don't get me wrong, football pants are tight, but I guess the boys playing baseball just have better butts, or maybe it's just me. Really that's about the most exciting part of the game too. Is that sexist, or is that taking it too far?

I return my attention to the gym floor and realize Cam's in play now. Hopefully she didn't notice me not paying attention. She's in the back row. I don't remember the technical name for it, but she looks ready. Her eyes are focused down-court and her feet are spread even with her outstretched hands. I thought she was supposed to... Never mind, there it is. She clasps her hands together, ready to spike the ball, I think. Well, once it comes over the net. I guess you can't be *too* ready.

I hope they win—just a little team spirit, by which I mean I think I'm required by some unspoken rule to feel that way, but mainly it's because I really need Cam to be in high spirits when I tell her I'm gay tonight.

Yeah, I'm going to do it. I've been saying that for a long time, but tonight should work. Parker's still grounded, so he's not here and he won't be going out with us to eat afterward either. That's when I'm going to tell her.

The other team spikes the ball and the Wonders — that's our mascot — go into action. One of the girls returns it and the back and forth begins. Macy returns the next round, but the tall blonde chick on the other team fails to keep it going and the ball crashes to the ground. The back and forth starts up again, and this time Camila dives in for it. I jump.

"Get it, Cam!" I scream before I realize what I'm doing.

I recoil into myself, plant my butt back on the bleachers and shoot my eyes over the stands. No one's looking. No one cares, I have to remind myself. It's sports, people do that shit. I take a breath and giggle inside. The game goes on like this for another five minutes before the coach takes Camila off the court again and I lose interest.

I take in a fresh gulp of musty gym air. I'm going to do this. But my heart is already racing. The game isn't over, I've probably got another half an hour, and my heart's all fucked up already. I swallow and glance to my left where most of the crowd sits. It feels like everyone is looking at me again, like they know my filthy little secret.

Stop it, Noah. It's not a filthy *little secret, it's a* wonderful *huge secret. You have to stop thinking of it like that.*

My phone dings and vibrates on my thigh, saving me from myself. I retrieve it and pull up the text message. It's from Cam. I glance down to the court and find her looking at me. I grin and read the message.

The girls want me to go out after the game.

Oh. I read it again, hoping somehow the words will rearrange themselves into something better, like maybe *the girls want me to go out tomorrow after school.* That I wouldn't mind. This, though, this puts a fucking wrench in my plans. My smile falters, but I'm quick to raise it again because I'm pretty sure she's still looking.

I'm frustrated, but I know I can't be angry with her. She can't read my mind. Oh, if she could, though, this would all be so much easier. But then again, considering some of the thoughts that go through my head, it's probably best she can't.

I sigh and type back a quick reply.

Ok.

I hope it doesn't come off short and flustered, but I don't feel like saying more right now.

I chance a glance at the team's section on the bleachers. Camila is smiling up at me. I'm not sure if she read the message and all is good, or if she just hasn't read it yet. I'm going with she's already read it.

Don't worry about it, Noah, she'll be good. I'm the one who's stuck now. Not only do I still have *to hold my secret close, now I have to get Mom or Dad to come pick me up.* Maybe that's how I could make her confirm she's ditching me. I open our message thread again and start typing.

I guess I need to get a ride?

I send it and wait. It takes no time for the little message bubble to start flashing, and I can see Camila typing on her phone. Her message pops up.

Sry. Only if you can. If not, I can still take you home.

That's Camila for you, but I guess I'm a lot like that too.

Change plans, then I feel bad for changing the plans and agree to go out of my way to make it up. I'm not doing that to her. I'm about to reply, but I pause over the digital keyboard. Although if I did, that means I could still tell her, I could still do it. *No, Noah. If you do that and she doesn't take it well, it'll be a big mess, and even if she does, I doubt she wants to think about gay Noah while she's trying to enjoy time out with the girls. No, you can just wallow in your self-pity one more night, or a few, or maybe a week. Hell, maybe another month or year.*

I do my best to keep the emotions tossing in my chest from surfacing while I type my reply.

Nah. I'll get Dad or Mom to pick me up. Have fun!

I go to send the message but stop short of tapping the little blue arrow. Hmm... Maybe I can still make this work. Maybe I can just tell her after the game, before she leaves with the team. No, that's dumping the news and running. But I need to get this off my chest.

Can we talk after the game before you leave? I have something I need to tell you. Don't ask.

Before I can make myself erase the entire thing I send it.

Dammit, Noah. This is such a bad idea. I pocket my phone and cup my face in my hands. My breath puffs off my palms. It's hot and nervous, like everything else about me.

I look up and check to make sure no one saw my little breakdown. All looks good. Down at the sidelines Camila turns and eyes me suspiciously for a moment, then smiles jokingly. I want to scream, but I grin instead. She shrugs and gives me the thumbs up. I shudder and give her a super-fake smile. Damn, I hope it doesn't look as fake as it is.

A minute later I've confirmed that Dad will be here to pick me up after the game. Mom's cooking, so Dad got chauffeur duty. Camila is back on the court, and I hope she's for-gotten all about my poor smile and awkward text. I try to do the same and get back into the match. I shout my encour-agement, and maybe one or two heckles at the other team. It seems to be working. The tension in my shoulders has eased and I'm not thinking about what I'm going to say or how I'm going to do it.

But the match is winding down, and with it, my heart winds up. I exhale a pent-up breath and clench my fists. Just a few more minutes and this will all be over. I'll either be free and excited, or I'll be embarrassed, terrified, and down a friend. *Stop it, you know better than that. She's going to take it great.*

But what if she doesn't?

I stop myself there and shift my butt on the bleacher. *Get yourself together, Noah, it's not that bad. It's just you. You're the only one worrying about it like it's some big deal.*

A yell breaks out on the court and everyone stampedes off the bleachers. It's the team, the entire A.L. Brown Won-ders volleyball team. It takes me a second to realize what's going on. The game is over, and we won! I manage a smile, and for a second, it's genuine and I'm happy. Camila did it! They won the match.

I get up and rush down the bleachers. The whole way down I search for Cam in the crowd of screaming and jump-ing bodies. She finds me first and nearly knocks me to the ground. I hug her and attempt to keep time with her jumps. She's really excited and I'm happy for her, I really am. She's like a sister after all, and a win for her is definitely a win for me.

But I have bad news for her. Dammit. I don't know if I

can throw it on her now. She's so happy, so ecstatic. I don't think I can do it.

"How about I at least walk you to your ride since technically I ditched you?" Her forthrightness is something I expect but I doubt I'll ever get used to.

I put a smile on. At least I don't have to make up some stupid excuse to get her to follow me now.

"Sure! I would make some remark about you being a bitch for ditching me — see, it even rhymes — but I won't," I tell her, a mischievous grin plastered across my face.

"Uh, thanks. I guess." She gives me the slant eye.

We turn and head outside, but I'm burning inside to use an Ms Moem quote on her. I have the perfect one. I chew my lip and decide yeah, why not. It's just for fun.

"But Moem did say, 'A true friend won't ditch you when something different comes along.'"

"So much for *not* calling me a bitch."

We both break out laughing, and I pull her in for a forgive-me-but-it-was-too-good-to-pass-up hug.

"I love you. I promise!" I tell her.

"Yeah, yeah." She shakes her head, but she's still grinning. "Who's Moem, anyway?"

"Don't really know. I think she, or maybe he, is a poet. Maybe. I found their stuff on the internet a while back, and you know me." I'm glad to have a distraction from what I really need to talk about. I know I should hurry and tell her, but instead I think I might continue this conversation all the way to Dad's Jeep once I find it.

"I know," she pushes me away playfully. "So, you said you had something to tell me?"

It comes off more as a question than a statement, and I

think for a moment that I should just say no, I don't know what you're talking about, you must be mistaken. But I'm positive it'll come off defensive, and all she has to do is read her texts and she'll know I'm lying. And that'll make it even worse tomorrow.

"Uh...yeah," I stutter. I try to fight it, but my mood flips like a light switch. The excitement of the team's win that got me this far is replaced by fear, a heavy crippling fear.

I've never come this close to actually saying it. I mean, I'm not there yet, I haven't told her I have a secret, or that there's something she doesn't know about me. All the things I've planned to say before I utter those two damned words... But my chest is already tightening.

When I don't say anything, she shakes her head and her eyes grow wide.

"So..."

"Yeah, I uh..." I want to take in a deep breath to calm my nerves, but it'd be so obvious, so I clench my fists instead and smile. Damn, I bet I look awkward anyway. I steal a quick glance around and inventory my choices.

We're walking down the main path with everyone else. Anyone could hear my admission if I do it here, and that's simply not how this is going to go down. Ahead is the parking lot. It's maybe ten yards away, just across the road, but of course I suck at eyeing distances, so maybe more, maybe less. Behind us, inside the gym, I imagine the ass-end of the bleachers, fully open minus the metal supports. For a second, I consider dragging Cam back inside and pulling her under them and doing it there, but that would definitely attract attention. I mean, two eighteen-year-olds climbing under the bleachers isn't exactly normal. Well, unless they're planning for a little privacy to make out, and ew, no.

Ahead the pathway veers around a big tree. There's plenty of room in the mulch bed under its weighty branches. I think I could tell her there. I doubt anyone else would hear, and it wouldn't look *too* suspicious. I glance at Camila again and jut my chin toward the tree.

"Can we go over there first?"

"Sure." I think she's trying to hide her suspicion, but she's failing.

I don't say anything as we close the gap. When we get there, I pull her to the side closest to the bleachers and away from the stream of people escaping to their cars. I take one last glance around to calm my nerves. It doesn't work.

"What's going on, Noah?" she asks.

I can see a sliver of worry eclipse the excitement in her eyes. Damn, I'm about to ruin her day, but it's too late now.

My arms and hands are shaking. Hell, my entire body is shaking. I'm having a hard time breathing, and even if I wanted to talk right now, I'm not sure I could. I squeeze my fists. *Come on, Noah, just do it. Just fucking say it.*

"Noah!"

I jump and snap my eyes away from the mulch bed. Dad's craning his neck out his window. I glance nervously at Cam and then back at Dad. I bet we look odd standing here by ourselves.

I guess that's it. I exhale and let the pressure slip from my lungs and fake another smile. I wave at Dad to give me a second. I'll only need a second now.

"Uh... You know what, don't worry about it," I tell her and thank Dad and all the gods of Greece for saving me from this moment. "Have fun with the team."

It's rude, but instead of letting her stop me, I turn and jog to safety, aka Dad's Jeep.

"Are you sure?" I hear behind me.

I turn, walking backwards with a super-fake grin on my lips. Hopefully I'm too far away for it to be obvious.

"Yeah, it's all good. I don't know what got into me. Bye!" I open the Jeep door and jump in as she gives me a not-so-sure-about-that grin. I let my smile falter as I lose her in the crowd.

Dad's looking at me from the driver's seat with his brow raised as I shut the door. "What's that all about? Everything okay?"

"Definitely! All good," I tell him. I don't want to get into this with him. I love him, but Dad's the last person I want to talk this over with, especially right now.

Actually, what I want now is to punch the dash over and over again. Sure, I'm not nervous anymore, which is great, but instead of calm filling its place, I feel like such a loser. I almost did it. I almost told her. But no, I let Dad pull me away. No, it's not Dad's fault, I let him give me an excuse. *Get it right, Noah, you're the coward here.*

"Did we win?" he asks, and I wonder why we're not leaving yet.

"Yeah."

Dad turns and leans his head out the window. "Go Wonders! Congrats, Cam!"

I find her in the crowd just before she turns and smiles. I think she's laughing, too, just like a number of other people in the crowd. I slink farther into my seat, wishing I was any-where but here right now. Really, Dad?

"Woah. Noah, I'm so glad you never wanted to dress gay

like that." Dad nods toward a group of three emo guys walking in front of the Jeep. I don't know them, they must go to Cox Mill, but a fire jumps in my chest.

"They're not gay, Dad, they're emo. There *is* a difference, and there's nothing wrong with it even if they were gay," I bite. Oh my God, did I just do that? Please tell me I didn't raise my voice like I think I did.

"Sorry." Dad pulls his hands from the steering wheel in surrender. "I didn't mean to offend."

I shake my head and look out the window. Seriously?

Calm down, Noah, you need to calm down. He doesn't mean it bad, he's just a dad. He doesn't know any better, so how can I expect him to know how much it hurts when he says stupid shit like that? He's not even talking about me, and he'd probably be all happy about the gayness if I came out, but he likes to joke.

He just doesn't realize I'm the butt end of the joke.

Tuesday
September 4, 2018

Well it's another day, another day in my cowardly closeted life.

I'm in the lunch line with, of all people, Camila. Nothing unusual there, except I'm horrified she's going to ask what I wanted to tell her yesterday. I still can't believe I chickened out.

Now it's the last thing I want to talk about. I mean, yeah, I want to tell her, but last night's epic failure is sort of eclipsing that want.

"You should have come with us last night," Cam says, throwing her hand in the air and almost toppling her tray to the floor. I grab my tray instinctively, just in case. "We had so much fun, but I think it would've been better if you'd been there. They all like you anyway."

"Like me?" I ask without turning. I pay for my food and lead Camila to our table. "What do you mean 'like me?'"

"Like, like-like you. Like, think you're cute, like you. Well, some of them, at least." She smirks.

I cringe. "What? Why? I mean seriously, I'm a nerd, like maybe a four out of ten," I tell her. It's only half defensive. I really am a nerd, I own it.

"Really?" She shoots me this crazed look. "I mean, don't get me wrong, I'm your friend. I don't like you like that, but you're super cute. You're at least a solid six, maybe even a seven."

"Sure." I don't know what else to say. I prefer this train to stop right here—no, better yet, I'd rather it derail and die a fiery death so it never comes back up. Lucky for me Parker appears and takes his seat next to Cam. "Hey, Park!"

"Hey, man!" He stuffs a chicken nugget in his mouth and doesn't wait to finish chewing before talking again. "Is your car out of the shop yet?"

"Nah." I have to work at keeping my eyes up. His shirt is a little snug today. The contours of his chest and the ball shape of his shoulders tug at the fabric. He's not ripped, but he's fit. "It's fixed though. Dad's taking me to pick it up after school."

"Did they ever figure out what was wrong?" he asks.

"Yeah, that's how they fixed it." Cam gives him the you-dumb-fuck look before I can react, and I cough out a laugh.

"You know what I mean." Parker grins.

"Yeah, but it was a stupid question," she says.

"Whatever." Parker waves her off.

"Yeah, there was something about engine mounts and seals. What that means, I don't really know, but Dad does so it's all good," I tell them. I'm not the best at car stuff. I think I could change a tire, maybe. And I know I can switch out the windshield wiper blades and fill up the water and oil, but otherwise, I'm content just knowing how to put gas in the tank.

"Speaking of your dad." A light bulb flashes in Cam's eyes and they fixate on me. Dammit. "Right before he picked you up last night, you were trying to tell me something."

I try not to slump my shoulders, but it's an absolute failure. My chest tightens and my mind races to find a way out. I know what she's going to ask.

"What was it?" she asks, just as expected.

I gulp. She's staring me down, and suddenly Parker gains interest. Suspicion paints his face. I don't want to do this. Not here. Not now. Not with *him* present.

It's hard to breathe. I hate lying to them. I really do, I swear, but I'm not doing this.

What the hell do I say? I'm not telling her here, not with Parker, and sure as hell not with the entire fucking school present. *Come on, Noah, think of something.*

Cam's chestnut eyes become slits, and the corners of her mouth rise into an impish smile.

"It's about a girl, isn't it?" she beams.

I don't deny it, and my face twists into an embarrassed and frustrated scowl, which only emboldens her.

"Is it?" Parker leans in.

"It is, isn't it?" Cam keeps on, pausing between questions. She only gives me enough time to look guilty in between. "Who is it? It's not Macy, is it? I know it's not Laura, you've always been so anti-Laura."

Oh my God, Cam, just stop. Please just stop. It's what I want to say, but I can't form the words. Instead my mouth hangs partially open with the syllables dangling at the tip of my tongue, begging to be let loose. All I can get out is a repeated "No."

"Okay, then, did you have a sex question? You are using condoms, right?" she prods.

"Noah! You're really surprising me," Parker jumps in and eggs her on. "I didn't think you were the type."

"No, I mean I would, but... No," I stumble over the

words. "Oh my God, really guys?"

"So it's not about a girl?" Camila can't seem to stop. I shouldn't be surprised, but it still has me shaking. "So is it a guy?"

I freeze for the tiniest of seconds, but it feels like an eternity. I have to remind myself to breathe. What the hell? I'm suddenly weak and nauseous. My head tips toward weightlessness and I have to grab the table to steady myself.

No, stop. She's just shitting you.

I let go of the table. I'm gripping so tight that my fingertips are white.

"Fuck no!" I blurt. I wish I could take it back, that I would have said something more tempered. The pit of my stomach grows more nauseated by the second. "Really, Cam? Really?"

Parker is obviously amused with all of this. His hand covers his wide-open mouth under squinted eyes. I catch a sliver of his intoxicating laugh over the drone of the cafeteria. He has the most amazing laugh, but even that cadence can't calm me right now.

I stare Camila down but force myself to soften, to get control of myself. I'm being obvious.

"So what was it?" she asks.

"I was just going to tell you how absolutely awesome you were at the game last night, that's all," I say, making sure it's sarcastic as fuck. "I mean, obviously."

"Oh, right. Okay." She rolls her eyes, but I catch something caring in them. If I didn't know better I'd think she knows something is up, something serious because she drops it. And just like that, what I thought was the end of the world is over.

"So what was it?" Park asks, oblivious that Cam just gave up.

She looks at him like it's obvious and basically repeats my words, but makes it sound more genuine.

"You heard him, he just wanted to tell me how I great I was last night."

"Yeah, I'm sure that's it," Parker laughs.

I'm still not out of enemy territory, but at least now I have an ally.

"Are you okay, Noah?" Parker's voice changes. I think he's actually worried. He's good like that. He can joke and be sarcastic, he can be the typical rowdy guy, but he's not a douche.

How the hell do I answer that? I don't have a clue, but I start talking anyway.

"Yeah, I'm good. I'm just nervous about our chemistry exam." I make it up as I go. It's not actually a lie. Technically it's the truth, so win one for me.

Parker can't deny it. He's in the same class and we have our first test of the semester in fourth period today. Plus, it *would* be a lie if I said I was ready for it. I spent last night moping about not telling Cam my secret instead of studying.

"Oh God, you're right. It's going to be so bad," Park says. He slaps his hands on the table and his eyes grow wider. "I swear I'm going to fail."

I manage a smile and my muscles ease up. Camila grins, and if I didn't know better, I'd swear she just winked at me. I squint back but quickly act like nothing happened.

Thursday
September 13, 2018

"You owe me forty bucks," Cam says without so much as looking at me. Her eyes are tracking the guys down the football field chasing a soccer ball.

Isn't it funny when you think about it? Playing fútbol on the football field. Okay, maybe it's not that funny. Never mind. The point is that this is a sport I can enjoy—boys' soccer. Despite that, I look away from the field.

"Huh?" I ask.

I don't have a clue what she's talking about. Forty bucks?

"Yeah, for your ticket."

My ticket? What is she talking about?

"What ticket? I don't—"

"The BVB tickets... October," she reminds me.

Sweet! In an instant I'm beaming. I'm so glad she remembered because I completely forgot.

"Black Veil Brides, Bad Omens, and Imminence, right?" I ask. This is awesome. I've wanted to see Brides and Omens for years, and now Imminence. Yes!

"Yeah, who else is BVB?" She grins sarcastically.

"I don't know, I just... Never mind," I tell her. "That's awesome! You got Park's ticket too, right?"

"Of course. What type of friend would I be if I didn't do that?" Cam jeers. "I got them during P.E. I have told you how pointless that class is, haven't I?"

I roll my eyes. Has she told me? The better question is how *many* times has she told me.

"At least a few times, maybe a couple hundred."

She giggles, and I return my attention to the guys on the field.

"It's not looking good for Park," I tell her.

The score is zero to two in Hickory Ridge's favor, not ours, and there are only another ten minutes in the game. We're just not holding our own, but then again, like most sports with the exception of swimming, I don't really know enough to comment. What I do know is that Parker and Mateo are both on the field, and Mateo's looking fine.

"Yeah, he's going to be pissed if—" she starts; I can't help but correct her.

"When."

"—they lose." Cam eyes me disapprovingly. "Maybe the tickets will cheer him up."

I nod. He's not the one I'm worried about right now.

* * *

A few hours later we're leaving the sub shop. It felt sort of bad going without Park, especially after that game.

He didn't talk much when we met him on the field at the buzzer. Park can be intense like that sometimes. Cam didn't even get to tell him about the tickets, but he didn't exactly give us a chance either. I think he was just ready to go, even if that meant going back home since he's still grounded.

"You're saying there was a *second* post-credit scene in *Deadpool 2*?" Camila asks. Her eyes are squinted and honestly, I'm surprised I have to answer this question.

She's not the biggest Marvel fan of all time, or even DC;
she's more of a Trekkie, but she does like them. I thought
everyone knew to stay to the very end of a comic book movie.

"Yeah, I'm not going to spoil it for you though," I assure
her. There's a special place in hell for people who spoil movies, a *really* special place. "I'll just say that it's great and it's
even better after watching *Infinity War.*"

She purses her lips and ducks into the passenger seat,
and I start up the engine. It hits me what I'm about to do the
moment I shift it into reverse. *Just stay calm, Noah, it's not like
you're kidnapping her and dumping her in a sewage drain.* I put
the car in drive and we're off.

"Really?" Cam asks and reclines her seat back. I can barely see her without turning.

"Huh?" I ask. For a second, I forget what we're talking
about as I prep myself to tell her my darkest secret. Is it my
darkest secret? Should I call it that? I mean, I'm good with it
now, right? It's a good thing? I'm normal. Yeah, I'm normal,
just not *that* normal.

Dammit, this sucks.

"*Deadpool…* The post-credit scene…" She lets her words
hang. I can hear the derision.

"Oh yeah, that," I start back. I try to focus. "No doubt.
It's great!"

We took my car on my insistence. I didn't want to allow
myself a way out tonight, but now I'm wishing I had. Damn,
I need to think more positively.

I've got it. Think of it like losing your virginity, which I
haven't done, for the record. It should be exciting and a little

bit terrifying, right? In a way it really is like that. Once I tell her, I can't ever take it back, and I shouldn't want to. Maybe that's a bad analogy. I don't know. Maybe.

"I'll have to check it out," she says. "Speaking of checking it out, did you see Kenan tonight?"

First, yes. But second, probably not like she thinks I did. Kenan's on the soccer team. We didn't know him from Adam until our freshman year. He also happens to be Cam's biggest crush.

"I saw him," I acknowledge and roll my eyes. He's cute, but even if I was ready to talk guys with her, I wouldn't have chosen him. He's not my type. Too tall and bulked up for my taste, and at the risk of sounding fucking horrible, he's not white or Latino.

I shift in my seat. Suddenly I understand why my dad says they're uncomfortable. A soft green glow laps over my face as we drive through an intersection. School isn't far. God, I'm not ready for this conversation.

"So, you *did* notice him?"

I know she's grinning, but I'm not looking to confirm it.

"Yeah," I start and then try a joke of the Lemony Snicket variety. Total truth under a tease. "He's not really my type."

She laughs, I laugh, but I know it comes out awkward.

"So what *is* your type?"

I can hear the accusation in her voice, and it sends me into cleanup mode.

"I was just kidding..." I start, but I let the words trail off as I pull into the school parking lot. I know I should make it clear, but I don't want to. No, what I want is to close my eyes and throw my face into the steering wheel, but I'm still maneuvering us through the lot to Cam's car, so I hold back.

That was horrible. Not only did I just make a gay joke, I then denied it and even failed at that.

This has to stop.

My arms are shaking as I park next to her Scion. It's the only vehicle in the parking lot—well, besides mine.

I need to distract myself. I bet we look downright shady, like a drug deal going down in the middle of the school parking lot. Like that hasn't ever happened before. I try to laugh but I can't. My throat is dry, and my palms are sweaty and stuck to the steering wheel. I stare straight ahead and let the silence suffocate me.

"Are you okay?" Cam asks. It's hard to take her seriously as her seat rises back to the upright position, but I also can't laugh. I think I might have just put myself into a situation I can't get out of, and I'm horrified.

"Uh…" I stumble and pry my hands from the wheel. I cup them together and squeeze. When I open my mouth to speak nothing comes out at first, and I can't get myself to look at her, I just can't. "I, uh… I need to tell you something."

She doesn't say a word. The air in here is heavy. I know she's not trying to intimidate me, but I bet *I'm* freaking *her* out right now. Hell, I'm freaking *me* out. I dart my eyes from the empty parking lot to the steering wheel and then to my fidgeting fingers.

"I…" I stumble yet again.

Why the fuck is this so hard? I swear there's a damn wall in my head keeping the words from flowing out of my mouth. It's so frustrating.

"It's okay, Noah." Her voice is soft, understanding. It's a Camila I rarely see behind the sarcastic face I usually deal with. "Take your time. You can say whatever you need."

"I don't know how to do this. Um... I, uh... Damn, why is this so fucking hard?" I'm so frustrated. This shouldn't be so difficult.

I shake my head furiously, trying to take that next step without drowning my leather seats. I want to, but I'm not sure I can. I've screamed it to an empty house when I knew no one was home, I've typed it repeatedly on Facebook only to delete it, I've even watched coming out YouTube videos to see how best to do this, but to actually say it to another person—why is it this hard? I take a deep breath and grab the steering wheel again for support.

"Take your time, Noah." She puts a hand on my shoulder.

"I'm g... I'm, uh..." I stop, but *this* has to stop now. I can't stand this anymore. "Oh my God! I'm gay!"

I nearly scream it. I glance at her from the corner of my eye, fully expecting her to scowl at me and barrel out of the car. But she doesn't move. No. She's smiling and bobbing her head.

"I'm sorry," I start when I realize it's done, that she knows. But instead of feeling free, I'm even more horrified. "I shouldn't have done that. I—"

"Stop, Noah!" She puts a finger on my lips and then leans in and hugs me. I don't move. I just sit with my hands gripping the wheel and her arms draped around my neck. I don't feel like I deserve this. "Don't apologize. You have nothing to apologize for. I'm your friend, I don't care if you want to fuck girls or guys, or if you like Reese's better than PayDays, even if that last one *is* a little fucked up."

For a brief second, I nearly laugh, and the tremors in my chest ease. It's typical Cam, a bit on the crude side but genuine. The best part is that my body relaxes a little. I can breathe, and I let my hands fall from the steering wheel.

"How long have you known?" She twists around and sits on her leg so she can face me.

I look at her, but I'm still not that comfortable, so I turn and stare at the rough, cracked concrete. They really need to patch it.

"A while," is all I say at first. I take my time and keep my eyes averted. This is all new territory and I don't want to mess it up like I have everything else. "I think I was twelve."

I turn to find her still looking at me. Her eyes are soft. There's an understanding in them, but I also see something more. Hurt. I'm not really sure how to take that, so I keep talking.

"I thought it was a phase, you know? But it wasn't. It's not." I had wished it was for a long time before I finally accepted it. That was both relieving and terrifying, but she doesn't need every detail. Like she doesn't need to know I was finally one hundred percent certain I was gay when I fell for Parker in the eighth grade, even if I didn't understand it then. "I finally accepted it our sophomore year. Like two years ago."

"You've kept this a secret for *six* years?" she asks, squinting her eyes. "I'm so sorry, Noah. I can't even begin to imagine. Hold on, you've told your parents, right? *Right?*"

I don't say anything.

"Oh." She looks out the window and then finds me again. "Who have you told?"

I keep my eyes on her. "Just you. I was freaked out. I was pretty sure you'd be all right with it, but I was still afraid. Hell, I still am."

"Why were you afraid?"

"I don't know. I just didn't want things to change between us. I know I shouldn't be, but it's just…hard for some reason. So we're good, right?"

"Of course we're good!" She looks at me like I just said the stupidest thing in the history of stupid things, and for once I like it.

I cry a happy tear. It's crazy awesome how happy that one sentence makes me right now.

"You know what this means, don't you?" She sits up straighter and her eyes widen as though a grand thought just slipped its way into her brilliant head.

"That I'm out?" I skew my lips, not really sure what she's looking to hear. "Technically I'm just out to you."

"No, dumbass," she says. "Now we get to talk guys!"

There's the Cam I know. And yeah, she's right. I've actually been waiting for this, though I'm not sure I'm ready for it.

"I guess so." I tilt my head and shrug, chuckling.

"No, this is happening. So, who's your crush? And don't tell me you don't have one," she jumps in, ready to devour this new tidbit of my life without wasting a second.

It's not like I don't know the answer, but telling her is another big step. Just like speaking those two little words.

"I do have one, maybe a few, actually…" I let it hang there. My mouth is dry again, and my lungs are pumping hard. It's so stupid. I just told her I'm gay, it shouldn't be hard to admit who I like. I force his name out quickly. "Mateo."

"Oh!" She grins. "And do tell why?"

"Everything?" I actually ask. Immediately I wish I could

reform the word as a statement, because it gets exactly the response I feared.

"That's cheating. *What* about him do you like?"

I groan. I think it amuses her, which oddly enough helps take some of the scariness out of it. I shake my head and grin. Let's start this out less graphically.

"Well, he's the reason I'm taking weight lifting. I'm not real fond of squats, but watching him do squats… Well, you get the idea."

Her grin turns devious. "Bad boy! Hold up. You mean to tell me all those reasons you gave me were total bullshit?"

"Oh my God!" I sweep my eyes to the blank ceiling and chuckle. "That *would* be what you take away from that."

Then, suddenly, it hits me that she knows my secret. A shockwave ripples through me, and abruptly I'm nervous someone else might find out. "You can't tell anyone. Not even Parker. You know that, right?"

"Of course!" She almost looks hurt by the unspoken accusation. I feel bad, but I can't risk it. Not until I'm ready. "I won't tell a soul. That's up to you. But you really should tell your parents."

I nod. I know.

* * *

I'm going to do it. I'm going to tell Mom and Dad. At least that's what I keep telling myself in the bathroom mirror.

I really need to get more sun. Thank God my eyes are a lighter steel-blue color, otherwise they'd be a real shocker cast against my pale skin. Of course, my choice of t-shirt doesn't help matters. It's a black tee sporting a singular white

Nike swoosh front and center, paired with some baggy *Dead-pool* pajamas. My hair is disheveled, so I run a hand through it, but it doesn't help.

"Come on, Noah, you've got this," I tell myself for at least the tenth time. I think I might actually be to the point of believing myself too. "You told Cam, you can tell them. They'll be happy, they'll understand."

But will they? Will Dad like that he has a faggot for a son? *Just stop it. It's going to be all right.*

After I dropped Cam off, having finally gotten the biggest secret of all fucking time off my chest, I came straight home. I hope I'm not the only gay person in the world who finds it funny any time I say I did something "straight." I mean, it's not like I can say I went gay home. That just sounds weird.

My point is that I made a promise to myself, and to Cam, that I'd tell Mom and Dad tonight, and I'm determined I'm going to keep it. But even after telling Cam I'm still hyperventilating. I can't get my hands to stop shaking and sweating.

"It's time to do this."

I force my legs to move and carry myself into the hallway. It's a short walk, but it feels like one of those massive never-ending sprawls in a mental ward right now.

I've got this.

My phone rings and the room fills with the familiar voice of Eddie Berg singing "This Is Goodbye." It's a ringtone assigned to the one and only Parker Evans. I sigh. Really? But I stop halfway down the hall and take out my phone anyway. I'm confronted with Parker's face on the screen. He's not just calling, he's FaceTiming me.

Just put the phone away and keep walking, Noah. I lower it and take another step. Call him back later. But on the other hand, what's a little delay? Before I can reason myself out of it I raise my phone and swipe to accept the call. Parker's face fills the screen. He's sitting on his bed in the Batman t-shirt I got him last year for his birthday.

"Hey, man!" Parker practically yells. I think typically the person answering the phone says hey first, but that rarely works with Park.

"Hey," I try to sound excited. I am, I actually am excited to talk to him because it means I don't have to do what I was planning yet, and that puts my body at ease.

"Cam told me!" he shouts, his eyes wide and excited.

I'm positive mine are wider. My heart jumps into my throat and my nerves flip out. My mouth has to be on the floor, and I don't know what to say. What was she thinking? I told her not to tell Park, not to tell anyone! I'm not ready for this! How could she do this?

"What the fuck?" is what comes out.

"Huh?" Parker's mouth twists, and he suddenly looks confused.

"She told you?" I start in on him.

"Yeah," he chuckles. "She got the tickets."

I freeze. What the hell just happened? Did I just freak out on Parker because Cam told him about the concert? Oh hell.

"Oh, that!" I say. How the hell do I fix this? "The concert."

"Yeah, what else would it have been?" Parker asks.

I can see the wheels working in his head. I think I just threw myself under the bus.

"I don't know. I was just thrown off by the call. Wasn't

expecting it with you being grounded and all." At least half of that's true.

"You sure?" He draws out the words. He doesn't believe me.

"Yeah, that's it. Sorry." I try to cover my tracks with a big smile and a few nods. Oh, how big a hole I'm digging.

"You're hiding something." He grins mischievously, knowingly. "You're not that good of a liar, Noah, you do know that, right?"

I laugh, and instead of answering I move the conversation back to the concert. I must not be *that* bad of a liar.

"So, are you excited about the concert?"

Friday
September 14, 2018

I made it out of Parker's FaceTime call unscathed last night, mostly. I looked guilty as hell, but as long as he doesn't know what for, I think I'm good.

I went straight to bed after that. Sure, my plan had been to come out to Mom and Dad, but that got rescheduled to this morning. And on that, well, that didn't happen either, again. I sat down for breakfast and had planned to talk it out, and I was about to, but before I could work past the writhing sensation under my skin Dad was out the door.

He had to go in early today so, in his words, "Daryl doesn't screw up the promotion again." He's a software developer, so I'm not really sure what that means, and I guess it doesn't really matter.

I'm still angry with Daryl, and I don't even know the man.

After failing last night, I wanted to get it over with this morning, but I couldn't do it without them both present. I don't think I can tell Dad on my own. I'm too afraid what he might think, and somehow having Mom there feels like he'll take it better.

After school I went to the range with Parker; well, Parker, his dad, and his brother, Joshua. We go every few weeks, sometimes more. It's one of those things that's made it easier to keep my cover. For some reason no one expects a gay boy to go target shooting. But I really enjoy it. It's relaxing, usually.

It was everything I could do today not to imagine Daryl as the black silhouette targets down range, whatever the hell he looks like. Fuck Daryl.

Mr. Evans was, well, he was Mr. Evans. He's a deputy with the Cabarrus Sheriff's Office, and a marine before that, prior to moving my best friend to Kannapolis. That's when Parker transferred in. His dad is a nice guy, but he's really old-fashioned. Strict and religious.

It's not a bad thing, I swear. I'm not super religious, but I'm not exactly an atheist either. The best way I've found to sum up my views on God is a Lex Luther quote from the unfortunately disappointing *Batman vs. Superman* movie, the one with Affleck. It's when he said "...if God is all-powerful, He cannot be all good. And if He is all good, then He cannot be all-powerful." I know, it's a movie quote, not Buddha or Jesus, and it definitely doesn't help that it comes from a DC movie, but it makes sense to me. It doesn't mean God isn't real but that maybe He's not as loving as people want to act like He is. I don't know, I'm just saying that's a possibility, and it helps me rationalize people like Mr. Evans.

He's well intentioned, I know, but if he were my dad, there's no way I'd be thinking about coming out right now. No way in hell.

"So where are we hanging the target?" Back home, Parker unrolls the paper on my bed.

"Don't know." I eye the hole-ridden paper for a moment. Not too bad. Five out of the fourteen holes are clustered in and around center mass, with the other nine varying from decent to embarrassing.

"How about here?" Park nods toward a blank space above my desk by the closet.

"Why not." I shrug and pin it to the wall.

"Now we just need a place to sit," Parker says.

My room's a mess as always, and the only place to sit is my bed, even when it's clean. And that's covered in a heap of clothes. I shake my head and transfer my clothes from the bed to my tiny desk chair, and we sprawl out and play FIFA.

Suddenly I find myself thinking about telling Parker my secret. I mean, I want to tell him, but I just can't do it. He'll have to find out later.

"Have you ever wondered if we're the only ones not listening to country music at Cook Out on Friday nights?" I distract myself.

It's a Friday night thing. Every week teens from all over Concord and Kannapolis go to the local Cook Out and fill up the parking lot. I'm talking every space filled with jacked-up pickup trucks and the occasional rice burner, and then half of us end up parking on the lawn.

"Or rap. Don't forget Stony's crew." He doesn't take his eyes off the television screen. "He's *obviously* got the best amp and sub."

Damn right. Stony and his friends, Nathaniel and Cameron, pack into a tiny Civic every Friday night and wedge between a pair of trucks to blare Drake and other rap I don't know. I can't wrap my head around why they come. It's even more baffling than us. They just sit in their car while everyone else walks around and swaps tailgates all night.

Actually, come to think of it, why do we go? We just sit in Park's truck and listen to our own music for an hour or so.

But we *are* in a truck, so we don't stand out too much.

Tonight's playlist consisted of a mix of Five Finger Death Punch (the modern gods of rock), Bad Omens, Bad Wolves (lots of Bad), some Halsey, a little Starset, and a few songs from The Weeknd and Diamante. Oh yeah, and some depressing but cool nothing,nowhere.

"Yeah. How could I forget Stony?" I roll my eyes. "Other than them, in that case."

"Probably," he says, but I can tell he's focused on the game.

He scores a goal because I let my guard down. I jump when he thrusts his fist in the air and shouts victoriously.

In the moment, between my heart racing and settling, something switches in my head.

"I need to tell you something," I blurt before I can think better of it. It's not the worst of it, but it's a start. I guess I'm doing this now.

I remember when being this close to Parker was problematic, not for him or anyone else, just me. Until our sophomore year I was obsessed with him. I'd have him come over just so I could do this, except I'd let my arm touch his every now and then. Now I don't. I got over him a few years ago and part of that involved keeping a certain physical distance. I need him to be my friend. He understands me—well, most of me—and I get him. The last thing I want is to fuck that up, which is exactly why I'm so scared right now.

But he is my best friend. He'll understand, right? But what if I'm wrong? What if it makes things weird, and he can't handle having a faggot as a friend? I know I'll still have Cam, but I don't want to lose him. I inch away and grit my teeth.

Maybe this wasn't such a great idea.

"Yeah?" He pauses the game and shifts onto his side to face me.

I don't want to do this anymore. I try to look him in the eye but fail. Surprise!

"I... I..." I try, but all he gets is babble. "Never mind."

"Nah, man," Parker drops his controller on the bed and tilts his head. His eyes gain this edge, like they know something's up, but at the same time there's a softness in them I rarely see. He can tell the wheels in my mind are turning. Dammit. "Are you okay?"

"Uh, yeah. I'm good." I kick myself for lying, but it's what I'm used to in these situations. It's easier.

Parker analyzes me for a moment. His lids constrict around chestnut eyes. I look away when it hits me how pretty they are. He's got these long, gorgeous eyelashes.

"Come on, Noah, I'm not an idiot," he tells me. A comforting smile rises on his lips. "Something's bugging you. I know it's not quote-unquote *manly*, but fuck that shit, if you need to talk, I'm here."

I don't know how, but in the same instant I both love him and hate him. I'd hoped he might let it go. Sure, I know he's willing to talk if I need it, I'd do the same for him, we have before, but not now. Just let me be a coward in peace.

But now he keeps looking at me. He's not letting it go so easily, so instead I drop my controller and grip a thick helping of my bedsheets in both hands and squeeze.

"I, uh." I look away. The air is trapped in my throat. I squeeze my eyes shut and take a deep breath. "I'm... Ugh! I hate this."

"Noah," Parker shifts back. I won't look at him, but I

know his eyes are drilling into the back of my head. Then he places his palm on my shoulder. A chill runs down my back and I have to rebound from the additional nerves. I know he means well, but it's not helping.

I suck in another breath and let it work its way through my lungs. Okay, I can do this, I have to do this. Without turning—I'm not that ready—I open my mouth.

"I'm... I'm gay."

A silence breaches the space between us. My chest tightens. I think I freaked him out, but I can't look. I feel the bed jitter, and for a moment I imagine him springing off the edge like a scared frog. But he hasn't moved. I hear him clear his throat just behind me.

"You're kidding, right?" he asks.

For the shortest second I contemplate saying yes and taking it all back like some big joke, but I don't. I can't. I shake my head vigorously.

"Really?" I can't tell if it's excitement or disbelief, but then he starts over in a softer tone. "I mean, really?"

"Yeah, really." I don't turn to face him. My hands aren't shaking as bad as last time, but I'm still embarrassed.

"That's...uh... That's great," he says.

I'm not sure how to take that. The silence, the question, then this. It's great? Is it? If I take it one way he sounds horrified, but in another he almost sounds thrilled.

"That's great?"

"Of course," he says with conviction. "Why wouldn't it be?"

"You're not disappointed? It doesn't bother you that your friend's a fag?" I ask.

"Are you serious, Noah? Look at me," he says.

I do, but I'm quick to divert my gaze to the wall where a painting of Carnage I got from a con last year hangs.

"Noah."

He's not having it, so I swallow back the fear and look him dead in the eye.

"I don't give a fuck if you're gay. You're Noah. You're *my* best friend." Parker's mouth forms a hard line each time it closes. He's serious. Seeing that it means that much to him pumps courage into my veins.

The hardness in his face goes soft and a smile tugs at the corners of his lips.

"Thanks, Park. I, uh…" I struggle for the words. "I was just afraid… You know, that it'd make things weird be-"

"Never! Stop it." He punches my shoulder playfully. I don't think Thor's hammer could wipe the grin from my face right now. "You're not getting rid of me that easily."

"You sure about that? What about when the guys at school start calling you the gay guy's friend or fag lover? Yeah, because I almost guarantee you someone is going to do that."

"Hmm… Well, the way I see it, only *I* get to call you a fag," he tells me. Immediately my eyebrows raise, but the smile doesn't fade. "Jokingly, of course."

"Oh yeah," I laugh. I'll call myself that, but yeah, it'll be different when someone else does. Park's on the approved list though. "You're good."

"So how long have you known?" Parker becomes quiet. I think he's unsure if he should ask, but I don't mind.

"I think I was twelve," I tell him. Suddenly I want to tell him how he was my first real crush, but he doesn't need to know. I'm about ninety-nine point nine percent sure that *would* strain our friendship.

Instead, I give him the short draft.

"While you all were crushing over Black Widow and Jennifer Lawrence, I was crushing on Captain America and Spider-Man, and maybe a little Andy Black."

"I wish you would have said something," Parker says. He sounds genuine, and it sort of hurts to know that I could have told him years ago and avoided all the close calls and junk. "I mean, I can only imagine what that's like. It can't be good to hide like that. And I'm sorry about all the gay jokes."

"It's all good." I nod my head. Yeah, no doubt. It's hell, a hell I'm finally crawling out of, and even though I'm only on the brink, it feels great.

"I still have to tell Mom and Dad." The words come out without my even thinking about it. I guess it's been an ever-present thought lately.

"You haven't told them?" Park sounds surprised. "You told me first?"

"Don't get too excited." I put a hand up to calm him. "I've already told Cam, but that's it."

"What?" He frowns, but I can see right through his charade, which makes me grin even more. "You told her first? Well, that bitch."

"That's our bitch you're talking about."

We laugh, and it feels good. I've just told one of my favorite people in the world what I've been hiding for years, and instead of losing him, I'm feeling better than I have in a long time.

"I was afraid. I didn't want anything to make you *not* want to be around me." I shake my head. "I know it was stupid now, but... I didn't know."

"Well, you have nothing to worry about, just like you have nothing to worry about with your parents. It's not like you live in *my* house." He raises his brow and forces a puff of air for emphasis. "Now that'd be a different story."

"Yeah, you're probably right."

"No, I *am* right. There's a difference." His smile intensifies. "So you're going to tell them now, aren't you?"

"Like now?" My brow crinkles. "Like right now?"

"Yeah." Parker shrugs. "Why not?"

Uh, because you're here, you don't want to be here when I do this, Park. Plus, I'm still mortified to tell *them*. I don't want to tell him that, but I am.

"Come on." He isn't letting up. There's a determination in his eyes, and once that sets in it's hard to dissuade him. "I'll even go out there and stand with you if you want me to. I'm just not holding your hand."

"Fuck you, Parker," I blurt with a smile tugging at my lips, but then I pause. "You'd really go out there with me? Wouldn't that be sort of odd for you?"

"Hell yeah!" he jokes. "But if you need it, I'm here for you. Mental backup."

I turn and peer at the television screen where digital recreations of soccer players are huddled, waiting for us to continue the game. Then I find my desk, the newly hung target, and my clothes on the desk chair, but I'm wondering if I could actually do it now.

Maybe. No, not maybe. I swing my head around and look Parker in the eye.

"Let's do this."

* * *

Mom's in the kitchen. Her awful jazz music is playing over the racket of some kung fu movie Dad's watching in the living room.

With more than a little prodding from Parker, I'm standing under the archway between the hallway and the living room. Dad's sprawled out on the couch.

I try to retreat back to my room, but Parker grips my arm and holds me in place. I turn and let my eyes plead their case yet again. I suddenly don't want to do this. Dad's busy anyway, and I'm sure Mom is occupied with whatever she's doing too. They don't need the stress.

Parker tilts his head and his lips form into a tight line under stern but caring eyes. I slouch and frown. Seconds ago this felt like it was going to be so easy. Parker's pep talk worked, I felt ready. And, crazy enough, it was easier to tell Parker than Camila, so I thought maybe this would be even easier. Surely the third time's a charm, right?

Nope.

My heart knocks against my ribs and my arms — hell, my whole body — are shaking again. Even with Parker standing his ground between me and surrender, I want to tuck tail and run back to the safety of my room.

He squeezes my arm again. Apparently I'm taking too long. Damn, I don't want to do this. But I need to. Before I can let adrenaline-induced panic win, I force a cough. One of those   I-don't-want-to-bother-you-Dad-but-I-need-to-talk type of coughs with some it's-probably-going-to-get-weird-as-fuck thrown in.

"Oh hey! I didn't see you there." Dad jerks around. He nods when he sees Parker. "Hey, Parker, you leaving already?"

I can tell Park doesn't want to start talking by the way he keeps his voice low. He wants me to talk.

"Uh, no, Mr. Andrews. Not yet." He stops. It's awkward.

I guess I'm supposed to talk, but my mouth is stiff.

"So, did you two go parking at Cook Out tonight?" Dad asks, but it sounds like he's joking.

We both nod. I look at Parker. Good, I'm not the only one who's confused as to why Dad's laughing.

"Never mind," he laughs and shakes his head. "Did you need something, Noah?"

That's my cue, the words I've anxiously awaited but hoped would never come. Well, I guess I did hope they'd come, but now that they have, not so much.

Parker nudges his fist into the small of my back. He's not giving me an out this time. If I was psychic like Professor Xavier or Jean Grey, I'd either telepathically thank him or melt his fucking brains for making me do this. His chances are fifty-fifty right now.

No, he's right. I'm sure he doesn't realize how much it means to me, even if a small part of me hates him for it.

"I need to talk to you about something, uh," I stumble for a second, but rebound quickly, "you and Mom both."

"Maria!" Dad raises his voice above the TV. He doesn't get up, but he does shift in his leather recliner to turn down the volume.

I'm glad he doesn't leave us here in the room by ourselves. If he did I'd probably shove Parker back, run to my bedroom and lock the door, where I'd then hyperventilate until I calmed down.

I ball my fists and chew on my lip. I have to do this. I don't want to, but I have to. No, I *do* want to.

Mom walks in from the kitchen. My legs grow weak, but I catch myself. I need to sit down. I look at Parker as if he knows what I'm thinking and start for the couch. He follows and takes a seat next to me.

Is it wrong that I'm too weak to do this without him? Is it wrong that I let him be here? I mean, I could do it alone, but I don't want to.

"Hey, Parker." Mom smiles. Dad reaches up and puts an arm around her waist and she plops down on the arm of his chair.

Seeing her smile disarms me for a second and then immediately puts me on edge again. I can't help but wonder if she'll be smiling or crying in a few minutes.

"Hey, Mrs. Andrews."

"How was the range?" she asks.

I'm thankful for the distraction, but I can tell Parker's trying to find a way to steer the conversation.

"It was great. Noah's finally improving. Right, Noah?" He laughs quietly and looks at me. He's expecting me to talk, but I don't think he cares what I have to say about the range and my sharpshooting skills.

I don't say anything. I'm frozen inside. It's like all my guts have squeezed together into one big mass. It's difficult to breathe as silence envelops the room and everyone waits for me to say something.

Finally, Dad breaks the ice. It's awkward, but at least he says something.

"So, Noah, you said you needed to talk." Okay, maybe I'm not glad he said something. I clench my fists again and again and swallow back a nervous gulp. Dad squints. "I guess it's okay for Parker to hear?"

"Yeah," I blurt. *Don't make him leave, please don't make him leave.*

Damn, that was awkward. Too loud, too quick. I go quiet again, and I can feel Parker's eyes digging into the side of my face.

"Okay." It's Mom this time, but she's lost her cheer. "What's going on, Noah? Is everything okay?"

"Uh... Yeah, everything's okay."

Is that a lie? *Is* everything okay? *Of course it is, Noah. The only thing not okay is how much of a fucking pussy you're being.*

"What is it, honey?" Mom asks. She shifts an inch closer to Dad, worry creeping into her green eyes. I don't want to make them sad, disappointed. But I have to do this.

I look to the floor and then the ceiling, and all around the room, searching for anything but them as I try to build up the tiniest sliver of courage. Finally, I find it, but it's not really courage, I don't think. No, it's one of those get-a-fucking-life-and-just-do-it moments, but I'll take it. I level my eyes on Mom. I can't look at Dad and say it.

"I'm gay." My voice is just above a whisper, but I shoot it out like a high-speed train about to derail.

Silence suffocates the room for an eternity. No, it's only a second, it only feels like an eternity. The look on my parents' faces morphs from marginal worry to this blank confusion. I'm not sure what it means, but I don't like it.

"Noah," Mom starts, and a subtle smile laces its way along her lips. She tilts her head forward, as if to look deeper into my soul, and places a thoughtful pause between my name and her next words. "I love you. *We* love you. No matter what. You know that, right?"

"Yeah," I push the word out. I'm shaking even more

now, and I want to cry, for some reason I need to cry. I try to dam it back, but a tiny droplet breaks free and trickles down my cheek. Then another, and another. Through the tears, the anxiety in my chest seems to seep from my bones and relief floods over me.

Somehow in the same moment I know she's telling the truth, I know they love me, but I doubt it too. It's so stupid, but I can't help it.

"It doesn't matter one way or the other, you're still my little boy." A smile I can't hold back takes over my face. Mom's voice goes softer. "How long have you known?"

Everyone asks the same question.

I finally look at Dad. He's here, but I think he's still in shock. He's looking past me, past their open bedroom door. I quickly pull my eyes back to Mom. I don't want to think about it now.

"A long time. Since I was twelve," I tell her. That seems to register with my dad.

"Twelve?" he asks. Something changes in his face, and he looks sad, but not a disappointed sad. A sorry sad. "You've known for six years? You've dealt with this for six years without saying anything?"

I can't seem to say yes, so I nod instead and glance at my feet.

"Noah, son, you could have told us," Dad says. Deep down I know, I knew, but he can't even imagine how hard it is. "We love you no matter what, and this isn't a bad thing. You do know this isn't a bad thing, right?"

"I know," I tell him, and I think I finally believe it. Hearing him say it means the world to me, and despite the nervous churning in my stomach, I feel free finally. Free.

There's another pause, and I use it to find Parker. I almost forgot he was here. Maybe I could have done it alone. Either way, he's still sitting next to me, smiling proudly at me, and I'm finally able to grin myself.

"I'm sorry for not seeing it," Mom says, and she starts to cry, which only makes me cry more. "I should have known."

"No, Mom, it's okay," I tell her.

She gets up and almost runs over. Before I can move she's hugging me. It *is* okay, but at the same time I wish they would have known, that they would have been the ones to say something years ago and save me all this anxiety. But no, it's okay.

"Please don't hold anything back like this, Noah, ever," she tells me. "Even if you don't think we'll get it, please talk to us. You're our little boy. Well, big little boy."

Mom lets me go, but she doesn't leave my side.

I nod and grin behind wet cheeks. It's awesome to finally get this off my chest, to feel the weight lifted and *me* finally surface. I know it's not all over, I still have the entire world to confront, but the world doesn't matter as much as Mom and Dad. I don't know what I would do if they didn't understand.

"So, are you two a couple?" It catches me off guard. My eyes dart to Dad. I can tell by the way he says it and how he's squinting that he knows he's treading on thin ice.

"What? Us?" I glance at Parker and then back to Dad.

"Yeah," Dad shrugs, trying to act like it's no big deal.

"Oh! Are you?" Unlike Dad who's trying to play it cool, Mom doesn't attempt to hide her excitement.

"No!" Parker and I shout at the same time. Suddenly my heart is thumping again. *Really?*

How did I not realize this would happen? My best *guy* friend since seventh grade basically walks me in and sits with me while I tell my parents I'm gay, and I never once thought they would think he's my boyfriend. The typical guess-what-this-is-my-boyfriend-and-oh-yeah-I'm-gay coming out talk. I'm *so* sorry, Parker, I should have known.

"We're just friends," I go on. I look at Parker and skew my face in a silent *I'm sorry*. His eyes are flared wide and he's pinching his lips tight.

"Yeah, I mean… Not that it would be a bad thing, but you know… I'm straight, I…" Parker is desperately trying to save himself from the hole Dad threw him in. It's actually sort of cute. "Yeah."

"Okay, I was just asking," Dad says. He slides back in the recliner. "Sorry, that probably shouldn't have been my first question."

"It's okay," Parker says.

"Oh, but that would've been so cute!" Mom starts up.

"Hold it right there, Mom." I stop her. She'll go on and on about it if I don't slow her down, and poor Parker doesn't need to go through that just because he's a good friend.

"Okay." She stops and cups my cheek in her palm. I cringe because I know it's about to get serious, probably mushy. "Noah, we're so proud of you. We've always been proud of you. The courage it took to come and tell us was enormous. You're a strong boy, but don't forget that every once in a while, you need to let others share your burdens. Your dad and I will always be here for you no matter what. You can always come to us."

I look away shyly and nod. "I know."

"We love you, Noah." Dad grins from his recliner.

"Of course we love you," Mom says. She lets her hand fall to my knee, and I catch a witty smile transform her face. "But I'm actually sort of disappointed you and Parker aren't a thing. I mean..."

"Mom! Just stop!"

* * *

I'm supposed to be asleep. It's like eleven, but I can't.

Today's been the most amazing day ever in the history of days. I did it. Who I am is no longer this secret thing, and it's not as scary as I thought it would be. With the help of Facebook, and obviously a little pushing from Parker and Camila, the world now knows.

I haven't been able to stop checking the comments since I clicked Share an hour ago, and they keep coming in. It's actually sort of overwhelming the amount of support I'm getting. I thought there'd be a lot more of the you're-going-to-hell crowd than the be-you and we-love-you crowds, but it's at least forty-to-one in my favor. It's awesome!

I went with a simple status. Maybe it could have been more elaborate, but I figure it's best not to bore people with my story—it's not that exciting anyway. So instead, I just told the truth and ended it with the first verse from one of my favorite songs.

I've kept this secret long enough. I'm gay. And no, I'm not joking this time.
"Are the secrets that you keep,
All the company that you need?
Is the way that they eat you alive,

And you break down and cry,
Worth the reason that you bleed?"
-Imminence, Coming Undone

Those lyrics have brought me through a lot. It's one of the reasons the band means so much to me. My secret *was* eating me alive.

Regardless, it's better than what it would have said if Camila had her way. Just a simple *I'm gay. Get over it.* Sure, it would have been funny, but that was the problem, I've joked about it for so long I didn't want *anyone* thinking I wasn't serious this time.

It's dark in my room. Only the hard light of my phone penetrates the black, and I can only imagine the look on my face. The excitement, the smile that I can't erase. It grows wider when I see Parker has entered the fray of commenters. It's a simple comment, but I laugh anyway.

I'm proud of you, man. Remember, I've got your back.

Yeah, Parker was clear on that point before leaving half an hour ago. Apparently if anyone so much as looks at me wrong, he's going to "destroy their face." It's a nice, although violent, sentiment. I have to admit I find it comical, though. Parker isn't puny, but he's no bodybuilder or jujitsu expert. I'm afraid it might not end exactly as he thinks it will if the wrong person looks at me wrong.

I continue scrolling. There are so many comments, so many from people I wouldn't expect, like Hunter from third period, who I thought was a super conservative, and Gabriel Ellis, *the* gorgeous Gabriel Ellis. I don't even have to worry about the haters. Everyone else pounces on them before I have a chance to read them.

I put my phone down and stare at the ceiling. It's hard to believe this day's finally come. I'm free. I can actually be me, which really isn't any different. I'm still the same guy I was yesterday, and the day before, and the weeks, months, and years before that. I'm just not shackled by what I thought everyone expected of me anymore.

My phone dings. It's a tone I haven't heard in a while, and I can't place what it's from. When I activate the screen a notification from the TMS app comes up. That's one I haven't used in a long time; damn, it's probably been a year, at least. I'm surprised it even works.

TMS stands for *Tell Me a Secret*. It's not exactly original, but what do you expect from a high school senior project. It's sort of like a local version of *Sarahah* where you can send an anonymous message to someone with the app as long as you know their handle.

I purse my lips and stare at the little *1* hanging over the app's icon. If they couldn't say it on Facebook, do I really want to open it? The obvious answer to that is no, but I can't help but wonder what it says.

I click the app. It takes a few seconds. It's not the most efficient app on my phone, but it comes up and a message pops onto my screen. In all capital letters, it proclaims, *FUCK YOU FAGGOT*.

What the hell? I swipe it from my screen and take a deep breath. *Just ignore it, Noah. Just ignore it.*

Hold on, why do I even have this stupid app still? No one, well, hardly anyone, apparently, uses it anymore. I tap and hold the icon, but before I can move it to the trash, another notification from the very same app dings on the screen. Inadvertently I let go and stare at the notice.

I should probably ignore it, just let it go forever unread in whatever online cloud it's stored in, never to be seen. That is definitely what I *should* do. But instead I tap it and open the message anyway.

> *Hey Noah,*
>
> *I just saw where you came out on Facebook. I think that's awesome! Really brave. Unfortunately, I'm not that brave. You see, I'm gay too, but I'm scared to tell anyone, except in a place where they don't know who I am. I wish I could.*
>
> *I don't want to freak you out or anything, I know you're probably being buried in support right now, but I have to tell you something.*
>
> *I like you. A lot. I have for a long time.*
>
> *Yeah, I know you, and you know me too. We go to the same school. I'd really like to talk if you don't mind, not in person, but here. Maybe we could email each other.*
>
> *Oh, and you can call me Altair.*
>
> *Altair*
>
> *altair022000@gmail.com*

I'm gawking at the screen. I think I'm in shock. This can't be real. Whoever this Altair joker is must be teasing me. He's probably sitting behind his phone or computer laughing at how he's messing with the new gay kid.

But what if I'm wrong? What if this person, this guy, really is opening up to me? Hell, what if he really does like me? I can't even begin to register that thought. It's too soon. It was only a few days ago I thought I'd forever be locked in my own mental cage, and now there might be a guy out there who knows me and likes me? It can't be.

I'm guessing that Altair isn't his real name. I don't know anyone at school named Altair, right? It only takes a few moments to take a mental inventory, and no, there's no Altair in my circles.

I should just drop it, but I can't. I want to know who's behind the message. Could it be Mateo or Gabriel? No, that's a *major* long shot. They're both extremely straight. But who? That name sounds so familiar.

My eyes hover over the email address in the message. I guess I could write him back. Maybe see how it goes. If it's a joke, it's only words. It can't be too bad, right?

I tap the screen and copy the address. A second later I have Gmail open. But what do I say? I look around my room searching for the words I should tap on the screen.

> *Hey Altair,*
> *You've got it wrong. I'm not brave. Not at all. I just got tired of holding it all in and I couldn't stand it anymore. Fortunately, I have some great friends who helped me.*
> *I don't know any Altairs at school. Are you sure I know you? There are a lot of guys at Brown. Are you a senior? Do we have any classes together, maybe lunch?*
> *You like me? Are you sure about that?*
> *I don't know what to say. I mean it sounds great, but I don't know who you are. No, it doesn't freak me out, it's all good there. I've just never had anyone tell me that who I'd be remotely interested in, you know, a guy. And to be honest, it seems weird that anyone would like me.*
> *Noah*

I stare at my message for a minute. I go over every word

and piece of punctuation to make sure it's the way I want it. I'm sure there's probably something wrong, something that autocorrect screwed up or some messed up grammar I won't notice until after it's sent, but I'll be damned if I don't at least attempt to check it first.

Satisfied, I hover my finger over the Send button. I wait. Am I sure I want to do this? I mean, if Altair is real and he actually, *somehow*, does like me, then I'd be a fool to not respond. Right? But what if he's ugly? *Noah, it's about more than looks, remember that.* Of course, that's easy to say. Ugh! Okay, but what if he's one of those idiot jocks I always complain about? They might be pretty, but that's about all they have going for them. I think I'd prefer ugly over stupid, maybe. What the hell, just do it.

I tap Send, and immediately it hits me that what I've done I can't undo. For a moment I think I'm going to hyperventilate, but I close my eyes and let my hands fall to my sides. *Calm down, Noah, it's going to be okay.*

I stare anxiously at my phone, waiting for it to light up with a response. Finally it dings. I unlock the screen and shiver. It's from Altair. A smile pulls at my lips, and I'm hoping and trusting that it's not an I-got-you-stupid-fucking-faggot reply.

    Noah,

    First, yeah, it was really brave of you to come out. Don't downplay it. Because there is no way in hell right now that I'd come out publicly. It sounds like you have some good friends.

    Yes, you know me. I hope you don't mind, but I'm not going to answer if we have any classes or lunch together, that might tell you too much, but I am a senior. And you might

*have guessed this already, but Altair isn't technically my
name.*

*Of course I like you. Is it really that hard to believe? I
mean honestly, you're super cute, maybe even bordering on
hot. There, I said it. Damn, I never thought I'd tell anyone
that, especially not you. WOW! I think I'm going to go climb
in a hole now.*

Altair

Cute? Hot?

Yeah, I'm majorly blushing right now. Thankfully it's
dark in here and I'm alone. This is surreal, but I *think* it *is* actually real. I want to pinch myself like they do in the movies
and the books I read, but it seems stupid in real life, so I
don't.

Okay, so Altair is not his real name, which was easy
enough to guess. Why does that sound so familiar, though? I
spin the images of every guy I can think of at school like a
carousel through my mind, but I come up empty again.

Hold on. Altair… Isn't Altair the name of the guy in the
Assassin's Creed games? I think it is.

I throw off the blanket and jump out of bed. Typing messages like this is easier on my laptop, so I yank it from my
desk and jump back in bed. Once the screen comes to life, I
open a browser and log into Gmail again.

I click on Altair's message and hit *Reply*.

Altair,

*Uhm… Thanks. You probably have bad eyes though if you
think I'm "cute" or "hot." Do you wear glasses?*

So, do you like video games? Maybe Assassin's Creed?

Noah

My eyes don't leave the screen after I hit send. I hope that wasn't too big of a question too soon. And God, I'm too anxious to go to bed now. I want to know more about this boy. Who he is, what he likes, what he looks like, anything, everything.

My computer dings and I rush to open the new message.

> *Noah,*
> *My eyes are just fine. Glasses? Wouldn't you like to know? Nice try though.*
> *YES! I'm definitely a gaymer. See what I did there? :)*
> *I take it you caught on to my pseudonym. Assassin's Creed is my all-time favorite. Of course, there's also Mass Effect, XCOMM, and I could go on for a while about this, but I'll spare you.*
> *So, are you a gaymer too?*
> *Altair*

I don't waste any time.

> *Altair,*
> *I was trying so hard. Haha! Oh well.*
> *Even if you had said you didn't wear glasses, which is what I'm assuming now since you said your eyes are fine, it'd only cut out like an eighth of the guys in our class. So I think your secret would still be safe.*
> *Don't worry. I'm not going to try to steal a kiss from every glassesless (is that even a word?) dude at school to find you. Just saying. I mean, it'd be fun, but I think I'd prefer to keep my face "cute" as you put it.*

On that note, I don't mean to push. I know what it's like to have this secret. So don't let me push you. I can be like that sometimes. I promise I don't mean to be.

And yes, I guess I'm a "gaymer" too. Haha! I'm pretty stoked I caught the name reference. Altaïr Ibn-La'Ahad. I had to look up the full name on Wiki, but I knew what it was from! My best friend loves that game. I'm more into the new Mass Effect right now, and I really like XCOMM too.

You can talk about games all night for all I care. :)
Noah

I could do *this* all night. Another message pops up and I'm giddy with excitement. Yeah, giddy.

Noah,

Well it seems your best friend has great taste in video games. I'm glad you're a gaymer too. If you weren't I'm not sure I could like you anymore. I'm just kidding, it'd be good either way.

I'm going to get some sleep. I hope we can talk again in the morning.
Altair

Hope? You better believe it!

Monday
September 17, 2018

Altair's favorite book is *The Maze Runner*. I'm getting the picture it's about the only book—well, series—that he's read. Strike one. But I guess not everyone is perfect.

His last reply included that little tidbit when I asked what his favorite book was, because naturally I always forget that not everyone loves to read like I do. Apparently it enrages him, just as much as it does me, how different the movies are from the books.

Right now I'm sitting in the school parking lot with my eyes jumping between three points. First, the school doors where my schoolmates form a steady stream into the building. I've had the whole weekend to prepare for this, but I still don't feel ready. I barely left the house on time, so it's not like I interacted with many people except Parker.

I can't help but wonder what everyone here is going to think. They know who I am now. I mean, they already knew who I was, but now they know a part of me I held back.

The second point is my phone, which has remained mostly dormant the last twenty minutes. I keep hoping I'll get a new email from Altair, a response to my latest question.

How the hell do you not like Reese's cups? I mean they're like a tiny piece of heaven wrapped in chocolate. The peanut butter being heaven of course. Don't want any confusion.

I'm beginning to wonder if I should have held back on the sarcasm. I know how it can get lost in written form, and I don't know him that well. What if he doesn't get it? *Dammit, Noah! Good going.*

The last thing to brighten my phone was the text from Cam agreeing to meet Parker and me in the parking lot. I'm not walking through those doors alone, not today.

That brings up the third point. The gate into the parking lot where I'm waiting for Parker to pull in. I'm always here before him, but today it feels like he's pushing it so much further. I check the clock on my dash.

It's 7:39 a.m. Okay, he has plenty of time.

I go back to refreshing my Gmail for the hundredth time. Still nothing.

Altair did volunteer one new little snippet about himself this morning in his blasphemous anti-Reese's email. I'm not sure he meant to, I think it was a slip. Apparently he has biology at some point in the day, and I know there are only a finite number of biology classes, so that narrows down the possibilities. I don't know all the classes, so it doesn't immediately help, but I do have my resources.

Parker. He's taking AP Biology this semester during second and third period. I'm thinking of asking him to scope out the room for me. He's probably not going to be too excited about it, but we'll see.

A knock on my window makes my nerves jump. I throw my phone and dart my eyes up to find the man himself, Parker. He's bent over laughing next to my door, his hand still plastered to the window.

"Really, Park?" I mutter.

I search for my phone. It's lying face down on the passenger seat. I pick it up and huff while I shove the door open. It pops against Parker's thigh and he stumbles back, but he doesn't stop laughing.

"Hey, Noah." He finally calms down and straightens. "What were you doing in there? Watching porn?"

"No!" I give him my best stern eyes as I get out of the car. "I'm just nervous."

His eyes soften. "I know, man, I'm just trying to lighten the mood. Hey, are your clothes gay too?"

"What the hell? What type of question is that?" I ask.

"'Cause they look like they just came out of the closet."

"Really? Really?" I stare him down wide-eyed. The more I look at him the more nervous Parker looks too. I have to stop just thinking about me. He's about to walk into school with the "new" gay guy. "Sorry, I'm just really tensed up right now. But that *was* lame as shit."

"Yeah, I know," he chuckles.

I smile when he plants his palm on my shoulder and gives it a squeeze. He's an idiot, but he's my idiot, so it's okay. I turn and search for Cam. I'm not moving until she gets here. It's the whole squad or I'm getting back in the car and going home. Sorry, Parker, but right now I need all the support I can get.

Lucky for him, here she comes, swaying in a pair of white shorts and a tight-fitting flowery t-shirt that exposes her arms.

"Noah!" she yells and starts into a jog. She practically jumps me, wrapping her arms around me and kissing me on the cheek. "Are you ready?"

I think she's still extremely proud to have been the first I told. She reminded Parker several times over FaceTime chats this weekend alone.

"I guess." I know it's not convincing, but I think I'm ready. I don't *want* to, but I chose this. It's about the only thing with this whole ordeal that I actually had a choice in, and I'm not holding back anymore. If people can't take it, that's not my fault. At least that's what I keep telling myself.

"You guess?" She's in my face. I swear she's about to grab my cheeks and give me a pep talk like her volleyball coach when the score is skewed in the other team's favor.

"I mean, I just thought I wouldn't be so nervous by now," I tell her.

"It's going to be okay," Camila says, but I know she can't tell the future and she can't make everyone at school like me.

"Noah, she's right. You're going to be fine. You've got us," Parker says. "Don't worry about what anyone else says. That's our job."

I know what he's saying, and I immediately imagine Parker trying to take on Uriah Byers, Brown's star quarterback, for saying something shitty. I'm nodding. Parker probably thinks I'm agreeing with him, but I'm actually assessing how badly bruised and bloodied Parker's cute face would be after that fight.

Damn, I really need to be more optimistic.

"Yeah." I try to put a little more enthusiasm, maybe a little more courage in my voice and purge a battered Parker from my thoughts. But it comes out over a sigh. "Let's do this."

"Come on!" Camila spins and throws an arm around my waist.

I guess that means we're off. We head toward the school, and even with Cam wrapped around me and Parker on my other side, I think I'm about to break into a sweat. I squeeze and release my fists as we get closer.

Just think of something else.

Altair's favorite color is yellow, not just any yellow, burnt yellow, like on a Camaro or Mustang. He doesn't know who Eddie Berg is, which was a bit of a disappointment, but understandable. I guess not everyone in the States has to know about a Swedish metalcore lead singer. But he does like hard rock, at least a little. He's more into pop and some R&B. He specifically mentioned Khalid and Troye Sivan, and to be fair, I didn't know who Khalid was until Altair mentioned him. Now I might be a little obsessed.

"Oh yeah, Park." I get his attention even though he's right next to me. It's a habit. "Altair said he has biology. You wouldn't happen to have any prospects in your AP classes for me, would you?"

"I don't know," Parker gives me a questioning glance. "I obviously don't have a great gaydar, so I'm not really sure."

I shrug. I assume he's talking about missing that I was gay this whole time. That's a fair point.

We're entering the crowd of students trying to push through the single set of entry doors. I throw my eyes around the flood. Hailey Holmes from third period is up ahead with her arm wrapped around Jacob Liles' waist. She doesn't see us yet. Riley Morrow is coming up from the left. We've known him since middle school.

He sees me. I try to look away, but it's too late.

"Hey, Noah!" His voice is deeper than I remember it. I guess I haven't talked to him for longer than I thought.

"Congrats, man!"

He slaps me on the shoulder and he's off. A smile creeps onto my face before I can think to grin, but I look away.

Camila squeezes me as if to say *See, what did I tell you?*

We keep walking. My nerves *have* relaxed a fraction. I'm still nervous, but that first kind word did a lot. For the most part no one notices me, just like any other day walking to class, and I like it like that.

"I'm proud of you, Noah!" It's... Actually, no. I don't know who it is. I mean, I've seen her before, I think she's a sophomore.

"Hey, Noah!" Another girl's voice reaches me before I can respond. I turn to find Veronica. I went through elementary and middle school with her and I can't even remember how many classes here at A.L. Brown High. "I'm so happy for you!"

I nod and smile, but I tighten my arms around my body. Cam pulls me closer. I want to thank her, but I keep quiet.

This is good. This *is* good.

It suddenly hits me that Altair could be close by. I wish so bad I knew who he was. My nerves heighten again, and my eyes jump around the crowd, but not in that nervous, jittery type of way, more like an I'm-going-to-find-you type of way. Of course, I'm *not* going to find him. I don't know what he looks like. I'm not even sure if he wears glasses, but I'm pretty sure he doesn't.

I do know he's single, he did clarify that point Saturday morning. He doesn't like the idea of having a girlfriend to fool everyone. I get that. Hell, I wish I'd had that mentality years ago when I thought I needed a girlfriend to be normal.

His relationship status doesn't really help though. I don't

exactly keep up with the latest who's-dating-who gossip. It's boring, not to mention a little invasive, in my opinion.

Camila and Parker help push me through the throng of students. It feels like everyone is looking at me now. They're not, at least not all of them, but it's still overwhelming. I hate being the center of attention in big groups, and the middle of the school hallway just before class qualifies as much more than a big group.

I get some odd looks. I'm not sure if they're disgusted, indifferent, scared, or what, but whatever. I take a glance at Parker and I think he sees them too. His lips are curled into a forced grin and his face is a little red.

We make it to Parker's first period class and he wishes me luck and disappears inside.

"You can go, Cam," I tell her. "I'm good."

"You sure?"

"Of course, I did ask for this." I huff.

"I don't know about that, but okay. I'll see you at lunch." She hugs me and walks off to the science wing.

I hold my head up and walk past a bunch of people I don't know. They don't notice me, and it amazes me how great that is. A minute later I step into Mrs. Simmons's room and take my usual seat behind Kary.

"Hey, Noah," Kary turns around and whispers. She's got this broad smile across her face. "I'm so happy for you. I can't even imagine what it's been like living in the closet for so long."

"Uh… Thanks." I squint and try to sound confident, but my voice betrays me. That's definitely not how I would have phrased it, but okay.

She turns around when Mrs. Simmons gets up and starts

the lesson.

Okay, this isn't so bad. So far, we're good, right? Yeah, all's good.

Then, out of the corner of my eye, something catches my attention. I twist my neck around to check it out, and I wish I hadn't.

Carter Underwood, the varsity second-string quarterback with something to prove is sitting a row back to my right, but he's not paying attention to the lesson. No, he's staring at me with fake longing while he pushes a banana in and out of his mouth. I clench my jaw and grip my desk, but I refuse to look away. Instead, I force myself to give him my best evil eye, which is probably pretty pathetic right now. It's probably more scared and confused than intimidating.

His friend and likely accomplice, Aiden Waylon, bursts into laughter behind me. That cuts off Carter's next go at the banana prematurely. He falls forward on his desk and loses it.

"What's going on back there?" Mrs. Simmons cuts through the laughter, and I snap my attention back to the front of the classroom.

This is going to be a long day.

* * *

Altair emailed me between first and second period. Apparently he saw me in the hallway.

Something about it puts a little extra pump in my step as I head to the lunchroom. It was about the only thing that got me through weight lifting too. Yeah, that was a bitch.

I'm not proud to admit it, but after half the guys in the

gym started dry humping each other as a joke, I spent most of the class in the bathroom. The worst part is that Mateo was in on it. I've crossed him off the list of possible Altairs. I was about ninety-nine percent sure he wasn't before, but still.

I was shaking, humiliated, in the toilet stall for a full five minutes before I managed to calm down. That was when I got Altair's message. It couldn't have come at a better time.

I sent him a quick reply, just a quick note about how mean people can be. I didn't give him any details. I didn't want to put it on him. Then I thought about how pathetic my email sounded, and I sent him another telling him not to worry about it.

It's okay. I'm okay. I'm good now. I swear. I knew it wasn't going to be a cakewalk. But damn, really?

When Altair replied I tried to imagine him, whoever he is, sneaking his phone out in the middle of class. I wonder if he was in biology?

He told me not to worry about what anyone says. Some motivational bullshit about how I was brave enough to come out, and to not let the haters bring me down. I don't know about this brave shit people keep bringing up. I wasn't brave. No, I was fucking mortified when I came out, and when I practically sprinted out of weight lifting. So maybe I still am, to a point, but it's still better now. There's a freedom in my veins I haven't experienced in a long time, a lightness even with the junk. Everything feels new again, like virgin territory.

By the time I grab my food and drop my tray on the table, Cam and Parker are still in the lunch line. I got here early. Not actually attending class has its perks. The crowd is much thinner. Of course I'm not telling them about that whole fiasco.

"Noah." Camila sits down. "How's it going?"

"It's good, mostly." I almost leave the *mostly* off, but I know she'll see through it if I hold back that much.

"Mostly?" Parker asks before shoving a fry in his mouth.

"Yeah, most are just treating me like normal old Noah, which is great. That's what I want, by the way. Mrs. Simmons sent Carter to detention for harassing me and then went out of her way after class to tell me if I needed anything to let her know." I was planning on skipping the whole banana charade, but I don't think Parker is going to have it.

"Detention?" he asks. "Which Carter? Football Carter or Carter from middle school?"

"Football Carter, second-string Carter." I make sure to add in the second-string part. It never seemed important before, but right now it does.

"Underwood." Parker exhales Carter's last name like he's brewing over it—hard.

"Yeah, him." I sit back and roll my eyes.

"What did he do?"

I was really hoping to avoid this. Hell, why not?

"He decided to blow a banana in the middle of class." I shrug. "His friends thought it was great, but Mrs. Simmons let him have it."

"He brought lunch just to torment you?" Camila scowls. Carter never brings lunch. He's one of the rich guys. Well, his family is. "That's messed up. Fuck him."

"Yeah, fuck him." Parker leans in with his fists balled up.

"Calm down. I'm not breaking down over here," I tell them. It's a half-truth. I'm not now, but... Well, I'm not now.

"Everything else go fine?" Parker probes. "How was second period?"

"It was okay. There were some jokes, but it wasn't bad." Now I'm full-on lying. Lovely. But I'm *not* telling them about second period. A little fib is way better than telling them I bitched out and ran to the bathroom. I swear it'll get better. I've been bullied in the past for being nerdy, so I know I can deal with it.

"You sure?" Parker asks again. "You don't sound convincing."

"Yeah, it wasn't bad. Suffice it to say that Mateo is *not* Altair."

"Oh, I'm sorry." Cam leans over the table and cups her palm over my hand. I dig my fork into a slice of pizza and cut off a piece. "I know you liked him."

"Mateo?" Parker asks. "You liked Mateo?"

"Uh... Sort of." It's still weird talking about it out loud, and I haven't talked about guys with Parker, period. It just seems weirder than with Cam. It's all so much easier in my head. "I did."

"Sorry." I can tell Parker doesn't know how to talk about it either, which gives me the tiniest bit of comfort.

"So what about Altair?" Cam steers the conversation to better waters. "Have you heard from him today? How's that going?"

It works. I'm smiling again. Somehow just the mention of his fake name uplifts my outlook on life.

"You're blushing." Parker sticks out his tongue between his teeth like it's some big thing. That only makes me blush more.

"Yeah." I can't help it. "He emailed me between classes. Apparently he saw me in the hall. I wish I knew who he was, but I don't have a damn clue."

"Really? None?" Camila leans over the table with her arms curled under her smiling face.

"So what *do* you know about him?" Parker asks, which surprises me. I figured he'd just sit this one out.

"Well, his favorite color is *burnt* yellow. I'm thinking he doesn't wear glasses, but I'm not really sure on that one. He's more of a pop music guy, but he likes a little rock. Uh… He's taking biology. Any luck on that front by chance?" I stare Parker down.

"Uh, no. I mean, I don't know. You want a list of guys?"

"Nah." I smile. "That might be a bit much."

"Get him the list." Cam nudges Parker.

I can't help but laugh. She's always proactive about guys. I remember her asking Cooper to homecoming last year. I don't think he was expecting it, but he did say yes. That was one of her many short-lived relationships.

"Oh yeah, he's not a big reader, which obviously is a bit of a blow, but I'll live." They laugh at that. I sort of wish he liked to read, to be honest. "But he loves *The Maze Runner*. Both the movies and the books, apparently. Aren't those the ones you like, Park?"

"Yeah," Parker nods. "The movies were better, though."

"Oh! Parker! Are you Altair? Are you Noah's secret lover?" Camila bursts out. Her voice carries farther than I think she was expecting, or maybe it's just farther than I want it to go.

Parker, on the other hand, gives her the look of death. "No. Seriously?"

That's all she gets before we both break out laughing. The thought of Parker as Altair is both funny and exciting at the same time. He's definitely not Altair. If he were gay I'd have noticed it by now. I'm not that blind.

I lean against the table and raise my brow at Parker. "Are you sure you're not Altair?"

"Nah, I'm pretty sure." Parker laughs. "If I was, I have to say I'd be a great catch. I mean, just look at me."

"Whoa!" Cam scowls over a smile she can't contain. I'm doing the same.

"Someone's confidence might be a little too high today," I say, shaking my head. "I have told Altair about you two, though."

"Oh really?" Cam asks, and Parker leans in. "And what *did* you tell him?"

"Wouldn't you like to know." I grin. I'm not telling them, not because it was mean or anything, but just to keep them in suspense, mainly Cam. She hates that shit. I know it'll eat at her all day now. Parker probably couldn't care less.

But even if I did tell, I wouldn't tell them everything. Altair asked when I knew I was gay in one of our emails on Saturday night, and I told him the full truth. The same truth I abridged for everyone else. I told him how it was the crush I developed on one of my best friends during eighth grade that confirmed it for me, I just didn't name Parker. I even told him how I loved watching his hands when he painted, drew, anything. Parker can't ever know that.

"I wonder if he's in here right now?" I pose the question and scan the lunchroom. I wish I knew.

"Maybe he is," Camila says.

"Maybe." Parker shrugs.

"I bet he is." I don't have proof, but for some reason I just feel like it has to be true.

Wednesday
September 19, 2018

I can't remember the last time we sat at the dinner table as a family, at least not intentionally. But that's where I am now. I would say I'm warming the side chair, but there is no head of the table.

With only my brother Zach and me, I guess my parents never saw a reason for anything bigger than the square table in our modest kitchen-dining room combo. So yeah, there's really no *head of the table* seat. Lucky for Zach that he's missing all this fun while he's away at college.

They didn't say it, but I know my parents want to talk. I've already loaded my plate with fried rice and a helping of sesame chicken bought from the tiny Chinese joint down the street. I'm thinking the 91 printed on their health inspection rating is a misprint, but hell, the food's great.

I want so badly to tell my parents about Altair, but the more I think about it, I don't think it's the best idea. Technically I don't know who he is, and the more I ponder it, the creepier it sounds. I mean, I am talking to an anonymous boy through email who says he knows me and who claims to like me. But he's Altair, whoever that is, and I don't want to lose him. I just need to figure out who he is.

"So how was school?" Mom asks.

She's barely eaten a bite. I know what this is. Even if I

didn't get it at first when she said we were having a family dinner. Her "no phones" policy at the table was telltale enough.

"It was good." I take a bite from a wonton. I know she wants more, but I'm not going to just sit here and paint them a picture. I want things to be normal. And while family dinners could be a nice little change from time to time, *this* isn't normal. Plus, my phone just vibrated and I'm dying to know why.

"So…" she continues, eyeing my dad across the table. He looks at her blankly and then something sparks. Here we go.

"Uh, yeah. So no one…" I wait for Dad to find the words, "…bothered you?"

"No," I lie. I really don't want to do this. Telling them about Carter or the pricks in weight class isn't going to fix anything. What it will do is make me look like a weak little bitch and possibly prompt Mom to come to school and make an issue out of it. And that is the absolute last thing I need.

"Are you sure?" Mom prods.

"Can we *not* do this right now?" I plead. Mom's mouth twitches, and she looks away. I use the moment to pull my phone out and place it on the table. She doesn't stop me.

"Honey, we're just concerned."

"I know, but I really don't want to talk about it," I tell her. "Can't we talk about something else?"

"You going to Camila's game tomorrow?" Dad asks, more than happy to oblige. I think he's almost as relieved as I am.

"Yeah." I give him a knowing grin, which he's smart not to return. "And I'm going to the coffee shop between school and the game."

My phone vibrates again, and the screen lights up. I take a peek. It's a text from Parker, and it looks like Cam was the culprit earlier.

"So you won't be home until late, I guess?" He keeps the conversation rolling.

"Yep," I tell him, avoiding eye contact with my mother. "I think we're going out to eat afterwards, like usual. Probably Firehouse."

"Gotcha. Does Camila think they have a good chance?" Dad asks. I think he's genuinely interested. He's even come to a few of her games. I guess that's what happens when your son grows up best friends with the girl and he had to shuttle you to every game.

"She's hopeful." I bob my head from side to side. At lunch she was going on and on about their chances. I still have trouble with some of the lingo, but I did gather that she thinks they can pull off a win. Apparently the other team isn't that good.

"When's that concert you're going to?" Mom pipes up. I can tell she's really trying.

"October. I think it's the first," I tell her. The only thing that's kept it off my mind is Altair. "I can't wait!"

My phone vibrates again. A new email. I squeeze my fists together in excitement. I don't know for sure that it's Altair, but I don't usually get much in my inbox, so the chances are good.

"Can I be excused?" I ask. Is that how this works? We have *family* dinners so infrequently, I'm not really sure if I have to ask to be dismissed or not.

"Sure." I can hear the resignation in Mom's voice. "Just… If you need anything, let us know."

I get up and pocket my phone. I just don't need the extra attention right now.

"I know, and I will," I assure her, then leave for my bedroom.

I'm not even halfway there before I pull my phone out and go through my notifications. Two texts from Camila and one from Parker, plus the email. I force myself to go through the texts first. I open Camila's.

U are coming to my game tomorrow, right?

Still talking to Mr. Anonymous?

I shake my head. In all the years I've known her I might have missed like three games. I type out my reply.

Of course I'll be at your game. As always. And yes, I'm still talking to Mr. Perfect.

Mr. Perfect. I hope it's true. It sure feels like it right now.

I grin at the thought and open Parker's text. It's a meme with Anthony Hopkins as Hannibal Lecter with *If people make you sick, then maybe you should cook them longer* written around his face. Wow, Parker, just wow! I shake my head and send him back a slew of crying laughing emojis as I jog into my room and flop on the bed.

It's time for the main event. I open up my email and find a new message from Altair. I'm already grinning, and I haven't even read it yet.

Thursday
September 20, 2018

My last email to Altair ended on a serious note.

Do you still believe in God?

It's a question I've asked myself a lot, and though I waffle around on the issue, I always end up saying *yes*. I don't know if it's simply need or lack of imagination or what, but it seems more fathomable to me that there is someone, something, watching over us, or at least out there somewhere. It can't just be us. We can't be the biggest fish in the pond, right?

I admit it's comforting, too. Knowing, hoping that there is something bigger out there, something waiting for us, waiting for me. It's a whole hell of a lot more exciting than trying to wrap my head around my light going out and then nothing. I mean really, I can't even begin to be all right with that.

I'm sitting at the coffee shop with Huxley's *Brave New World* in my hand, which, come to think of it, is probably why I asked Altair the God question. We're reading it in English, and I'm sort of surprised how messed up some of it's been already. The orgies and God as a myth stuff. Yeah, not what I expected from required high school reading. I know it's not the 1950s, hell, even the 1990s, but still.

Sipping on my frappe I try to read, but my focus is divided between the page and the hope for a reply. I want to know his answer. It won't change anything, but I want to know how someone who grew up in a much stricter religious household deals with this. I've had my issues with faith, but my family always said that God loves everyone. From what Altair's told me, that's not how his family portrays it. They claim God loves everyone, but He's still sending you to Hell for being gay, for being the way He made us. Of course, *they* don't say God made us this way, and all their condescension is in "love." I think my psychology teacher last year would have called it cognitive dissonance.

The door chime rings and I gladly let my attention wander. Cam? I thought she'd still be at school waiting with the team.

"Hey, Cam." I wrinkle my brow and drop the book on the table.

"What are you doing here?" she asks, as if this isn't my normal habitat.

"I'm engaging in lines of text and adventure." I close my mouth and immediately wish I could take the words back, but I keep a smile on. Damn, that was stupid, so stupid.

"Uh huh," Camila says with just enough sarcasm. "That good, huh?"

"Oh yeah." I nod jokingly. I laugh and shake my head. "It sounded a lot better in my head the split second before I said it."

She chuckles, that almost bending over and covering your face type of laughter.

"I bet it did." She purses her lips. "So you *are* still coming to the game, right? You're not going to sit here all evening?"

"Of course, for the last time, I'll be there. Since when

have I missed a game?"

"Uh, freshman year, game two against North Stanly."

"You're never going to let me forget, are you?" How the hell does she remember this shit?

"Nope." She grins. "It's all good. I'm going to get a drink and then get back to school for warm-ups."

"Get your damn coffee," I tell her.

She heads to the register, and I check my phone. It's blank, so I pick up my book and try at the lines of text again. *Oh my God, that was stupid.* I don't get three words in before my phone dings. It's Parker.

Am I still picking you up?

Why does no one believe me? I text back that we're still good and that I'll be waiting at Editions.

Before I can try my hand at reading again Cam interrupts me.

"I'm off. Enjoy those lines of text. See you tonight."

"Yeah, will do. See you." I shake my head. I don't think she's going to let that one go for a while.

I try again to get back into my book. I'm reading, but I'm not really reading. My eyes catch the words and maybe a fraction of the meaning behind them, but for the most part it's like I'm looking at an object without value. What I really want is to hear from Altair.

I keep at it for another twenty minutes. So far, the main thing I've gleaned from Huxley's classic is that apparently he envisioned regular people having their own rocket ships. I can go for that.

Finally my phone dings and I nearly throw the book on the table scrambling for it. As I hoped, it's Altair.

Noah,

That's a hard subject.

I've typed this message a few times just to erase it and start over again. Hopefully this is good enough.

Yes. I do believe in God. No, it's not easy for me.

I already told you how my family is. They're really strict, my church is really strict, and from what they say, God is really strict. They say He loves me but hates "what" I am. They say – if they knew about me, at least, they would say – that if I don't change myself, I'm going to Hell. And somehow that's supposed to be just.

How exactly is that just?

I didn't choose this. I'm sure you know that. And I wouldn't have if I had the choice. Who would? I hope that doesn't sound bad.

So to me that means God made me this way. How can He make me this way and hate me? How can He do that and then say I have to burn for it? How is that love?

Maybe God isn't all-loving, or maybe He's just spiteful. I don't know, and that feels really bad to say, but I can't shake that there is a God.

I hope that makes sense and that I didn't sound like I was rambling or some fence rider. Yeah, so that's that.

Altair

My heart is sad for Altair. I never had to delve that deeply into it. I came close, but not that far. In his words I can sense the hurt, and it bothers me.

I want to know who you are, Altair. I want to be able to really talk to you. I need to know. But I can't push him to tell me anything more than he wants.

I'm about to reply, but Sandra walks up.

"Hey, Noah," she says. I didn't realize she was here. She must have snuck in after I arrived. "You good?"

"Hey. Yeah, I'm good." I simultaneously lie and tell the truth, again. Altair's email did hit a sad spot, but I'm just happy to be talking to him. Am I really that transparent? Do my feelings show that much?

"Looks like you finished that Rollins book. What are you reading now?" She nods at Huxley's classic next to me. She always notices when I switch books. I guess that's sort of her job.

"*Brave New World*." I lift it to show her the cover.

"Ah, Aldous Huxley." She purses her lips in what I think is approval. "That's a good one. It's strange, but it'll definitely make you wonder about the direction we're heading."

"It's crazy." I haven't got that far, so I'm sort of talking out of my ass. I'm not going to tell her this, but the book's portrayal of sex is disturbing. It's like it's become meaningless in Huxley's vision of the future, something simply to pacify, a thing void of any real attachment or meaning. Don't get me wrong, sex is on my mind a lot, a whole lot, but not like this. I mean, I read the word orgy in the book and was like *oh hell*, but it wasn't what I was expecting. "It's for English. I *think* I like it so far. It's definitely no *Sigma Force*, but it's all right."

"It was required reading for me in high school too. I didn't read it until I was out of college though." Sandra smirks. "Yeah, I was that kid."

I let a grin slip. Seeing Sandra as the teen girl who doesn't do her homework, and of all things doesn't read the required books, is out of place in my head. But it does make her more real.

"Me too, actually," I admit. "This one's just weird enough, though, that I might finish it."

"Do. It's actually not that bad. So I wanted to admit that I sort of guessed your secret weeks ago," she tells me. "I hope that's okay."

It's a cryptic statement. My brow scrunches as I try to figure out what she's talking about. She comes over and takes the seat opposite me at the table.

"That you're... gay." She grins lightly. "Weeks ago you came in and I could tell you were fighting something. I don't know if you remember, but I asked if you needed to talk and you didn't want to. I wasn't going to push it, I never will, but you said enough. I know I've already told you I'm happy for you, but I just want to say that I'm proud of you too."

Yeah, apparently I am that transparent, dammit.

Sandra shifts in her chair. She eyes me the way Mom does when she's being overly sentimental. I'm trying to figure out what to say, and in the meantime, I just stare back at her, chewing on my lip. I'm not one for being sentimental, but it doesn't really bother me either.

"I know I'm just the crazy bookstore lady, but I consider you a friend. I mean it. I'm really proud of you. What you did, what you went through before, and honestly will from now on, it's not easy. You might not see it, but there's something brave in that. *You* did that."

"Thanks." The word isn't remotely adequate, but it's all I can muster.

I'm trying not to tear up. Dammit, I swear she seems like my second mom right now and I want to hug her for it. I don't, though. I sit in my chair and focus on breathing. "It doesn't feel brave. It feels... It's nerve-wracking at times, but it does feel good. It being out there. Yeah, people make their jokes and junk, but still. What did Jennifer Garner say in that movie... 'You get to exhale now.' I get to breathe."

She smiles at me, and a tiny laugh escapes her lips. "Yep, still the same old Noah. You even got your quote quota in."

The edges of my mouth lift to their max and I laugh. I guess I did get my quote in. But I do get to breathe now, and it feels so good.

"So, one other thing," Sandra says.

"Yes..." Something about her expression changes, losing a bit of its mirth to something the slightest bit resembling gravity.

"What would you say if I offered you a job, here, at the shop?"

"You want *me* to work here?" It comes out wrong. The tone is off, more like I'm offended than surprised. I definitely meant surprised.

"Of course." She grins.

"Let me think about it," I say, but I'm already grinning. Considering my track record of keeping secrets from her, I'm rather sure she already knows what I'm thinking. I'd love it. Dad even mentioned I could get a job to make a little money before leaving for college. Working here would be awesome.

"Good. You do that." Sandra pushes her chair back and gets up. She's about to walk to the barista area but stops and turns around. "And if you need to talk, if you *ever* need to talk, know that I'm here."

I nod. When she goes to leave it hits me that maybe I *could* ask her something.

"Sandra..." I stop her.

"Yes?" She spins around and eyes me.

"There is something, if you don't mind," I say.

"Of course." She smiles and sits again. She's almost jittery.

I've only told Cam and Parker about Altair, but I'm thinking it might be good to talk to Sandra about him too. See if I'm being crazy from an adult's perspective who isn't Mom or Dad.

"The night I came out, this guy from school emailed me. We've been emailing back and forth ever since, but..." I hesitate. I don't know how to tell her. It just sounds crazy telling an adult.

"But what?"

"I don't know who he is."

"You don't know who he is? What's his name?"

"Yeah, I don't know that either. I mean, he goes by Altair in his emails, but that's not his real name. He's afraid to come out, so he doesn't want me to know who he is."

"So does he like you or something?" She squints.

"Yeah." I look down like it's something scary, but I'm quick to regain eye contact. I don't want to look squeamish. "He's real, though. We've talked a lot now. I don't know what he looks like, but he seems amazing."

"So it's like Tinder but through email?" She grins.

"No!" I almost yell. "If he just wanted to fuck he'd tell me who he is."

"Hey, hey!" She puts her hands up. "Tinder is not just about sex. I met my husband on Tinder."

"Oh, sorry. That's just all I've heard about it," I say. "But am I crazy for talking to him?"

"I don't think so." Her voice is tempered. "I mean, it's sort of a sticky situation. I take it you care about this guy…Altair. But you don't actually know who he is. I assume you hope to meet him eventually, so you just have to be careful. Don't go meeting in dark alleyways or a hotel, and don't go alone. But the big question is, is he ready to meet?"

"No," I tell her. "He's not. I want him to be, though. I know it's only been days since I came out, but…"

"I understand. But you have to give him time, just like you needed. Remember how hard it was for you, but also remember that his circumstances might be different. It might be harder for him, or not."

She's right. Sandra doesn't even know Altair and she's so right. Which sucks, because it reaffirms that I might have to resign myself to a senior year or longer with an anonymous boyfriend.

Boyfriend. Is that what he is to me?

"Do you have any guesses who he might be?" She grins mischievously.

"Not really," I tell her. "He hasn't given me much to go on. I know he goes to Brown too, and he's apparently taking biology, but I don't even know how many biology classes there are this semester. He may or may not wear glasses, but I'm thinking he doesn't." Sandra's eyes beam with excitement, and it only eggs me on. "That also doesn't help, because the *vast* majority of boys at school don't wear glasses. Uh… He doesn't like Reese's, and he's not a big reader. Oh yeah, and he's a guy."

I leave out the God talk. It just seems too deep to bring up.

"Yeah, that's not much to go on," she agrees. "He doesn't like Reese's?"

"I know, right?" I laugh.

"Eh, you can get over that." She grins. "Nothing else, though? Is there anyone you wish he was?"

I get that same mischievous grin again. She wiggles in her chair like she's ready for the juicy details. I bite my lip nervously and look away, then refocus.

"Yeah, that's all he gave me. I mean, I know he likes yellow, he likes the type of music I do mostly, and he's a gamer, but any number of guys could match that description and I just don't know it," I tell her. Then I move on to my wishes. There are many, but I just name one, the former number two on my list. "But who I'd like him to be…" I pause in mock contemplation. "Gabriel Ellis," I tell her.

Before this week I would have said Mateo, but he got marked off the list on Monday, permanently. Yeah, he's still nice to look at, but that's it.

"And why?"

I knew it was coming, but I was still hoping to dodge it.

"He's super cute… Great butt." I almost don't say it, but what the hell, she obviously wants details.

"Oh really?" She grins, and I'm one hundred percent sure my face is blood-red now.

"He comes here for coffee, I'm sure you've seen him," I tell her.

"You'll have to introduce me next time he comes in. Do tell me more."

I tilt my head down in embarrassment. "Yeah, that's not happening. But he's got short brown hair. A light tan, slim. Not tiny, but not a jock either. I remember hoping he might be gay when I first met him last year, but then he got a girlfriend."

"So he has a girl?" Sandra sounds genuinely interested.

"Well, he did. They broke up over the summer."

"Oh, so he's single…" She lets the thought hang.

I bite my lip and huff.

"Yeah, but that does—" I stop mid-sentence when my phone vibrates on the table. I peek at the screen. It's Parker. "That doesn't mean he's gay. I can dream, but I don't think he is."

"Well, most people didn't think you were either until last weekend, honey," she reminds me.

I nod and open Parker's text. Apparently he's sitting outside waiting for me. I check the time. 5:20 p.m. Damn, time flew by quick.

"True." I tuck *Brave New World* under my arm. "Well, Parker's here. I've got to go. Thanks for the talk."

"No problem." She grins. "And enjoy the game. Oh, and don't forget about that job offer."

"I will," I say, and then think how it sounded. "I mean, I'll enjoy the game. I won't forget about the job offer."

* * *

Dinner was quick.

But that's typical when Cam loses. It wasn't a slaughter, but it wasn't exactly what you might call competitive.

"So have you talked to Altair today?" Parker asks on the way home.

I give him the *really* look. Of course I have. I can't tell if Park's genuinely taking an interest in my secret and potential love life or if he's just trying to *sound* interested. You know, be supportive. I think it's the former, though.

"I'll take that as a yes," he laughs.

"Uh, yeah." I chuckle. "We're on the religion talk now."

"Oh really?" Parker raises his brow. He steals his eyes from the road long enough to glance at me. "Religion, huh? Getting serious."

"Oh, stop it," I tell him.

"Come on, you don't talk about religion with your boyfriend unless it's getting serious." Park nudges me with his elbow. He has to lean over the middle seat to do it, and he pulls at the steering wheel. The truck jerks to the right, but he's quick to regain control.

"Yeah, you stay over there," I suggest.

"I got it." He rolls his eyes, but I catch a smile.

"And yeah," I tell him, "I think maybe it *is* getting serious. I mean, maybe not, I still don't actually know who he is, but... I... I don't know, I think I like him. It's hard to tell over email though."

"Yeah, not knowing who it is sort of fucks things up," Parker agrees.

"Yeah, tell me about it. It sounds stupid. Believe me, I know, but there's something about him." I look out the window. The trees open up to a small strip of failing brick buildings and a traffic light ahead at the intersection. "I feel like I know him. It doesn't make a lot of sense, but I feel like I do."

If I'm honest, I'm afraid to look at Parker. I can imagine the crazed look on his face. He's probably wondering when I totally lost it.

"That's awesome," he says.

I swing my head around. I'm the one with the crazed look on my face. I'm the one having a hard time believing it, and he doesn't even sound like he's just agreeing to be agreeing.

"Really?" I ask, squinting. "You don't think I'm crazy?"

"Of course not, I already *know* you're crazy." He smiles. "That was never in question. But no, really man, I think that's awesome. You probably *do* know him. That's what he said, right? You just don't know *which* guy he is."

I nod. He's right.

"So what did he say about God?" Parker asks.

"That's between us," I grin. "I'm not telling you everything we talk about."

I let it hang; Parker can take that as he may.

"Fair." He pulls the car into the coffee shop parking lot and takes the spot next to my Nissan. I open the door, but a hand grips my upper arm.

"Noah." Parker lets go of me. He swallows but doesn't say anything.

"Yeah, man?"

"Uh. It's not important and it sounds sappy," he tells me.

I'm not letting him off the hook that easily, though.

"No, you can't stop me like that and then say never mind." I grin.

His cheek twitches.

"I was just going to say that if you need to talk about any of this, I'm here. Please don't think it's going to weird me out. I'm your friend. Just because you like guys doesn't mean you can't talk to me."

My eyes soften, and my smile grows less accusing.

"I know."

"Good. Now that I got that off my chest, just think, you'll be starting here tomorrow," Parker says, changing the subject.

I grin.

"Yep, right after school."

Saturday
September 22, 2018

I keep waking up early, too early. My mind is constantly wondering when the next message will arrive from Altair, even while I'm asleep.

I just read his last email. Normally I wouldn't be awake right now on a Sunday morning, but it's worth it, even if his message was simple. He wanted to know how work went yesterday.

It was my first day at Editions, and I already love it. To be fair, I loved it before I got the job too. Sandra was like family already, but now I get to stick around longer. Plus there's L.A., Macy, Andrew, Dawn, Gavin, and Tina, all of them, at least the ones I worked with Saturday. They're all great. And I finally found out what L.A.'s real name is. It's Leigh Ann, but she prefers L.A.

I type Altair a quick reply about how crazy Tina is even though I think I'm going to like her, and how I get a discount on my coffee now. Of course, since he doesn't care for books as much as me, I throw in a little snippet about how "fucking awesome"—my exact words—it is to be around books all day.

Rolling over, I lie on my back and stare at the ceiling. It's still hard to believe I'm talking to a guy. It was barely two weeks ago I thought I'd never be out of the closet. Now I'm talking to a guy, and not just any guy, one that actually likes me, or at least he says he does.

My laptop dings and I twist a little too hard. I start tumbling over the edge of the mattress just before I catch myself and grab for the computer. My heart thumps a little harder when I see it's a new message from Altair, or maybe it's from the near face-to-floor moment.

> Noah,
>
> I'm glad you like the job. They really sound nice. Andrew and Gavin aren't cute, or worse, hot, are they? I don't need competition.
>
> As for the books, nah. I think I'm good as long as I read a handful a year. Actually, no. I think one or two might be enough. Maybe too many.
>
> So, I don't think we've talked about college yet. I'm assuming you're going. Any idea where you want to go?
>
> Altair

My lips pooch when I read his second paragraph. He's definitely not a bibliophile, but I guess that's okay. No one's perfect, and I like him too much already for it to matter, like books would have gotten in the way anyway. And competition? I mean, Andrew's definitely cute, but he's younger, and I'm already talking to Altair.

I hit reply and tell him he has no competition. I only have eyes for him, even if I haven't actually seen him yet. I throw in a joke that we'll have to work on the book situation, then tell him yes, I do know where I want to go to school. I literally just finished my application to NC State last night, so I tell him about that and submitting to UNC Charlotte and U of I last week.

I tell him how I want to go to Illinois most. Their architecture program is amazing, but it's competitive, so I'm not holding out much hope, to be honest. I also admit to Altair that I'd go to NC State even if I do get accepted at Illinois if Parker ends up at State. I end my reply on a funny note, telling him that none of it's going to matter, though, if Mr. Richter's chemistry class keeps kicking my ass.

I roll back over. My dream is Illinois, but I made a pact with Parker this summer. If we're both accepted to State, no matter who else accepts us, we're both going to State. It's the one school we agree on, and neither of us wants to venture off to college alone, if we're honest. Well, if I'm honest. I guess he doesn't want to either.

Parker's going to major in biology and pre-med. He wants to be a doctor of some sort, he just doesn't know what type yet. His heart is set on Michigan and Berkley, though. So I don't really expect him to make good on our deal. I'm not saying he's a liar, but it would be hard to pass those up. I'd have a hard time deciding myself. Plus I think he really wants to get out of Kannapolis, and Raleigh doesn't seem so far.

My computer dings again. I swing around, more careful this time, and open Altair's message.

> *Noah,*
> *You shouldn't worry about chemistry. You're smart, you'll be fine. I finished two apps last week too. Maybe I'll tell you where someday. :)*
> *Maybe soon.*
> *Altair*

I scrunch my brow. He thinks I'm smart — that's good. It means I've got him fooled. But that ending. *Maybe soon.* That's just so wrong. I want to know now. And especially after asking me where I'm applying.

The computer dings again, and my inbox lights up with a new message from Altair. That was quick.

> *Noah,*
>
> *I wasn't going to say it, but I saw you this weekend. It's eating at me. I had to tell you. I swear it nearly killed me to not walk up and say, "Hey, I'm Altair. Surprise!" I couldn't do it though. I've been thinking about it all weekend.*
>
> *I think I'm ready. I'm 100% freaked out for you to know who I am, but I can't wait anymore. I want you to know.*
>
> *Altair*

I swear my heart stopped on that last sentence. He's ready. He's finally ready!

And he saw me this weekend? Who is he?

He could be anyone. I saw Gavin at work on Saturday. I haven't talked to him at school before, but we talked a little on my first day at the coffee shop. I saw Andrew in passing — his shift ended when I got there. Gabriel, Zayne, and Liam came by the shop for a drink, and I think I remember seeing Jacob and Carter on the highway going home Sunday.

I don't waste any time.

> *Altair,*
>
> *Are you sure you know who I am? I only saw a few guys from school this weekend, and I'm certain you're none of them.*

You're freaked out about meeting me? Why?

I'm so ready to meet you! Just say when and where. Tues-day evening would be perfect. But whenever is good.

So do I get to know who you are now? I'm dying to know.

Noah

I hit send and wait. I wish we could meet tonight, but I don't want to rush him. I mean, I do, but I don't.

The digits on my computer's clock are moving so slow. Minutes drag on. I tap the edge of my keyboard and puff my cheeks. Patience might be a virtue, but it's one I don't possess. Finally a new message comes in.

Noah,

I'm sure I know who you are. Haha! :)

You have deep steel-gray eyes and dark-chocolate hair that's just enough neat, just enough messy. You're slim, and your skin is this subtle pale color that matches your kissable pink lips (yes, I said it). You're not uptight. No, you're down to earth. You're nice to everyone and a little self-conscious at the same time. You're also not afraid to have fun or make an inappropriate joke (which I find awesome).

I seriously don't think you know how gorgeous you are, though. Hmm... Maybe I shouldn't inflate your ego too much. :)

As for seeing you, maybe I was hiding in the bushes com-mando-style, stalking you. Nah, I promise I wasn't stalking.

I'm going to let you decide where we meet. Tuesday even-ing works great. How about 6 p.m.? That'll give me enough time to have a total nervous breakdown in peace. I promise I won't back out, I'm just being melodramatic. At least I think that's the word I'm looking for.

And no, I'm not saying who I am yet. I'm still really nervous about that. You'll find out Tuesday though. I hope that's all right.

I'm excited. Nervous as hell, but excited!

Altair

Did he just admit he's thought about kissing me? A shiver runs up my spine and I can't drop the grin from my *kissable* lips. I read over his description of me a second time. It's over the top, but I guess in some ways I do fit it—my eyes are gray, I do have dark-brown (not so sure about chocolate) hair. My dad's side of the family did curse me with pale skin, tanning isn't a thing we do well. I just burn.

Altair,

Okay, you might know who I am, then. I so wouldn't use "gorgeous" to describe myself though. More like "nerd" or something.

How about Five Guys across from the mall? Six is great!

I can't wait!

Noah

I send the message and have to remind myself to breathe. I'm going to meet him. I'm finally going to meet Altair, and I'll finally get to put a face to the name and a real name to a face.

Tuesday
September 25, 2018

The old analog clock above the classroom door ticks so damn slowly. I packed my things minutes ago and I'm dying to get out of here.

Mr. Richter drones on about the periodic table, but his words are at best a distant thrum. They're competing with the rain slapping the windowpanes and my distracted mind and losing gloriously. The clock hand ticks off another minute. Two more.

I glance at Cam. She's staring me down with one eye wider than the other like I'm crazy, but there's this understanding, humored grin too. She knows why I'm ready to get out of class, even if I do still have another period to labor through. Tonight I meet Altair. It's grated at my nerves the last two days. I've counted down the hours, and now I'm counting the minutes.

I'm nervous. I'm scared. I'm petrified he won't like me once we talk. I'm afraid he might be someone like Drake Easton, the chubby gamer with the unibrow in my English class. Or maybe Kenan Fletcher, who I had P.E. with last year. I was afraid to tackle him in football, or rather when I was forced to play football. Actually everyone was afraid to tackle him. He's so frail we thought he might snap a bone.

I know I shouldn't think like that. I have to look on the

inside, at what I've seen in our emails, not the outside. But the outside is so damn hard to overlook. Is that shallow? Am I already a petty gay? Please, no.

The bell rings, and I jump. I don't know why. It's not like I get to sprint to my car and run home or like he's waiting in my next class. No, I have a whole fucking ninety minutes left. I stop before I can get far and squeeze my fists.

"Damn, you're on edge," Camila jeers.

I barely hear her over the ruffle and clacks of others packing their bags and rushing out the door.

"I'm good," I lie. Well, not really. I'm just nervous. "Just ready to be out of here."

"I can tell," she laughs. "Excited about tonight?"

We squeeze between the desks and people who are still packing and pour into the hall.

"Yeah. Is it that obvious?" I ask.

"Well, to me it is," she says. "I don't think anyone else is going to know why, but I'm sure anyone can tell you're a little on edge."

"I'm not on edge," I retort. "I'm just excited."

"Right…" She nods.

I'm about to reply when Gabriel walks by. He's gorgeous, but I guess I don't really know him. I've never talked with him. I wonder if he ever goes by Gabe? Does he game any? Does he like burnt yellow? Maybe he's Altair, just maybe. He does have biology this semester. I can thank my group sessions with Kary in English for that little tidbit.

"Gabriel?" Camila asks.

I pull my eyes away from him and grin awkwardly at Cam.

"Why not?" I ask.

"I don't know, I...just..." she stammers, which isn't usual for her.

"No, you're probably right." I shrug. "I'm like ninety-nine percent positive he's straight. But there's always that one percent."

I go back to scanning the crowd. It's one of those useless tasks, but I can't help it. I've noticed the way people look at me is back to normal. Sure, I still get the occasional stare or nervous glance, but I doubt that'll ever really end, and I don't mind.

It's just crazy to think I could literally walk right by Altair, my arm could brush against him, I could even talk to him, and I'd never know it.

"So where are you two going?" Camila asks.

"I'm not saying," I tell her yet again. "I don't need you or Park showing up and making things awkward. I'm nervous as fuck as it is."

"What are we nervous as fuck over?" I know that voice. I roll my eyes. It's Parker.

"You know exactly what," I tell him as he comes up on my left. I texted both of them last night as soon as Altair agreed to meet.

"Oh yeah, that," Parker says.

Cam puts on a pouty face and completely ignores Parker. "Come on, Noah. You shouldn't be meeting with strange anonymous people without at least telling someone where you'll be."

"He's not strange," I tell her, but she has a point on the anonymous part.

"Whatever, just don't think this means you can start keeping secrets from me," she tells me. "The gay thing doesn't count."

"Yeah, no more secrets," Parker agrees.

I laugh and sling my arms around them both. I love my friends.

Cam ducks under my arm. "I've gotta go. Can't be late for P.E. again, unfortunately."

"Gotcha." I grin.

"But in case I don't see you before your little date—"

"*Meeting*," I correct her.

"As I was saying, *date*, have fun. And while it's perfectly acceptable to fuck on the first date, at least wear a condom."

"What the hell?" The heat's blazing in my cheeks. I glance at Parker for a little backup.

"Yeah, she's right. Safe sex or no sex, man," he says. "But maybe oral's best for the first date anyway."

Cam sticks out her tongue gleefully and high fives Parker before running off.

"Really, guys? Seriously? This is your pep talk?" I throw a hand over my face. I have the worst friends ever, but that's why I love them, I think.

Parker punches my shoulder. "You're going to be fine tonight."

"I hope so," I tell him.

* * *

I'm early.

The clouds paint a tender orange glow behind the Starbucks, Five Guys, FedEx, and the Beef Jerky Outlet complex. It's warm but not hot enough to keep my windows up and the A/C going.

I swallow an invisible lump and stare down the entrance to Five Guys. Now that I'm here, now that it's time, I'm *really* nervous. I guess I was nervous at school today, but nothing like this. The thought of finally seeing the face behind the email is exciting, but it's scary too.

It's twelve till six. I didn't want to be late on my first date. Yeah, it's a date no matter what I told Parker and Cam, or didn't tell my parents. They think I'm off to a movie at the mall with Park, and of course being the awesome person he is, he's covering for me.

"All right, let's do this." I grip the door handle and let myself out. It takes every ounce of strength I can muster to defeat the mounting anxiety in my chest, but I do it.

My legs are shaking. My face is warm, and I'm danger-ously close to sweating. Dammit, I don't need to sweat right now. I'm not sure if it's more excitement or fear, but either way I stiffen my legs and walk inside.

It's cool and smells of French fries and grease. The smell actually helps calm my nerves while I place my order and take a seat. I bounce my eyes around the bright white-and-red dining area. It's not exactly the most amazing first-date-ever location, but I'm not exactly rolling in cash either.

The tables forming the perimeter around me are empty. In a row to my right sits a family of three. The parents might be in their mid-thirties and their daughter looks to be in her early teens, maybe. Next to them is a group of loud teenag-ers, none of whom I recognize, and they're all girls. Their voices carry above the rest of the conversations in this annoy-ing cacophony. I glance to my left and it's more of the same—no one close enough to my age and mostly women.

A cold smirk draws on my face. *It's still early, Noah. He's got...* I check my phone. Three minutes.

The guy at the counter calls my number, eleven, and I get my food. I slip back to my table and set the food aside. I'm waiting for Altair.

I check my phone again. It's one till six. I huff and stare down the entrance. It opens, and a familiar face walks in. I lean back and swallow another invisible lump. It's... Uh... I think his name is Oliver. I barely know him, but he's in my fourth period this semester. He usually sits on the far end of the room, near the front—about the opposite of my usual position.

He sees me and grins. On autopilot, I mimic him. Is he Altair?

This feels so awkward. I look away like it might harm my eyes to keep looking. He's cute. Well, sort of. I mean, he's not *bad* looking. He's my age. Auburn hair arches over his forehead and nearly touches his shoulders. I'm not usually a big fan of gingers, but he's not bad. I can't remember what color his eyes are, and I'm not looking to find out while he's at the counter. He's slim, maybe a little *too* slim, and he doesn't really have any shape below the waist. Yeah, I can't help it, I look.

I've talked to him a little. I could count the number of times this semester on one hand, and the rest—ever—on the other. Honestly, I can't really remember much else about him except he goes to the same school and we have a class together, and we've had a few others together since freshman year.

Maybe that's a good thing. Maybe not knowing him much already is a good thing. I mean, at least I don't have many preconceived notions. I think he's more of a nerd than

I am, but that's not a problem.

The girl behind the counter calls out a number and Oliver takes a bag from her. I straighten my posture and steal my gaze away when he turns. It's stupid, I shouldn't be this nervous. If he's Altair, then he expects me to look, right? So I look up again just as he walks past the tables next to me. He sees me looking and waves. I throw my hand up before he shoves the door open and disappears.

I slump and grind my teeth. Guess I can mark Oliver off the list.

I check my phone for the hundredth time. It's four after six now, and there's not so much as a single email from Altair. Cam's filled up my screen with texts. A bunch of hearts, smiley faces, and *You've got this, lovebird* notes. I roll my eyes and bite my lip. He's late. Our first date and he's late.

Give him a break, Noah, he said he was nervous. He's just late. It's okay. Anything could have happened.

Maybe he got caught up at home or took a wrong turn. Maybe traffic is bad, and he's stuck in the perpetual construction zone known as I-85.

I'm impatient by nature, at least that's what I always tell Mom when she asks me to wait. Five more minutes pass and there's still no sign of Altair. The family of three gets up and leaves, and a group of guys around my age walk in. I search their faces. I don't know any of them, so I stop looking.

I fidget my fingers along the grease-soaked edges of my food bag and sigh. Whatever. I open the bag and lay out my burger and oversized cup of fries, but I don't feel like eating. My index finger skates along the tabletop, skidding across a stain of something sticky and red, probably ketchup. My eyes jump from the tip of my finger to the door. Still nothing.

It's *eleven after*, and with each passing second my heart beats more harshly against my chest. It's not nerves anymore. It's disappointment, letdown, maybe a little broken pride. My first date is a no-show. I chew on my lip and throw my eyes to the wall, ignoring the newspaper plaques hailing how amazing the restaurant is and focusing on the bland white instead.

This sucks so hard. It's like a cruel joke. Hell, maybe it was a cruel joke.

The door swooshes open and someone's feet tap across the threshold. I don't look. I don't need the extra disappointment of seeing some teenage girl or old fart, but curiosity gets the better of me, and as if some invisible force is controlling my destiny, I look anyway.

My body relaxes a tiny bit. I should be mad that he's here. He's probably been spying on me since I left the house this evening. I guess he finally decided I was too pitiful to leave alone any longer.

"Parker," I say. It comes out just like I feel, cold and empty.

In response, he grins cheesily and waves with his fingers forming a peace sign like he so often does. "Hey. Uh… Let me get my food and I'll be right there."

I don't say anything. I just nod with half my mouth turned up and the other dragging on the floor. How long has he been waiting to come in? Has he been out there this whole time? Why didn't he come in minutes ago? He probably feels guilty. And damn right, Parker, you should.

No, be nice. I should be glad he's here, right?

I'm feeling a little nauseous, but I really would like to eat, and I'd rather not be alone right now. My food is sure to be cold already, but that's the least of my worries. A missing date being numero *fucking* uno.

I look up to see if Parker's on his way yet. Nope. He's waiting by the pickup counter with both hands stuffed awkwardly in his pants pockets.

It's only been a few weeks since I came out. Sure, Altair's a bust, but there will be others. Right? Right. Patience. I just need to learn a little patience. That should be easy. Dammit.

Hell, he must have been nothing more than some jerk at school playing a cruel joke. Carter. I bet it was Carter or one of his friends. Yeah, I can see them behind the emails. I squeeze my eyes shut in frustration. And to think I poured my heart into them.

I open my eyes and Park is standing at the opposite edge of the table. He's got this uneasy look about him, like he doesn't know if it's okay to sit.

"What are you waiting for? Is Cam here too?" I throw up my hands. It comes out a little harsher than I intend.

He jerks his head in what I guess is a no on the Cam front and takes a seat. He folds his lower lip in.

"Sorry, I don't mean to be mean. I'm just... Uh... You know."

So he came alone. Surprising. I figured Camila would have been in on it unless he didn't tell her.

"I know." He's quiet and his eyes keep jumping from the table to me. I keep my eyes on him. If there is one thing I can do, it's keep eye contact, usually. I mean, it *is* Parker.

I'm about to lay into him. I need to get this junk off my chest, even if it isn't his fault. He did follow me after all, so he does have it coming.

"So—" I start, but Parker opens his mouth before I can

say more.

"I'm sorry for being late. I, uh…" he stumbles over his words. His brow creases and I notice a tremble in his hands. They're gripped tight, causing his food bag to shiver. "I shouldn't have…"

"Late?" I tilt my head and straighten my back. What does he mean, *late*?

"I was supposed to be here at six," he tells me. Finally he looks me in the eye again. "I was too nervous. I almost left."

"What are you talking about, Park?" I ask. "You aren't supposed to be here at all. I specifically didn't tell you where I was going for that very reason. This was supposed to be *my* date with Altair. And yeah, that's what it was, a date. But no, he didn't *fucking* show up. And now I just have you."

He jerks back. I hurt him. A sting jolts through my mind and I hate myself for saying it. That's not what I meant. I put my hand up and try to soften the blow.

"I'm sorry, I didn't mean it like that, Park. I swear. It's just I… I was really looking forward to this. I had my hopes up so much, you know? Talking to Altair was amazing. He seemed so great. But I guess he wasn't real. Probably a bunch of pricks at school made him up to torment me." I can't help apologizing and unloading the hurt I'm feeling on Parker all at the same time. Yeah, I'm glad he's here. I really am. "Thanks for coming, Park, even if you weren't supposed to. I'm glad you're here."

"Noah. Um… You didn't get stood up for your first date. Altair was… Uh… He was just late. I'm here now." Parker's pale lips turn up, but they waver.

What? *I'm here now.*

I fall back in my chair and throw my hands to my forehead. I rake my fingers through my hair and lock my gaze on Parker's stunning chestnut-brown eyes. As I regard him, all the feelings I buried for this boy since middle school seep back into my chest. *No, stop it, Noah.*

"What are you saying, Park?" I know what I think he said, but I need to hear it come from his mouth. "And don't fuck with me right now. I'm not in the mood for it."

"I'm not, I swear. Noah, I'm Altair." Parker—Altair—leans over the table like he's about to divulge a dark secret. "I'm... Uh... I'm... Dammit, Noah, you know what I'm trying to say."

All I can do is nod. I know exactly what he's trying to say. It's the one thing I've wanted to be true since eighth grade, the desire I buried under what I thought was reality, that fire I never truly managed to douse.

"Well, say something, please." His eyes beg for understanding.

"You're Altair..." I say it just above a whisper, my gaze jumping around the woodgrain tabletop. Is this really happening? I gulp and meet his scared gaze. "You're gay?"

He nods and opens his mouth. At first nothing comes out. I remember this moment clearly just weeks ago when I came out to Cam, then Parker, then my parents. I know how it feels, all the emotions, the fear and excitement, the desire to throw it all off, but the need to keep it safe, the sheer weight of uttering that little three-letter word, an admission of something I felt was too scary for the world to know about me.

Then he finally says it. "Yeah."

"And *you* like *me*?" As soon as I say it I wish I hadn't. I know those aren't the first words I should say to Park right now. They're not the words I wanted to hear when I came out. Well, maybe I *would* have been fine with it if Parker had asked. "I'm sorry, you don't have to answer that. I mean, that's wonderful, Park. I had no idea!"

"No, it's okay." He exhales, and a grin takes over his face. I can see the weight lift from his shoulders and it reminds me how it felt for me. "And yeah. I do like you."

His eyes shy away and he smirks under a quiet giggle. I chew on my lip nervously. Yes!

"I knew about the same time you did, I think." He finds me again. "I was like twelve. I can't remember exactly."

"Yeah, that's about the same."

"I've liked you since seventh grade, Noah," he blurts. For a second his eyes widen. I think he's terrified but excited at the same time. It's so cute. He giggles again, and a smile settles on his lips.

I want to say something, but my chest is fluttering out of control. He's *liked* me since middle school? He actually likes me? There has to be a catch, how am I just realizing this? There's nothing I can think of that I've ever wanted more.

"Believe it or not, I hated art before we met." He laughs nervously, and I find myself watching his lips move. I haven't allowed myself to do this in years. "I took art in middle school because I had a *major* crush on you."

"But you love art, you paint all the time," I insist.

"I do, but I didn't then. Back then I was just a kid with a crush on a boy." He looks away. "The hard part was that how I felt never changed. I couldn't stop, and I couldn't ignore you because we became best friends. I've been stuck in this cruel game for years, and then you came out to me that night and everything changed. Everything. I can't begin to tell you how hard it was not to say something right then, but

I was too scared."

His eyes meet mine. I look away but quickly find him again. It hasn't been this hard to look at him since his family moved into the neighborhood. He has no clue how hard I tried not to like him, how much I wanted to tell him for so many years. He doesn't have a clue.

"Park, I have something to admit too," I tell him.

His eyes become slits, but he doesn't stop smiling. I don't think he could if he wanted to, and I don't ever want him to.

"You know how I told you in our emails that I realized I was gay when I started crushing on a friend, but I'd buried it?"

"Yeah." He nods slowly. If he understands, he isn't letting on.

"No joke, it was you, Park, it's always been you," I admit, and damn, it feels good. "It sounds cheesy now that you basically said the same thing, but I tried so hard to end it, to stop liking you because I just *knew* you were straight. I was the closeted gay kid in love with his straight friend. I thought I was the only guy going through that."

I don't think I can smile any bigger than I am right now. The urge to lean across the table and kiss him is almost too much, but I hold back. I've never kissed a boy.

"You were definitely wrong," Parker says over nervous laughter.

"I almost got over you, Park. Almost," I tell him. "You're so beautiful!" I blurt before I can tell myself I shouldn't. I've wanted to say that for so long.

"Lies. All Lies." Parker shrugs and his eyes drop to the table again.

"No, you are," I tell him again, and thankfully it's easier

this time.

He shrugs again. He doesn't see it. I can tell I'm making him nervous, but I think it's in a good way.

"I'm sorry I couldn't tell you like you told me that night," he apologizes.

"No, don't do that."

"I was pathetic, as usual," he keeps putting himself down. "I was too scared, too *fucking* pathetic to just say it like you did. Instead, I had to do it in secret."

"Parker, stop it!" I raise my voice a little. I don't like that he's kicking himself. Not one bit. "You were brave, you *are* brave. We all do this at our own speed. Hell, Altair was brilliant. It gave me an escape, a hope that I'd never felt. Honestly, I might have freaked out had this all happened when I came out. I wouldn't change it, Park."

"Really?" Parker finally looks at me again.

"Really. But we *do* have a few things to talk about," I tell him. I put up a faux serious demeanor. "You lied to me in your emails."

"Huh?"

"You said you didn't know who Imminence was." I can't hold it back, I laugh. Parker shakes his head and joins in.

"You do realize most people around here don't have a clue *who* or even *what* Imminence is, right?" He cuts at me, all in good fun though. "They sure as hell *should*, but they don't."

He pauses, and for a moment we just look at each other.

"I figured if I, the random dude behind the email, knew *them* of all bands it would tip you off. It would have been obvious who Altair really was, and I wasn't ready for that. I swear I love them, and yes, Eddie is super cute."

"Well that's better. As long as we've cleared that up." I'm grinning ear to ear. Should I be talking to Parker about other guys? Yeah, it's okay. "I understand, I just wanted to give you grief over it. Honestly though, I probably still wouldn't have guessed it."

"You can be rather oblivious sometimes, but I wasn't taking any chances. And, uh… You're really cute too." He throws that last sentence out at hyperspeed.

I'm blushing. I can feel the red build on my cheeks.

"Really?"

"Um… Yeah, you really are. The cutest guy I know." He smiles.

I have to look away for a second.

"Did I seriously just come out to you without even saying the word?" It seems random, but that is the Parker I love.

"Yeah, you did." I shrug. "It's okay."

"I need to say it. You know what I mean, right? I need to say it," he insists.

"I know. It's hard, it's so much harder than it should be." I know how he feels. The need to say it, but the fear that comes with it. "But you can do it."

"Okay. I'm…" he tries. "I'm… Uh…"

I reach across the table and lay my palm over his hand. I've touched his hand before, back when we used to have a secret handshake in eighth and ninth grade. I forgot how soft it was.

"Take your time," I tell him.

"I'm… I'm gay." He releases a deep breath and smiles at me. "There it is. I said it. I'm gay. I'm *fucking* gay, and I want you to be my boyfriend."

A shockwave knocks me back. I want it more than anything, I have for so long, but to hear him say it sends my heart into a volley of flips and shudders. I don't know if it's because I thought I'd never hear a guy say that to me or just because I never believed it would come from him.

"Deal," I say. Oh my God, is that seriously the best I've got?

"Okay, I guess that works."

"I mean, yeah, definitely. I'd love that." I bite my lip. "I can't believe this is happening. Am I dreaming, Park? Did we seriously just become a thing?"

He laughs. "Yeah, I guess we did. We're a *thing*. Boyfriends."

The next few minutes fly by in a blur as my mind and heart try to catch up with each other. We talk about eighth grade and how we both were thinking the same thing all this time. He makes sure to let me know he liked me first once he realizes he had the upper hand. That's probably going to stick. He developed a crush on me in seventh grade, but it took me a year to start crushing on the new transfer student. I tell him that beyond how cute he was, his laugh is what really did it for me. It still does. He laughs when I say it and a chill runs up my spine.

It's getting late, so I suggest we head out. We get up and walk to my car.

"I've been wondering," Parker starts. "Why did you choose Five Guys?"

"I don't know. I like it," I say. "It's not really first date worthy, right?"

"Oh, it's not that. It was great. You sure it wasn't anything else?" He gives me a sideways glance and we stop next to the driver's side of my car.

"I don't think so."

"It's stupid probably, but I thought maybe it had something to do with it being one of our favorite places," he says.

I grin. Maybe. I don't know, though. I didn't think about it like that, but maybe. It could have been a subconscious thing.

"It was probably just me trying to find meaning out of nothing. I swear my head was running on overdrive before I walked in there." Parker nods at the restaurant. "One more thing."

I take a quick glance about the parking lot and take a chance. I take his hand in mine and squeeze it. It feels so good. I think it catches him off guard for a moment, but he rebounds quickly.

"And what's that?" I'd like to say he's smiling more but something dims in his eyes.

"I, uh, I'm not ready for anyone else to know," he says. "You know, that I'm…gay, and that we're a *thing*."

I love hearing him call us a thing, but it still feels like a little paper cut on my heart. I know it shouldn't though, I should understand. But like a paper cut, it still hurts like hell.

"I understand," I tell him. "Take your time. It's not easy, I know."

"It's just… Well, you know my family." Parker shifts to my left and bunches his lips nervously. "They're not going to like this. I don't know how they'll react, Noah. And I'm afraid to find out. Actually, I'm terrified."

I don't know what to say. He's right. They won't like it. Hell, they don't even like that he cusses.

"I won't tell anyone. And when you're ready, I'll be there for you just like you were with me, if you want." I squint, thinking back on the night I came out to my parents with Parker sitting next to me. "Now it makes more sense why you were willing to sit with me when I came out to my parents."

He smiles. Most of the fear is gone from his brown eyes. I grunt happily. He stares at me with this twinkle in his eyes. Then he leans toward me. Time slows, and his eyes are locked on mine. They're so beautiful. That's when I realize what's happening. He's going to kiss me. He inches closer, and my heart begins to pound. I want this so badly. I've wanted it for years. Our lips are an inch apart, and his eyes close.

I'm about to close my eyes and let it happen, feel the softness of his lips on mine, but I freak out and turn away. His lips tap my cheek, and I immediately regret it. *Dammit, Noah!*

He pulls back. There's a sliver of confusion in his eyes and he's chewing on his lip in that way he always does when he's unsure or nervous. He looks away at the traffic rushing above the line of bushes dividing the parking lot from the road.

Seriously, Noah! What were you thinking?

"I'm sorry," he says, but he's still not looking at me. "I should slow down."

"No." I reach for his face and cup his cheek in my palm. I turn his face so he'll look at me again. I look into his eyes and smile before leaning in. Time blurs again, but I'm ready this time.

I close my eyes and let it happen. Our lips touch and it's everything I ever dreamed of and more. I don't want it to ever end, and for a few seconds, it doesn't. Then we part, and

I open my eyes.

My heart is thumping like a jackhammer and probably skipping a few beats too. Before me is everything I ever wanted, and he's finally mine.

Wednesday
September 26, 2018

No one realizes how happy I am, how happy I've been all morning. And speaking of happy, the reason for my smile just walked around the corner. It's a struggle, but I hold back the urge to rush him and plow down anyone who stands in my way.

He's the Parker I've known for—what, six years?—but he's completely new. It's weird. He's the same guy I rode bikes with in middle school on the greenway, the same guy I've played every iteration of *Assassin's Creed* with, the boy I talk shit to and depend on, even if I never admitted it until now. But he's new, too. There's this new piece of him I never got to see. I guess it was always there, right in front of my eyes, but I didn't see it.

I wonder if he feels the same about me?

"Hey." He grins with this smile that says he knows something no one else in the room does, but I'm in on the secret.

"How was biology?" I ask.

I still can't believe I missed all the little hints; it was all right there in front of me the entire time. I knew Park had biology, hell, I asked him to scope out the guys in his class. Damn, that sounds so bad now. And of course there was his name, Altair, one of Park's favorite video game characters. I was so fucking blind.

"It's biology." He rolls his eyes, but I know better. He loves science, he always has. Why else would he be taking college level biology if he didn't, and especially one that takes two whole class blocks?

We turn and make for the cafeteria. I want to hold his hand like we did last night by my car and this morning for a brief second in the school parking lot, but I don't. I can't stop myself from looking at him, though, and frankly, I'm not going to try.

"Right." We weave through the rush of people, and the lunch line comes into view ahead. "So… We doing this?"

"Yeah." Parker takes a deep breath.

Once I got home last night, I spent the rest of the night on the phone with Park and in a flurry of texts. He wants to tell Camila. I told him I'd be there with him if he wanted, so he chose to tell her today at lunch. He's braver than I was at this point.

"I think I can do it," he says.

I let the back of my hand brush his, and it nearly takes my breath away. It's crazy. I still can't believe this is happening. I woke up this morning convinced it was all a beautiful dream, one of those you wake up from and want to go back to sleep and continue inside its lie forever. But it's not a dream. It's so much better.

"You've got this," I tell him. "I'll be here too."

He's not ready to come out to the world yet, or to his family, but he's doing it, he's making progress. I guess he's a lot like me in that way.

We finally get through the line and find Cam already waiting for us. Thankfully we don't have any stragglers trying to take up residence. I tell myself it's for Parker, that I want him to feel free to tell Camila, that I know it's going to be hard. But I think it's more than that. Yeah, I want to tell everyone that we're together, but at the same time there's this little part of me that's still scared about what people might think.

"Where've you been?" Cam's looking right at me. It's almost like Parker's not even here.

"Huh?" I'm taken off guard by the question as I sit down opposite Cam and next to Park.

"You weren't waiting upstairs like usual." She raises her eyebrows, which isn't good.

Then it hits me. In my excitement to see Parker, I forgot about Cam. Dammit. I left her standing in the hall. I can only imagine the texts I've probably got on my phone right now. I eye Parker with an I-might-have-screwed-up look.

"Oh my God! I'm sorry, Cam!" I blurt. "I, uh—"

"You told him first, didn't you?"

"What?" I'm not following. She's still pissed, but is she still talking to *me*? She's looking at me. What did I tell him?

"You told Parker about your date, didn't you?" She's smiling. Thank God, I'm safe. She eyes Park. "All I got were a few texts. Apparently it went okay after the asshole got there late. No offense to him, but I don't like that he almost stood you up. He's going to have some explaining to do when I meet him."

I grin. It's equal parts I've-just-been-caught and oh-take-that-Parker. I glance at him. He's smiling nervously, probably unsure how to approach it now as the asshole who almost stood me up.

After our date I fed Cam a few tidbits via texts about my night. I told her how Altair was late, how I almost left, but then how great he was when he did get there. She begged to know who he was and what he looked like, and of course she wanted to know if we kissed. I refused to give up anything, especially the best part—that's for Parker to do. Yeah, she didn't care for that.

"We wanted to tell you in person. You're the first, I swear," I say to her.

"Like hell, I'm the first. Did you not hear a word I said?" she asks.

Park shifts in his seat. I notice his hand in his lap, so I slip mine under the table where no one can see and lace my fingers between his. He gives me a faint grin, but it's laced with anxiety. *You can do it, Park.* He has to be the one to do it, we talked about it last night. It's the only right way.

"Cam." He turns to her. They lock eyes, and his voice shakes. "You are the first. We promise. You see, I...I'm Altair."

"Huh?" Cam asks. It's about what I expect. I guess it's probably more shocking and confusing than if he'd just said, *I'm gay,* but that's coming too. Brace for it, Cam.

"I'm gay too." Park grips my fingers. His hand is quaking.

I shift my gaze to Park and bite at my lip. He's not smiling. There's this uncertain look in his eyes. I squeeze his hand while the wheels keep turning in Camila's crazy brain. She leans away from the table and plants both hands next to her tray. Her eyes blink rapidly like she's fighting to keep rain out of them.

"You're gay?" she asks. "I mean, that's okay—no, actually that's great. It really is. But...whoa, this is a lot for one month, guys." She pauses, and a light goes off in her eyes.

"Wait, you're Altair. You two are dating?"

I want to squeal, to scream *yes*, but I hold it back under a flurry of exaggerated nods. Parker's doing the same, just not as crazily.

"Yeah," I tell her once I've gained control of my excitement. "We are. And what I didn't tell you last night was that I've had a crush on Parker since eighth grade."

"Rea—" she tries, but Parker cuts her off.

"I've got him beat. I've been crushing on him since seventh." I think the barrier broke. I thought it'd take him longer, but he's already going at it like the Parker I know.

"Let me get this right." Camila throws her hands up for us to shut up. I can't stop grinning. "You two are telling me you've *both* been closeted since middle school, *and* you both had a *fucking* crush on the other?"

I nod, but it probably looks more like an uncontrolled neck spasm. I want to lean over and prop my head on Parker's shoulder, but I remind myself that's not okay, not yet.

"Crazy, isn't it?" I say. I mean really, what are the chances?

"You know I was there when Noah told his parents, right?" Parker asks, and Cam nods. "When he told me I wanted to burst. I wanted so badly to tell him that I was g-gay too." He turns to me. "And then sitting there with you while you told them…"

He drifts off, looking into space, or maybe it's the tack board at the edge of the lunchroom with the sports schedule. I have an idea what he's thinking. We talked about it last night—his parents. He's certain they won't take it as well as my mom and dad. I grip his hand a little tighter to let him know I'm here.

"Oh," Camila says. The realization brightens—no, darkens—behind her brown eyes. "You haven't told your parents yet, have you?"

Park shakes his head and drops his eyes to his plate. When he looks back up, he sighs.

"They're not going to like it, not one bit," he says. "I'm probably going to hell, that's the first thing they'll say without actually saying it probably. I bet they'll try to make me go to *'counseling'* with our pastor too. I've thought about it all. Over and over again, all the damn time. Get why it's taken me so long, and why I'm still not ready for them to know?"

"I'm sorry." Cam reaches across the table in a gesture of sympathy. "It shouldn't be like that, and you don't have to tell them now."

Parker and I bob our heads.

"I know," he says. "It's just... I don't know, it's messed up."

"We can keep it quiet until you're ready," I assure him. I know how it feels. I won't rush him, even if I do want to shout that I'm dating the most beautiful boy in the world to everyone in the general vicinity.

"Agreed, take your time," Camila says. "I won't say anything, promise." Her tone then shifts from quiet and consoling to the normal Camila. "Oh, and I was going to say sorry I called your new boyfriend an asshole earlier, but hey, it's Parker, he probably deserves it for something."

"Bitch." Parker smiles brightly.

"But I'm your bitch." She grins right back. "Sweet! I can say that now and it's not weird."

"Oh my God, really?" I roll my eyes.

"Oh yeah."

She's proud of herself, but I shake my head, and Parker's blushing.

"Oh, I almost forgot to ask!" Her eyes light up and she wiggles closer to the table. "Did you two kiss?"

"Shhh!" I put a finger over a mischievous grin. She almost yelled it. When I look at Parker, he's doing the same, finger and all.

"You did," she whispers. She opens her mouth in a wide O. "That's so cute!"

Thursday
September 27, 2018

"I sent in my app to Michigan last night," Parker says.

"Ann Arbor?" I ask. I know which one he's talking about, it's the only school in Michigan he's interested in. I don't know why I ask, or maybe I do. I don't want him to go and leave me, I guess.

We're on my bed, eyes glued to the TV screen. Park is playing the new *Assassin's Creed*.

"Yeah. That was my last one," he utters between button combos.

I'm all too aware of how close we are. His arm is touching mine, and it's almost all I can think about. Damn, if Mom and Dad knew Parker was gay, there is no way in hell they'd let him in my room like this.

It's actually sort of funny. Years ago, before I came out, Dad made it clear that no girls were allowed in my room. Apparently teenage urges are too strong to be allowed near a bed, as if that's the only place you can do it. But now that I'm out, the same rule doesn't seem to apply to boys. I guess it's harder to decipher, plus if the other guy's not gay it shouldn't matter anyway, right?

I look at Parker. He's engrossed in the game, so I simply admire him. *Mine* is the first word that comes to me. Those chestnut-brown eyes, that perfect nose. I linger on his mouth.

It's small, but his lips are thick and pink, and my, do they taste amazing. I unlock my gaze and trace the gentle rise of his chin and drastic fall under his neck before the taut curve of soft, tanned skin disappears under his collar. Damn. He inches closer. It's like he knows what I'm thinking. Our arms press together. I close my eyes for just a moment and let the electricity settle.

"You're still aiming for Berkley or Michigan, right?" I ask. Anything to ignore the churning in my chest. If I'm truthful, I'm conflicted on the whole college thing. I want him to get what he wants. I really do. I want him to be happy, but what about me? Now more than ever it hits me how much I don't want him to go away. What if what we each want isn't the same thing? How does that work?

"Yeah," he says. His eyes drop from the TV and he pauses the game. "Technically. I've been thinking about that a lot lately. I'm going to keep our promise. Don't worry about that."

Damn, Park, was I that transparent? What has he been thinking about, though?

"Ever since you asked me—well, you asked Altair—where I wanted to go to school—"

"Which you wouldn't say," I interrupt.

He chuckles and nudges closer. "And reveal who I was? I think not."

I nod and chew a little on my lower lip. It's hard to ignore that his face is only inches away.

"But college. I still want to go to Berkley or Michigan, mainly Michigan, but..." He stops and sighs. "I never thought I'd actually have you, like *really* have you. Sure, part of the college excitement is getting away from Kannapolis, the independence and all that junk, but it was also putting distance between *us*. I hate to say it, but I wanted to put enough space and time between us that I'd stop liking you. It was stupid. Hell, it sounds horrible now, I know, but, yeah. There it is."

"Oh," I say. "So *would* you have kept our promise if I hadn't come out?"

"I think." He grips my wrist. "I...I hope." He looks away, then comes back around. "But now... Now I'm not so sure I want to go off to California or Connecticut. Sure, they're awesome schools. I'd be stupid to not want to go, but now I don't want to be away from you. I don't *need* the space. I don't want it."

There is this part of me that wants to demand he cancel his applications, to not open any letters he gets from Berkley or Michigan, to make it final. I want to tell him he should stay with me, but I can't. That's the selfish part of me, the person in my head who only thinks of himself. In my defense, two weeks ago I didn't think I'd be sitting here with Parker as my boyfriend. No, Park was my friend, he was the perfect straight boy I'd never have, not the boy I'd kiss. Now everything's changed, and I'm not really sure how to react.

"There's always FaceTime, Facebook, probably some other face app." I'm grinning, but I'm sad inside. I'm thinking of all the ways I can make him go to college with me, but the words I hear coming out of my mouth tell a different story. "It'll be all right. We've been friends for what, like six years? I think we can get through college together even if we're not at the same school."

"You're right." Parker's frown flips, but I'm wishing I didn't have these conflicting thoughts. I should be happy for him.

"Of course I am." I grin and pull back my shoulders to emphasize the point.

"Right." Parker shakes his head. I think he's about to go back to his game, but instead he shifts onto his side and props his head on the pillow. He looks at me and gives me this subtle smile. "Do you know why it took me two weeks to tell you who I was in our emails, or, well, I guess meet you as Altair?"

"'Cause you're a faggot?" I know from the serious look on his face I probably shouldn't be joking, but it just sort of comes out.

"Haha, funny." Parker rolls his eyes. He slips his hand over mine. "No. It's because I was afraid I'd lose you."

"Lose me? Why?"

"I don't know, but I couldn't shake it." He glances at the sheets. "I mean… I guess I thought you wouldn't want to date your best friend. I thought it might freak you out and things would get weird. And honestly, I think I could handle not being your boyfriend if that's what it came to, but losing you completely, hell no. That scared me."

"Oh." It's barely a whisper. Now I understand. I remember feeling the same way when I debated coming out to Parker. I was sure it would ruin our friendship.

"I almost didn't show up Tuesday. And then when I did show up, I almost didn't come in. Of course you know that." He grimaces. "But I'm glad I did. Plus it would have been a real douche move."

"You had nothing to be afraid of, Park." I squeeze his hand. "But I get it. I do."

"I didn't know that. You had nothing to fear coming out

to your parents, to Cam, and definitely not to me, but you were still afraid. We were both afraid."

He's right. I was horrified, I was scared to death of something that never was, of some rejection that would never be.

"The only thing I knew I had going for me was that you had come out already. I knew you were into guys, that's it." He laughs. "It at least opened the path for the thing I wanted most. You."

My cheeks spring up, and I bury my lower lip under my teeth.

"Stop biting your lip." Parker purses his lips. "It gives me shivers."

"Oh, does it?" I ask before leaning in for a kiss.

It's beyond amazing. The feeling of his lips touching mine, of his mouth opening. There's the slightest hint of something fruity, but I can't place it.

Suddenly the red alert klaxon from *Star Trek* goes off next to my head, and I jerk away from Park. It's his damn alarm. It must be later than I thought.

"Dammit." Parker checks his phone.

He has a strict ten-thirty curfew no matter where he is.

"Can't you stay longer?" I beg. I know it's pointless, but I do it anyway.

"If you want me grounded again, sure, but that'd mean I don't get to kiss you for a while."

"In that case, leave! Leave now!" I swing my legs over the edge of the bed and thrust my fingers toward the door. He shakes his head and gets to his feet.

Before he can get to the door, I grab his arm and pull him back around. He smiles as I bring him in for another kiss. I let my eyes close and enjoy the fleeting seconds that we're touching. He pulls away and I have to catch my breath.

"I really have to go," he tells me, but he's grinning from ear to ear.

"I know," I whine. "I'll walk you to your car," I offer to make up for it.

"That might look a little suspicious," he tells me. "I mean, you never did before."

"*Burn*, but true," I joke with him. He shakes his head. "I'll walk you to the front door, then."

"That'll work."

He turns, and I follow him to the foyer.

"Night, Parker." It's Mom. She's sitting in the living room, probably watching one of those how-to-kill-someone-and-get-away-with-it shows masked as a criminal investigation documentary.

"Good night, Mrs. Andrews." He waves.

Well, there goes my chance at another kiss.

He turns back around as I'm opening the door. I want so badly to at least give him a hug, but I know it'd be a bad call; I never hugged him in the past either. Instead, I smile and watch him cross the threshold.

"See you tomorrow," I call after him before he can dismount the porch steps.

"See you then." He grins back.

I want to watch him get in his big truck and drive off, but that might look odd if Mom happens to notice, so I shut the door and start back to my room.

"Night, Mom."

"Night, Noah. Love you," she calls after me.

"Love you too."

Before I reach my bedroom, I slip off my shirt, then lose

my shorts once the door closes behind me. I'm about to jump in bed when there's a knock on the door.

"Noah," Mom calls.

"Yeah?"

"Can I come in?" she asks.

"Yeah," I say, like I really have the option to say no. "Just let me get some clothes on."

"It's not anything I haven't seen before." I think she's joking. Surely she doesn't think that matters.

"Don't care," I yell back, slipping on a pair of Deadpool pajama pants with *Maximum Effort* stenciled in bold red down the right leg and throw the shirt I was wearing a few seconds ago back on. "Okay, good now."

She opens the door and walks in. At first she doesn't say anything. I don't know if I'm supposed to talk or what, but she starts walking around, skating her fingers over the knick-knacks scattered on my TV stand. It's mostly trophies from middle school, some from elementary school too, the participation kind.

Is she crying?

"Mom? You okay?" I step toward her.

"Yeah." She wipes her eyes and faces me. A second or two passes and neither of us speaks. Finally she breaks the silence. "I'm sorry."

"What? Why?" I don't like that she's crying, and I'm not used to her apologizing to me. I'm not saying she has reason to often, it's just odd.

"I should have seen it. I should've known," she starts. "I feel like I saw the little things; I mean, I guess they're big things, but they seem so small now. I remember your first step. I remember your first word. And your first big word, which came out something like '*Piderman*."

I'm laughing, but a tear threatens to escape my eye.

"Then I always had these visions of you. You know? Of what you would be, what you would do as you grew up." She blinks and uses her sleeve to dry her eyes before sitting on the edge of my bed. I sit beside her. "The sports you'd play in high school, the girl you'd date, the kids you'd have… I was actually angry this past week that I'll never get grandkids from you, but it was so wrong of me. I guess I'm just trying to say that I missed something big. I should have known. I should've realized there was something going on, that you were struggling. I should have been there to help. I can't believe I missed it. I'm so sorry. I hope I can make it up to you."

"Don't do that. You did everything right," I tell her. It was all me. I place more emphasis on my next words. "You're an awesome mom! I love you."

"I love you, too, honey." She snuggles up to me and hooks her arm over my shoulder.

"Plus, Zach can still give you some grandkids," I tell her. It's part joke, part truth.

"I'm beginning to wonder about that too." She smirks.

"You think he's gay?" I'm honestly surprised.

"No, that's not what I meant." She laughs. "Not that it'd be a problem, obviously, but no. It just doesn't look like he's settling down any time soon."

"Oh yeah, that," I agree.

"I love you, Noah." She gets up and starts to leave.

"I love you too, Mom."

She stops at the door and looks at the floor and then me. She wipes the last of the tears from her eyes.

"Are you two dating?" It comes out of nowhere.

"Huh?" I ask, trying to play dumb. "What are you talking about?"

"You and Parker?" She nods toward my door.

"No!" I assert. It's one of those things that's hard to keep my cool over. On one hand I want to scream yes, but on the other I have my promise to Parker. "That's insane. He's just a friend, plus he's straight."

"Do you like him?"

I'm beginning to feel like a prisoner of war in an interrogation cell instead of her son. I guess I can answer that one honestly, though.

"Yeah," I whisper, letting my head tilt down, playing the part.

She skews her mouth. I think she's trying to decide what to say. "How long have you liked him?"

I look back up as she takes a step toward me and stops.

"I don't know, a while. Eighth grade."

"I'm sorry." Her eyes are soft, and I can tell it does something to her. "It's no fun to like someone who can't like you back. Don't let it get you down, honey. That's just life. You'll find someone. You have plenty of time."

Do we have to do this? I give her my best sad grin, trying not to admit I'm a fucking liar and I have another secret.

The sympathy etched across her face morphs into an amused grin. "Plus, you're my little boy, which means you're downright adorable. Some guy *will* be extremely lucky to have you some day."

"Thanks, I guess." I blush and roll my eyes.

"Oh, and one more thing," she says. "Your dad and I have been talking, and we think it best that Parker doesn't come to your room alone anymore or stay the night… Any boys, actually."

"Oh my God! Are you serious?" I guess I knew it was coming.

"Dead serious."

"Parker's just a friend, and I *am* eighteen," I remind her.

"I know, but you're also living in our house." She squints.

"Come on, Mom," I beg. There has to be a compromise. "What if I promise to leave the door open? Plus, if Parker can't come back here, then I'll have to move my PlayStation to the living room and you won't get to watch Netflix as much."

I guess that last one isn't the most valid. Technically they could tell me I can't play video games so they can watch Netflix, but it's the best I've got.

She sighs and grimaces.

"All right." She puts her finger in the air. "As long as your door stays open *all the way*, Parker can still come back. But no other boys."

"Thanks!" I say, probably a little more happily than I ought.

She grins and shakes her head. "Good night, Noah."

"Night, Mom."

I can hear her mumbling on her way out. Something about how she's going to explain this to Dad.

Monday
October 1, 2018

"Morning, Park!" I yell across the school parking lot.

He's only now climbing out of his truck. His head swivels toward me in surprise, and his eyes, as gorgeous as they are, tell me he'd rather be in bed. But I'm not about to give him time to gain his bearings. What type of friend, or boyfriend even, would I be if I did that?

I glance to my left and make certain no one's speeding up the row to get that last-minute spot before running over to Parker.

"Morning." He shakes his head, but he keeps grinning.

I stop next to him. It's only noticeable this close that he's taller than me. It's only an inch, but it's there, and no, it's not his shoes, he is taller. I dart my eyes behind him and take a quick glance to my six o'clock. The coast is clear.

I jump forward and plant my lips on his mouth, but I don't linger. Any more than a second would be asking for trouble. If I'm honest, I think I sort of want to get caught, but I can't do that to him. I'm smiling so hard, and although he's trying to be serious, he can't stop himself.

"Noah!" he chides me. "Not here."

"I know, sorry," I say. Is it really better to just do it and ask forgiveness later? Hell yes. "I had to, and I made sure no one would see first."

Parker huffs. "Right. Just be more careful, and no boy-friend junk at school."

"I know." I keep my chest up and try to avoid rolling my eyes.

"Come on."

He takes off and I follow. A few minutes later we're sift-ing through the crowd. It's still all so new. To be honest, it's both exhilarating and debilitating. There's something awe-some about holding this secret, but at the same time it nags at me. It's like knowing how a really fucking awesome book is going to end, but your friends are still reading it, so you have to wait to talk about it. That bursting-at-the-seams feeling.

"You excited about the concert tonight?" I ask, trying to ignore my nerves.

"Hell yes!" Parker barks. "I've waited so long to see BVB, and of course Imminence!"

"I know! And Bad Omens! It's going to be fucking in-sane!" I love concerts, and I love these bands. "We have to get their autographs! All of them!"

"Good luck with that." He smirks. "Don't you have to pay for that?"

"I don't know."

I see Cam up ahead. She's waving at us before I have a chance to lift a finger.

"Hey guys!" she squeals, still a full first down away. I think that's about twenty feet, right?

"Morning, Cam." I wait until we're closer. No need for everyone in the general vicinity to hear too.

"Morning," Park echoes.

"You two ready to rock out tonight?" She's still squealing, but at least now we're making progress down the hall.

"Hell yes!" I steal Parker's line before he can use it again. He looks at me and chuckles.

"Definitely." He takes my usual.

"It's going to be great! The Brides, Omens, Imminence!" I think she might be more excited than I am, but I doubt it. "You two might have to keep me off Andy. Oh wait, *God*, I might have to keep you two off Andy. Do you think he's cute?"

"First off…" I nod at Parker, then shake my head, trying to get the point across that she shouldn't refer to him when she says gay shit like that. She apparently gets it. Her mouth and eyes go wide, and she mouths an *I'm sorry*. Parker smiles and shakes his head. "Second…yeah."

She's shrieking again, and suddenly her hands are grappling my shoulders.

"Calm down, Cam, seriously!" She's too cute sometimes.

"Sorry." She smiles.

Something clicks in her eyes, and she lowers her head.

"So how's the new no-boys-allowed policy going?" she asks.

She's being quiet about it, but I'd prefer her not to ask me *that* in the middle of the hallway, period. A fleeting glimpse at Park tells me he feels the same, except he looks a bit more on the shut-the-fuck-up side than me.

I messaged them both after Mom gave me her little speech last night to fill them in. I omitted the part where she asked if I was dating Parker.

"It's not technically a total boy ban," I whisper. I keep my head low as if it might help dampen the acoustics. It seems logical. Then it hits me how stupid I'm being.

No one here, with the exception of Cam and me, know

Park is gay. So why are we worried about talking about my parents' new little rule for *me*? I shake my head.

"So just Park?" she asks.

I tilt my head and give her a grimace.

"No, any boy. Mom and Dad don't know about..." I don't say his name, unlike Cam. Instead, I jerk my head toward him. "It's no boys, except for Parker. I just have to keep the door open when he's there. Oh, and I can't complain if they come and check on us."

"Yeah." Parker grins. "I'm the *only* one allowed."

"Talk about ironic." She raises an eyebrow.

"I know, right?" I'm beaming.

"So I guess it's *not* because of anything you two did, then?" Cam grins.

"*No!*" I shrug. It was just in the making, one of those things where I guess the light went off in my parents' heads and they had to act. "Not yet, at least."

"Oh!" Camila says.

"Really?" Parker looks at me with this questioning gaze.

"I'm just kidding." I punch him lightly.

"So now we're not?" He grins.

"Oh fuck off." I shake my head. I can't win.

"That's not *too* bad, then," Camila bobs her head. She's right, it really isn't.

"Could be worse," Parker tells her. "Noah's not allowed in my room, *period*. Hell, as soon as they found out he was gay, that's the first thing they told me. I swear they think you're going to butt-fuck me the moment you cross the threshold, even though I'm 'straight'."

If I hadn't expected it, his parents' decision would probably have bothered me more, but I knew it was coming. I was actually more surprised they said I could still come by at all. It's not like I'm going to, but at least the option is there.

"Yeah, see?" I tell her. "Not that bad."

"I just don't understand people like that," Camila starts up. "I mean, really. It's the twenty-first century. It wasn't that long ago the same people would have condemned their precious white kids from marrying us *colored* folk."

"Calm down, Cam," I beg her. Parker doesn't need to hear it. Yeah, I don't like it either, but they're still his parents. They're actually nice people, just a bit misguided, I guess.

"Sorry, Park," she says.

"It's okay." He shrugs it off, but I think it bothers him more than he lets on.

"You know what just hit me?" Camila asks. I can see the light bulb shattering behind her brown eyes. "I used to be the odd one out here. You know, the only minority, a black girl hanging out with two nerdy white boys. Now we're all minorities. A black girl and her two gay friends."

"Oh my God!" I drop my gaze to the floor and sigh.

"That's what you're taking from this?" Parker is laughing now.

"It's true." She shrugs. "I'd love to stay and talk, but I'm already going to be late for astronomy, and Mr. Brock's been on my ass about my tardies. So adios!"

"See you," Parker calls after her as she half-runs, half-jogs down the hall.

I throw up a hand and wave at her.

"You should probably get moving too," I tell him. I know I won't be late for class. I have another half minute, and I'm standing next to the door to Mrs. Simmons's room.

"Yeah," Parker agrees.

He eyes me for a second, and I wonder if he's thinking about hugging me. I know that's what I'm thinking about; well, and a quick kiss. He smiles and shakes his head. "See you at lunch."

"See you," I tell him and watch him sprint two classrooms down to Mr. Anderson's room.

Wednesday
October 3, 2018

Sandra's behind the register ringing up some old dude that comes in every Wednesday afternoon. He's one of those Mr. Clean look-alikes, except I don't think he ever got the earring memo. I still can't remember his name.

I'm still learning the process and all the terms, but he's easy. He just wants a coffee, black with today's brew, which just so happens to be Organic Colombian.

He pays with cash as I top off his cup.

"Here you go, sir." I hand him his coffee.

"Thank you, son." He nods and disappears into our indoor porch.

"I think you're getting the hang of it," Sandra says, nodding.

"It was only a drip." I wrinkle my brow. It really isn't a hard one. It's the damn frappes, the ones I like, and lattes that I have to follow the directions on her little white index cards. "I'm not totally incompetent."

I know she's a friend, but she's also my boss, so for a moment I wish I would have kept my mouth shut.

"Well, you could have fooled me your first few days." She's grinning.

My mouth drops, and I'm sure my eyes are beaming surprise. "WOW!"

"I'm just kidding." She pats my chest with the back of her hand and laughs with, or at, me. "But seriously, you're coming along great. I might train you on the register later tonight too."

"That'd be cool."

"Oh, I about forgot," she lifts her brow, "how was the concert?"

"It was fu-" I catch myself. I actually don't think she'd mind swearing, but I'm not testing it—not now, at least. "It was great! I could literally feel the bass in my chest, it was *that* hard. And I got those autographs!"

"Really?" she asks. "All of them?"

"Well, most of them." I shrug. "I got Andy Black's, Eddie Berg's, Nicholas Ruffalo's, and Noah Sebastian's. I didn't get Harald Barrett's, though. He wasn't at the table when I got there."

"Did you tell the one guy you share the same name?"

At first, I look at her like she's crazy, but I break down quickly and roll my eyes. "Yeah, I did."

"And was the one as crazy good-looking as you thought he was?" she asks.

"Huh?" I ask. I mean, I think I know who she's talking about, but I don't know how she knows to ask, plus there's more than one. I think she's talking about Eddie, though, or maybe Andy.

"I can't remember which, but I've heard you and Camila talking about them for weeks now." She smiles and steps around the register. "No, I wasn't intentionally listening. You two aren't exactly quiet."

Well, I didn't think we were that loud. There's no point in depriving her, though.

"Yeah, they were." I think I'm blushing.

The front entry chime rings and my attention jumps to the door. A grin peaks at the edges of my mouth when Parker walks in. I've been expecting him. He told me after lunch that he planned to stop by today before church. And here he is, strutting into the veranda in khaki slacks with those beautiful chestnut eyes bouncing between Sandra and me. He swipes a hand through his hair. It's disheveled as it is, but it settles over his forehead, matching his eyes perfectly.

"Hey," Parker says.

That's when I realize I'm staring and suddenly unable to form a single syllable. My chest is heavy. I'm holding my breath. I shake my head and exhale, and my reply comes out in a stutter.

"H-hey, Park."

"Parker." Sandra nods. "How are you?"

"Great, you?" He nods back, but his eyes gravitate back to me.

I shy away so I can beam in peace for a moment before meeting his gaze again.

"All's good here. So what can *Noah* get for you?" she asks. Normally it's *what can* we *get you*, but not this time.

"I'll take a mocha frappe," he tells her.

"Oh good, he needs some work on those anyway." She smiles at Parker and then eyes me.

"Oh boy." Parker widens his eyes. I *think* it's mock fear. It damn well better be.

"I've got it." I roll my eyes. They're not going to see me fail now. I turn and find the little index card titled *Mocha Frappe* and get to work.

"So did you have fun at the concert?" she asks Parker.

From the corner of my eye I can see Parker perfectly, and I can just make out Sandra's elbow leaning on the counter. "Noah and I were just talking about it."

"Yeah, it was awesome!" he says.

"Which is your favorite band?" Sandra's good at making small talk. I envy how easy she makes it look. If it was me and a random customer, I'd be standing there staring at them trying to find something to say that doesn't sound awkward like *that's a nice blue shirt*. Except the main thing running through my head would be wishing they'd just leave.

"That's *so* hard," he says, but I'm certain it isn't. I've heard him talk about it ever since we left the concert Monday night. "They're all *so* good! Black Veil Brides is my favorite of the three, but the energy that Bad Omens put out was insane. They probably had the best set of the night."

"So what were they again?" Sandra asks. I made her listen to one song by each of the bands when we first got our tickets. It's her fault, she asked me the same question. I guess she forgot, or maybe this is how one makes small talk.

"It's all hard rock," he reminds her with a tilt of his head. "Omens is more of a grunge sound, I guess. That might not be the right term. Industrial, maybe. I don't know, they're awesome, that's all that matters."

"I guess so," Sandra concedes just as I'm finishing up Parker's frappe.

"Here we are. A mocha frappe," I announce proudly and pass the drink over the counter. My fingers brush Park's, and I have to swallow the flutter in my throat.

"Are you sure this is right?" He grins.

I could smack him right now. I really could.

"Only one way to find out," Sandra laments and winks at

me. "I think he got it right, though. Believe it or not, I was watching him make it."

I shake my head but let out a chuckle, too.

"If you say so." Parker smirks. His eyes flick between Sandra and me. "I'll be out here for a little bit."

"Enjoy," I tell him.

He turns just as he's making the bend onto the porch and smiles at me. Then he disappears, and I'm left with Sandra, trying not to let the waves in my heart surface.

"I'm going to check the thriller section while you clean up." Sandra walks around the counter. "Some little asses wreaked havoc on it before you got here."

"I've got it," I tell her, but she's already gone. I turn around and gather up the supplies and start cleaning. Hopefully I'll have time to talk to Park once this is done. While I'm dunking the blender shell under the faucet the entry chime rings again.

When I turn, the first word that comes to mind isn't the loveliest.

Fuck.

It's Carter from school and two of his football buddies, neither of which I'd call friends or even friendly. To his right is one of our first-string tackles, the blonde-haired wonder boy, Aaron Lydell. On the other side is Taren Niger. I think Cam said he's a halfback, whatever that means.

There's already a smug smirk drawn across Carter's face.

"What can I get you guys?" I manage a bit of hospitality.

"Nothing," Aaron says. It doesn't matter how good-looking he may be, he sounds like a douche.

I squint. For some reason I don't see them coming here for the books, so I'm not really sure where this is going.

"Nah." Carter laughs at Aaron and then faces me as he puts his hands on the counter. "Hmmm... Let's see. I'll take a caramel faggot. Oh, I'm sorry, I meant frappe."

A lump builds in my throat and my arms tense. It's nothing I shouldn't expect from him, but I guess it's different when it actually happens as opposed to just imagining it. I concentrate on slowing my pulse before I open my mouth.

The sound of a chair screeching on the wood floors out on the porch jumps over the whirr of the air conditioning. *Just serve them and they'll be gone.*

"And what about you two?" I ask the others.

"I'll take a caramel *faggot* too." Taren stresses the F word with a glee that punches me in the gut yet again.

"And I'll take a coconut *crème* faggot." I think Aaron is especially proud of himself. The others obviously approve. They're bent over in laughter.

"*Damn* man, *that's* fucked up." Carter is hysterical at this point.

I definitely get it, and no, it's not funny.

"What's your problem?" I know that voice. Parker's standing in the doorway. His face is hard, the anger burning in his eyes.

I lock my gaze on Parker. I need something good to focus on, and at the same time I need to tell him not to worry about it. I'll be okay. Yeah, it fucking sucks, but I'll be okay. I shake my head, but he's not having it.

"Apologize!" Parker raises his voice.

"Apologize?" Carter steps toward Parker and juts out his chest. "For what?"

"You know for what."

"Oh, for calling your little homo friend a faggot?" Carter

becomes prouder by the moment, I swear. "No."

"What's your problem with it?" Aaron shifts to Carter's left. "You a fag lover?"

"No." But there's no conviction in Parker's voice. He rebounds and puffs his chest too. "Why can't you just apologize? You know you're being jerks."

That only makes it worse. Carter takes a few steps back to stand directly in front of me across the counter. He looks me dead in the eyes.

"*Fucking* faggot. *Fucking* little faggot ass *bitch*."

I gulp. Electricity pulses through my veins. I tell myself that it shouldn't bother me, I am gay and they're just words. Who cares if someone calls me a faggot, but it's how he says it. It's the venom behind his tongue, the spite in his words that cause my heart to beat out of rhythm.

"What the—" Parker starts to yell.

"What seems to be the problem?" Sandra interrupts. Her voice booms in the small space.

I didn't see her walk in.

"Nothing's wrong." Carter's speaking for the three of them. "We're just waiting for our drinks."

"Uh-huh? Is that all?" Sandra throws her palms to her hips and does this sassy little sway. "Because I was standing right back there this entire time and my hearing is rather good. You either apologize to Noah *and* Parker and then we'll get your drink, or you three can walk your pathetic little asses out the door."

"What?" Taren seems confused.

It's everything I can do not to smile. Seeing Sandra like this is empowering.

"*What?*" I'm pretty sure Sandra just mocked him. "I said

apologize or leave. You're not going to come in here and treat my employees or customers like that."

"We're customers too," Carter counters. Apparently it's just too difficult to apologize.

"It sure doesn't look like it. Get out!" she demands. Her command is met with wide, surprised eyes but no movement. "I *said* get out."

"Fuck you!" Carter spurts, but he's leaving anyway with the others on his heels.

The door slams shut behind them. Sandra waves at the door with her middle finger and sighs.

"Are you two all right?" she asks, but she's looking at me.

I nod, and Parker says yeah. His shoulders slump and his chest rises and falls with a deep breath. I give him a weak smile and he does the same.

"High school. Oh, how I don't miss it," Sandra sighs.

"Yeah, it sucks," I agree.

"You good, Noah?" Parker steps up to the counter next to Sandra.

"Yeah. They're jus jocks. They don't have anything better to do," I explain. Yeah, I'm fine, but it doesn't mean it didn't register. Damn, I hate those guys.

Sandra leans over the counter. She's about to say something, but Parker speaks up first.

"I have to go. I'll see you later." His cheeks are full-on red, hot with anger, I think. It actually makes me happy that it bothers him so much.

"Okay." I nod, but I don't want him to go. I know he has to, but still. "I'll call you later."

He exchanges goodbyes with Sandra and then he's gone.

I hate that he had to be here for that, but I'm glad he was too. I mean, it's better not having to deal with it alone, but at the same time I hate it. I can't say for sure, but having to deny he likes me probably did something to him, at least I hope it did. I know that sounds bad, but I do.

"Noah," Sandra starts off quiet. I can tell this is going to be serious. "If something like that ever happens while I'm not here, you have complete authority to make them leave. If they won't, you call the cops. They have no right to come in here and treat you like that. You hear me?"

"Yes, ma'am." I smile. My nerves are finally settling, and I can breathe normally again.

"Now I do have a question for you. I wanted to wait for Parker to leave first anyway."

My jaw tightens. I'm not sure where this is going, but it sounds serious too.

"Are you and Parker dating?" She grins mischievously.

"You're just like my mom." I give her a sideways grin, hoping it throws her off. "She asked the same thing."

"What did you tell her?" she asks.

"Just because he's my best friend and I'm gay doesn't mean we're dating. No." I bounce my head up and down like it's final.

"So you lied." I don't know how she does it, but it comes out as a statement rather than a question.

My mouth drops and hangs there for a second. I know what I need to say. I know the single two-letter word that I should say without hesitation. I need to tell her no, I didn't lie, but that'd just be compounding one lie on another. And for some reason, I don't have the willpower to do that. Instead, I stand speechless, flicking my eyes away to the white chocolate-flavor pump.

She smiles, but I'm conflicted. Did I do the right thing? She knows. I know she does. I should feel excited, and in a way I do, but I also feel dirty. Not a minute ago Parker stood up for me, and here I am, too fucking weak to simply say *no* to defend him.

Thursday
October 4, 2018

If anything is worse than chemistry, it's sitting through Mr. Richter's chemistry. He's so damn dry. I didn't care how electrons, protons, and neutrons bond before class and I definitely don't care now.

What I do care about is the boy sitting in front of me. I've had a lot of time over the years to examine his neck from this vantage point, and that's exactly what I'm doing now. It's crazy. It's just a neck, but there's something mesmerizing about how it gently slopes away beneath his hairline and disappears under his shirt.

For years I imagined what it felt like, how soft it must be to the touch. I can't even begin to count the times I wondered. A chill of satisfaction runs up my chest that I now know.

We'd thought about switching things up after we made our relationship secretly official: sitting side by side in class instead of Park taking the desk in front of me. In the end we nixed that. Like so much else, it just felt like it would say too much.

Actually, over the past week I've found us walking farther apart in the hallway, talking to each other less in class, and debating whether we should even walk to our cars together after school. I feel like we're trying too hard, but at the same time I know he's afraid someone is going to find out. I can't help but wonder if maybe we're actually being more obvious than if we didn't change anything.

My phone vibrates in my pocket and interrupts what's at least my twentieth inspection of Park's neck since class started. I check the front of the room as my phone vibrates. Mr. Richter is facing the dry-erase board writing an equation. More math.

I slip my phone out and hold it under the desk. It's my brother, Zach. I check again to see if anyone's watching. All clear. I tap out a quick text reply that I'll call him back after class, then pocket my phone.

When I look back up, Parker's bent around smiling at me. I shrug, and he shakes his head. Damn he's gorgeous.

A few minutes later the bell rings and we make our escape. It's school, every bell feels like an escape, but even more so now.

"Who's calling you during class?" Parker asks.

"You're not jealous, are you?" I smirk. "And how did you know?"

"First, no. And second, your phone's not that quiet," he says and then gives me a sideways grin. "Plus, you know I can't help but turn around every once in a while."

I know what he's saying even though he leaves off the part about how it's to see me. It still feels so unreal. He likes me. He really likes me.

"It was Zach. I'll call him back in a little." I shake my head and purse my lips bashfully.

We push through the crowd and manage to make it outside. It's cool out today. I'm not a huge winter fan, but I do love autumn. The clouds are out in full force, but the sun still peeks through, and the leaves are just beginning to turn.

"I'm still angry about last night. How Carter and his ass-holes treated you," Parker says. "I mean, really?"

"I know. It's stupid, but whatever." I shrug. "There will always be a Carter."

"Not the point. It's so messed up. Taren's in my first period. Spanish. He absolutely sucks at it, but that's not the point either." I can tell Parker enjoys saying it. He swings the driver's side door of his truck open and throws his backpack over to the passenger seat. "I stared him down the entire class. I think it freaked him out. He either thinks I'm psycho or gay now, and honestly I don't really give a fuck."

"Probably psycho," I say, hoping that's what he wants to hear. Then I lean closer and whisper, "But you're fucking gay."

"Shut up." He shakes his head, but he's smiling.

"You don't have to defend me all the time, you know," I tell him. I want so badly to step closer, lean my body against him, wrap my arms around his waist, but I know better. There are way too many eyes, not to mention cameras.

"I know," he says. "But I can't just stand there. Even if you weren't my boyfriend, or even just a friend, it'd still get under my skin. But *especially* because you're mine."

My mouth stretches into a massive U. I'm blushing. Just hearing him call me *his* boyfriend and *mine* sends my heart thumping.

"I get it," I tell him. "Damn, I've got a great support team."

"Tell me about it," he starts. "You've got me. Oh, yeah, and you have Cam, your parents, what's-her-name in your first period...Kary?" I nod, and he keeps going, "Then there's, like, all our teachers, and I'd definitely say your boss is on your side. Speaking of her, what's her name again?"

"Sandra," I remind him. At the same time, my conversation with her last night and what I didn't say hits me in the pit of my stomach. Suddenly I feel nauseous.

"Yeah, Sandra," he repeats. "I like her. She's pretty cool."

I smirk nervously. "Yeah, she's awesome. Uh...I need to call Zach back. You're still picking me up tonight, right?"

It's one of those things I don't need to ask, but the nervous me needs a way out so I don't have to face him feeling guilty. He nods.

"Yeah. You get off at eight, right?"

"Round about. Maybe a quarter after." It all depends.

"I'll be there by eight." He jumps into his truck.

I want to step onto the foot rail, lean in, and kiss him, but I tell myself I shouldn't. Hell, why not. Despite the look on Park's face, I mount the rail, jump forward, and plant my lips on his for a split second and then jump back to the ground.

I'm all smiles now. It makes me feel better about my fuck up. Parker, on the other hand, is a mixture of excitement and horror. I laugh at him as he checks for any onlookers. Once he's sure no one saw, he eyes me down and grins.

"*Don't* do that."

"Okay." I twist my body back and forth guiltily. "See you tonight."

He shakes his head. I let him shut his door before I take off to my car. I refuse to turn and wave once I hear his truck come to life, even though I want to.

In my car I rev up the engine as I connect my phone and dial Zach. He answers on the second ring.

"Hey, Noah." His voice is gruff, which I always find odd

since he's even skinnier than I am. But maybe that only makes sense in my head.

"Hey. What's up? I was in class when you called."

"Yeah, I didn't think about that then," he says. "But yeah, I'm planning a little camping trip in a few weeks. Thought you might want to come."

Camping? So hanging out in the woods all day and night, sleeping on hard ground, dealing with bugs. Not sure where he gets that I'd want to do that. Hell, camping has never been high on our list of family vacation ideas. Actually, that's partly why I was surprised when Zach decided to go to App State. I swear there's nothing to do up there except hike.

I'm about to ask why he thinks I'd want to go camping, but a thought clicks in my head.

"Can Parker come too?" I ask before I can tell myself it's a bad idea.

"Uh… Yeah, I guess that'd be all right," he says. "I was going to ask Dad if he—"

"No!" I blurt. *Dammit, what are you doing, Noah?* "I mean, I don't think he'd want to. You know they've never been big on camping."

I'm certain it's an epic fail on my part, but it's the best I can come up with on the fly. And it isn't technically a lie, which is sort of a plus.

"Sure." Zach drags it out, stopping short of questioning my motives. I'll take it. "I was thinking October nineteenth and twentieth. I checked your school calendar online and you've got a teacher workday that Friday, so you'll be free. I figure you can come up Friday morning and we can go up to Rough Ridge that afternoon, hike a little and then camp out that night. We could make it a two-nighter or come back to

Boone on Saturday."

"Rough Ridge? Hell, why not. Sounds good," I tell him. I'm still just glad he isn't questioning why I want Parker to come, or why I sound excited about it, for that matter. "Do I need to talk to Mom and Dad, or are you going to handle that?"

"I'll talk to them. Just don't make any other plans," he says. "Oh, and how'd that concert go?"

"It was awesome!" I tell him. He's not on the same wavelength with music; well, not completely, but he can appreciate a good concert. "It was so fucking heavy."

He laughs on the other end of the line. "That's great. I wish I could have gone."

"Maybe next time," I say.

"Well, I'm going to call Mom and make sure she's all right with me stealing you for the trip," he says. "I'll talk to you later, man. Love you."

"Love you too, bye!"

I guess I need to buy a tent for two.

* * *

"Noah, can you turn off the OPEN light?" L.A. nods toward the porch.

"Yeah, I got it," I tell her.

The sun disappeared about an hour ago. The street-side lamp posts and car headlights are all that illuminate the view of Main Street from the front porch windows. I walk to the corner and switch off the OPEN light and scan the street. Parker should be arriving any moment.

Instead, a tiny Honda speeds around a moped, and an

evening jogger passes by on the opposite side of the street. I head back to the bar and help L.A. with what's left of the closing checklist. It's been slow the last half hour, so we got a head start.

I keep wondering what Park did while I was at work. I mean, it's not technically my business, but maybe it is at the same time. Is it? Either way I want to know where the hell he is right now. I'm about ready to leave and he was supposed to be here a minute ago.

"So you hanging out with your friends after work?" L.A. asks.

"Yeah." I nod. I found out earlier in the week that she does, in fact, go to Concord High, which is why I didn't know her outside the shop. "We're going to watch a movie, I think."

"Like at the theater?" Her eyes light up. "I love going to the movies."

"Nah, we're going to Cam's." I shake my head.

"What are y'all watching?" she asks.

I still don't know her well, and our conversations always seem to end up like this. Random question to fill the void.

"I don't know." I shrug. "She wouldn't tell us. Apparently it has to be a surprise."

"That could be fun." L.A. widens her eyes sarcastically.

"Fun for her. Not so sure about us yet." I laugh. "Park's supposed to meet me here, actually," I tell her and peek out the front window again, "but I still don't see any sign of him."

"Probably just running late."

"Yeah, that would be Parker." But suddenly I'm worried. Why would he be late? Oh my God! Did he get in an accident? I fight the urge to pull out my phone and call him. I know I'm overreacting. It's stupid. I'm sure he's fine. Or did he forget? Damn, I'm not sure which would be worse right now.

"Well, we're all done here," L.A. announces.

"Sweet. Let's go," I tell her, even if I'm even more anxious now than I was.

She leads the way, but I open the door for her. I literally debated this one in my head a week ago. Should I still open the door for girls now that I'm out? Do they expect gay guys to do that? And that's what I find it comes down to. Expectations. I have to stop worrying about what people expect. And on that note, I decided I should just open the door like a kind and decent human being for anyone, guy or gal. It's simpler that way anyway, and it can't hurt just to be nice.

Outside she locks up and we say our goodbyes. I'm still wondering where the hell Parker is as I head down the ramp to my car.

Really? His truck is sitting in the space next to mine with the engine idling. I purse my lips and roll my eyes. He must have pulled in from the other entry down the street.

Damn you, Parker, you could have at least texted me.

I huff and wave. He waves back as I open the passenger door and crawl inside.

"Hey!" Parker sounds excited. He looks me over before leaning in and kissing me. "Have I told you how adorable you look in your work apron?"

"Huh?" I look down. I forgot to take it off before leaving again. Dammit. "Thanks, I guess. You know, you could have texted me to let me know you were here."

"Why?" he asks. "I told you I would be."

"Yeah, but I was expecting you to come driving by out

front. You know, using the *normal* entrance that *normal* people use."

"Since when has either of us been *normal*, Noah? I mean, really?" He smiles widely at me.

"You got me there." I laugh. He has a point. "Whatever. Let's get going."

Parker nods and in a matter of seconds we're heading down Main Street. Park's pushing at least ten over the posted speed limit. I can't really say anything, but I also can't help noticing it.

"So do you have any idea what Cam's trying to make us watch?" I ask.

"Not a clue. All she told me was that it's a comedy," he says, tilting his head toward his window and pursing his lips. "I'm just hoping for the best. I mean, it can't be that bad, right?"

"Hehe... Yeah, it can," I tell him. "Remember when she made us watch *Batman & Robin* — you know, the George Clooney one? That was horrible."

"Oh my God, yes!" I see it click in his eyes. "That was the worst! And she actually likes it."

"No, she likes Clooney. Don't know why, but that's what she liked. Did she never tell you that?"

"I don't think so." He chuckles and makes a turn off the main road. "Wouldn't surprise me, though. I definitely don't see it— —Clooney, that is."

"Yeah." I nod and then change the subject. "So would you like to go camping in a few weeks with my brother and me?"

"Camping?" Parker takes his eyes off the road for a second, and I catch the incredulous look in his eyes. "You want to go camping? Who are you?"

"Okay, okay. Calm the fuck down." I shake my head and sigh. He doesn't like camping any more than I do, but I think in the end he'll want to go. If I hadn't thought so, I wouldn't have agreed to it myself. "It'll be fun."

"Camping and fun don't belong in the same sentence, Noah." He's grinning when he says it, but he's also not lying.

"Yeah, I know." I unbuckle and slide to the center seat and buckle up again. He eyes me suspiciously as I lean over and lay my head on his shoulder, resting my palm on his thigh. It feels good to be so close. "But I think it'll be fun this time. I mean, you'll get to go with *me*."

"Okay…" I don't think he's catching my drift.

"Come on, Park." I'm almost pleading now. "Other than Zach, it'd just be you and me, nature, and the stars. It actually sounds sort of nice. Don't you think? We'll have our own tent."

"And the cold." He's looking up at the ceiling contemplatively and darting his eyes back down to the road between each point he makes. "And spiders. And lots of walking. And bugs. And bears. And did I say spiders already?"

"Yeah, you said spiders twice." I've got this giant grin going now. Neither of us likes spiders much, but Park's the polar opposite of a fan. "And yeah, all that's going to be there too, but I'm sure it's not *that* bad. I mean, it's October, so a lot of the bugs won't be out, and maybe the bears will be hibernating."

I don't know about that last part. I'm basically talking out of my ass, but it sounds good. Park purses his lips. I think he's contemplating it.

"Oh, I almost forgot. It also means sleeping on hard, uneven ground and hiking. That one alone is a real *fun* downer," he says sarcastically.

"For God's sake," I start up again. "You're not three hundred pounds, Park, you play fucking soccer. I don't think hiking is going to hurt you."

"And you like it?"

"Well… Uh…" I struggle for a moment. I'm not going to lie. "No, not exactly."

"Aha!" He holds up his head in victory.

I shake my head. I think I'm losing.

"You're impossible," I tell him.

"It's okay, Noah, I'm going." He takes his eyes off the road long enough to shoot me an I-got-you look.

I punch him on the shoulder, which is probably a bad idea since he's driving. We're still on the road, though.

"Really?" I wobble my head. "You were just leading me on?"

"Of course," he tells me. "You had me the moment you said we'd have our own tent."

You sly, beautiful boy. His entire tone shifts now that he's not shitting me.

"I love camping now."

Friday
October 5, 2018

It's killing me.

My nerves, that is. I'm on my way to Editions even though I don't have to work today. Parker is meeting me for coffee before we head to Concord Mills for the evening. There's this sweet electric go-karting place near the mall we plan to hit up. Apparently it's been here a few years, but I'm somehow just now hearing about it.

That's beside the point, though.

I'm riding Parker's tailgate down Dale Earnhardt Boulevard debating whether I should tell him what Sandra knows about us or not. I still can't believe I was so stupid. It didn't bother me so much yesterday, but last night it hit me hard. Why couldn't I just say no? Why couldn't I just tell Sandra that I wasn't dating Parker?

It's been eating at me, and it's coming to a boiling point.

In my defense, I didn't say a word. I didn't technically answer. So when I really get down to it, I never told her we're dating, and I definitely didn't tell her Parker is gay. But yeah, that stupid-ass *but*. I didn't deny it. That's the problem. No, I sat there and looked away like some guilty criminal. I'm not sure I was thinking straight, to be honest. It's like I thought not saying anything was enough, that she'd assume she was wrong. She knows, though.

Of course, being the awesome boss she is, Sandra swore she wouldn't say anything. Hell, she even apologized for asking, but I still have this overwhelming feeling that I've betrayed Parker.

He takes a right on red in his hulking Ram, and I try to draft in behind him, but I'm not quick enough. I watch him turn and speed off down Main while a minivan and some dude on one of those souped-up-looking three-wheeled bikes cuts by me.

I need to tell him. If nothing else, I'll feel better about it. The problem is I don't know how he'll react. He's only out to Cam and me, and I know he's still horrified to tell anyone else. But maybe it's just his parents he's really worried about, not everyone else.

Oh my God! I don't think I can do this. Why can't I have one full week without any stupid complications?

The light turns green and I swing onto Main. A few blocks down I pull up in the coffee shop's driveway and park next to Parker. I sit quietly for a moment, staring out the windshield at the railroad tracks running behind the shop. I wish the North Carolina passenger train would speed by about now, so I'd at least appear like there's something there to look at.

I should tell him. No. It'll be better if I don't. He doesn't know, and Sandra isn't going to say anything. She promised.

Taking a deep breath, I get out. Park's already waiting behind my car.

"Cam must be running behind." He nods toward the empty spaces. There are only a few vehicles. Macy's Camaro is parked at the edge of the lot and Sandra's 4Runner is nestled in behind the shop, but there's no Scion.

"Didn't she leave before us?" I ask. Anything to get my mind moving. But then it bounces right back.

"I thought," Parker says.

He starts off toward the shop, but I can't move. My stomach is clenched up and my lungs feel heavy. I have to tell him.

"Park," I call, and he swings around. "Can we talk in my car for a second?"

"Sure." Parker grins impishly.

Dammit, he thinks I'm being naughty. That just makes it worse.

I wait for him to jump in and close the door before I do the same. Inside I try to grin but give up. The lines on his forehead crinkle. I think he's finally getting the idea I wasn't asking him here to make out.

"Is everything okay?" he asks.

"Uh. Yeah, well, I mean, sort of." It's a bad start. How do I do this? Do I just look at him and say *I betrayed you*? Or should I be more subtle about it? *Just talk, Noah.*

"Sort of?"

"Yeah." My hands are shaking. "I might have made a mistake Wednesday after you left the shop."

He doesn't say anything, and I'm not sure if that's a good thing or not.

"You see, uh…" I chew on my lip, but it's not the sexy type that he likes. "After you left, Sandra asked if we were dating."

"And you told her no, right?"

I don't like the way he says it.

"Not exactly," I whisper. I still can't look him in the eye.

"Not exactly?" Parker eyes me.

I don't want to do this. This was such a bad idea.

"You told her?" His voice isn't exactly accusing, but it's questioning.

"No," I say.

"Huh?" He pushes back in his seat. I can't tell if he's scared or angry. "You either did or didn't, Noah."

"I didn't, but I guess maybe I did, too," I tell him. "She asked, and I know I should have just said no, but I couldn't."

I stop and let my gaze escape to the train station. I trace the aged red brick and cracked concrete leading up to the platform. I wish I had kept my mouth shut.

"I just didn't say anything. I should have, but I didn't want to lie anymore. I just didn't answer, and then she knew. I wasn't thinking straight."

It's the truth. That should count for something, right?

When Parker doesn't speak, I muster up the courage to face him. He's pressed back against the seat, eyes piercing the ceiling. They're sort of glossy and his mouth is hanging open. Disbelief, fear. Maybe a little of both.

"Okay. So you didn't tell her, but you didn't deny it," Parker recounts my mistake. Maybe he's hoping I'll contradict something he thought I said, and then it'll make sense. "Maybe she doesn't really know, maybe she thinks you were just nervous."

"No, Park, she knows." I admit. I don't want to lie to him, but his reaction hurts. It hurts that he doesn't want her to know about us. It hurts that he's trying to act like it's just not happening. But it also hurts to see him scared like this, because of something *I* did, because *I* hurt him. It's like a knife slicing a hundred tiny cuts in my heart.

I fucked up. I *so* fucked up.

"How could you do that, Noah?" He's talking fast, and his eyes are pleading. "That was a secret. That was *our* secret. It wasn't for her to know. *You* know how hard this is."

"I didn't mean to." I try to defend myself and at the same time hold back my tears. "I really didn't, Park, I promise. I just didn't know what to do. She asked, and my heart wanted so badly to say yes, but I didn't. I knew that would be wrong, but I jammed up. I couldn't talk. I'm so sorry! I'm so sorry, Park. I promise she won't say anything. She's really good about this stuff."

"Yeah, but we're talking about *my* stuff. *I* was supposed to decide when anyone else knew. Not you, Noah!" He's almost screaming now.

I jerk back and clamp my mouth shut. A tear rolls down his reddening cheeks. I've only seen him cry a few times, and I'm not sure I can stand it. What have I done?

"I'm sorry," is all I can think to say. I'm crying too now, but unlike his single tear I'm a rain cloud that decided the weight was just too much. "I didn't mean to, Parker, I swear."

"But you did." His words are a hammer. "You and Cam enjoy the karts, I'm going home."

"Come on, Park, don't do that." I reach for him, but he's already got the door open and he jumps out. My finger brushes his arm, but I can't gain purchase. Before I can say anything more, the door slams in my face. "Parker!"

I sling my door open and run after him. "Parker! Stop!"

I barely notice Cam stepping out of her car. The look on her face says it all, but I don't have time for that.

"No, Noah," he barks back and slams his door shut.

I slap my hand against the gray paint below his window

and let my wet eyes plead with him to not leave.

"Noah?" It's Camila, but I don't turn.

"Parker, come on!"

The truck's engine revs and I step away as it jolts back. He whips it around and barks the tires as he speeds away. I watch him disappear, leaving me alone in the lot.

"Noah?" Cam calls again, and I remember I'm not alone, which just makes it worse. I glance at her but shy away to wipe at the tears covering my face. "What's going on?"

What's going on? I fucked up, that's what's going on. I fucked the hell up.

* * *

By the time Camila pulls away from the drive-thru, I'm still brushing away tears. I'm not bawling anymore, but I can't seem to stop crying.

We didn't stay at Editions. Cam didn't understand why at the time, but there's no way I was going in there and facing Sandra, especially like this.

She'd see right through me and I'd probably fuck something else up. I think I've done that enough, plus I don't really want to go in anywhere right now. Thankfully, Cam didn't push for answers at first. She didn't even protest when I said we should just go to her place the rest of the night instead of the go-kart track.

As she drove, I finally told her what happened. How I messed up. How it was eating at me all week. How I thought I could make it right by coming clean. She didn't say much at first. I think she wanted time to think it over.

"I didn't mean to mess up, I really didn't." It's probably

the fifth or sixth time I've said it.

"I know." She doesn't even sound annoyed by it. "But why didn't you tell him earlier? I don't know if it would have helped, but why?"

"I was afraid," I tell her. "I knew I should have. I just couldn't. I was too scared of how he'd react. And I guess I was right."

"I get it, but Park deserved to know," she tells me. She's looking at me instead of the road more than she probably should. "It isn't just you anymore. It's you *and* him. And this was definitely something he should have known about. Yeah, it probably wouldn't have made it any easier. You know that. This shit *isn't* easy, and it might even be harder for Park."

I want to say it was just as hard for me, that I had just as much to worry about, but it's a lie. I nod. She's right. He has so much more to lose.

"That's why I told him. I couldn't keep it a secret, I felt horrible about it," I explain.

Cam grins at me. Her eyes are warm and there's a kindness in them beyond her usual awesomeness.

"That's sweet, Noah," she tells me as we pull down her street. "Other than the whole gay thing, you've always been a pretty open book. Lying really isn't your thing, at least I don't think it is, and that's a plus, really. I think Park knows that. It sucks right now, but I think he'll understand in time."

"How long?" I ask. "We haven't even been dating for a full two weeks and we're already fighting. We never fought before this. And it's more than just while we've been dating. We never fought when we were just friends either."

"Couples always fight. Jaylen and I fought too," she tells

me.

"You and Jaylen broke up." I cock my head sideways, and I'm about to start crying again, but I dam up the tears.

"Okay, maybe that wasn't the best example, but every couple fights. It's just how it is." We bounce up her driveaway and circle behind her parents' house. "It'll be okay."

She parks the car and unbuckles. Instead of getting out, she twists in her seat and digs her gaze into me. I swallow back the need to cry.

"You're both in the wrong, though," she tells me. "You *should* have lied, as odd as that sounds, and in the end Park should calm the fuck down. It's not the end of the world, but he's afraid, and that's okay. You know that. At the same time he also has to understand that he's no longer dealing with just his own feelings. He's got you. You two have to work this out."

I don't know what to say. Cam said it all so perfectly. It's like she's this wise old person for a moment. I finally smile, even if my heart is still breaking.

"You know, Cam, you're like this small, skinny female Buddha right now." I try to make it sound funny, but I can't do it.

"I'll try to take that as a compliment." She strains out the words and raises her brows in disbelief.

"It is," I tell her. "This all sucks so bad, and I don't know what do to, but thanks, Cam."

Monday
October 8, 2018

Hell if it isn't raining. I wonder what else can go wrong today?

I've checked my phone incessantly this morning. But there's nothing interesting, nothing I want to see. Hell, I swear that Tom Holland or Chris Evans could show up to school today and I wouldn't be interested. I only want one thing.

I check my texts again, and even though I know it's useless, I tap on Parker's name. The last message is from me. Well, actually, every message on the screen is from me. He hasn't responded since our fight and he won't return my calls.

I squint through the rain pelting the windshield. He's still not here. Honestly I shouldn't expect him. It's 7:38 a.m. He never gets here before 7:40 a.m.

People probably think I'm watching the rain, but all I can see is the look on Parker's face when I told him I messed up. The fear, the hurt. It twists my heart into knots. I even thought about going to his house and apologizing in person, but the more I considered it, the worse the idea seemed.

But at school he can't avoid me entirely.

Halsey's playing from the speakers, probably a little too loud, but I'm not bobbing my head to the beat like usual.

Typically I can lose myself in the music, even when things are bad, but I just can't seem to do it. I check my phone again and think about sending him another text.

No. Just wait. He'll be here any minute.

I check the time again—7:43 a.m.—and peek through the rain. Either he's running behind, or he really is trying to avoid me.

No. There he is.

I scoot forward and loop my arm through my pack while I grip the door handle with my free hand. He pulls up the usual row and takes a space near the end. I bite my lip. If I get out too early he'll see me, and he might go back to his car, so I wait. He gets out and starts off toward the school.

When he's directly in front of my car, I jump out and take chase. The rain pops my face and hands, but I don't care.

"Park!" I try not to yell, but it comes out loud anyway.

He ignores me. He seriously keeps walking as if I'm not here, as if I didn't just say his name. I try again.

"Parker!" I speed up and close the gap with the rain now slapping my face.

He still doesn't answer and the silence is burrowing into my chest. It's like I don't exist, like it's just him, the cement beneath his feet, and the rain splattering against his frowning face.

"Parker!" I say it quieter this time, but I grab his arm.

"What, Noah?!" He swings around and pulls away from me. His mouth is taut, and his cheeks are flushed under angry eyes.

I reel back and squint before breaking eye contact.

"I'm sorry!" It's the same thing I've been saying since Friday. It's the same message I've sent him over and over again, but I'm not sure what else to say.

"Yeah, I got that the first twenty fucking times," he bites back. More like the hundredth, I think. I swipe away the water building around my eyes.

Before I say anything else, he turns and takes off. *No, just wait. Give me a chance, Park.*

"Come on, Park," I call after him. "Please! I don't know what else to say. I *am* sorry."

"Are you now? Who else have you told?" He swings around again. His hair falls over his forehead and sticks just over his eyes. "Your mom and dad? Zach? Facebook maybe? Who else have you told I'm a…"

I stand like a dead log, which means I'm dangerously close to falling. My body's shaking. My heart is rapping at my ribcage and I want to scream. But I don't know what to say. I just want him to understand I didn't mean any harm — that's the last thing I want. I want him back.

"No one," I tell him again. "I promise on my life. I've told no one else. And I didn't mean to tell Sandra. You know that. I didn't mean to hurt you, Park. I like —"

Parker throws up a hand. "Just stop, Noah. I don't want to talk about it."

I want to say more. I want to tell him I was excited. I was so happy, maybe *too* happy, to be with him that I couldn't deny it. It felt wrong, even dirty to say no. I want to tell him that I like him so much, maybe even love him. No, I can't say that yet. But maybe. Do I?

He drops his eyes to the concrete. For a second I catch a sliver of doubt, a split second of something that isn't angry, but sad. Before it can form into anything more he spins around and practically runs for the building.

I don't move. I want to run after him, but I don't. I just stand, stuck in the rain.

Friday
October 19, 2018

I'm not sure what sucks more right now. The fact that Parker and I are finally talking again but we're *taking a break*, or that I don't know if Parker is still going on this damn camping trip anymore. I wouldn't have agreed to go if I thought he wasn't going with me.

My backpack, the one I use for school, is thrown in the back of my car along with our, or I guess *my*, tent and the blow-up air mattress and bicycle pump. Dad had to remind me last night that the electric pump wouldn't work in the middle of the mountains. Apparently there are no outlets up there. Damn nature.

I mentioned the trip again to Parker on Wednesday when he finally started talking to me again. He got quiet and instead of answering, all I got was a shrug. Then I tried again yesterday, but he said something about not being sure. It was more of a mumble than anything.

Of course, I've texted him since then, but he hasn't responded. He'll text back about anything else, just not that. I tried again this morning until about an hour ago, and I'm still waiting on a response. If nothing else, he knows I'm leaving at ten thirty with or without him.

I really don't want to leave without him.

I've been up since the sun showed its ugly face behind a

scattering of rain clouds. And it has nothing to do with being *excited* about going camping. It doesn't even have anything to do with seeing Zach, which I actually *am* excited about—it's been a few months. No, it's my damn mind running nonstop all night and waking me up every hour just to wonder whether Parker is coming. I really should assume he's not. I mean, that is what everything is pointing toward.

Though I'm reluctant, I check my phone again. 10:26 a.m.

I sigh and push off my bed. After one last glance around my room, I shut the door and go to the living room to say goodbye to Mom. Dad's at work, so I told him I'd see him later last night. Mom's waiting for me, all smiles.

"Well, I think I'm off." I put on a fake grin for her.

"Where's Parker?" She gets up from the sofa and hugs me. "I thought he was supposed to go with you?"

How did I not think of this? I had to argue with her and Dad the night Zach called so Park could go with us. Apparently it was a violation of the new bedroom rule, but eventually, with a little help from Zach, I won. Now it looks like all of that was for nothing.

The original plan had been for him to meet me here and then take my car up to Boone. I guess that's not happening. So I lie.

"He's running behind. I'm going to pick him up at his place instead." I cringe inside.

"Okay." Mom nods and follows me out the front door. "Well, you better leave so you're not late too."

"Yeah," I say, trying to hide the disappointment raging in my chest.

I make it to my car, and before I can get in Mom yells from the house, "I love you! Have fun. Tell Zach I said hey and I love him too."

"Love you too! And I will," I yell back and drop my butt in the car. It's not raining yet, but it looks like it could start at any moment. I really hope it's clear in Boone. It's going to suck enough as it is, the last thing I want is to have to hike in the rain.

My eyes stall on the passenger seat. Parker's supposed to be there. His perfect ass is supposed to be planted next to me, going with me to Boone so I'm not stuck out in the middle of fucking nowhere without a good reason. But no.

I check my phone again. I know it's stupid, but I can't stop myself. As expected, my screen is blank. I shake my head and grip the steering wheel. If it was a neck I swear I could squeeze the life right of out it. *Just go, Noah, just go.*

Finally, I drop the shifter into reverse and start moving back.

I slam on the brakes just in time to avoid backing into the idiot that just swerved into our driveway. Wait. What?

Parker's truck barrels around my back end and screeches to a stop. My head bangs against the headrest, but my eyes are stuck on the gray paint. I'm not sure how to feel. I look up and he's peeking over the passenger window. He's smiling at me. He's actually smiling.

My first thought is to be angry, to rip him a new one. But that smile. I wasn't expecting that. Hell, I wasn't expecting him.

Hold on, he's smiling. I can't seem to process anything else.

Finally I peel my eyes away and realize I'm smiling too. He came.

Mom's standing out on the porch, and I can see the confusion in her eyes. Dammit. How exactly am I going to explain this?

He came, and he literally just smiled at me. That's a first for a while now.

It takes me a moment to realize I haven't moved yet. I snap myself from my moment and jump out of the car. I make a mental note not to look too excited for Mom, and before Parker can get out I yell an excuse, another lie.

"I missed his last text. Guess he wasn't going to be that late."

"Sorry, Mrs. Andrews." Parker waves to my mom. Good. He caught on.

"That's okay, Parker. You two be careful now." She waves.

"We will be," he tells her before I can answer.

He's coming around the back of his truck with his pack in tow over his shoulder. It's cool, not cold, but he's still wearing those shorts that don't quite reach his knees. Our eyes meet, and suddenly I can't breathe; I wonder if that'll ever go away. I hope it doesn't.

"Hey, Park," I whisper in a nerve-laced stutter.

"Hey, Noah." He sounds more confident.

"I didn't think you were coming," I tell him.

He walks up within inches of me, and I wonder if he's thinking this through, because he grabs my hand. I swallow back the exhilaration of touching him again, and just as quickly, it's over. He yanks his hand back and his eyes dart toward my house. Mom's not there, though.

He averts his eyes for a second and then finds me again. I haven't left, and I don't plan on it.

"Sorry." Parker skews his mouth and puffs out a nervous

breath.

"For what?" I ask. Maybe it's for not talking to me for days. Maybe it's for acting like I didn't exist for days before that. Or no, maybe he's sorry for leaving me in the dark about *us* or not answering my texts about the trip. As much as I want to be angry, I can't do it. He's back, and to be honest, what I did to him was worse than any of his wrongs. I mean, if they can even be considered wrongs.

"Being late." He shrugs. He looks at me for a second, and I can see something deeper in his eyes. I swear he's looking at me like he did the first night we kissed. "And for being such a douche. I should—"

"Stop, Parker." I put my hand up. "Let's do this in the car."

"Good idea." He nods.

I stop with my hand on the door handle before he can get around the car. "I'm glad you came."

I swear his cheeks go from tanned to red. We get in the car and he grabs my hand again. I look down at our intertwined fingers. I want to hold his hand forever.

I angle my left hand awkwardly around the steering wheel and start the car. I'm not letting go if I don't have to, but he sees I'm struggling, and he lets go. I grin and shift the car into reverse and pull out of the driveway.

I find his hand again and give it a tight squeeze.

"So." He coughs. "I'm sorry. It doesn't matter what happened, I shouldn't have treated you like that. I was just scared. I'm sorry for being distant, for ignoring you. For everything."

I let him talk. One, I need to hear this, and two, I'm waiting to apologize myself.

"I've made this a lot harder than it should have been, and I guess it all hit me this morning," he says. My gaze is set on the road, but I glance at him. His eyes are genuine, almost pleading. "I'm sorry, Noah."

"It's okay," I tell him. But I can't help wondering if that's what I really think. I say a lot of stuff because it just sounds good, sometimes because it's what I think I *should* say. I mean, things are better now, or at least they should be, now that Parker's talking to me again, but does that really make it all okay? Maybe it does. "I'm sorry too. No matter what, I should have thought more. I should have kept your secret better. I should have known how that would hurt. I didn't mean to hurt you."

"I know," he says. "I know that now. I guess I did then too, but I was just so scared. Damn, I was terrified. All I could imagine was that my dad would find out, and then Mom. That they'd make me go to counseling, ground me as long as I lived with them, if they even let me stay. He probably wouldn't let me talk to my friends, and definitely not to you. I realize how stupid I was now. *I* wasn't letting myself talk to you because I was afraid *he* wouldn't let me. Dammit, I'm so stupid sometimes."

"It's okay, Park." I don't get it necessarily, but on some weird deep level it makes a lot of sense. I mean, we do stupid shit when we're scared. I think I heard someone say that before. I can't fault him. He has a lot more to worry about than I ever did. His family isn't exactly accepting. I can't imagine what that feels like.

"I hope I didn't hurt you," he whispers.

I'm about to lie, but I decide against it. I'm going to be truthful. I let my eyes wander out my window at the cars zooming by under us on the interstate I'm about to pull onto.

"I...I'd be lying if I said it didn't hurt. Not being able to talk to you. Being ignored when I walked by you," I tell him. "I hurt you too. Let's just call it even and move on."

I think he nods because he doesn't say anything. We're merging into interstate traffic, and a tiny water pellet splatters on the windshield, then another and another. I turn the wipers on.

"Are we going to be okay?" I ask him.

We've definitely had our first fight now. They say it makes you stronger, that it makes your bond greater. Or am I thinking of something else? I don't know. What I do know is that I *still* want him more than anything. I want to be his and I want him to be mine. That never changed.

"Of course we are." He sounds surprised. "Noah, it was just a fight. We're both stubborn." Parker shrugs and laughs. "Okay, I might be a little more stubborn than you, but it was just a fight. Everyone fights. We'll be good."

I nod. "I know. I mean, I guess I *knew*. I just wanted to hear it."

"Noah." Parker's voice sounds different. There's something longing in it and he squeezes my hand. "I love you."

My hand clinches around his and I think my heart just seized up. I shouldn't, but I take my eyes off the road and lose myself in his gaze. In that brief second I can see it in his eyes. The desire, the caring, the *love*. It stirs through the air and in my chest where it soaks every part of me. I've wanted to tell him the same thing for so long, but I was too chicken-shit to do it, and then the fight happened. But I never stopped needing him. I never stopped loving him. And now I know he feels the same.

"I love you too, Park," I tell him. "I think I always have."

Parker smiles childishly and he holds his chin up a little higher.

"We're going to be fine," he assures me. "You just have to give me time. And then, when I'm there, I'll shout my gay boy love for Noah Reid Andrews from the fucking rooftop of the school gym!"

"Your gay boy love?" I don't think it's possible to smile any bigger than I am now. He's such an idiot when he's happy, but I love it. I love him. "That's the best you've got?"

"I said from the fucking rooftop." His eyes widen to emphasize the point. "*Of the school gym.*"

I laugh with him. Or maybe it's more at him, but it's just as good either way.

"Gotcha," I giggle. "You don't have to do that, but I won't stop you either. Well, I might. That might be a bit embarrassing."

Parker shakes his head, but he's still beaming.

"But I do want to make you a promise." His voice steadies. "I decided this morning on the way to your house."

I glance at him again. What is he about to do?

"I *will* come out by the time we graduate."

"You don't have to do that, Park. You really don't," I tell him, but inside I'm wishing he'd do it sooner. "Whenever you're ready is all that matters."

"I promise."

There's no changing his mind. At least not now, but I'm not going to hold him to it. Well, I'll try not to hold him to it.

* * *

The last text I sent was nearly half an hour ago. That's how long I've been without a signal, and we're still not at the trail.

I check again anyway. An unsent message sits at the bottom of my screen telling Camila I'm about to lose the signal. Oh, the irony. In place of my signal bars there's an X hovering under the reflection of treetops passing overhead.

"Did I tell you I hit four hundred and fifty on my squats last week?" Zach juts his chin.

"No," I say. Ever since Zach found out I'm taking weight lifting this semester, he has this idea that I love lifting. I mean, why else would I take it? I guess coming out didn't explain it.

"I thought I mentioned that." He shrugs, weaving us through the mountain up a slim country road. I'm honestly surprised it's paved, and I'm not too fond of the abrupt drop-off on our right.

"That's awesome, though," I tell him. Three months ago when he'd tell me his new max, I'd grin and nod like I understood. Sure it sounded heavy, but I didn't have a clue. I'm still no judge, but at least I have an idea of what he's talking about now. I sure as hell can't squat four hundred and fifty pounds. My last max was three weeks ago, and it was less than half that.

"And I hit three forty on bench press." He's nodding now. "What are you up to?"

"It's only been since August," I say.

"He's still a scrawny bitch," Park pipes up from the back seat.

"Scrawny bitch?" I crack my neck around to face him. He's sitting in the back seat cheesing. I try to stare him down with a look that could kill, but all I muster is an amused smirk.

"Damn, Parker," Zach huffs, then gives me a once-over and shoots his eyes back to the road. "He is scrawny."

"What the hell, guys?" I puff my chest; I'm not *that* scrawny. "I just started."

"So what's your squat up to?" Parker's enjoying this now.

"One sixty." I roll my eyes and show him my middle finger. "And I'm benching one thirty."

"That's not bad. Especially at your size. What are you weighing now, anyway?" Zach asks.

"Uh… I think I'm at like one forty or something," I tell him. My coach at school has tried to explain all the BMI stuff and how the goal is to reduce body fat and increase muscle, and how that doesn't necessarily mean losing weight. I think I get it. I signed up for the view, so I haven't bothered paying *that* much attention.

"So I guess you *didn't* just take the class for the scenery?" Zach's proud of himself. He's grinning widely. I swear he read my mind, even if he got it dead wrong.

I chuckle. "Well, actually, that's exactly why I took it. I don't give a damn about weight lifting."

"You told me you wanted to look like a Greek god." Parker almost sounds offended.

"I lied." I smile.

How else was I going to explain it? I wasn't going to be like, hey Park, I'm taking weight lifting because I want to see Mateo shirtless and maybe see his ass in the locker room. Nope. There was no way in hell or any other universe that was happening. And I'm definitely not fessing up to it now.

Parker huffs, and I purse my lips at him.

"It's not like I was going to tell everyone the truth back then," I explain.

"Good point," Zach admits. He takes a left onto yet a smaller road, which I didn't think was possible. "You sure you don't want six-pack abs? You don't want to look good for Parker?"

"What?" I come out of my seat and twist my whole body to face him.

"Huh?" Parker leans forward, his face hanging over the tiny center console.

"Woah!" Zach throws one hand in the air while he steers the Jeep around another curve. "Just a gay joke, I didn't mean it. Sorry, Parker. You're not going to get offended at gay jokes, are you now?"

"Uh, no. You're good." I struggle at first. That was close.

"I was just kidding, I promise."

"Yeah, all good." Parker's nodding hard. It's a bit much. "You had me there for a sec."

"So what else is new with you two?" Zach laughs and changes the topic.

I glance out the window to calm my nerves, hoping Parker might answer first.

It's still early in the day, and autumn has taken hold of the forest. The leaves are painted like one of the old patchwork quilts Mom has in her bedroom. A little red, or maroon maybe, over here, some amber, or maybe it's just yellow, over there. The constant green of countless evergreen needles break up the autumn-colored ceiling here and there under a cool blue Carolina sky. It's beautiful really, but I'd still trade it for cell service.

"Swim team is starting back up," Parker speaks up.

"Practice started last week. I think our first meet is in November."

"Really?" Zach asks. "How long does it go?"

"February, just like last year." I turn and answer his question. Swim team is the only sport Parker and I both do each year. I love being in the water. It's calming, even when you're diving in and rushing across twenty-five yards of it. I can't explain why. It just is.

"Maybe I'll make it to a few meets over winter break, then." Zach sounds happy about that.

"That'd be great." He better. I know he tries, but sometimes it's hard with his school schedule and living over two hours away.

For a brief moment, no one talks, and the deep screaming voice on the radio fills the void. It sounds like death metal, I swear. I'm not a fan, but hey, it was Zach who got me into rock in the first place, just not *this* rock.

"You know," Zach starts up again. He glances at me and I think he looks at Parker in his rearview mirror before putting his eyes back on the road. "I never thought I'd be in the car with two gay guys. I never thought."

My tongue freezes and my head swivels to lock my horrified eyes on him. What did he just say? I keep turning until I find Parker. He's staring right at me, and I can see the accusation in his dark brown eyes.

Hell no!

"What are you talking about?" I force my tongue to move, and suddenly I'm talking fast and loudly. "What do you mean?"

Parker is paralyzed in the back seat.

"Yeah, you and Parker." He looks at me with this confused expression. "I mean, he *is* gay too."

"I'm not gay!" Parker barks.

My eyes jump back to Parker and then fall on my brother again. He's not joking anymore. He's not fucking joking. He's reached a new level of insanity.

At the same time something about the way Parker denied it squeezes in my chest. It's sort of like when we hold hands back home and someone comes around the corner and he lets go. I know why he does it, but I still hate it.

"Really?" Zach jumps his eyes from the road to me and back again. "I know you're gay. You made that public. But Parker, man, if I'm wrong, I'm sorry, but are we sure? I know it sounds odd, but I've known you a long time."

I'm surprised the conversation is still moving. But at least I think it's clear to Parker now that I didn't say anything.

"I don't mean to step on your toes, but uh... How to say it..." Zach ponders. "The way you two act around each other, it's different. It's not bad, but it's different. To be honest, I knew Noah was gay years ago."

I swing my head around and bore my eyes into him. How? And what the hell?

"Yeah," he shrugs. "I don't know exactly what it was, but the whole lack of girlfriends, lack of interest, except that one short-lived one. There were other little things, but mainly that. That's just not normal for a teen boy. I know."

I shrug and let out a sigh. He's got a point there, and I actually think I like this revelation. Somehow, in some weird way, it's actually comforting. But Park? How does he know about Park, and why the hell would he bring it up?

"And you, Parker," he starts. I tense again. "Sort of the same thing. I keep thinking you had a girlfriend, but I can't remember for sure. Plus Noah was determined Dad shouldn't come on our little trip, but you should instead. Like really insistent."

Parker nods, but instead of beaming with anger, there's something calm in his eyes.

"I know guys hang out, but you two have been inseparable. And the way you keep looking at each other. I mean, it's okay. You don't have to say anything, Parker, I'm not going to say anything. I know your family. I went to school with your brother, Joshua. I won't say anything."

I peer back at Parker. I think he knows what I'm asking because he drops his eyes to his lap.

"Uh... Yeah," he mutters.

The sound of the music seems to dim to nothing. The weight of the warm air pushing through the vents feels hotter and the high-mountain pressure weighs on my ears. Parker finally looks up and meets my gaze. I thought he might be crying and afraid, but I smile when I find a grin on his lips. He looks nervous, but I think he's good. He nods at me and he does something I definitely don't expect.

He reaches for me. I tilt my head, but he nods again, and I slip my hand around his.

"You're right," Parker whispers in the back seat. His next words are louder, prouder. "I'm gay."

"So you two are dating?" Zach asks.

"Yeah." I smile so big.

"Yeah," Parker mimics me. "We're dating."

I throw myself over the center console and drape my arms over Park's shoulders. He grins at me just before I plant a kiss on him.

"That's seriously awesome, guys," Zach says. "But I'm

not sure I'm ready to witness a full-on gay make-out session. So let's hold off on that, okay?"

"Hater much?" I joke and slide my butt back into my seat. I steal another glance at Parker and take in a deep breath.

"Seriously though, guys, I'm happy for you. I really am," he says. "And I'm no homo, but Parker's a good choice."

"Really?" Parker leans forward with a crooked grin.

"Don't get me wrong, you're no Chris Hemsworth, but for Noah you'll do." Zach smiles, looks at me, and shrugs. "Hey, you don't have to be gay to have a man crush."

I shake my head and throw a smirk back at Parker. He's beautiful. Of course he always is, but there's something about how he's beaming right now. His chestnut eyes gleam under the natural light, and his nose is so fucking cute. I just can't stop looking, and the awesome part is that he doesn't mind.

"So, Zach." Parker keeps his eyes locked on mine, but he shifts in his seat. "Did you really know a long time ago? About me?"

Zach doesn't pause to think, he just speaks. "Yeah, but don't worry. You're not that obvious."

"Are you saying I am?" I crinkle my brow.

He shakes his head and chuckles. "Nah, man. Well, not over the top, at least."

* * *

I'm not the most fit dude, but hell, I thought I was better than this. This trail is kicking my ass and we're only half an hour in with God only knows how many more hours before we hit the peak. This already sucks.

"Nine people have gone missing on this trail," my brother informs us. He's not even out of breath.

"When?" I can see the creases form on Parker's forehead. I squeeze his hand and bob my head.

"Ten years ago, I think," Zach says. "It was some old white dude, apparently. They say he'd take them, strip them, and then peel their skin."

"That's fucked up." I step over a felled branch. "Like some Ed Gein shit?"

"Is that the skin suit guy Mom's obsessed with?" he asks.

"Yeah." I nod. I swear my mom's not insane. "That's the one."

It's still light out. We have a few hours of sunshine left, I think. The clouds are sparse, and the breeze is light. It nips at my neck and I swear it's trying to snake up my pant leg and down the collar of my red NC State hoodie.

"They got him?" Parker poses the real question.

"Yeah, a few years ago." Zach twists around and walks backwards up the trail. It's not exactly the brightest idea, but he pulls it off with ease. "I heard someone else went missing a few months ago."

"Huh?" Parker stops. The slack in our arms goes taut and I'm pulled to a halt. I grin at Parker and shake my head.

"He's joking," I tell him and then look at Zach. "You are joking, right?"

Surely Zach's not stupid enough to bring us on a trail where people are going missing *again*.

"Nope." He stops and starts walking toward me. "Some Asian chick was up here by herself about a month ago. She never came back."

A lump rises in my throat. Parker's fingers latch tighter and we exchange a nervous glance. It sounds stupid in my head, but it's awesome getting to hold Parker's hand in front of someone other than Cam. That's not what I should be thinking about now.

"Nah," Zach blurts. "I'm just shitting you."

"Fuck you!" I shove him with my free hand, but I'm still chuckling. "Seriously? You know I'm skittish."

"Yeah," he says. "Plus I know Parker loves a good scare."

"Yeah, fuck you." Parker's all grins.

Zach throws his hand at us dismissively and laughs it off. He turns and starts back up the trail.

Parker's walking again by the time I finally get moving, pulling me along. I catch up and lean on his shoulder to get around a particularly large rock sitting dead center in the trail.

"So how much farther do we have?" I ask.

"Please tell me you're not going to be asking me that all day?" Zach asks.

I shrug. "We'll see. So how long?"

"Oh my God!" He throws his head back. It's almost like he's actually begging God now. I giggle inside. "I don't know. It shouldn't be too long. Maybe a few more hours."

"A few more hours?!" Parker's eyes are glowing. "You don't call that long?"

"In comparison," Zach peers over his shoulder and tilts his head. "On another topic, how long have you two been dating?"

My eyes dart to Park, and my first thought is whether I should subtract the days we weren't talking. I don't, though.

"Exactly five weeks today," I tell him while I'm counting

down the hours. "Minus like six hours."

Zach gives me this skewed grin. I smile and look at Parker.

"You know down to the hour?" Parker raises his brows.

"Yeah," I tell him. "You want to know the minutes?"

"Sure." Parker nods questioningly.

"Okay, I'm not that hardcore," I admit.

"So five weeks," Zach says. "You could have just left it at that. A couple hours aren't going to hurt anything. Next question."

"Okay." I let it hang there.

"Since Parker isn't out, how the hell did you two hook up?" he asks. "Did y'all already know about each other *before*?"

I'm beaming. Parker's smiling too, and before I can say anything he jumps at the question.

"No, we didn't," Parker says. "Noah didn't know I was…uh…gay, until five weeks ago actually."

Zach stops and turns to face us with his lips pursed.

"That seems awful quick to get together."

"It wasn't that simple," I tell him.

"Yeah, we'd talked about it for a week or so before that," Parker says. "Except he didn't know it was me. I've had a crush on him going way back. So when he came out I messaged him on that old TMS app. You remember that? The anonymous messaging one."

Zach nods. He seems intrigued.

"Well, I messaged him and told him I was gay, too, and asked him to email me, but I didn't tell him who I was." Parker wraps his arm around my waist and keeps talking. I watch his lips move and his eyes switch between Zach and me. "He emailed me, and we talked until I finally got the courage to tell him who I was."

"Really?" Zach asks.

"Yeah. We met at Five Guys over by the mall," I continue our story. "I didn't think he was coming at first, but then Parker shows up, and I thought for sure I'd been stood up. I actually thought Parker had followed me."

Parker's beaming. I squeeze him and find Zach again.

"But it *was* Park. The crazy part is that I've liked him a long time too. And here we are."

"Here we are," Parker repeats.

Zach nods. "That's awesome, guys. Super gay, but awesome."

* * *

The heat of the fire licks at my cheeks and wards off the cold in my bones. I knew it would be chilly, but damn, it's colder than I expected now that a bazillion stars float in a perfectly calm sea of bluish-black above us.

"So I might have a girlfriend." Zach says it like he's not really sure.

I pull my eyes away from the sky. We found a small clearing to make camp in, so for the most part I've got a clear view. Even where the trees hang overhead, their branches are mostly bare. It's nice, actually.

"*Might?*" I raise my brow.

"Yeah," he says and tosses a twig in the fire. "We've been talking for a few weeks, maybe two. I like her. I think. I don't know, maybe."

"Who is she?" I ask.

Parker's ass is planted next to me on a log. His cheek rests on my shoulder and his arms drape over my chest and back. His soft hair is tickling my face. It's weird, but his hair smells so good. It's like this manly strawberry scent, and I can't get enough of it.

"Her name's Allie. Allie Winger," he tells us. He keeps looking down and then back up again, and there's a certain perk underlying the nervousness in his voice. I know that feeling. "She's a freshman English major. When I found that out, I spoke before thinking and told her she was basically going to school to be a housewife."

"You said what?" Parker asks. I just know his eyes are bugging out of his head.

"Yeah, I thought I'd made a big mistake," Zach admits. "You two know my humor."

"Yeah, that's definitely you." It's one of those things he didn't mean. It's just a joke, but sometimes he doesn't filter those around the right people.

"I didn't mean it." Zach puts his hands up in mock defense. "Well, it is sort of true — what are you actually going to do with a degree in English? But I *was* joking. The crazy part is she got it. She thought it was great. That tells you all you need to know about her."

"A keeper," I tell him.

He nods. "Maybe. I was honestly just trying to get in her dorm room at first, you know? But that never happened. Probably best it didn't. But I guess it's going well. We're still talking."

"That's awesome," I tell him. "So do we get to meet her while we're up?"

"Let's hold off. We're just talking right now." He grins

wryly and stands up. "And on that note, I'm heading to bed."

"It's only like ten," I say.

"Yeah, time for bed. I'm old and tired." He smiles and heads for his tent. "Oh, and just to be clear. I'm not an idiot. I know why you didn't want Dad coming."

I swallow. I guess I assumed he knew after our little exploratory session in the Jeep, but at the same time I didn't *really* think so. I don't say anything.

"Just be safe." He puts his fist to his mouth and coughs suggestively. I roll my eyes. "And keep it quiet. Tent walls are thin. I support your gayness and all, but I don't think I can take *that* much gay."

"Oh come on," I say, but the heat in my face isn't just from the fire. Park lifts his head from my shoulder. He's blushing hard. I smile and bite my lip.

"Just... Just, yeah," Zach stutters. He waves at us when he can't think of anything to say. "Goodnight."

"Night, Zach," Parker says.

"Night," I echo my boyfriend. My *boyfriend*.

I wait for Zach to disappear behind the relative safety of his tent before looking at Parker again. I start giggling the moment I find him. He leans forward and touches his forehead to mine and I look into his eyes. Something about the glow and shimmer of the fire makes them appear deeper than usual, almost enchanting. I chew at my lip and then kiss him.

When we separate, I lock my eyes on him again. I can't stop. I'm here with *him*.

"Are you tired?" I shuffle on the log.

"Nah," Parker says. He looks up, staring at the stars between the bare branches. "It's beautiful up here."

"Not as beautiful as what I'm looking at." I move my eyes past his chestnut browns, down his cute nose and pale lips, and trace the slope of his chin and then back up to his eyes.

He pulls his gaze from the stars and looks me dead in the eyes.

"But you can't see what I see." He grins.

If anyone else had said it at any other time, I'd cringe, but instead a tingle slips down my spine. I shy away and scan the browning pine needles scattered at the base of our log. How anyone can find me attractive I still don't get.

Parker lays his cheek on my shoulder and wraps an arm around me. He rests the other on my thigh and I have to catch my breath. I look up at the stars to distract myself.

"The stars really *are* gorgeous, though," I say.

"We can actually see them *all* up here," Parker agrees. "Back home there's too much light pollution. And has it really been five weeks?"

I turn to look at him. He's still staring at the sky, but I know he sees me looking at him.

"Yeah, it has been," I tell him. His lips twitch and he pulls his gaze from the stars. The way he peers at me causes me to swallow nervously. What does he see in me? Then he leans in and kisses me gently on the cheek.

"It's hard to believe this is real. I didn't think I'd ever tell anyone, especially you."

"Especially me?" I squint and slide my arm around his waist.

"Yeah." He shrugs. "You were my friend. I thought it'd be me just telling you and you being like no, no, I'm straight or something, and then we'd be all awkward."

"I understand," I tell him. "Same here, I guess. I knew I'd come out eventually, but had you not messaged me that night, I don't think I would've ever told you I liked you. I had finally gotten over you. At least that's what I told myself."

"I'm glad you didn't *really* get over me," he says. "I never got over you. I couldn't. I'm glad I don't have to. It'd suck being that gay guy who can't get over a straight dude."

"I love you, Park," I breathe. I love him, and I love saying it.

"I love you too." He's smiling so big, and his eyes sparkle under the stars.

"I think I'm ready for bed now. How about you?" I chew on my lip.

He looks at me sideways at first. I'm not sure if he caught my meaning, but then he giggles and nods mischievously.

"I'd love to."

Saturday
October 20, 2018

Zach's apartment shrinks in my rearview mirror and disappears as I pull onto the highway.

"Well, that was *actually* fun," Parker says, puffing his exposed chest and squeezing my hand. I don't think he's let go since last night.

A briar caught his shoulder on the walk down. It was wrapped around an innocuous-looking plant when Park ran into it, and it ripped half the fabric off his arm. Luckily it barely touched his skin. There's a razor-thin mark etched along the front of his shoulder, but that's it.

The moment we left Zach's and the heater came on, Park lost the shirt. He could have kept it on, it's not torn that badly. But who am I to complain? It just makes it harder to keep my eyes on the road, and like I could wipe this grin off my face anyway.

"Yeah, it was," I agree. "Course, that's mainly because you came."

It was great catching up with my brother, but I think I would have found myself wishing for my own bed back in Kannapolis more had Park not come along. And the walking, all that walking. Damn, yeah I definitely don't think I would have cared for that if it had just been Zach or Dad. Don't get me wrong, they're great, but there's a point where your greatness has to outweigh how much I fucking hate hiking.

"Aw." Parker shrugs, all grins. "You would have had Zach if I hadn't come. He's cool. You two get along now anyway, you would've had fun."

"Yeah, dad jokes and all since Dad would have been there too," I remind him. I divert my eyes from the road and steal a glance at his stomach. How it felt under my palm last night sends a shiver up my spine.

Parker's checking his phone, so he doesn't notice.

"Dad jokes rule, man," he laughs. "If only because they're stupid, they're awesome."

"Sure…" I let it hang there.

"Cam's blowing up my phone," he says. I think he's looking at me, so I look over and catch his glowing brown eyes. "I think she wants an update."

"Call her," I tell him. "Hook it up to the car so we can both hear."

"Okay." Parker switches the cord from my phone to his and waits for my car to register it. "There we go."

On the second ring Cam picks up.

"Tell me everything!" She doesn't waste a second.

I look at Park and wrinkle my brow. He's doing the same, and we laugh.

"*Hey* would have been nice," he says.

"Oh come on. You've been holding out on me since yesterday," she complains.

"We haven't had a signal since yesterday," Parker reminds her. "And we told you we'd call on our way back."

"Yeah, yeah. Whatever." I can imagine her waving us off back home as if we can see her. "So…"

"It was great." I finally say something.

"Oh, so I'm on speakerphone," she says with that very familiar sass breaking out. "Aren't you supposed to inform your victims before they say something stupid?"

"It's more fun when they find out after," Park grins at me. I'm positive he's remembering the same incident.

A grin pulls at my lips when I think about it. It was a few years ago, our freshman year, I think. Park and I were hanging out in his room when Cam called. She was going on and on like she tends to do, and Park put her on speaker while mocking her silently where only I could see it. Well, it wasn't half a minute later when she told Parker what she was getting me for my birthday. I couldn't help it, I spoke up after that. Parker dealt with her wrath for at least a month.

"Whatever, I'm FaceTiming you, then," she says, and a second later her face pops up on Parker's phone. "Better. So, how'd it go?"

"It was a lot of fun, actually," I tell her.

The dude in front of me is creeping down the mountain, so I gun it and pass him on the right, because no one seems to know what the left lane is for. The view is breathtaking here with the Blue Ridge Mountains off to the right. They really do look blue.

"It was a little cold," Parker complains.

That was the only complaint I think I heard from him the entire hike. It *was* cold. I think it might have topped out at fifty with the sun at its peak.

"Come on, details, people." She's begging now.

"You want to know about the trees, the squirrels, and the birds too?" I ask without looking away from the road.

"Haha," she mocks me. "You know what I mean. And why don't you have a shirt on, Park?"

"Oh that." Parker winks at me mischievously, then leans over and kisses me on the cheek. "I ran into a briar or something. It ripped my sleeve right off."

"You sure it wasn't Noah who ripped it off?" I'm not looking, I refuse, but I know she's grinning.

"Funny." I cock my head and smirk.

Parker smiles deviously at me, and I have to swallow back my nerves.

"Yeah, other than the briar, it was great. Well, and the cold," Parker says. "It's beautiful up here. The views are incredible, and it's so clear at night. You can actually see *all* the stars."

"I bet," Cam says. "There's too much damn light down here, you can't get away from it all. You both hate camping, though, you sure that's it?"

She knows us so well. Too well, maybe.

"Normally," I blurt without thinking. "But it was great this time. I had someone to make it more than just dad jokes and acting like we're roughing it."

"That's great. Not what I was asking, but okay." Cam drops it. "I'm so glad you two are back together. For the record, you're horrible apart."

"Is it really that bad?" I ask, stealing a glance at Parker. Damn, I can't stop smiling.

"Hell yes!" She rolls her eyes when I take a glance at the screen and then smiles. "I hate playing both sides. It sucks! But now that you two are back together and you had your little camping trip, I take it you made up?"

"Definitely." Parker nods and grabs my free hand on the center dash. "We're back to normal. All good."

"I figured that, but did you two *make up* last night?"

I shift my bottom jaw and shake my head. I know what she's thinking even if Parker seems clueless. Or maybe he just hides his understanding better than me.

"Really, Cam?" I ask.

"Huh? Of course we made up. That's why I went." Parker genuinely doesn't seem to get it.

Camila is grinning mischievously on the phone screen, but she isn't saying anything.

"Parker, babe." I eye him and can't help but blush. I just called him *babe* for the first time, and I think I like it, but I think I'm about to have to lay it out for him.

My mind drifts to last night. The smooth texture of his rippled stomach, the sensation of lying underneath his body, the puffs of fog each time he breathed, the sound of his voice. I clench the steering wheel and have to catch my breath.

"She's not asking if we're good now."

"Huh?" He looks at me and suddenly it clicks. "Oh! That."

"You did, didn't you?" She's leaning closer to the screen, and she's almost squealing.

I lick my teeth nervously. I should have known she'd ask. She's not stupid. And do I really care if she knows? No. I don't.

I glance at Parker and ask him, without speaking a word, whether it's okay to answer. He smiles and his eyes dart away from me nervously for a fraction of a second before coming back. He nods, and the smile on my own face only grows.

"Yeah, we made up."

Monday | Halloween
October 31, 2018

It's Halloween, aka the best day of the year.

Other people love Christmas or Independence Day or Easter, but on which of those can you dress up as anyone you want, and no one questions your sanity? Okay, there are caveats to that. You can at comic cons, and even on Halloween some people get their undies in a wad if you dress up with a poncho and mustache or an Indian headdress. But that's not the point.

"Here you go, sir." I hand Waldo one of our hot specialty drinks, the Jack-o-Latte. It's probably childish of me, but I can barely contain myself when people ask for it. I mean, really? As for Waldo, though, he's dressed up in the red-and-white striped shirt and blue jeans I remember in the old picture books Mom showed me from when she was a kid, and he's even wearing the matching toboggan. According to Sandra, his partner is Carmen San Diego, but I'm not really sure who that is.

He says thanks and the two walk out the door after corralling three rambunctious kids. They seem awfully young to have three kids, but whatever.

The coffee shop is quiet and it's almost closing time. I can hear Sandra moving around somewhere in the back, probably straightening books or sweeping. Macy's doing the dishes while I clean up the espresso machine.

I check the clock behind me. It's analog, so I have to count off the ticks until I get to the hour and minute hands. Why can't it just be digital? It's 7:12 p.m., so I have another eighteen minutes. I'm leaving early to go home and change into my costume for the party.

When I found out I had to work on Halloween, I was a little distraught, but it worked out. Since it falls on a Wednesday this year, Parker isn't free until about half past eight because of church. His parents aren't about to let him miss for the "devil's holiday"—their words, not mine—so I just had to ask to get off a little early.

Plus, it's been an eventful night at the shop. The city is doing construction across the street. The entire downtown strip is cordoned off while the old buildings are being stripped down and readied for demolition. So randomly Sandra and Tina got this bright idea that we should all run across the road and do a little Halloween night trespassing. You know, see what's left, illegal shit. So we had L.A. and Becki, one of our local authors, stay at the shop to keep watch while we had a little adventure.

After about half an hour a truck pulled up outside. We ended up walking out with headlights blaring our shadows bigger than life on the brick wall of one of the abandoned houses. We might as well have been holding numbers like in some criminal lineup. I can only imagine how it looked, but it turned out all right. The cop didn't really care. He just stopped because he was called. So my record's still clean.

"Noah, can you sweep the nonfiction and children's sections before you leave? And no trespassing this time." Sandra pops around the corner.

"Sure." I nod and make my way to the back of the store to fetch the broom.

She's apologized a dozen times for the little schism between Parker and me. That might be one reason it was so easy to get off early tonight. I mean, I haven't asked for much yet, but maybe.

This past week has been great too. It's like nothing ever happened between us, like those days of not talking to each other never were. Instead, we've laughed and hugged and kissed the week away. I can't remember being happier.

I finish up the sweeping and check my phone. There's a text from Parker.

Can't wait to show you my costume.

I just wish I knew *what* he's going to be. He's playing a Camila and won't tell me. Apparently it needs to be a surprise. He already knows what I'm going as, I told him before I realized we were keeping secrets. I send him a quick text back.

Shouldn't you not be texting in church? Isn't that a rule or something? Can't wait.

I pocket my phone and go back up front. Macy and Sandra are helping another customer, hopefully our last. My phone vibrates in my pocket. I guess that's a no from Park.

I check the clock behind the counter again. 7:28 p.m. That's close enough.

"Sandra, it's time for me to go," I say. It's more of a question, really.

"All right. You two have fun tonight." She smiles.

"I forgot to ask," Macy peeks around the man at the counter who apparently doesn't participate in Halloween. "What are you going as?"

"Andy Black, or Biersack, whichever you want," I tell her. Technically it's Biersack.

"Who?" she wrinkles her brow. Yeah, I should have known she wouldn't know the rock demigod.

"I'll send you a picture," I tell her and wave goodbye to the pair of them. "See you tomorrow."

"Bye, Noah," she calls out and waves in the middle of stirring the coffee for the dude at the register, and I head outside.

I grab my phone and check Parker's last text.

Technically, yeah, but I think I do a lot of stuff they don't like…

A chuckle jumps up my throat. Yeah, that sounds about right. I smile and send him another text before getting in my car.

Maybe we can do some other stuff they don't like tonight.

* * *

I'm almost there.

Apparently Park just left church. They must have run late tonight. It's nearly half an hour till nine and the party started at eight. I knew we were going to be late, but not this late.

I lower my phone and check my face paint in the bathroom mirror again. It's nothing extravagant, just a thin black line running from ear to ear under my eyes and over the bridge of my nose. It was Andy's usual facial decoration before the *Vale* album when he lost it and after they stopped going full-on Kiss. I'm also wearing black skinny jeans and a sleeveless black vest jacket with an upturned collar, sort of like the one Andy wears. My eyes fall below my neckline where my collar is usually close to my neck. I feel sort of exposed without a shirt on underneath this vest, especially with it zipped up only halfway, but hey, it's how Andy wears it. Plus I'm pale like Andy, so it works.

Looking back up, I tilt my head and look into my own eyes. I wonder what Parker sees in them. He's always telling me I have nice eyes. All I see is the gray irises I wake up to every morning. I mean, I'm not even muscular. I guess it really does take more than three months in weight class to get a six-pack.

My phone vibrates.

I'm here.

I have to stifle a jump. I can't wait to see what he's dressed up as. I jog to the front door and swing it open. He's standing on the front steps waiting, but he's not in costume. I guess that makes sense.

"Come on, you need to get changed so we can go." I rush him through the door.

"Well, hey there, Andy." He grins mischievously. I blush when his eyes drop below my neck for a moment and he smiles. He whispers, "Looking sexy."

"Stop it." I swat his shoulder.

He purses his lips into an air smooch and scopes out the living room as he passes by. "Are your parents not home?"

"Nah, they're at my dad's work party. One of his friends decided to throw one at the last minute." I follow him to my bedroom.

"That means I can do this." He stops so abruptly that I bump into him. I see a flash of a grin before he plants his lips on me. We stand in the hall for what feels like a beautiful eternity locked together before I lean back and bite at my lips.

"Did they know I was going to be here?" he asks as he stops at the bathroom door.

"They know we won't be long," I tell him, pushing him into the bathroom. "Now get changed. I want to know what you're going as, plus we're already late."

He shakes his head and disappears behind the door. I go to my bedroom and pace the floor. I close my eyes and imagine the feeling of his soft lips, the heat of his body, the sensation of my palms wrapped around his waist. He's perfect. He's absolutely perfect.

A few minutes later the bathroom door creaks open and his footsteps thud down the hallway.

"Are you ready?" he calls around the corner.

"Definitely." I'm bouncing on the balls of my feet.

"Okay," he says and jumps around the corner into a crouch. He has one arm extended, his fingers outstretched in red-and-black cloth. He's fucking Spider-Man! Yes!

"Fuck yes!" I grin. This must be why he wouldn't tell me. He knows Spider-Man is my favorite. "Park, you look awesome! Damn!"

"It should have come to me earlier, but it just hit me this week that when you say my name, it'll be just like you're calling me Peter Parker," he tells me. "I mean, they do call him Parker in the movies half the time anyway."

"Yep, my Peter Parker," I tell him. "This might sound bad, but can you turn around?"

I can't see it through the mask, but I'm pretty sure by the way he angles his head he's smiling at me, but he does it. And oh my.

"This thing fits tight as shit," he says. "You like?"

"Yeah," is all I can say, and he turns back around.

"You're blushing, Noah." I can hear the smile in his voice.

"Oh shut up." I jump back. "I'm going to the party with a superhero. Ain't that cool?"

"Well I'm going with a rock star." He walks up and puts his arms around my waist and touches his forehead to mine. "Just don't try singing, please. I've heard you in the car before."

I push him away playfully and laugh. "Oh fuck off. We need to go."

* * *

It's sort of disappointing how few people dress up for Halloween or decorate their houses. I miss all the tombstones and skeletons dotting the lawns as you ride by. Sure it's tacky, but it was cool.

I'm in the passenger seat of Spider-Man's truck switching my gaze between the road and the curves in Parker's suit where his chest dips at his stomach, and then back out my own window at yet another bland yard.

My lips move in sync to the music, Black Veil Brides's "In the End," my absolute all-time favorite BVB song. I'm not actually singing though, just lip syncing.

"We're here," Parker announces. He settles on a street spot behind an older Chevrolet Malibu and we get out.

Instinctively I pull the top of my jacket together to cover my chest.

"Stop that," Parker tells me. He reaches over, and instead of helping me, he pulls my jacket open further. "It looks good."

I can't tell if he's smiling or smirking, but I huff and go with it. I can't hold it closed the entire party anyway—whatever's left of the party, at least. Well, I could, but that would just be weird.

"If anyone should be self-conscious, it's me." Parker throws his hands out, pointing at himself. "This is so fucking tight."

"But it looks good," I purposely mimic him with a smile.

He shakes his head, and I wish I could see his eyes. I bet he's rolling them.

"Come on." He waves, and we take off down the pavement until we reach the sidewalk leading up to Grady's house. He's this rich kid at A.L. Brown. He's a good guy. Tall, really tanned with this majorly contrasting blonde hair.

The path to the house is narrow, so I drop behind Parker. I want so badly to reach out and grab his butt, but I don't. Suddenly it hits me there will be music and dancing, and I'm wishing I could dance with Parker, but that's not really an option. We're just "friends" at a party.

Parker opens the door and a massive bass note pounds me in the face. It's only off-putting for a moment before my ears adjust, and then the beat becomes familiar. I don't know it technically, but I think I've heard it somewhere. It's some rap song I'd never listen to voluntarily.

I follow Park inside. It doesn't take him any time to start moving his shoulders to the beat. Me, on the other hand, it's going to take a little longer to be that comfortable.

"Come on, Noah!" Parker turns and pulls me onto what might be considered the dance floor. We slide a pack of comic book and horror movie characters.

Parker's dancing and I'm just nervous. I gulp back an imaginary ball of spit and glance around me before finding Parker again. He's swaying his hips and raising his arms. Why am I so nervous? Everyone knows we're friends, and don't teen friends do stupid shit? I shake away the jittering in my nerves and let my body move to the beat. It's nothing fancy, but it feels good with my eyes locked on my Peter Parker; well, on the huge white Spidey eyes.

"There you go," Parker says.

I take a quick look around to check out who else is here. I can't tell who half of the people really are with their masks on, but I do see Drake and Kary—not together, separate. Drake's dressed up as Rick from *Rick and Morty* and Kary looks like she's trying for Black Widow, but I don't know if it's the lack of red or white hair or what, but it just isn't working.

Traven, David, and I think Kyler—I could have his name wrong—are hanging around the food bar. None of them are dressed up. Actually most of the people in here are not dressed up, which is a bit of a bummer. At least the room is covered in black and orange streamers. The lights are low and there's a strobe light going. It's a bit much but it works. I don't know the rest of the people.

"Where's Cam?" I ask. I thought she'd be here already.

"I don't know, man, I haven't seen her either." Parker stops dancing, and I follow him to the finger food platters.

Some chick in a super stereotypical black witch gown, pointy hat and all, shimmies in between us. My mouth drops when she gropes Parker's butt. He jumps, probably thinking it was me and wondering what the hell I'm thinking.

"Well hey there, Spidey," she hisses, trying to sound sensual.

I bite my tongue. I want to say something, to tell her to keep her fucking hands off my boyfriend, but I can't. I take a deep breath.

"Hey." I can hear the tension in Parker's voice when he realizes the hand that grabbed him isn't mine.

"You want to save me upstairs?" She pooches her lips at Park.

"No," I blurt. Dammit, keep your mouth shut, Noah. I tighten my fists into balls and breathe.

"I didn't ask you…whoever the hell you're supposed to be." She crinkles her brow, and her long fake nose wiggles. I want to slap it right off. "I was talking to Spidey here. So what do you say?"

Parker takes a step around her, a step closer to me. "Nah, I'm good. Someone else'll have to manage that."

I hold back a huff, but I can't get rid of the if-it-wasn't-illegal-I'd-kill-you-right-now look on my face. She gives me a dirty sneer and jerks her head away all snooty before walking off.

"That was awkward," he says.

"Yeah," I agree and grab a cracker from one of the trays, stuffing it in my mouth nervously. "Dirty bitch needs to keep her hands to herself."

He leans closer. "I thought that was your hand."

"I know. Believe me, I thought about it."

He turns and pours a Sprite.

Contrary to how the movies make it look, not every teen party has alcohol. We're not all that lucky. I pour my own and wait. Parker lifts his cup and nearly spills it on his suit before he realizes his mistake.

"Really, Park?" I laugh. "Really?"

"Shut up." He shakes his head and pulls the bottom of his mask over his nose, keeping his eyes covered, and takes a sip.

"There's Cam." I point past the crowd, into the next room.

She's in a short red dress—Uhura from *Star Trek,* just like she promised. I nod my head for Parker to follow and lead us across the dance floor between a pair of sort-of-dancing couples.

Cam's talking to Stephanie. They've been friends since eighth grade, I think. They're not as tight as our little threesome, but they still talk. She sees me, and I almost feel bad at how quickly she ditches Stephanie, but the girl doesn't seem to mind. She's a little socialite, so she just moves on to the next victim.

"Uhura!" I yell and throw my arms around her.

"Andy!" She hugs me and then eyes Parker with a hint of curiosity. "And Spidey must be Parker."

"Right," he says, and before his Spidey senses can deflect it, she rushes him with a hug too.

"I should have known you'd dress up as Spider-Man." She puts her hands on her hips, then looks at me. "That's Noah's big movie crush."

I try not to blush, but my cheeks are already warmer. It's not like he doesn't know, but hearing it spoken in public still riles up a bit of embarrassment.

"Cam," I chide her.

"I know." Parker is obviously talking to Camila, not me. I shoot him a pleading look.

"Not here, guys," I try.

"Oh, I think we're embarrassing him." Cam raises her shoulders and grins. "He's blushing. It's so cute!"

"Oh my God!" I plead.

"Calm down," she tells me and grabs both of us by the hand. "Come on, let's dance."

I don't have a chance to rebuke her before she pulls us into the other room and onto the dance floor. I still don't know the song, but it doesn't matter. Cam's already dancing and so is Parker, so I join in.

"I really suck at this, guys," I say. And damn, do I suck at it.

Earlier was no better, but with both of them it feels more obvious somehow. Maybe it's how Cam at least has rhythm in her body, and Park seems to be able to dance to anything you give him. I'm the odd one out here.

"Who cares? Just let loose," Parker tells me.

"Well, try a little," Camila says jokingly with a light-hearted glare.

"Not helping," I quip but laugh.

After a second I don't care if anyone's watching or that I probably look like an idiot. Nope. I'm here with my two favorite people, and the smiles on their faces, or at least the one I'm imagining behind Parker's mask, are enough fuel to keep me going and love every minute of it.

The song ends, and there's that moment when everyone's waiting for the next one to start up. Parker pulls his mask back and lets it hang behind his neck.

"It was getting hot in there," he complains. His forehead is sweating, and he puffs his cheeks.

I like the costume, but I like his eyes better.

"I bet," I say.

"They should play some Black Veil Brides," Camila comments. "Then you could lip sync, not actually sing, we don't need that."

"You too?" I throw my hands up. "Park's already told me once today."

"Sorry, not sorry," she beams. "It would be cool, though. I mean, other than your hair, you look sort of like him."

I raise an eyebrow critically.

"Okay, maybe it's not that close. Andy is skinner." She stops and thinks about what she just said. "I'm not saying you're fat. You're not, at all. I promise. Oh God, I just need to shut up and dance."

Parker's laughing. "Wow, Cam. Yeah, just shut up."

"Nah, I get it," I tell her. Andy's not unhealthy skinny, but he is skinny, not to mention super pale, and I wasn't going that far. I at least pulled off the spikey hairdo. "He's *skinnier* than me."

I think Cam's extra glad when the music starts back up. It's not BVB, but it's something to move to and move on. I'm swaying back and forth when I bump into someone.

"Sorry," I say before turning to see who it is. A pair of hands shove into my chest before I have a chance to get all the way around.

Carter.

"Ugh, get off me," Carter shrieks, like I was purposely gyrating my ass on him.

"Sorry, man," I try, but his expression changes.

He gives me a once-over and starts to laugh. "Oh look! The fag's dressed up as another fag."

"Andy's not a fag, you fucking inbred," I yell.

It probably isn't my best comeback ever, or the wisest,

but it's out of my mouth before I have time to think rational-
ly. Out of the corner of my eye I can see Camila give me her
really look, and what's happening is just now registering with
Park.

"What did you call me?" Carter steps forward and grabs
me by the collar. He pulls me in when I don't answer. A
lump builds in my throat, and even though the music is still
playing, I can feel everyone's eyes on me.

"A *fucking* inbred," I repeat. I don't know why, but something has emboldened me, and somehow I say it again. Strike
two.

Apparently there's no strike three in Carter's game. Abruptly he shoves me back and I fall to my ass. It hurts, but
I'm hyper-focused on Carter. He lowers his center of mass
and curls his shoulders forward. Oh no. This isn't over yet.

He's about to lurch, and I can imagine how badly that's
going to end, but Parker jumps in between us.

"Woah!" Parker puts his gloved hand up in Carter's face,
and the football player stumbles to a halt. He stands up
straight, but he clenches his fists. "He didn't mean it."

No, I meant it. Maybe it's because he's a stupid jock or
that he's a homophobic pretty boy, but something broke my
give-a-shit the moment he threw out the F word. I know I
really ought to consider how he could beat my head in, but
somewhere along the line that got blurred.

"So now you're reading his mind? I thought Spider-Man
only sensed danger," Carter says.

I can't see Parker's face, but the way his hands ball up
and his head tilts I can imagine the look he's giving Carter.

"How many times have you blown him?" Carter blows
his cheeks in and out. He's proud of himself and I'm begin-

ning to boil inside. I don't give a shit about what he's saying to me now, but what he's doing to Parker? Hell no.

"W-what?" Parker stutters. "No."

"Oh, you like it better when he fucks you in the ass, right?" Carter keeps it up.

Something in Park's demeanor changes. If there was any doubt before, it's obvious when he opens his mouth that his give-a-shit just flew out the window too.

"You know man, you're about as useful as Anne Frank's drumset."

"Huh?" Carter's nose crinkles, and he looks back to his ever-present buddies, Aaron and Taren. They share the same blank looks.

They don't get it. Oh my God, they seriously don't get it. All at once the heat in my face starts to dissipate. I don't know what's funnier, the joke or the fact that they don't understand.

"Really?" Parker puts his hands out, palms up, giving them another chance to catch the insult. Apparently he's giving up because he throws out another that doesn't take as much of an IQ to get. "Damn, it's so hard to believe you were the best sperm your dad had to offer. Your mom must be really disappointed."

"Fuck you!"

Parker doesn't have time to move before Carter's fist catches his cheek.

I stiffen at the smack of knuckles against skin. Parker stumbles backwards. What the hell? I jump to my feet and tackle Carter.

"No!" I scream as we fall to the floor. I swing weakly at his face.

Carter grunts, but he's quick. After only one punch he gets his arm around me. He throws me off and starts in on my face. Pain blossoms up my jaw and scatters behind my eyes and forehead. Somewhere nearby I hear more impacts. Parker!

I squirm and manage to slide away just enough to grip the foot of a chair and reel myself away a few inches. Carter follows, his fist pounding into my side.

"Stop!" Cam yells. I don't think I've ever heard her that scared before. "You're hurting him, stop!"

Finally the beating stops. I dart my eyes about me fearfully as a pair of hands grab me. I jerk away before I realize it's just Cam.

"I'm all right," I tell her. On my feet, I swivel my head around searching for Parker, but I find Carter first. He's up. Traven and Drake have their arms locked around his forearms, and Kyler and some boys I don't know are holding Aaron and Taren back.

"Parker!" I start to run, but it's too quick. A wheezy feeling catches me and my vision blurs. I drop to my knees and grunt. I have to give it a second to pass. Finally I'm up and running across the room. I shove some random girl in an Elastigirl suit out of my way and drop to my knees beside Parker.

He's still on the floor. Blood oozes from his lip, his nose, and even a little above his left eye. My heart skydives a thousand feet.

"Park? You okay?" I lean down and cup my hand under the back of his head. I don't give a fuck what anyone thinks right now. I just want to be sure he's okay. My other hand shakes over the wound on his lip.

"Yep." It's quiet and strained, but he manages it.

"You sure?" My voice is shaking.

"Are you positive?" Cam drops next to me.

He nods and forces a smile through swollen bloodstained lips. Somehow a tiny laugh jumps from my mouth.

"Let's get you up," I tell him.

He puts his elbows back and we help him sit up. I give him a second to catch his breath before getting him to his feet. Once he's up I realize how quiet the room is. Everyone's just standing around, gawking. The music is still playing, but the party's stopped.

My eyes land on Taren and then Aaron. My nose flares and I want nothing more than to feel my fist slam into their smug faces. Then there's Carter. I hate him. Yeah, I hate him. But at least with him I get the satisfaction of seeing him bleed. His mouth is busted open. I can't remember if I did that or Parker. I hope to God it was me.

"What are you all looking at?" I shout at the room.

Apparently that was all they needed. They snap out of it and everyone goes back to their talking and dancing, but I bet most of the talks are going to be a little different now.

"Let's get out of here," I say.

Cam's eyes are wet, but she nods. As I help Parker walk out, she gives Carter and his gang the most intense look I think I've ever witnessed. That's also when I notice the fire in my stomach and chest. Damn, it hurts.

Outside I search for Park's truck. Argh! It's down the street.

"Cam, can you go get Park's truck?" I ask. "It's just down the street. He doesn't need to walk that far."

I don't know if it's that bad. It's probably not, but I can't stand to watch him cringe with each step, not all the way down the street, and Cam doesn't protest.

"Got it," she says.

"Thanks." Park tosses her the keys and she jogs off.

I settle on the porch steps with Parker. It's all I can do not to wrap my arms around him to comfort him. "You sure you're good?"

"Yeah, yeah." He shakes his head, but he can't hold back a grimace. "He shouldn't have called you a..."

"True," I agree, but then I cringe a little inside. "But I probably shouldn't have called him an inbred either."

Parker laughs. "Yeah, I got your back either way, but I don't think you should go around defending Andy Black's honor that much."

I'm laughing even though it hurts my stomach.

"Not my crowning moment," I admit.

Even with the blood on his face, Parker's smile is gorgeous. I wipe some of it from his chin and cheek.

"I'm sorry," I tell him. "I should have known better. Thanks for standing up for me."

"No thanks needed." He locks his eyes on me. "You're mine, that's my job."

I'm beaming while I look him over. "So I guess now you're going for the Spider-Man look after he got his ass kicked?"

His eyes narrow into slits and he pooches his lips.

"I'm just teasing you. You even look good as Spider-Man when you're all bloodied up. That's an accomplishment."

"Really? Better than Holland?" Parker puffs his chest.

I wrinkle my brow and roll my eyes.

"Now let's not be stupid," I lie. He gives me that cute faux hurt look. "Of course you do. Way hotter."

A moment passes and neither of us says a thing. I think he's contemplating the same thing I am because he's not looking me in the eyes either. But we both know better. Even a simple kiss would hurt too much right now, and we're still sitting outside the party.

"Well…" Parker's suddenly amused by something. "This is definitely going to reaffirm my parents' anti-Halloween convictions. And probably anti-party convictions too."

Thursday
November 8, 2018

"Can you hand me the rice?" Dad stretches his arm over the tray of remaining taco shells.

I hand him the bowl and go back to piling beef in a shell, a little lettuce, a lot of cheese, and then top it all off with a little hot sauce. Unless I'm wrong, most families in the South have stuff like ham and mashed potatoes for dinner, or pork tenderloin and collard greens, although to be honest, I don't really know what that is. We're having tacos, rice, and some freezer section Mexican dessert that I think is supposed to be a churro.

"You did a great job tonight," Dad says.

"Thanks. Second place. I still can't believe it," I tell him. "I didn't think I'd get higher than, like, fourth."

"You do great." Mom nudges me. "Have a little confidence."

I shrug. I love to swim, but it's not my best sport. I'm better at lacrosse, but I had to pick one once I started working at Editions because I knew I wouldn't have time for both, so I chose swimming because Park doesn't play lacrosse. I'm honestly surprised I took second in the freestyle.

"And Parker did good too." Dad nods across the table. "What'd he come in at?"

"Third in breaststroke," I remind him and start in on my

taco.

"That's good, right?" Mom asks.

I smile at her questioningly.

"Yeah, third is good." I nod. "I mean, he would have been happier with second or first."

"You know what I meant." She shakes her head.

We've been having these family dinners a lot more lately. I'm not one hundred percent sure why, but I'm thinking it's my mother's doing. I don't believe Dad would think like that. I could be wrong, but I think the reality that I'll be heading off to college next year might be setting in.

Tonight would normally have been a night laughing at bad jokes with Parker and Cam at Five Guys or Firehouse, but Mom insisted. Plus, Parker's parents have done the same a lot lately. A lot. It's actually made me nervous the last few days. The thought hit me the other night that they might know about Parker, but he says they don't.

Parker's face is finally healing up. The bruising went down a lot quicker than I expected, but the places where his skin broke are still bruised. At least a little bit. His parents took it about as well as we expected, maybe a little better, if I'm honest. They weren't happy that Park got into a fight, but to their credit they didn't ground him.

"Has Parker finished his college applications?" Mom asks.

I cock my head to the side. Definitely not the question I expected.

"Uh… Yeah, I think so," I say. "Actually, yeah, he has."

"Where'd he apply?" she leans back in her chair.

I gather the list in my head. It's not hard, I've known for months where he planned to apply.

"NC State, Carolina, Charlotte, UC-Berkley, Yale, and Michigan." Charlotte was the only one that surprised me. I didn't think he planned to submit there too.

"Damn, that must have cost a fortune." Dad shakes his head, his mouth half-full.

I nod. "Oh yeah! I think it cost his parents like five hundred bucks or something in the end."

"And that doesn't even include the cost of taking the SAT." Dad swallows. "Then there's tuition, room and board, books—oh my God, books. For his parents' sake, I hope he either gets a lot of financial aid or ends up at State or Charlotte. Honey, how much did it cost again for Noah?"

"For what? His applications?" Mom asks.

My eyes jump between them. I'm grinning. If Dad only knew how much I agree with him. State or Charlotte would be great, because then I could go with Parker.

"It wasn't any more than say, three hundred bucks." She shrugs.

"Thank you, Noah." Dad laughs.

"No problem." I grin.

Mom gets up and takes her plate with her. She swings around Dad's end of the table and gathers his plate and then mine.

"I'm going to clean up and then watch some ID Channel." She raises her eyebrows. "They're having a serial killer marathon today."

"Oh my." I shake my head and look at Dad, who's rolling his eyes. "If you ever die under questionable circumstances, I swear I'm telling the police that Mom's their prime suspect."

"You hear that, honey?" he yells into the kitchen. "You won't get away with it unless you take Noah out too."

I angle my face away with an amused grin. Dad shrugs and pushes away from the table.

"You don't expect me to be on your side, do you?" He grins. "I have to deal with her."

I cover my mouth to dampen a laugh.

"Yeah, I guess so."

"Night, buddy, see you in the morning." Dad pats me on the shoulder on his way out of the kitchen. "Love you."

"Love you too, Dad, night," I call after him.

I'm alone at the table now, so I get my phone out and check to see what I missed. It's not much. Cam wants to go to a show at the Comedy Zone in uptown Charlotte Saturday night, but I'm not sure I can make that with my work schedule. I shoot her a text telling her it *might* work.

There's a handful of messages waiting for me on Snapchat too. Kary with her beloved Dalmatian in one of those time-loop videos. Zach sent a picture of him with Allie in some bar up in Boone, I'm assuming. They're getting pretty serious.

I tap through a few more. I always save Park's for last.

I roll my eyes once I do open it, though. He used the dog ears filter—so unoriginal—but there's no getting around how cute it is. I tap to the next snap and he's blowing a kiss at the camera and there's a heart at the bottom.

Mom comes in from the kitchen, so I swipe the app off the screen and smile. I try not to look suspicious, but I think it only makes it worse.

"You want to watch TV with me?" She keeps walking and plops down on the sofa.

"Why not?" I say under my breath and take a seat on the opposite end of the sofa.

She turns on the TV and flips to the ID Channel. She wasn't fibbing. There is a documentary playing about a serial killer.

"Oh! They're talking about H. H. Holmes."

I'm not sure whether to be impressed or worried that Mom knows which mass murderer they're talking about. The TV's only been on for like five seconds and his name is nowhere to be seen on the screen, just his face. Finally a little bar pops up at the bottom of the screen with *H. H. Holmes & The Murder Hotel* written across it. Yep, she got it.

"You do realize it's super creepy you knew that so quick, right?" I ask her.

She shrugs but her eyes never leave the television. "Eh."

I shake my head, smiling, and go back to messing with my phone. Parker's family dinner is over, too, based on his Snapchat story, but his brother and sister have him playing a late-night game of Scattergories, so he's not texting back so quick. It's been forever since I've played that game. Everyone in my family tries to come up with the most inappropriate words for each category. It gets really awkward, but I guess that's what makes it fun.

I refuse to be the super clingy, I-need-a-text-every-two-minutes type of boyfriend, so I let him have his Noahless time. Don't get me wrong, I would like a text every two minutes, but I'm not going to push it. Pursing my lips, I hold back the desire to text him anyway and send Cam a snap of myself grinning stupidly with Mom in the background glued to the TV. I complete it with the caption *Serial killer in the making*.

A few minutes pass of the mildly interesting documentary and a storm of snaps ranging from doggy ears to flamingos and sunglasses to my all-time favorite, the one that makes your mouth huge and your voice squeaky. I'm getting tired, so I throw my feet off the couch and make a start for my bedroom.

"Hold up, Noah." Mom stops me before I reach the hallway.

I turn, and she lowers the volume on the TV.

"Yeah?" I squint.

"I really don't want to intrude, but..." She pauses and looks around the room. Her eyes stop on a family photo hanging on the wall next to me. I think I was three or four. I still had blonde hair, and my dimples hadn't moderated yet. "I have to ask, though."

"What, Mom?" I take a step back into the living room. I'm nervous now. I hate it when a conversation starts like this. It's sort of like when Dad had *the talk* with me when I turned twelve, or somewhere about there. That was interesting, considering.

"I know I brought it up before and you said no, but *are* you and Parker dating?" She sits up taller on the sofa. I can tell she knows I don't really want to talk about it.

I want to say yes. I always want to say yes, but I won't have this on me again.

"No." I try to play it cool, but I think it came out a little jarring.

"Noah, you do know you can tell me if you are, right?"

"Of course." I shrug, but I'm jittery.

"I actually think it'd be great. You two would be so freaking adorable together. He *is* cute."

I swallow back a nervous ball in my throat. If she only knew how badly I want to agree and how great it is to hear her say it.

"Stop it, Mom." I shy my eyes away. "I already know you think it'd be great. We're just friends, just like always. You're looking way too much into things."

"Okay," she says and gets up and comes over to me. She puts her hands on my shoulders and looks me in the eye.

"You're a good-hearted boy, Noah. You're handsome, you're smart. You've got a good head on your shoulders, and even though you never clean you room when I ask you to, I love you." She puts her forehead against mine and smiles. "You'll find someone."

"I know." I roll my eyes and pull away. "I love you too. I'm going to bed now."

She grins and lets me go after giving me a quick hug and ruffling my hair. I'm about to turn and make a run for my room when she opens her mouth one more time.

"Just so we're on the same page, though." She smirks. She's clearly amused with herself for something. "You're a terrible liar."

"Huh?" I swing around.

"You and Parker," she tells me, shaking her head. "I'm not stupid."

"Well, I did pretty well hiding the whole gay thing." It's all I've got.

"Touché." She grimaces, but it turns back into a smile quickly. "Good night, Noah. Your secret's safe."

I grin but turn and make for my bedroom as quick as possible. Oh my God! How the hell does this keep happening?

In my room I let the door shut behind me. I throw myself on the bed and roll onto my back. How the hell was I able to keep being gay a secret so well for so long, but I can't hide how I feel about Parker?

Maybe love's harder to hide.

Tuesday
November 20, 2018

The sky is clear tonight, so Parker and I drove out to China Grove to escape the city lights to see the stars better. It's not as secluded as the mountain, but it's better than Kannapolis.

We had no clue where we were heading. We just drove until we found a place off the road next to a massive hay field with enough space to park his truck and get away from the road. It's been quiet the last ten minutes. We're only about twenty minutes from my house in the suburbs and another twenty from uptown Charlotte, but it's more country out this way.

To battle the frigid temperatures, we're lying tangled together in the truck bed. Parker's chest is pressed against me and my leg is wrapped around him. My eyes are closed, and I press my hand to his cheek as we kiss, or make out. Yeah, make out is definitely more accurate.

While I nibble at his lip my mind takes me back to our first kiss and a smile pulls at my cheeks.

"What is it?" Parker leans away and eyes me with suspicion.

"I was just thinking about us," I tell him. "Our first *date*. Our first *kiss*."

I throw up air quotes with my free hand.

"I think about that a lot." Parker bites at his lip. He rarely does that, and oh my God, I wish he would do it more. "I still have a hard time believing this is real."

"Yeah. It's like some perfect dream, and I'm terrified I'm going to wake up." I lie back and let my head settle on the hard metal truck bed. Next time we have to at least bring some blankets. It's cold and I need something to prop my head on. My jacket's barely doing its job, and if it wasn't for the warmth from Parker's body, I'd be freezing right now. "I never thought I'd actually *really* be with you. It was nothing more than a fantasy."

"A fantasy?" He squirms on his back, but I know he's looking at me with that mischievous grin of his. "You haven't told me about any fantasy yet."

"And I'm not going to now." I laugh. "All you need to know is I thought about it *a lot*."

We laugh together for a minute before silence overtakes us. I stare at the sky. It's late, but it's not that late. We're on fall break so there's no school tomorrow, but both our parents still expect us back home by eleven. Well, Parker's expect him by ten thirty, but we've still got a little time left.

It's a lot like our camping trip, except the sky's not quite as clear and the crickets and katydids are silent tonight. It's just the gentle whistle of the wind and the puffs of our own breaths.

"Did your dad really cuss out Dylan's dad?" Parker asks.

I grin at Park. The rose in his tanned cheeks is all but gone from the cold, and his lips are facing the sky. With the last of his injuries healed, his skin is back to perfection.

"Yep." I giggle.

It was at our last swim meet a week ago. I didn't hear the whole conversation, just the tail end, but the gist is that Mr.

Kowalski felt I shouldn't be on the team. Apparently having a gay kid in the locker room with his straight son was dangerous. My first thought, almost simultaneous with thinking he was a hateful fuck, was that there was no way in hell I'd ever do anything with his son.

I mean, I'll talk to him in a totally friend-only way, but that's it. I don't have anything against Dylan, he's just not my type. Too tall and skinny.

Dylan hated that his dad made a scene, he even apologized at school the next day. My dad, on the other hand, didn't just hate it, I think it enraged him. He replied immediately with a few choice words in the middle of the YMCA. The look on Mr. Kowalski's face was priceless.

"I hate I missed it." Parker laughs. "My parents made me leave as soon as the meet was over. Hannah wanted to go to the mall before it closed for some outfit she wanted."

"It was great." I let my hand fall from my chest and search for Park's hand. When I find it I lace our fingers together. They're so cold, but I guess mine are too. "Coach had to make Dad leave. But once they got outside, he told Dad he wouldn't cut me from the team on account of some homophobe and that he'd even fight it if Mr. Kowalski took it above him."

"That's awesome." Parker nods. "Coach A's a cool guy."

We're quiet for a little bit. As odd as it would have felt months ago, lying here, saying nothing, just being together is enough. Everything in this moment is enough. No, it's more than that. It's perfect.

I'm out and open. I'm no longer afraid of what people think of me, for the most part. The boy I've always crushed on is lying next to me under a clear country sky in the middle of autumn. I turn my head and trace the outline of his face against the wheel well, every perfect inch.

He's not just a crush anymore. Not at all. I love him, and he loves me.

I twist to my side and lay my arm over his stomach and nestle my nose under his chin. I breathe in his minty musky scent. It's the same cologne he's worn since sophomore year, and I love it. I kiss him. He arches his neck and I keep kissing him.

"Ugh," I huff when my phone vibrates and breaks the moment.

"What?" he breathes.

"It's just my phone," I tell him. "Don't worry about it."

With an impish grin I go back in for the attack. My lips brush his skin. Then my teeth for a brief second. I can hear his breath intensify. It's like music to my ears, so I keep it up.

My phone starts vibrating again. I grunt and slump back onto my ass.

"Dammit," I groan and pull out my phone. I stare at the name on the screen. "It's Mom."

"Just answer it. It's okay."

"No." I shake my head and swipe the call away. "I'm here right now for you and you only."

He grins, but before I have a chance to get back to business, my phone starts up again. I roll my eyes.

"Answer it," he tells me. "Just tell her she has to stop interrupting our make-out sessions."

I shake my head and a giggle escapes.

"Right." I know he's joking, but the thought of actually telling her that is hilarious. I answer the call.

"Hey, Mom," I huff.

"Noah." Immediately my insides stiffen at her voice. There's something different, something scared behind her tone. "You need to come home."

"What's going on?" I sit up, propping myself up with my free hand and looking down at Parker. There's silence on the other end, and I think Park notices that something's up because he sits up too.

"Zach's been in an accident." She starts to cry. "We're on our way to the hospital now."

"What?" My body locks up.

Zach was on his way down from the mountain tonight for the Thanksgiving holiday. An accident? Oh hell. No. How bad? Is he okay?

"They airlifted him and Allie to NorthEast." She's barely holding her voice together.

"Airlifted?" I ask. I get to my feet and jump off the back of the truck. "How bad is it?"

"I don't... I don't know, honey," she says. "Just meet us at the hospital. I have to go."

The call ends, and that's when I notice I'm shaking. I turn to look at Parker. What's happening? How? Please be okay, Zach! Please!

"Is everything okay?" Park asks.

"No." I shake my head briskly. "Can you take me to the hospital?"

"The hospital?" Parker jumps to his feet, and he's slinging his legs over the side of the truck bed before I can get around to the passenger door.

I don't bother answering until I'm inside.

"Zach was in an accident." I clench my teeth, but that doesn't stop my eyes from watering. I shoot my blind stare to the ceiling and try to stop, but I give up. *Please be all right, Zach.*

"Oh no," Parker utters. There's a sort of disbelief in his voice, a lot like how I'm feeling right now. Then his eyes harden. "Let's go."

Thursday | Thanksgiving Day
November 22, 2018

This isn't how I imagined spending Thanksgiving.

The sterile smell of disinfectant, the quietness of bland hallways, Zach in a hospital bed. All of it. How could this happen?

The police said the asshole that hit Zach on Highway 321 was drunk. Typical. Stupid. Selfish idiot. He put my brother in more than one cast, and the stitches on his forehead and cheek are probably going to leave scars. But that's nothing compared to the emotional damage.

I've only left to sleep since Parker rushed us to the hospital two nights ago. Everything was so hectic and scary the first night. We didn't know what was happening and no one would give us a straight answer. I guess that's normal, but when your brother is stuck in the emergency room for hours, you get antsy.

When they finally told us something it was bittersweet. Zach was recovering, but he was in a lot of pain. He'd sustained cuts and bruises to his head, and both legs had been crushed under the console when his Jeep slammed head first into the bridge supports. He had multiple broken ribs and he'd lost a lot of blood. But they said he was going to be okay. They were going to keep him medicated, but he made it.

I remember feeling a wave of excitement as I hugged Parker. But then things came to another crashing halt. Zach's girlfriend, Allie. She didn't make it. She lost too much blood en route to the hospital. They lost her before they made it to the emergency room.

That was the hardest part. I didn't even know her, really. I've seen her on FaceTime and some of Zach's Snapchat stories, but I never met her in person, none of us had. That was actually the plan, to meet her on Thanksgiving.

Watching Dad tell Zach that Allie was gone was the absolute worst. I've never really lost anyone close to me before. My grandparents are still living, my aunts and uncles, cousins, all of them. At least the ones I know. It didn't matter that I didn't really know her. Zach did, and watching him cry broke my heart.

He's doing better now, he's asleep. When Zach's awake I can tell he's in pain even under all the meds. But I don't think it's physical. The thought churns my stomach incessantly.

I squeeze Parker's hand under the blanket we're sharing. Mom and Dad are sitting a few feet away, but no one cares right now, and even if they did, I don't think anyone would notice. We're just two teen boys sharing a seat that's barely big enough for the two of us because there aren't any more chairs. I guess we could ask for one, but I don't want to. I need him right here, right now.

Parker's come back both days since the wreck and he's stayed most of the day each time. I know he has better things to do, even with school out for the holiday, but he stays anyway. Cam's come by a few times too and stayed while Parker left long enough to grab a bite. I want to lean my head on his shoulder, something to ease the stress in my veins, but I think it'd be a step too far. I *almost* don't care.

As I watch Zach's chest rise and fall under the blankets, I think about what it'd be like to lose him. I keep doing this to myself even though I know I shouldn't. I grip Parker's hand a little tighter and he reciprocates like he knows what I'm thinking. Does he? What about Parker? Oh God, no. I couldn't stand to lose him like that. Hell, I don't think I could handle it. It'd be like losing family.

I can deal with physical pain. The slice of a knife, the blunt impact of a hateful fist. But the emotional pain...I don't know if I could handle that.

A tear trickles from the corner of my eye and settles on my lip. I brush it away and sniffle back the rest.

"You okay, Noah?" Mom asks.

"Yeah," I whisper.

Am I? Is being all right just a series of comparisons? I'm positive I feel better than Zach right now. I'm better than if Parker wasn't here. I'm better than...I'm better than Allie. I'm doing better than her parents. Damn, they're making arrangements right now for a funeral up in some little town I'd never heard of until this week called Elkhart Lake. I think it's in Wisconsin, or maybe it was Nebraska. I don't remember. It doesn't matter.

But I'm not okay, not really. I mean, I am, but I'm not at the same time. I'm in this sort of limbo. It's like I'm stuck between this lurid happiness and an all-consuming sadness, and I don't know exactly how to feel, which side to settle on. I mean, how am I supposed to be thankful right now? It's Thanksgiving, right?

My brother's in the hospital. He's struggling, he's hurting. And the idiot who thought it was okay to get behind the wheel of a car totally fucked, he's up and about. Sure he's in a jail cell somewhere, at least he better be, but he's still breathing, and the police said his injuries were minor.

Stop it, Noah. Stop moping. I have plenty to be thankful for. Zach is alive, first off. I've got my parents. They love me, no matter what. And my friends. I have *the* best friends, and of course, Parker. I have Parker. I allow a sliver of a grin to turn my lips up and I tug at Parker's hand again. I wonder if he's getting tired of me doing that. He looks at me and mimics my weak attempt at happiness.

Yeah. I have a lot to be thankful for. A whole hell of a lot.

"We're going to have Thanksgiving here tonight." Mom points at the floor. She says it with purpose and determination. She's trying so hard to be strong.

Dad hugs her and nods. "All right, honey."

Thanksgiving in a hospital room. I sigh. Who would have thought?

Tuesday
December 4, 2018

It's been two weeks since the wreck, and Zach is improving. He's still not walking on his own yet, but the physical therapy is helping.

My teachers are treating me normally again. It took a week for them to realize I'm not a fragile little snowflake. Yeah, it was a bad week, but Zach's okay, so I'm okay. I know it sounds bad, but I think they thought I was going to be grieving heavily over Allie, but well...

I'm just glad things are mostly back to normal. Zach is still in the hospital, but he's recovering. He even sent me a happy birthday text this morning.

Oh yeah, it's my day. As of exactly 9:11 this morning, I turned nineteen. So that's one whole year as a so-called *adult* and two years away from getting to drink legally.

Mom was the first, not counting all the people on Facebook, to wish me a happy birthday. She nearly pounced on me when I left my room to use the bathroom this morning. Scared the shit out of me, actually. I was still half asleep when she bounced around the corner singing. I almost— almost—screamed the F word, and I'm not talking about faggot. That would have been a fun way to start my nineteenth year. Grounded. Well, maybe.

Either way, like every year, I refused to accept her birthday wishes until 9:11 a.m. on the dot with a sly grin. I didn't turn nineteen for a few more hours technically, so all her birthday singing didn't count until after that. Also like always, she just shrugged it off and kept going.

"So how's it feel to be nineteen?" Cam asks.

She's sitting across from me with her arms crossed and resting on the lunchroom table. I shrug and quite intentionally brush my shoulder against Parker.

"Same," I try. "Like eighteen. I mean, you're seriously still going to ask that question?"

"I'll ask that question until the day you fucking die, Noah." She grins.

"Oh God." Parker throws his head back. "I'm with Noah on this one. That's one of those questions that only makes sense if you're, like, under ten or over seventy or sixty — whatever 'old' is."

"Hey, my mom is fifty-eight." Cam gives Parker her laser eyes but chills it off with a flash of her pearly white teeth.

"Okay, seventy, then." Parker throws his hands up.

"How about we go with eighty to be safe?" I suggest.

"Nah, you're ancient once you hit eighty." He grins. "I mean, you could kick the bucket at any moment at that age."

"Wow," I gasp.

He shrugs in response.

The two of them, nearly simultaneously, sent me messages at 9:11 this morning wishing me a happy birthday. Well, Cam sent a text message. Park sent a Snapchat of the underside of his desk. It had a Bitmoji of himself screaming happy birthday and a buttload of Xs and Os. I've got good friends and a fucking awesome boyfriend. They both risked losing their phones for the day to wish me a happy birthday first. Technically Cam won, but as far as they're concerned, Parker sent his first.

"Here's your birthday cake." Cam passes me an oatmeal crème pie still in its plastic wrapper.

I raise an eyebrow as I look at the "cake." I love oatmeal crème pie, not as much as Reese's, but I still can't help but chuckle. My birthday cake?

"It's a little small," Parker says quickly before I can stick my own foot in my mouth. "Something tells me we don't all get a piece."

I laugh.

"Yeah, well, it's not like I could smuggle a whole cake in. Plus, Noah likes them," she reminds Parker.

"I know." Parker puffs his chest. "You could have at least got the double decker type, though. And one for each of us."

"Oh shut up, Park." She throws up a hand and settles on me.

"I love it," I tell her.

"What about the candle? No candle?" Parker starts up again.

I give him the eye and tear open the wrapper. He's just asking for it now.

"Fire hazard," is all she says.

"She's got a point." I nod at her while smirking at Parker and take a bite from my birthday cake—or pie, I guess. "Delicious."

"Oh, and this too." Camila reaches into her pack and pulls out a perfectly wrapped box. It's covered in Spock hands.

"How many times do I have say you don't have to buy me anything?" I plead. It's mainly because I always fail to get her anything.

"A lot, because I'm not likely to listen any time soon." She grins.

"Dammit," Parker grunts. "I knew I forgot to do something."

"Huh?" I ask.

Cam's mouth forms into a wide O.

"Oh, he forgot to get you a present," she tattles. "Didn't you?"

"Yeah." Parker shies away. "You're not supposed to show me up in front of my…"

He finishes up the sentence by mouthing *boyfriend*.

"It's—" I start, but Cam talks over me.

"I always do," she reminds him.

I'm about to shake my head, but she actually has a point.

"Yeah, yeah. I know." Parker shakes his head. "I guess I have to work on this whole boyfriend thing."

I ignore how he says boyfriend quieter than the rest and wrap my arm around his neck and shake him, but I'm sure to make it look like two stupid teen boys, not a couple.

"Nah. I think you're doing fine," I tell him. "You being mine is a gift every single fucking day."

"That's just cheesy, man." Park laughs.

"It definitely is, but technically I told you not to get me anything. So if we want to get down to it, you're being a great boyfriend," I remind him.

We decided in early November, when Parker first asked what I wanted, that we wouldn't get each other gifts until Park decided to come out. The way I saw it, we never did before, so if we start now with everyone knowing I'm gay, they might start drawing conclusions. I'm fine with that, but

Parker still just isn't there.

"Oh my God. Enough with the sentimental shit, I'm dying over here," Camila complains. "Open it already."

I shake my head at Park and rip into the wrapping paper. By the time I get it open there's fragments of Spock all over the table, and maybe a little on the floor. Inside there's a box. I tear off the tape and eye Cam before opening it. She's leaning across the table anxiously.

I open it and pull out a gray t-shirt. It's sort of plain. I hold it up and look it over.

"Turn it around, genius," she says.

"Oh." I flip it and then I see it. The front has this retro-looking rocket launching in shades of gray and orange with one of my favorite band names stamped at the bottom: STARSET. It's awesome!

"You like it?" she asks. "I wasn't sure if you already had it. You've got so many band tees. I have the receipt if you need to send it back."

"Calm down, I love it." I turn it side to side, letting the light shine on it at different angles. It's so cool. "And no, I don't have this one yet. Isn't it cool, Park?"

"Yeah, that's sweet." He nods.

"I figured it'd be best to give it to you now," Cam explains. "Because I'm sure I can't top tonight."

"Tonight?" I ask.

"Yeah, what's happening tonight? We're going to the movies, but something else?" Parker repeats.

"Not that I'm aware of," I answer.

Cam's grinning too big. I'm not really sure I want to know the answer.

"Birthday sex," she says, like it's a forgone conclusion. "I hear it's the best."

"Jesus Henry Christ, really?" I'm blushing, I'm certain of it, and she just shrugs.

"Maybe we should find out." Parker tips his head at me, and pooches out his bottom lip contemplatively.

"Seriously? I mean, uh…" I'm stuttering now. "But seriously? Here? In the middle of the school cafeteria?"

"No, in your room." Park sounds super serious.

"That's not what I meant." I put a finger up. "And who said anything about…*that* anyway?"

"So it's a no?" Parker frowns.

"Oh…" Cam's toggling her eyes between us, totally immersed in my embarrassment. I think she's extra proud of herself right now. She has a way of creating awkward situations for me, and she's making this one epic.

"You two are monsters. You know that, right?" I shake my head.

I love them to death, but they are masters at embarrassing me. It's not a bad idea, though.

* * *

The smell of popcorn butter and salt disappears the moment the theater doors swing shut behind us. I do love the smell and the popcorn, and well, the butter too, lots of it.

The cold late autumn air welcomes us with a bite under my nose. I squeeze my jacket tight around my chest, and I'm wishing I had worn a second layer of pants now, maybe some sweats under my skinny jeans. My legs are freezing.

"So what'd you think?" Parker asks.

Park took me to see the new *Robin Hood* movie for my

birthday. We ran off right after dinner with my family at the hospital, so Zach could be included. Mom and Dad had planned to take me out somewhere nice, but I wanted my birthday with the whole family. So we snuck in some Cook-out and had a little mini-party in Zach's hospital room.

"It was good," I tell him.

"Good?" He tilts his head back and gives me his I-don't-believe-you look. "Just good?"

"All right." I put my hands up in defense. I was trying to be nice. "It was okay. I think I was expecting a little more out of the new Robin Hood character."

"Egerton?" Parker asks.

"Yeah, I guess." I shrug.

"How do you guess?" Parker's in disbelief. "He's hot."

"So you're crushing on other boys on my birthday?" I raise an eyebrow.

"Uh... I—"

"It's okay, Park." I laugh. "I'm just kidding. He's hot."

"Damn, Noah, don't do that to me." Parker smiles.

"Is he hotter than me?" I ask. I'm definitely not *hot*, but I want to see how Parker squirms.

"Fuck no." Parker doesn't hesitate. After he makes his proclamation he stops and takes a quick glance around him before continuing a little quieter, "I mean, there's no contest. You are *so* hot."

I wasn't expecting such a quick and easy response. And it's odd, I know he likes me—well, loves me—but I still can't seem to understand how he sees me like he does. So hot? No. But I still like hearing it. I guess I can't deny that.

Instead of responding I give him this awkward, embarrassed smile and escape around the other side of the truck. I get in and push up the moveable center console. Once he's in too, I sprawl out on my back along the long bench seat. I let my legs hang off the edge and drop my head on Parker's lap. I look up at him and he's looking down at me. His eyes are soft in the low light.

"Hey," I say. I don't know why, but it just felt like the right thing to say.

"Hey," he giggles back.

"Thanks for a great night."

"We're not done yet." He grins.

He reaches into the tiny back seat and comes back with a wrapped box. It's about the size of those gifts that usually have shirts in them, like Cam's. The wrapping job is decent at best. Actually, that's probably being too nice.

"Your present," Park announces as if I hadn't caught on already.

"We had a deal," I remind him. "No birthday presents. Plus you just took me to the movies. Technically that was a birthday gift since you wouldn't let me pay."

He shrugs. "It's not like it's going to be anything amazing."

"So you're giving me junk for my birthday?" I purse my lips.

"For God's sake, just open the damn box." He drops it on my chest with a laugh. I brace myself, expecting something heavier, but it's light.

"Okay, okay." I put my palms up in surrender and pick it up off my chest. I give it a quick once-over and start ripping the paper.

"Yeah, okay, just throw the paper on the floor. Right." Parker rolls his eyes. I smile bigger. I'll get it up, but it's fun messing with him. He takes his truck seriously.

Finally I'm down to a white cardboard box. I lift the top and pull out something long, thin, and rectangular. When I realize what it is my hand goes to my open mouth.

"Parker." I think I might tear up a little. It's beautiful.

"It's not much. It's not even that good." He knocks his own work.

It's a painting, but not just any painting. On the canvas are two boys sitting next to each other in the mountains under a velvet sea of stars and a silver moon. I immediately know who they are and where they are. It's Park and me up in the mountains.

"How long have you been working on this?" I ask. My finger traces the outline of our bodies on the canvas. It's perfect. It's absolutely perfect.

"Since our trip. I started the day we got back home. So a little over a month," he tells me. "I finished it last week. So *technically* I kept our deal. I didn't buy you anything. I already had the paint and supplies."

"Technicalities," I say, but I can't take my eyes off the painting. "I *love* it."

I unglue my eyes from the canvas. Parker is looking down at me with this gentle, beautiful grin. He just stares at me like that for a few seconds and then he leans down and kisses me.

"And I love you. Happy birthday, Noah." He sits back up and sighs. "If you only knew, by the way, how hard it was to keep that painting private. Oh my God."

"I didn't think about that," I tell him. It's a good point. There's no way he could let his parents find out about it. Generally speaking, it could just be two random guys in a painting, nothing romantic about it, but then again, I don't know if straight dudes do that type of thing and then paint pictures of it. So yeah.

"Yes! I had such a close call a few weeks ago. Mom accidentally found it. She decided to do some late fall cleaning, which apparently included under my bed." He bobs his head from side to side. "It was only about half-painted then, so she didn't see us in it, just the sky. She liked it."

He's grinning and laughing. Damn, I love hearing his laugh.

"At least we know she approves," I joke.

"Ha, right." Parker's eyes widen, but he keeps smiling. "I've got an odd question. Well, maybe it's not that odd."

"Okay…" I let the word trail off. I hate those types of lead-ins.

"If you could have anything in the world, anything at all, what would it be?"

He's staring down at me with this intent look in his glistening brown eyes. I don't even have to think about it. It's all that's been on my mind lately. I want him, openly. I want to be able to call him my boyfriend around friends and family. I don't want to have to lie about our relationship. I want to hold his hand in public, to give him a hug without it being a scary thing. I want him to come out.

But I can't tell him that. I've already said it enough, or hinted at it, probably when I shouldn't have. No. I guess what it all boils down to anyway is just him. Parker Evans. I grunt happily at the thought. Even if he isn't out, I'm still happy with him.

"You." I smile up at him and wrap my fingers around his arm.

He puts his other hand over mine and our fingers lace together. I close my eyes as he raises my hand to his lips and kisses it.

"You don't have to say that," he says, grinning down at me. "It can be a car, money, anything."

"I'm serious, Park," I say. "You. Just you."

He lets out a happy sigh, and his eyes twitch away for a second.

"Is that really it? That's all?" Parker asks, as if wanting him isn't a cool enough thing.

Or maybe it's just me, but it feels like he's digging for something. Can he tell I'm holding back? Is that it? Maybe I should be honest—totally, brutally honest. Well, not brutally, but honest.

"Yes...and no," I admit. I rise and slide next to him so our sides are pressed together. "I do just want you. But I... Uh... I want you completely. I don't want to have to hide what we are. I want to be able to call you my boyfriend in public. To hold your hand in the hallway at school. To sit close to you like we did in the theater, even when people might be watching. I don't want to hide *us*."

Parker looks away. There's a hint of fear in his eyes, maybe a little regret, but what gets me most is the look of pain. Did I hurt him?

"Park, I didn't mean to keep on like that. I know—" I try.

"No, I understand. It's just..." he starts, but I put my finger to his lips to stop him.

"I know. You don't have to explain. All that matters is that we love each other," I remind him. "I'll be patient, I promise. I love you."

"I love you too," he says, grinning under my finger.

I lean in and put my cheek on his shoulder, and Parker takes my hand. The feeling of his fingers caressing mine causes a lump to rise in my throat. I swallow it and sigh. Just being here, like this, really is enough. But inside I know I want more. Why do I always want more?

"Park." I lift my head to look at him.

"Yeah?" He finds me with those beautiful brown eyes.

"Thanks for a great birthday."

He smiles, and I put my head back on his shoulder and snuggle closer.

"You deserve it. Almost forgot." Park jerks his head up. He rummages in the back again and comes back with candy. "Your birthday Reese's."

Tuesday | Christmas Day
December 25, 2018

Denny's is practically empty except for Parker, Camila, me, a couple a few tables over, and the bare bones staff they have on hand. I'd been trying to find a way for weeks to spend at least a little bit of Christmas with Parker, and I found it.

It was actually Cam who said we should go out for lunch. I thought essentially everything except the police, fire department, and hospital were closed on Christmas Day, but I was wrong. So here we are.

"My Uncle Darnell almost threw every bit of food on the floor last night," Cam says. Her dad's side of the family has their Christmas get-together on Christmas Eve like my mom's side. Nothing interesting ever happens at mine, though.

"How'd he manage that?" Parker asks and shovels more than a forkful of pancakes into his mouth. The syrup drips from his fork and sticks to his chin and lip.

I reach over and wipe the syrup from his chin and lick it from my finger. He shakes his head and smiles.

"Granny's tablecloth was frayed and his belt buckle grabbed it. When he went for the potatoes he took the table-cloth with him." She grins. "We did lose a few rolls, but everything else was okay."

"I've got a couple clumsy relatives, but mostly they're just crazy." Park smirks. "I've told you about my cousin, Randy, haven't I?"

I nod, and so does Cam. If I'm thinking of the right person, he's not the most upstanding guy in the world, sort of the relative the rest of the family tries not to associate with.

"He's my Aunt Sharon's kid," he reminds us, just in case. "He didn't make it to Christmas last night. Seems he's in jail. He tried robbing Walmart *again*. Dad said he tried stealing two big-screen TVs and a shitload of movies."

"Why the hell does he think he can get away with that?" I ask, but it's really not a question.

Parker shrugs and shakes his head.

"That's crazy," Cam says. "What about you, Noah, anything interesting last night at your…dad's family?"

"Nah, it's my mom's side on Christmas Eve," I correct her. "Don't worry, Mom has to remind me every year which get-together is on Christmas Eve and which is on Christmas Day. I can never remember. And no, nothing interesting. Just the usual. We went for dinner at my Mama Jo's, opened gifts, talked a little, and went home. My cousin Melanie was there, though, so that made it a little more exciting. You know how much I love her. And of course Zach made it."

"How is Zach doing, by the way?" Cam asks.

Our waitress, a heavyset lady probably pushing fifty with peppered brown hair hanging lazily over her shoulders, walks up to the table and asks if we need anything. I hate how they interrupt like that, but I know it's her job, so I just act like it's okay.

"I'm good." I look at the others.

"Could I get a refill?" Parker asks.

"Sure, it was Dr. Pepper, right?" she asks.

"Yes, please," Parker says, polite as always.

"Anything else?"

"Actually yes, let me get one of your peanut butter banana milkshakes." Cam eyes me, then Parker. "What about you two? Feeling like dessert?"

"I don't know." I rub my stomach. I rarely make it that far.

"Ooh, yeah." Parker looks up at the waitress. "Can I get your caramel apple crisp?"

"Sure." She nods and then looks at me expectantly.

I wasn't going to, but hell, it's Christmas.

"Why not, give me one of the apple pies too," I tell her.

Parker pats me on the back, and I wonder for a moment if he's going to tell me that I'm a good boy, like some dog, but he doesn't. I laugh off the thought silently.

The waitress walks off and leaves us to ourselves again. Park straightens up and pushes his empty plate to the center of the table. He looks at me.

"I do have a Christmas gift for you," he tells me.

"Park, we agreed not to do that," I tell him, and then smirk. "Of course we agreed on no birthday gifts too, but I guess we all know how that went."

I'm about to start having cold sweats. I didn't get him anything. We said we weren't going to, and I was keeping my end of the bargain. I even saw this cool LED charging base that would be great for Parker's PS4 controllers and the PS4 Virtual Reality setup. Of course, I couldn't afford the virtual reality goggles anyway, but I almost bought him the charging dock. Almost.

"I know, but this isn't like that," he assures me. I tilt my head and glance at Cam. She looks just as confused as me.

"It's a promise, not an actual thing."

He puts his hands in front of him like he's holding some-thing to make a point. I sit straighter in my seat. What's this about?

"Okay," I say. "So another technicality?"

"Yeah." He's proud of himself, I think.

"Go on." I lean back, intrigued.

"So I've been thinking a lot—" Parker starts, but Camila can't help but butt in.

"There's your first problem." She grins.

"Funny, Cam." Park rolls his eyes, but he's still smiling.

I don't say anything. This promise of his has me tensed up. I want to know what it is he's been thinking about.

"Thinking a lot about what?" I ask.

"Us… And me." He swallows and glances at the table. He's about to open his mouth when our waitress comes back with the desserts.

"All right. Here's your milkshake, peanut butter banana." She puts the shake in front of Camila and then sets our apple pies on the table. I just want her to leave. "And your pies. I hope you enjoy. I'm going to leave the tickets right here, but there's no rush. Just let me know if you need anything else."

"Thank you." I'm nodding and smiling, trying to look nice and patient. Finally she walks away, and I meet Parker's eyes again and wait.

"So yeah, I've been thinking about it a lot," he continues. "Especially after Zach's accident. I know you told me to take my time, and I did. But I think I'm ready. I think I'm finally ready to come out publicly."

"Really?" Cam says it before I can get the same word out.

"Yeah." He nods spastically, then returns his attention to

me. "I know you hate having to keep secrets, and it's selfish of me to keep asking you to."

"No, Park, don't think of it like that," I tell him. But in my head, I'm agreeing with him. I know I shouldn't be, but a part of me wants this more than anything, and I can't seem to shut it up. "You need to be ready, not me. It's up to you."

"I am, Noah. I'm ready." He dips his spoon into the flaky pie crust and scoops out a piece. It's steaming hot. He lets it sit on his spoon to cool down. "I want this. It's all I've been able to think about since Zach was in the hospital. How nothing is certain. I don't want to regret anything. And I know I'll regret it if I don't do this."

A silence hangs over the table.

"My parents aren't going to take it well, but I think I've finally come to terms with it." He bunches up his forehead and his mouth twitches. "I just don't know how it's going to be once I tell them."

That's a lot like how I felt before I told my parents. Trapped inside this cage of the unknown. But I had the distinct advantage of being ninety-eight percent certain they'd accept who I was, and I was right in the end. Parker has about a two percent chance they'll accept it, and that alone sends a pang through my heart.

"When?" I ask. It's not my job to stop him, and honestly, I don't want to.

He drags in a deep breath and exhales. Cam and I are both staring at him, probably making this more difficult than it should be. But I'm anxious. How much longer do I have to wait?

"Next week. New Year's Day. After the ball drops," he says and sucks his lips in nervously. "The way I see it, I'm going to start 2019 right. I'm going to be me no matter what and make it the best year yet. With you."

I thought I'd know what to say when he finally told me, but I don't. Somehow I'm at a loss for words. It feels wrong to jump for joy or tell him I've waited for this moment a long time. It's too selfish, but it's how I'm actually feeling.

"That's great, Park!" I say instead.

"Yeah, that's awesome!" Camila echoes. "I guess you'll let us know after it goes down since we're not all spending New Years together like usual?"

"Yeah." He nods. "That's the plan. I'll text you both or something. So uh, Merry Christmas, Noah."

I'm overwhelmed with a burning happiness deep in my chest. I throw myself on him and wrap my arms around his neck.

"Thanks, Park," I whisper in his ear. "Thank you."

Tuesday | New Year's Eve
December 31, 2018

"So are you really planning on going off to Stanford?" I play with the ends of Cam's wavy black hair. She usually keeps it up, but tonight she's staying over, so she let it down. We're lying on my bed facing each other.

"Maybe." She shrugs. "Yeah."

Her early acceptance arrived the day after Christmas. I've thought about it a whole lot more than I should.

I've grown up with her. I can't remember a week, except maybe a family vacation or something, when I haven't seen her at least once, usually a hell of a lot more. And now we're talking about Stanford in fucking California. That's literally two thousand seven hundred and fourteen miles from where I'm sitting right now and something like a forty-one-hour drive. That's insane, and yeah, I looked it up on Google. And even if I did go to U of I, it's still something like a thirty-two-hour drive.

Plus it hit me at the same time that I haven't hung out with her as much lately. Why does this all have to be so complicated?

"Yale's your top pick, right?" I skirt asking a question I already know the answer to. Her top pick has been Stanford since our sophomore year. The excitement in her voice when she told me she got accepted after the initial onslaught of texts was out of this world.

"No." She pushes me playfully. "You know I want to go to Stanford. Berkley would be nice, but Stanford's my dream, and as long as the financial aid shit comes together, that's where I'm going."

So yeah, I'm not keen on this leaving for California thing. Park and I received acceptance letters from State on Friday, so now I'm crossing my fingers she ends up at Duke, but I think I'm going to have to suck it up and get over it.

"I gotcha," I smile. "Honestly, I'm just not sure I like the idea of you going off alone to California. I've heard they're weird out there."

"Did you now?" She grins.

"Yeah." I nod. I can't just say hey, I don't want you going to college without me.

"I'm not going to stop being your friend." She pats my shoulder and eyes me crazily. "Just because I might be on the other coast doesn't mean we're going to fall apart. I'm not letting you get away."

"Yeah, but everyone says that's what happens when you go off to college," I sigh. I bounce my gaze from the riddled target on my wall and back to Cam. "We'll do better though, right?"

"Right." She nods. "Promise."

"Promise." I agree.

"So how do you think Parker's doing?" she asks. The look in her eyes changes. I'm positive mine look the same.

"I don't know," I admit.

"I hate this so much. It's been eating at me all day," Cam shifts on my bed.

"Me too." I hate that he has to go through this. I hate that he has to do it alone. I hate that it can't possibly turn out as awesome as it did for me. I hate that he's not here now. I hate every bit of it.

Usually the three of us spend New Year's Eve together and ring in the New Year with Sprite and Dr. Pepper in my parents' champagne glasses. Then we'd have a sleepover. We just never told Parker's parents Cam slept over too, even though she always stayed in the spare room anyway.

I wish I could be there with him when he tells them. He was there for me, and I know it made a world of difference, it made it easier. But I can't.

It's about ten to midnight now. I swallow a lump in my throat. Parker's probably scared to death right now. All his texts say he's doing good, but I know better.

"Just think," I start. "When we get back to school in January, I'll get to hold Park's hand in the hallway, and if people ask, I'll be able to say 'yeah, he's my boyfriend.'"

"And you two can kiss whenever you want," she reminds me with this naughty-looking smirk on her face.

"It's not like I'm going to be all over him at school. Come on." I let it hang for a second. "But that too. Give me a sec, I'm going to text him again."

I grab my phone and check my messages. Nothing new. I tap Parker's name and ask how he's doing and if he wants me to give him a call, mainly because I want to. It takes less than a second for the little bubbles to pop up on the screen and then his reply.

I'm good. Promise. I'm not backing out. Now's probably not the best time to call though.

It's a little vague, but I understand. I send him a quick *I love you, Park. You've got this* message and check the time. It's

11:57 p.m.

"He says he's all right. But he's got to be horrified," I tell her. She nods. I huff. "But, it's time for *us* to go watch the ball drop."

And wait for the real ball to drop at Parker's place.

My stomach churns as we walk down the hallway and scuttle into the living room in our pajamas. I'm wearing my Thor bottoms and Cam has a pair with the Starship Enterprise shooting down the leg.

"I was about to call for you two, it's getting close," Mom says when we round the corner.

I smile as best I can and take my Sprite-filled champagne glass. Only two more minutes until 2019. Only two more minutes until Parker breaks the news to his family. Only two more minutes until I get to tell my parents the full truth. Only two more minutes until my world comes together.

That was the deal we made over the weekend. He promised he wouldn't back out and that I could tell my parents we're dating at the same time he comes out to his. And even if he does back out, we decided it would still be okay. My parents will support him either way, and I know my mom already thinks it'd be *cute*. That much she's made abundantly clear.

And there's this quote that's been digging at my brain lately, though. I feel like it's sort of true, but at the same time not. It makes me think of Park and me. It's an Oscar Wilde one from *The Picture of Dorian Gray*. I've never read the book, but I found the quote online and I've kept it in my head like all the others.

He said, "*When I like people immensely I never tell their names to anyone. It is like surrendering a part of them. I have grown to love secrecy."*

One more minute.

Somehow, right now, on the edge of a new year, on the edge of telling my parents who I'm dating, who I'm in love with, I suddenly *love secrecy*. It's almost as if something might be taken from me if I tell them I love Parker, like Wilde's *surrendering a part of them.*

It's stupid, though, so I push it aside and smile at Dad. He's on his feet now. Mom jumps up next and wraps an arm around me, and I do the same to Cam.

Half a minute. Twenty seconds.

"Here we go!" Dad raises his glass when the ball at Times Square starts to drop on the screen and the countdown begins.

I join in on the count; it helps ease my nerves. Damn, Park's probably about to shit himself right now. I know the feeling.

"Five, four, three, two, one," I chant along with everyone, and then we all shout, "Happy New Year!"

Mom and Dad lift their glasses and drink up. I tap my glass on Cam's and we do the same, all smiles, even though I haven't been this worked up since September. I immediately pull out my phone and check for an update. It's stupid, I know it'll take him more than five seconds to tell his parents.

Patience is a virtue, Noah. Yeah, one I don't fucking have.

Before I realize what's happening Cam scoops me up in a massive hug and nearly lifts me off the ground. She lets me go and grins, then nods toward my parents. I know what that means. I inhale a gulp of Sprite like it's a swig of that God-awful vodka my Uncle Drew let me try last year at Thanksgiving, and I exhale. I don't know why I'm so nervous. Maybe it's more of the unknown, that I don't know how Parker's doing right now, or that whole Oscar Wilde bullshit or something. It's stupid, I know it is. I turn around and hug my parents for the new year and Mom kisses me on the forehead.

I check my phone again. I want to know how it went on Park's end. No new texts, but it's still midnight.

"Hey, I need to tell you two something," I speak up.

The drinking and revelry stop. They look at me and I get the immediate impression they're worried. I've really got to work on my conversation-starting skills.

"It's nothing bad or earth-shattering, I promise." I wave my hand to assure them it's okay. "Actually, I'm pretty sure Mom already knows anyway."

"What is it, honey?" Mom asks. Dad simply looks at me with this give-it-to-me-straight look.

I huff, it shouldn't be difficult, but it is. "Uh…" I grin and giggle stupidly.

"So?" Dad shrugs.

"Parker and I are dating," I blurt.

"Oh!" Mom throws her arms out and smothers me in a massive hug. "Of course I already knew. I'm so happy for you!"

"Believe it or not, I knew too," Dad chimes in.

What? He walks over and wraps his arms around both of us.

"Yeah, he did," Mom says. "This is great. You two are so cute together."

"Mom!" I eye her.

"But you are," she says. "Own it."

"You really are." Cam shrugs.

"There's no use trying to stop her, Noah," Dad tells me.

"You should know that by now."

I laugh, and Mom slaps at Dad dismissively.

"Well, I guess I'm glad we're all in agreement." I roll my eyes.

"Do his parents know?" Mom asks.

I find Cam and linger for a moment. She's not helping. When I find Mom again, she's waiting patiently. I wish I could be that patient.

"Not yet," I say. "At least, I don't know yet. They didn't. Park's telling them tonight. Probably right now, actually. I'm hoping for a text soon."

"Oh," Dad grunts. "He's a good kid. Good head on his shoulders, he'll be all right. His parents probably aren't going to take it well though. You know that, right?"

"I know." I nod, and I'm not smiling anymore. "That's why he waited longer."

"Let him know we're here for him if he needs anything," Dad tells me. "Anything."

I nod just as my phone vibrates. I throw it up to my face without thinking. It's a text from Parker, but a fissure cracks through my heart when I read it.

I did it. Meet me at our spot. :(

"I have to go," I tell my parents. They look at me oddly. "He did it. He wants me to meet him. Something's wrong."

"Go." Mom nods and waves me off. "Be careful though."

"And don't stay out late," Dad shouts after Cam and me as we make for the front door and past the porch.

"What's wrong?" Cam yells after me, but she follows anyway and jumps in my car.

"I don't know. He just said to meet him," I tell her and pass her my phone. "Let's just go."

Wednesday | New Year's Day
January 1, 2019

I'm driving faster than I should, but the growing pit in my stomach won't allow me to ease off the gas. I knew this was a possibility; hell, I knew it was the most likely scenario, but it still hit me like a rock.

"Slow down, Noah." Camila bears down on the suicide rail above her head. I'm not sure that's what it's actually called, but that's what I heard at least.

I don't reply, but I manage to ease off the accelerator. We hang one last curve and pass under a canopy of bare tree branches. There he is. I bury the fear in my chest and pull off the road next to his truck. I squeeze the steering wheel.

Am I ready for this?

I get out and round the hood. Cam meets me by Parker's door. It's freezing out here, but I barely notice. I can see him through the glass. He's just sitting there, head down, his eyes shied from view. I don't want to spook him, so I stand stonily for a moment and fight the urge to throw the door open and wrap my arms around him.

"Park?" I call through the glass. He moves, but it's just a twitch.

I let a breath whistle through my lips, and then I open the door. He doesn't move. He doesn't look at me. Instead, he sits like a statue. I bend down and look up at him to see his face. He's crying. I grit my teeth and hold back my own tears. He doesn't need that right now. He needs me to be strong.

"Park?" I whisper.

He finally looks at me. His eyes are puffy, and his face is wet. His chin is trembling, and he won't hold eye contact. I look away to gather myself.

You've got this, Noah.

I take his hand and offer him a weak smile, but he looks away and starts to cry again. My jaw starts to quake, and dammit, I'm crying too. I take a deep breath and exhale. A hand rests on my shoulder. I'd almost forgotten that Camila came too.

"What happened?" I talk slowly, my voice barely a whisper. It's a stupid question. I think I already know the answer.

He jerks his head side to side and tries to blink away the tears, but new ones fill their place.

"Scoot over, Park," I say and step up on the siderail.

I look back at Cam and jut my head to the side. She understands and goes around to the passenger side. Parker moves over, and I slip in beside him and wrap my arm about his waist. I let our temples touch and close my eyes for a moment.

"Talk to me, Park," I say as Cam shuts her door and layers her arm over mine.

"I, uh..." he tries. "I...I told them. At midnight. I told the... I told the whole family."

I'd completely forgotten about his brother and sister.

"I asked them to sit down, that I had something I needed...uh...that I needed to tell them." Parker leans over, cups his face in his palms and sobs. "It took me forever just to say it, but I did. I told them... Mom just cried. She wouldn't even look at me. Dad kept saying I was making the wrong choice over and over again. I tried telling him he was wrong, that it wasn't a choice."

Finally he looks up. His eyes are timid and pleading. I've never seen that look in his eyes, and it slays my heart.

"I would have never chosen this. Never! Why would anyone?!" He's yelling now.

I jerk away but quickly lean into him again. I understand the feeling. I felt that way a lot when I'd hear people say it was a choice. It's different now. Sure, I wouldn't have chosen it had it ever actually been up to me, but it's who I am, and it's who Parker is no matter what we want. I just finally came to the decision not to hate myself every second of the day, and everything changed.

"I know." I bury my nose in his cheek and cry with him. "I know, Park."

"It's okay," Cam whispers.

Parker is quiet for a moment, then he sits up. He takes a long breath, and I think it helps steady his nerves a little because he's calmer when he begins to speak again.

"He kept on saying it. Like I wasn't listening and that if he said it enough, I'd say I wasn't gay anymore. Like I hadn't thought about it long enough. Like I hadn't hated myself enough," Parker continues. "He said I wouldn't be *allowed* to be gay in his house. And maybe it wasn't the best timing—I was going to tell them eventually anyway—but when he said *that* it just hit me wrong, so I hit back. I told him I was dating you."

"Oh." The word hangs from my lip. That wasn't part of the plan. I was supposed to tell my parents, and then his parents were supposed to find out later once things settled down.

"He... He didn't take that well..." Parker stutters. "I should have waited. I don't know what I was thinking. He said that I'm dating no one, and I have to go to counseling with my pastor."

"Counseling? Are you fucking serious?" Cam says it before I can.

"Yeah," he nods vigorously. "That's when I left. I just ran, got in the truck and drove straight here."

"How can he make you do that?" I ask. "You're eighteen. Hell, you'll be nineteen in a month."

"I know, but..." He looks at me, and I can see he's searching for what to say. "I don't know. What happens if I say no? What if they kick me out?"

"They're not going to kick you out," I assure him.

But will they? Am I lying? No, surely they wouldn't do that.

"I don't know." He's crying again.

"I'm so sorry. I, uh..." I hug him tighter. I was about to say I understand how he feels, but I don't. I don't understand this. It would have been a lie. "I'm sorry. I know it can't be easy. I'm here for you, Park. I love you."

"Me too," Camila says. "I love you just like you are. Always have, always will."

We sit in his truck in this awkward but warm group hug, and we're all constantly wiping the tears from our cheeks. It's so messed up. I mean really, how can his parents be like this? Yeah, they don't agree. But he's their son. How can they make him feel like this?

There's a heat, a dark warmth, rising in my chest, and I know I should push it back, but I can't.

"I don't think they're going to let me see you anymore." Parker breaks our hug and looks at me. I can't stand to see him like this. The moist eyes. The downturned lips. The sadness.

"Not at school. They can't keep us apart at school," I tell him. "And I bet we can find ways outside of school too."

I squeeze his hand and raise it up so he can see it.

"You see this, Park?" I ask. "*We* are going to get through this. *We* aren't giving up. *You're* mine, and *I'm* yours. Nothing's going to stop that."

My heart leaps when a smile breaks through his frown, and a fleeting shimmer bursts in his beautiful eyes. He nods, and a tiny giggle graces my ears. It's such an angelic sound.

"*I'm* yours, and *you're* mine," he repeats, his eyes locked on me. He releases a pent-up breath in stutters. "Now it's time to tell the world."

"Huh?" I tilt my head.

"If I don't do it now, I won't get the chance." He lifts his phone. A list of missed calls occupy the front screen when he wakes it. His parents, I bet. When he unlocks the screen I see the status he's already prepared. I freeze near the end where he declares his love for me to the world. I have to read that part twice, and there's no use trying not to smile.

When I look up, he's smiling at me. I wish he was as happy as I was when I did this. I'd give anything to make him happy right now.

"I'm doing this," he tells us. I hold my breath, my eyes darting between his phone and the twitch in his eye. His finger hovers over the *Post* button for a fraction of a second, then he taps it and shuts off the screen.

"Oh my God. Did I just do that?" His eyes are wide. He

looks to me first, then Cam, and then back at me.

"You did." Camila is beaming.

"Yeah, you did it," I repeat. I go to hug him, but he diverts and catches my lips.

"I did it," he says when he pulls away. His smile is tainted, though, and it slowly droops back into a frown.

"Just ignore the haters. They'll always be there, but they're the minority," I tell him. "And no matter what happens at home, I'll be here. I love you, Park."

"I know."

Wednesday
January 2, 2019

Park's feed blew up on New Year's Day. I'm scrolling through it right now in the school parking lot while I wait for him to show up. It's the first day of second semester.

The comments are great. So many supportive thoughts and congratulations. I can't help but giggle every time I find one congratulating us on our relationship. And there are a lot of those.

The only problem is I haven't heard from Park since Cam and I left him at our spot on New Year's morning. It was a foregone conclusion his parents grounded him the moment he got home, but it still bugged me all weekend. However, I'm guessing they don't have access to his Facebook since his coming out post is still up.

Hell, to be honest, I don't even know for sure if he went home. That possibility has been absolutely destroying my nerves. I'm trying to trust he did, though. Running through the comments helps distract me from those unwanted thoughts, but I still have to keep telling myself over and over that he's okay, it's just me.

I check the parking lot again. Still no Parker. A group of girls walking by see me and start waving. I wave back while I try to remember their names. I suck at the name game. I think it's Amelia, Brittany, and… Oh God, I know I know this. Yes, Abigaile. For some reason her name has an E at the end, even though that doesn't make any sense, and she's always having to correct our teachers when they write it.

They each throw me a thumbs up, and finally I realize why they're waving. I blush. Then I see Parker's truck pull in and I completely forget about them. The weight on my chest melts away and I bite excitedly at my lip. When he finds a spot I jump out and practically run across the parking lot. I'm there before he has a chance to get out, and I wrap him in a tight hug the moment he does.

"Woah." Parker grins and hugs me back.

"I was so worried!" I tell him and grab his hands. "How've you been?"

"Let's walk." He tilts his head toward the school.

"All right," I agree. "Damn, I've missed you so bad!"

He's smiling, but there's a dreariness in the deep brown of his eyes. It's there, just under the surface in the way he's squinting and the way the edge of his lip twitches.

"You too," he says.

Suddenly my hand jerks back, and I stop. Parker's not moving. He's standing behind me, but he's not looking at me. He's looking past me. I follow his line of sight to the school.

"It's going to be okay, Park." I take a step toward him. "I'll be there with you, just like you were for me."

"I've been cooped up at home all weekend. How did everyone react?" he asks.

I know he saw the first few responses, but I guess he didn't have a chance to read the majority of them. He doesn't know how much support he's got.

"They're for you, Park," I tell him. "Just avoid Carter and

his fucktards and you'll be good. No making smart jokes at them either. It'll just piss them off."

He laughs and starts walking with me. "Deal."

"So I guess you're grounded?" It's obvious, but I feel like I should at least confirm it.

"To put it lightly, yeah." He rolls his eyes. "No phone, no Facebook, no Twitter, no internet. I can't leave the house without telling them where I'm going, and I definitely can't see you. Hell, I'm not even supposed to see you here, but fuck that shit."

"Not going to happen." I wrap my arm around his waist and pull him closer.

Ahead we merge into the flow of students, and Parker starts to pull away. I squeeze him. His head jerks around and I give him a big smile.

"It's okay," I assure him.

He nods and comes back to me.

"We're so happy for you, Parker!" a group of girls shouts as we pass. "Love is love!"

Parker smiles nervously. The attention is a little much right now. I know the feeling.

"Congrats, Parker!" It's Gabriel. He smiles before disappearing inside.

"Go Parker!" a girl I don't know shouts in passing. "You two make a super cute couple."

And there goes my head swelling.

"See, Park?" I tell him. "Just wait until I show you the comments on your post."

"Parker!" I know that voice. She screams again before I can find her in the crowd. I laugh when Cam bursts through the crowd and jumps Park. Once she's startled him enough, she envelops us both in a group hug.

"God! Calm down, Cam." Parker is laughing now. He's smiling. He's beaming.

Monday
January 7, 2019

"Didn't you already sweep the porch?" L.A. asks.

"Uh…" I look down at the floor. Hell, I did. "Yeah."

I sigh and put the broom away. It's closing time. Well, we've got another ten minutes, but there's no one here except L.A. and me. I stop by the ice box.

"Do I look as out of it as I feel?" I ask her.

I knew it was going to be difficult, or at least interesting. Maybe that's more like it. I thought it would be interesting. That once Parker came out, his parents would have a momentary flip-out and then it would be over, and things would go back to normal. I guess somehow I didn't really believe it would be this bad in the end.

But it is.

"Sort of," L.A. treads carefully.

"It's okay, you can be honest," I tell her.

"Yes." She nods and busies her hands with cleaning the main counter. "Are you okay? I know what happened. I mean, I get it, but are *you* okay?"

I shrug. Am I? I guess I am. It's Park who's not. I'm just stuck dealing with it, knowing he's sad and cut off, that he's being forced not to see me. That sounds really selfish now that I think about it, but I hope that's the case. No, I know it is. He wants to see me just as badly as I want to see him.

"We can talk about it if you like." L.A. grins. "You know, believe it or not, I sort of had a crush on you."

"I believe it." I giggle. It feels good. "I guess you're a lot like me. You don't hide it so well."

"Oh." She purses her lips and her eyes freeze up.

"It's okay, I promise." I wave it off. "It's all good."

"Well, if you want to talk about it, I can still listen," she starts again.

"Nah, I'm okay," I tell her.

I'll just unload on Camila once I get off. It seems like a lot longer, but I haven't seen Parker outside of school since New Year's. It's been almost a full week, and it's killing me. Yeah, we get to talk at school and even sneak in a few kisses here and there, but it's just not the same as spending time together without the entire school over our shoulders.

"Okay." L.A. nods and returns to cleaning up the last of the barista station in silence.

Damn. Was that harsh of me?

Parker's coming out post on Facebook is gone now. It disappeared on Saturday. My best guess is his parents made him give up the password. Probably his dad. It just seems to get worse each day.

Park was so quiet at school today. He wouldn't say why, and I guess I didn't really need to know. All of this is enough to bring anyone down.

The clock on the wall hits 8:00 p.m., so I switch off the OPEN light and check over the closing list one more time. Everything gets a check, and L.A. and I are out the door. I say goodbye to her and she walks off to her car.

Cam is in the parking lot waiting. I can hear the music beating at the windows before I knock on the glass. She jumps and almost drops her phone, which sends a small crack of a smile creeping across my mouth.

"Damn, Noah." She opens her door. "Give a girl a heart attack, why don't you?"

"I hardly think you're going to have a heart attack, Cam, you're only eighteen," I remind her.

"Whatever." She rolls her eyes. "Your car or mine?"

"Yours."

"Let's go, then." She gets back in. I swing around to the passenger side, and in a matter of seconds we pull onto Main Street.

"Have you heard anything from Park?" I ask.

"No phone, Noah." She doesn't take her eyes off the road. "Even I can't communicate with him telepathically."

"Fair," I admit. I guess the phone confiscation *was* total. "I really wish I could see him. Talk to him. Hell, a text would be awesome right now."

"I know," Camila says. "But you know Parker's parents."

"Yeah, unfortunately." I say it harsher than I mean to. "Sorry."

"It's okay. And stop telling me you're sorry." She glances at me this time. "It can't last forever, right?"

"I didn't think it'd last *this* long," I tell her. But that was stupid. I guess I didn't really believe it, I just really hoped. "But I was wrong."

"You thought they'd get over this in a week?" Cam asks.

"No…" I stare out the window. My reflection stares back, but I ignore its accusing eyes. Behind it, Moe's and McDonald's pass by. Where are we going to eat? I know we talked about this before work. Dammit, where did we decide? It doesn't matter.

My mind flashes to the painting Parker gave me on my birthday. What am I getting him for his birthday? Will I even get to? I wipe a single tear from my cheek and hope Cam didn't see it. I imagine the stars we watched that night on top of the mountain, the same ones Park so perfectly caught on canvas. The mountains around us, the sound of birds cooing and insects chirping, even the gentle chill of autumn air. Then cold, damp reality comes rushing back in.

"You're right," I finally admit.

Neither of us says anything for a minute. Then a thought hits me. "Remember how hard his parents pushed for the Marriage Amendment when we were kids? They even had Park work the polls with them. Damn. It just hit me how much that had to suck."

I think it was 2012. It was a divisive year, and oddly enough, the same year I realized I was gay. Yeah, that sucked.

"Oh my." Camila sighs. "Damn, you're right. But, we're all graduating in June, and then it's off to college after the summer. They can't stop him then."

"That's like eight months away, Cam." My voice rises. "Am I going to have to miss him for eight whole months? Hell, what about summer, I'll *never* get to see him if they keep it up."

"Just don't think like that." Cam's deep-brown cheeks gently rise over a sad grin.

"How?" I ask. How do I do that?

Tuesday
January 15, 2019

The cafeteria is abuzz with chitchat and the sound of sneakers squeaking on the marbled laminate floor. But our table is silent.

I force what might pass as a grin when Parker looks up from his plate. Still chewing, he manages a weak smirk, but that constant sadness lingers in his eyes. He's still so cute, though, my cute Parker. I want to keep thinking of him like that, but it's impossible to see past the storm in his not-so-present eyes. I hate seeing him frown, and that's what he's done most the last few days.

Things aren't getting better. I was wrong about that. When I do get to see him, I swear we talk less and less. Today's been the worst yet. He's barely said five whole sentences since I found him in the hallway. He even got to school late this morning, so I didn't get to say good morning.

I keep thinking this is all my fault. What if I hadn't pushed him to come out? *Is* this my fault? It's not like I didn't know his parents would flip. I knew they wouldn't let us talk outside of school and that it would cause problems. But I...I don't know. I guess back then, when it was all a secret, it all felt so amazing. I felt invincible in this weird sort of stupid way, like nothing could go wrong. I had Parker.

Everything was right, except the fact I had to hide it all.

And I was tired of hiding. Hell, that's why I came out. I think back on those weeks and months before New Year's Day and our first date at Five Guys. Did I ever stop to think how this would all turn out? Did I think how it would affect Parker? Did I really?

And now this. This bullshit.

"How can your parents force you to go to some quote unquote *conversion therapy* camp?" I break the silence, and I say it a little louder than I should. "You *are* an adult, after all—you're eighteen."

"Yeah, how does that work?" Camila leans in. I think she's ready to rid our table of silence just as much as I am.

Park looks away and leans back in his chair. He absently puts down the fry he was about to chew on. He still doesn't look at us, but at least he's looking between us, his eyes stuck on the kelly-green tabletop.

"I have to sign," he says. There's no emotion in his voice. It's just matter-of-fact.

"Well, *don't* sign," I tell him. That sounds easy enough to me. The way he made it sound a few minutes ago was like it was a directive. Like he had no choice.

"It's not that easy," he explains. He's being quiet, and his words come out in this slow, drawn-out cadence. "I *have* to agree. I *have* to sign. If I don't there's no way I'm going to college. They said they won't pay to send me to college like…like this, unless I agree to go to the camp. I can't afford college on my own."

At first I want to blow up. I want to say that he plans to agree to this shit just for college, but I hold my tongue. I think I understand. If he doesn't go to college, he's stuck in Kannapolis and he can't get the job he wants. They don't just hire random strangers in the medical field.

"Plus, if I go, then maybe they won't keep me away from you." Park finally looks me in the eye.

"Because you'll be straight?" I blurt and immediately wish I could take it back. But it's out there, so I roll with it. "That's bullshit, and you know it. I'm not even going to tell you the stats I found on depression and junk from people who go to those stupid fucking camps. They might as well be called death camps. It's some real Nazi shit, if you ask me."

I sit back and fold my arms over my chest. I'm fuming. Not at Parker, but his parents. How could they do this? How can they not see that Parker is a perfectly normal guy?

"It can't be much worse than these *counseling* sessions," he reminds us.

"No. I bet it can," I disagree. He's just trying to find something positive to cling to. I get it, but he's wrong.

Parker drops his gaze to the table and his shoulders begin to quake.

"I'm sorry, Park, I didn't mean…" I start, but he puts up his hand and shakes his head.

"No, it's not you," he manages between sniffles.

Cam reaches over and squeezes his hand. "It's going to be okay, Park."

I wish I could confidently say the same thing. But it feels like a lie. Instead, I lean my head on his shoulder and embrace him.

"We'll get through this, Park." That much I know. "I'm not giving up."

I'll find us a way.

Thursday
January 17, 2019

I came in fourth of five in my swim meet. I could have done better, I know I could have, but all I could think about is how Parker didn't get to swim.

His parents made him quit the team. Yeah, they literally made him quit the swim team because they thought he didn't need to be in a locker room full of boys. They didn't say it, but I'm pretty sure they basically meant me.

I'm supposed to be watching Jacob line up to swim the freestyle, but I'm focused on the stands. Park's up there with Cam. He's smiling, but I can tell it's put on, for show. He was so mad when they made him quit. I think he loves swimming almost as much as he loves drawing. It's almost cruel that he's here now, but he wanted to support the team.

I guess there is one plus, though. Yesterday his parents finally gave him his phone back. I think it was a compromise. He's just not allowed to use it in any way to contact me. No calls, no texts, no Facebook, Twitter, nothing. So on my end, basically nothing has changed, but I'm still glad for Park.

The last match ends and the crowd starts to peel away from the stands. I wait for Park and Cam to come down. I can shower and change once they're gone.

"Hey!" I yell.

"Hey!" Parker yells over Camila's shoulder.

"I still can't believe you came," I tell him. "Or that they let you come."

"Gotta support the team." He winks.

Damn. I smirk. He's smiling. It's so far and few between these days I wish I could take a picture.

"Yeah, got to support the team, Noah," Cam echoes him. "Aka, it's the only way he was going to get to see *you* outside school."

I shy away. I want to hug him, but I don't.

"And you *should* have placed *at least* second," Parker tells me.

"Huh?" I shrug. He's right, but I'm not giving him the satisfaction yet.

"You could have easily placed second," he repeats. "You weren't *in* it were you?"

"Not exactly," I admit.

"I bet Coach A noticed." Park pooches his lips.

"Oh boy," I say. I guess I'll be hearing about this more in the locker room and at practice. I change the subject. "Are you going with us to Five Guys?"

It's a stupid question, but it can't hurt to try.

"No." Parker frowns. "Dad said I could go to the meet, but I have to come straight home once it's over. So technically, *this* isn't even allowed."

"Naughty boy." Cam slaps Park's shoulder.

We both give her our best *really* look, and she shrugs.

"Well, I've got to go," Park says, but he lingers.

"Come here," I tell him, and before he can protest, I wrap him up in a hug. I don't want to let go, but I don't need to get him in any more trouble either. "Love you, Park, good night."

"Love you too. Night."

Saturday
January 26, 2019

I don't think Park's parents realize all the stuff you can do with Instagram, namely its direct messaging feature. At least if they do, they don't check it.

That's why I'm sitting in my car at our spot in China Grove. Parker sent me a message asking to meet about twenty minutes ago. I could have been in the middle of the most intense level of *Mass Effect* and I would have dropped it, saves be damned, and rushed out the door. Hell, I don't even use Instagram much. It's just a bunch of pictures I don't care about, but right now it's the most awesome app on the face of the whole fucking planet.

The car's running and the temperature gauge reads twenty-eight degrees. Heat blasts through the vents, and I'm wearing my thickest leather jacket. I don't think it's moved north of thirty since Monday, maybe further back than that. It doesn't look as if the little dusting we got on Thursday is going away any time soon. It's layered everything in a thin blanket of soft white snow.

The sound of a racing engine approaches and I poke my head around to scope it out. It's not Parker, though. It's an old, rusty pickup.

I'm jittery. Not because of the cold, that's bearable. No, it's the first time in over three weeks that I'll get to be alone with Parker. Don't get me wrong, I'm grateful to see him at school and when he comes to my meets, but I feel like I'm missing something important when I can't *just* be with him. We need to be able to talk, to work on what he's going through, what we're going through. I know I don't have the answers, but if we can just talk, maybe that'll help in some small way.

There's another car coming. I check again, and thank God, this time it's Park. I wait as patiently as I can for him to pull in, which isn't saying much. The moment he pulls to a stop I jump out into the shivering cold and grab at his door handle. I pull, but it doesn't move. My eyes barely reach over the bottom edge of the passenger door window, but I eye Parker. He's smiling, laughing actually. Hell, I can deal with the cold for that.

"Let me in! It's fucking freezing out here." I play with the door handle.

There's a click and it finally opens. He's hysterical as I climb inside and slam the door behind me. I eye him, a slanted grin on my face, and welcome the blaring heat.

"You're such an asshole," I jeer.

"But I'm your asshole," he comes back.

I tilt my head and shrug. He's got me there.

"I see what you did there." I smirk.

For a moment we stare into each other's eyes. His smile. It's perfect. And it's been so long since I've seen him look this vibrant. It actually gives me hope.

"Come here," he says, but I'm already moving in before he has a chance, and I kiss him.

It's at least a minute before I let him go, and I have to catch my breath. I sigh, but Parker's not smiling anymore.

He's not frowning, but it's like the sadness of the last month haunts his face. I don't mean to, but my shoulders slump.

"How are you holding up?" I ask.

"I'm making it," he says.

That's all I get before his eyes get lost beyond the windshield. I watch him contemplate every white-laced strand of frozen field grass and the way the white flakes coat the rickety wooden fence just beyond the hood of his truck. I know it's rude to stare, but I don't want to look away. Even like this, he's beautiful.

"So..." I start. "Your birthday is coming up in two weeks."

"Yeah." He nods slowly.

He's got something on his mind. It's not hard to tell, and I know he wants to talk about it, but he's not ready. Best to be patient with him.

"What do you want to do?" I ask. "I mean, *if* we can figure out a way to do something."

"Don't know." Parker's gaze drops to the instrument panel behind the steering wheel. "The family is taking me out for dinner, so we can't do anything on the second. As if we could actually get away with it anyway."

"Maybe we can, we're sitting right here, aren't we?" I remind him. I'm trying to be positive for him. Seeing his smile when he first got here was so refreshing. I need that back, so if there's a way, I'm going to find it. "What about a movie? I think *Glass* is still playing. You haven't seen it yet, right?"

I feel like I should know if he has, but with how things have been lately, I imagine I'm missing a lot. I hate that.

"Nope. I don't think a movie would work." He shakes his head. "I would have loved to, though. I hear it's good, but Mom and Dad know I don't like going to the movies alone. They'll ask questions, and that'll be harder to hide."

I sit back and think on it. How do I get him out of the house and with me without his parents finding out and not make it rough on Park? Damn. This might be more difficult than I thought. I hatched my original movie date plan last night in bed. I thought we could just get Cam to cover for us. Park could tell his parents he was going with her. Maybe he's right though. What if they found out? But isn't that the danger with any plan?

"You could say you're going for a swim, and you know, I just happen to show up." I wink at him. "Stranger things have happened."

He smiles, but he shakes his head.

"Okay, how about we go to the Basement Arcade downtown," I try. I've only been a few times, but it's so cool. It's packed wall-to-wall with arcade machines from, like, the eighties or something. *Pac-Man, Galaga, Street Fighter, Donkey Kong.* I think it even has *Frogger* and the original *Mortal Combat.* The last time we went I spent all my spare coins trying to beat the high score in *Galaga. Trying* being the key word.

"Maybe..." Park sounds more hopeful on that suggestion, but he wobbles his head from side to side and flares his nostrils. So I'm not entirely sure whether he doesn't want to or if he's afraid to.

"What about just going to the mall, Concord Mills?" I ask. It's not my favorite place, but at least Christmas is over and the traffic's died down for the most part. "We could walk around, and you could pick something out. Oh! I heard about this fortune reader downtown too. We could get your fortune read."

"Nah." He grimaces. "Right now the last thing I want to know is my fortune."

Ugh. I didn't think of it like that. Damn.

"Okay, how about…" I'm at a loss. There's so much to do around Kannapolis and Concord, especially with Charlotte so close, and of course the Mills area, but I can't think of anything else. Oh wait. Go-karting, we still haven't made it over there. I'm about to open my mouth, but Parker speaks up.

"I had my second *counseling* session today." His tiny sliver of happiness is gone. His body slumps, but his eyes are on me.

"And…" I brace myself. I'm not sure how to proceed, so I ask the first thing that comes to mind. "How'd it go?"

"About as well as you'd think." Parker shrugs. He puffs his cheeks and pooches his lips in frustration. His eyes jump to the ceiling before dropping down again. He doesn't look at me this time. "I believe in God. Sure, not like everyone else maybe, but I do. You know that, right?"

"Yeah." I nod. "So do I."

"Yeah, well, I was always told that as a Christian the one thing we are truly never allowed to judge in another person is their salvation. You know, it's between me and God, right?" he says more than asks.

I think I know where he's going with this. I nod. Parker looks away again. The frustration radiates behind his eyes and his fingers twitch. He's gripping the seat tightly.

"But today the main thing my pastor had to say, and he said it over and over again, was that I can't be gay and a Christian. I told him I didn't choose this, that I couldn't change if I wanted to. I've tried, but he wouldn't have it." I let him continue, but I reach for his hand. He takes it and grips tightly. If the heat in his voice wasn't enough to churn my heart, this is. "Apparently I'm living in sin, because I'm who God made me. I mean, I've heard all of this over and over again in the past, it's what he preached all the time. It's what my Dad always had to say too. But having my pastor look me in the eye and tell it to *me*... Hearing him... Well, apparently God made one huge fucking mistake, then."

Park's hand is shaking in time with his voice and droplets begin to pool in his eyes. I want to look away so I don't cry, so I don't have to see him cry, but I can't do that. No, I won't do that to him. The first tear breaks the surface and crawls down my cheek.

"Parker..." I squeeze his hand. He shakes his head.

"Why am I this way?" Park drops his head to the steering wheel and lets it all out, every tear, every sob, every last hurt and pain.

"No, Park," I try. He's perfect the way he is. "I know what you mean. I've dealt with the same thing. They don't understand. You *are* who you're supposed to be."

"But does God really hate me? How..." He stops to gather himself, but it's useless. "How can He hate me or say I'm evil because of the way *He* made me? It doesn't make sense. Am I going to Hell, Noah? I don't want to go to Hell."

"Parker, stop it!" I bark. "You're not going to Hell."

"But what if we are? What if somehow they're right, and we're messed up? What if we're the dark spots on God's record, the mistakes, the damned?" He begs for an answer through the monsoon. "I'm afraid to die, Noah. I'm horrified to die. But I want to at the same time."

"Parker, don't say that! Don't ever say that." My eyes fly wide open. My heart is bursting, like someone's thrusting a dagger in my chest over and over again, like they're not content with just killing me, but prolonging the pain. "You *know* you didn't choose this. I didn't choose this. I don't have the answers, no one does, but we're not going to Hell just because we love each other. And don't you ever say that again! Ever!"

He nods, but he can't stop crying.

"I love you, Parker, and I'm not letting you go." I scoot over and hug him. "No matter how hard it gets, I'm here for you. You know that, right?"

He bobs his head.

"And Cam too. Cam's always there for you too," I remind him. "And my parents. You've got tons of people at school who have your back. Hell, even our teachers."

I let him dig his fingers in my back and soak my shoulder. How can they do this to him? How can they make him doubt everything? Make him so scared and anxious?

"As for God, you know I believe, I really do. I don't know if He's really all love or even perfect. Maybe He is, maybe He's not, but I don't think He hates us. I think He loves us, just like anyone else."

"I don't know anymore, Noah, and that scares me so bad," Parker says.

"Just don't give up on me." I cup his cheeks in my hands and make him look me in the eye. It's a struggle, but I force a torn smile. "Promise me you'll never give up."

"I promise."

Friday
February 1, 2019

"Are you still meeting Parker tonight?" Sandra asks while she locks up the shop.

"Yeah." I pull my jacket tighter. A chill settles at the nape of my neck. Damn, it's cold tonight. "We're going to Denny's."

It's a lie, one I bet she sees right through. I swear the woman's telepathic. Bur if she does, she doesn't say it.

"That sounds nice." She nods. We start down the ramp and end up next to my Nissan. "It's his birthday, right?"

"Yeah, well not really. His birthday's tomorrow. But I won't get to see him then." I frown. Weekends are now Parkerless; well, they have been for weeks now. They seem so much longer without him, and not in a good way.

She nods.

Sandra knows all about the situation, the initial grounding, the slight relaxation but total prohibition on contact outside of school. All of it.

"So I take it his parents don't know you two are meeting up?"

"No." I shy away. I know she isn't going to say anything, but she's an adult, and suddenly I feel like I might have said too much. "They think he's going out with Cam for dinner and a late movie."

"You think that's a good idea?" She throws her hands up defensively. "I'm not saying you shouldn't, I'm just asking. I don't want you two lovebirds getting into more trouble or anything. I'd hate for things to become harder than they already are. Especially poor Parker. I feel so bad for him. I just don't understand. This might seem off topic, but have I told you that quote from Wilde?"

"Vague much?" I shrug. It wasn't exactly much to go on. I know a few Wilde quotes, but there's a bunch of them.

"Oh, right. Oscar Wilde?" she explains. I shrug again. "Well, he said, 'I think God, in creating man, somewhat overestimated his ability.' The people treating Parker like this, I think they fall into that category."

"Yeah, maybe so." I nod nervously. I'm not really sure what to say. "I think we'll be good though."

She does have a point. What if they find out? I don't know how much worse it could get, really. I guess they could take his phone away again, but there's not much else they can hold over his head.

"You know Parker's always welcome to come by the shop, right?" She bobs her head. "It's a public place. You two wouldn't be alone while you're here, so maybe his parents wouldn't mind as much. You can even tell them I'll be watching."

"Thanks, but I don't think that's going to cut it," I tell her.

"Well, keep it in mind, just in case. It can't be any worse than running around behind their backs." Sandra steps away and starts toward her car. "Have fun tonight, but be careful. See you in the morning."

"Bye, Sandra. See you," I holler back.

I have the morning shift with Macy. Sandra usually

shows up around ten, a good three to four hours after I get there. The perks of being the owner.

I slip into my car and start the ignition. The heater blares to life, and the yet-to-warm-up air blasts me in the face.

"Damn!" I fidget with the knobs and get the airflow under control until it manages to warm up a little, and then I turn it back up.

In the passenger seat is Parker's gift wrapped in Santa Claus wrapping paper. It was the first roll I found, and I wasn't really worried about it since he's just going to rip it to shreds anyway. In the box is the Spider-Man hoodie I got him. It's the only thing I could think of. Parker wouldn't tell me what he wanted, and unlike him I can't paint that well, so he's not getting anything cool and artsy from me.

I'm about to start off to our spot when my phone vibrates. I forgot to turn the ringer back on. I pull it out and find a new Instagram message. Before I can read the entire thing I close my eyes. A tear escapes anyway, and I have to take deep breaths to keep from crying.

He's not coming. Apparently his parents are being extra cautious. They called off his movie date with Cam, his night with me. I won't get to see him until Monday. I ball my free fist around the steering wheel and let my arms quake.

How the…

I slap my phone against the steering wheel.

"Fuck!"

Monday
February 4, 2019

The lunch bell rings and I throw my pack over my shoulder and heft Parker's gift under my arm. It's two days late, but it's not like I had any control over that. I didn't exactly get to see him. I push through the mass of bodies with my head down.

Mom says she's worried about me. Apparently I've been quiet.

This whole situation, it's got me down in this pit. I want to be excited when I see Park, and I am, but I also feel bad. When Mom wouldn't let me out the door without talking to her, I asked the only question I could think of. Why do Park's parents have to be like this? Why do they have to put him through all of this shit?

Hell, I even said *shit* in front of Mom and she didn't complain. She didn't have an answer either. Maybe there isn't one. I hate that idea. There ought to be a reason, a justification, some answer for everything.

Out in the hall I find Cam with Parker in tow exiting the English and history wing. I smile, but I only get one back in return.

It shouldn't, but deep down it still bugs me that Cam and Parker went out for his birthday Saturday. I mean, I get it. His parents found out that I'd be off by the time Park was "going to the movies" on Friday night and called it off. On Saturday afternoon I was stuck at Editions. So it was *safe*.

Cam told me that night how Park's dad threatened to throw him out if he went to see me Friday. That's why he canceled. I understand, I do. The thought of Park being kicked to the curb is maddening, but honestly, and I know this is selfish, it didn't make me feel any better when I found out. And it didn't mend the brand new crack running down my iPhone.

"Happy late birthday, Park!" It comes out as a spiritless cheer.

"Thanks, man," Parker says, and I hand him the package.

"Santa Claus wrapping paper? Aren't you a little behind?" Cam smirks.

"It was the first roll I found. I just went with it." I shrug. Park's looking at the box, but he doesn't open it. "Well, are you going to open it?"

"How about I wait until we get to the lunchroom?" he asks. I feel like he should be excited having just turned nineteen, but he's just here.

"Give the man some time." Cam grins.

I laugh because I think I'm supposed to.

No one talks on the way to the cafeteria. It's this deathly uncomfortable silence underneath the wretched noise of sneakers shuffling, the latest gossip about who the jocks are screwing, and the clack of trays ahead.

We get through the lunch line and claim our table. It's not our usual place from last semester. A group of freshman girls commandeered that the first week back, and it just didn't seem worth fighting over with everything else going on. I shovel a helping of public school's finest tasteless meatloaf and give Park and Cam a moment to situate themselves before talking.

"So are you going to open it now?" I ask. I nod at his present on the table. I really want him to open it. Maybe, maybe not, but maybe it'll cheer him up some.

"Oh, sorry, yeah." He shakes his head. It's like he's not even here. He rips at the paper, opens the box, and finally pulls out the hoodie. "Damn, that's sweet!"

Finally. A bit of life. I smile, proud of myself.

"So you like it?" I ask.

"Like it?" He eyes me. "I love it!"

There's the Parker I grew up with, the one I fell in love with, that I kissed under the stars. A smile raises my cheeks and suddenly, even if it's only for a second, everything feels right again.

Parker peels off the red Wolfpack hoodie he's had on all morning and slips into mine. He likes it. He really likes it. But then he stops and drops his attention to the table, like the meatloaf and potatoes on his plate might jump away. At least that's how I look at it because it's better than what's probably going through his head.

"Sorry, guys." He looks at me, then Cam, and rolls his eyes. "I swear I don't mean to be such a downer, but it's just… It's been a rough few weeks."

Cam pats him on the back, and suddenly I wish I was next to him so I could do the same.

"No, it's okay," I say. "We understand."

"This last weekend was just so odd," Parker starts. He finds Camila and gives her a half-grin. "I had fun Saturday, I really did, but it still felt wrong. It's nothing against you, Cam. You know I love you to death, right?"

"Of course," she says, then hugs him. "It's okay."

"I just really thought, after you and I finally got together, that I'd get to spend my birthday with you," he tells me. There's this longing in his eyes, a look that says he feels cheated. "I'd really looked forward to it, but then it all got fucked up. Hell, my family took me out to eat, and everyone acted like nothing was wrong. It was like I was the old fake Parker, like nothing ever happened. Almost like before. All just a day after Dad threatened to throw me out if I saw you."

"I'm sorry, Park." It's all I can think to say. I want to tell him that it's all my fault, but for some reason I just can't get myself to do it.

"Well, there was cake." Parker shrugs. "And they didn't make me go to counseling this week. So there were a few pluses."

"There you go, look at the bright side," Cam says.

I nod and pat Parker's hand on the table.

"Yeah, you can't knock cake."

Tuesday
February 19, 2019

"Fui a la estación de servicio," I reply to Ms. Anderson, our very much not Hispanic Spanish II instructor.

"Magnífico." She nods, and moves on to Deago behind me.

It's a daily ritual at the end of class. We each have to think up one full sentence in Spanish that another classmate hasn't already said before the bell rings. I chuckled, along with a few of the nerdier kids in the class when the teacher translated Camila's sentence before getting to me. Her *vida larga y próspera, ranúnculo,* or *live long and prosper, buttercup,* was just enough nerdy and just enough crazy.

Now that my turn is over, and I'm done frantically trying to think up something different, my attention wanders again. Not one time during the entire ninety minutes in class has Parker looked over his shoulder and winked or paid me any attention like he usually does, even though he's been in a better mood the last two weeks.

The first thing I noticed this morning was that he's not wearing his Spider-Man hoodie. I think it's the first time since I gave it to him that I haven't seen him in it. I guess it has to be washed every once in a while.

He's still not himself, though, and that's all right. It makes sense at least, and I think I'm dealing a little better with how things are going. It's all becoming normal, par for the course. Make no mistake about it, though, I'm still angry, and I doubt that's going to change any time soon.

I dare a peek behind me at the wall clock. Five more minutes.

We didn't get the sweet Valentine's Day I'd dreamt of. It wasn't going to be anything extravagant. Just him and me, dinner somewhere a little nicer than Five Guys this time, but nothing too much, and then a few hours cuddled up together in a blanket in the back of his truck with the stars overhead.

Instead, I ended up volunteering to work that evening. Most of the girls at the shop had plans, and of course I didn't. So I spent my first non-single Valentine's Day serving coffee and coffeeless drinks to more fortunate people than myself. Watching a bunch of couples sipping coffee together all googly-eyed was maddening.

And then this whole week Park's been quieter than usual. I swear he was getting better there for a few weeks. He was talking more, smiling more, even joking a little.

Then bam, it all came to an abrupt halt. He said the "therapy" sessions are getting to him. Apparently it's the same thing over and over again, that mentality that if you say it long enough and loud enough, it'll stick eventually.

But the real culprit, the thing that's been under my skin since Monday at lunch is so much worse. It took him a bit to tell us, but his parents finally made it clear he's either going to their little conversion camp up in the foothills over the summer or he can kiss college goodbye. I was so fucking angry. I slammed my fist on the table in the middle of the cafeteria and caused a bit of scene. Nothing major, but enough that people stopped and looked.

Those places should be called death camps, they should be illegal. From what I've read, that's where the mind goes to die. You don't come back the same. No, you come back saddled with depression, and your chances of drug abuse, criminal activity, and even suicide increase. Parker says he'll be fine, but I can't get the numbers out of my head.

The bell finally rings, and I take my time packing my things.

"Nerd much?" Julia cocks her pretty little head at Cam.

"Yeah, at least I didn't butcher mine." Camila bobs her head from side to side like only she can. I have to bite my tongue to keep from giggling when Julia's face scrunches up and she stomps off.

"Bitch." Cam laughs. "Let's get out of here."

"Coming," I say and throw my backpack over my shoulder. We walk up the aisle and meet Parker at the front of the room.

"Well, that's a wrap," I joke, but he doesn't look at me. I swear he's actually avoiding eye contact.

When he doesn't answer, I look at Cam. She shakes her head and shrugs. I don't know what to say, so I lead the way out. I don't like it. This has to stop. We have to talk. I need to know what's going on. I deserve to understand, right? And he should be able to talk to me.

At the intersection we swing left and follow the flow, making our mass exodus. It feels so awkward walking next to Park in silence, even if it has been going on for weeks to one degree or another. Hell, even Cam isn't talking, and that says a lot. Someone needs to say something now or I might lose it.

"Park," I say before we can get out of the building, before

he can escape to his truck and I'm cut off until tomorrow morning. I don't want to do this here, but I'm not waiting any longer.

He doesn't answer. Maybe he didn't hear me. It is loud in here.

"Hey, Park," I try again.

He looks at me, but he doesn't respond.

"Come on, man, talk to me," I try. When he looks away I grab his hand and plant my feet.

Our arms go taut and he almost falls back. I feel sort of bad for that one, but no, I need this. He glares at me. Camila sees it too and shies away.

"I'll see you two later, okay?" She gives me a weak grin, and I lose her in the crowd before I can say anything back. What was that about?

Never mind, I've got more important things to worry about.

"Park, I know things are tough right now. I do," I tell him. I squeeze his hand, but he pulls it away. I'm not sure how to react. He's hurting, that much is certain, but I'm here. "What's going on? I know something's up 'cause you're not talking."

Parker looks away. I can see his Adam's apple move nervously and his eyes roll up to the ceiling. He bites at his lips, but it's not cute right now. It looks angry.

"Parker. Please," I'm begging now. I don't want to make a scene in the middle of the school hallway, but eyes are already beginning to linger on us. Who would have thought I'd be begging my best friend, my boyfriend, just to talk to me? "I love you, Park. You know you can talk to—"

"Just stop!" he blurts.

My back goes rigid. I'm not sure what to think.

"Stop." It comes out with less strength this time, more weary. He looks toward me, but not at me. It's like he's looking past me, maybe at the lockers, but not at me, and he's crying. A chill runs over me. "Yeah, I'm not okay. None of this is *fucking* okay! *None* of it. It all *fucking* sucks, Noah!"

I want to shy away, but my back is already against the lockers. He's so angry. But I nod. He's right, I know that. There is nothing about this that makes sense. Nothing that's all right. But we have to talk about it.

"Park, I know. That's why we have to—" I try again, but he cuts me off.

"Stop, Noah." His cheeks blush over in an angry red under the tears. He shakes his head like a man whose mind is gone, and it's scaring me. "And why? Why did you have to say you loved me?"

"What?" I'm baffled. Why the hell wouldn't I? "Because I do. I do love you."

I almost forget we're in the middle of the school hallway and that dozens of our classmates are passing by. For a second, I want to ask him to move this conversation outside, but I don't want to risk him getting away.

"Dammit, Noah," he shouts. Everyone around us hears it. The looks on their faces make it plenty evident, but most of them keep moving. Finally the boy of my dreams looks me in the eyes. But instead of their warmth and beauty, all I find is coldness and regret. He opens his mouth to say something, but the words don't come out at first. He tries again. "I can't do this anymore. It's too much. It's over, Noah."

"What? What do you mean it's over?" I ask. Inside I know exactly what he means, but my heart refuses to accept the answer. It's not possible. We're in love. The river down my cheeks should be enough to tell him that.

"I'm breaking up with you." He can't look me in the eye when he says it. I don't know if it's because I'm crying, the way my lips are trembling in absolute panic, or the hurt in my eyes, but he won't look at me.

"Parker? No. Please, Parker, don't do this."

He shakes his head and instead of answering, he turns and walks away.

"Parker?!" I call after him. *No, you're not doing this to me. I deserve an answer.* I run after him and grab his hoodie, and it's stupid, but I suddenly understand why he's not wearing the one I got him. I let go. How stupid of me. He swings around, but he still refuses to look at me. "Please, Parker. Can't we talk about this?"

His mouth is trembling. His eyes are bloodshot, and the tears mark wild paths down his face. It breaks my heart in more ways than I thought possible to see him like this, even while he's breaking my heart in a completely different way.

"Don't..." Parker tries between sobs. "Just don't... Just..."

I'm about to beg again, but he spins around and runs. He runs...

I swear everything slows down. All I can hear is his feet beating on the cheap laminate floor, out of time with the pounding of my heart. Out of time.

I want to run after him, to tell him he can't do this to me, I won't let him, but my legs are stiff and rigid. This can't be happening. It's a dream. It's a cruel nightmare.

I rake my wrists over my soaked eyes, begging reality to set in, begging to still be in class reciting what little Spanish I know, to wake up from this nightmare. But I'm not asleep.

* * *

Going to work has never been this hard. Usually I'm good with being here, typically I'm glad to be. But today, the only thing that could raise my spirits is if Parker comes walking through the door and tells me he's sorry, and takes it all back, and takes me back.

"You okay?" Mrs. Gentry asks from across the counter. My back is turned to her while I make her espresso. She's one of our two local authors who come in weekly, sometimes more.

"I'm good," I say. It's all I can do to put strength behind my words. I fake a smile when I set her coffee down on the bar, but it feels as phony as it is. She smiles back, but I don't think she's buying it. She bobs her head and disappears around the corner, probably to set up in the memoir and cookbook section.

I shuffle by L.A. to get to the sink. She's smiling too, and I find myself hating her for it. Why does she get to smile? Why does she get to be happy? *Stop it, Noah!* But what did I do wrong? Did I push too hard? Was I not supportive enough? What did I do? Or is it something I didn't do?

I have to loosen my grip on the blender cup L.A. used for the previous customer before it breaks in my hand. I close my eyes and breathe.

"Noah." I jump at the sound of my own name. It's Sandra. "Woah there."

"Sorry," I say and drop the cup in the sink.

"You're sorry?" she asks. "I'm the one who scared you."

I nod quickly. *What are you doing, Noah? Get it together.* Sandra tilts her head to the side and eyes me.

"What's wrong?" she asks.

"Noth—" I start, but she points her index finger to the ceiling and stops me.

"And don't say nothing." She sighs and nods toward the covered front porch. "Come on, let's go sit down for a moment."

"I'm good, it's okay, really," I try.

"Come on, Noah," she insists.

I huff, my eyes drawn to the old wooden floors. But I walk past her to the porch and sit at one of tables set against the large scenic windows. Sandra sits across from me, but I focus on the little old brick building across the street. It's a cable company now, but I've always wondered what it used to be. There's a lot of little old buildings along this road like that.

"What's going on, Noah?" she asks again.

I don't say anything. I can't. So I keep staring out the window, watching the cars drive by, wondering if the people inside them are happy. I wonder if Parker's driving around somewhere right now, happy to be rid of me, or if he's second-guessing dumping me. It's the hardest thing to compute in my mind, but somehow, against all logic, I don't hate him. I can't, even if it feels like I should.

I notice my reflection in the glass. And damn, I look as bad as I feel. The gray circles under my eyes, the downward turn of my mouth, this dead look in my eyes.

"Noah…" It's just a whisper. Sandra gets up and moves to the chair next to me. She scoots it closer and pats her hand on top of mine. "Talk to me."

I pull my eyes from the glass and look at her for a second, then turn away again. I close my eyes. I haven't even told Mom yet.

"Is it about Parker?" I swear she's clairvoyant. It's either that or she's got one hell of an intuition.

I nod spastically.

"What happened? Is he okay?" She leans in.

I nod again, but I face her this time. My jaw is shivering, and my hands keep rhythm.

"He… Uh…" I cough, trying not to cry in the shop. "He dumped me."

Sandra squeezes my hand and puts her arms around me. Her chin settles on my shoulder and I let my cheek rests against hers.

"He dumped me," I say again.

"I'm sorry, Noah." She hugs me. "I'm so sorry. I know it hurts."

"But why?" I know it's an impossible question, but I want an answer. I need an answer.

"I don't know," she admits, but she doesn't stop there. "Love's like that. I think it was John Green who said, 'It hurts because it matters.' And it's so true. Parker matters to you."

She shifts in her chair. "I know this isn't what you want to hear, but Parker was your first love. If things don't work out, and hopefully they do, there'll be others."

"I don't want anyone else," I bite back. "I want Parker."

"I know, honey." Sandra strokes my hair back from my face. "I know. Maybe he just needs some time. You never know. You just have to be patient."

I squeeze my eyes shut and wipe the tears from my face. Patient. I have to be patient. I hate that word so fucking much. Why can't I just have Parker? Why can't things just work out?

The door chime rings and shoes plop into the veranda.

"You take your time out here," Sandra says as she gets up. "If you need me, just holler."

I nod and manage a weak grin before looking out the window again. It's nice out today. The sun's shining and the few clouds that dot the Tar Heel blue sky are puffy and soft. A couple walks down the sidewalk in front of the shop holding hands. They look happy. It's such a nice day, but it's also the worst day.

The worst.

Wednesday
February 20, 2019

It's early, it's cold, it's raining, and I'm walking into school alone. I hate it all, all of it.

I could probably count on both hands the number of times I've walked into school without Parker. Even when we were just friends I always waited for him. Today, I sat in the parking lot until his truck pulled in and then I bolted. I don't know why I waited. Maybe I needed to see him. Maybe I wanted to make sure he was okay even if he doesn't care that I'm not. I'm not sure, but I did.

On the way to school I considered stopping him out in the parking lot. I was going to tell him he can't break up with me. It sounds really stupid now. Like telling him I'm not ready for him to dump me is going to work. In the entire history of breakups I'm ninety-nine percent certain that's never worked. In the end, Mom's advice last night, combined with a little Sandra logic, won out. Patience, which sucks since I have so little of it. But maybe a little time will fix things.

The hardest part now is knowing he's somewhere behind me. That he's probably walking back there. That his deep-brown eyes probably aren't looking at me but avoiding me. That all I have to do is stop and turn around, and maybe it'll all change and yet knowing it's not that simple.

Cam's propped against the brick wall by the entrance.

She doesn't smile like usual. That's when it hits me. She knew, didn't she? That's why she was so quiet in class yesterday and why she ran off after.

"Good morning." She gives me a forced grin.

"Morning," I mutter.

I'm of a mind to just keep walking, but she holds her arms out and hugs me. I withhold the temptation to cry. I'm not crying, not now, not here. I huff, and she leads the way into the building. I catch up and grunt to get her attention. I have to know.

"You knew, didn't you?" I ask.

"Yeah," she whispers. I barely hear her over the sound of sneakers screeching. "Sorry. Don't be mad, please."

"I'm not," I tell her. I feel like I should be, but somehow I'm not. I can't blame her. Well, maybe I can, but it's a hard place to be in.

"Thanks…" Her voice trails off. "He told me after lunch. He wasn't going to do it in the hallway. It wasn't supposed to be like that."

"That was my fault." I pooch my lips into a sideways grimace. I'm surprised I admit it so quickly, but it's true. That *was* my fault. It doesn't make it any better, but I guess I did ask for that. "But why? Did I do something wrong?"

Cam shrugs and skews her lips, but she doesn't look at me.

"He just said it was too hard, something about needing space," she tells me. "Are you okay? I tried calling last night."

"I know," I sigh. I didn't feel like talking, so I didn't pick up. "Wouldn't it be easier together, though?"

"Maybe," she says.

It's not the answer I was looking for.

Thursday
February 22, 2019

There's this tiny hole in my bedroom wall next to the TV.

Dad's talking, but I'm not really listening. Instead I toggle my blank stare between the spot on the wall and Parker's painting next to it.

The hole is where Park tripped over something on my floor last year—I can't remember what, it's not important. He tumbled against the TV stand and crashed against my fifth-grade baseball participation trophy. The little gold bat punched right through the wall.

"You're probably tired of hearing this, but how are you doing?" Dad asks.

"Okay." I shuffle back a little farther on my bed. It's a lie, but I guess I'm good at that too, guess not that much has changed after all.

I wish I was back in the woods, back up in Boone or wherever it was Zach had us that night. To be lying on a blanket again under the stars with Park, just to be with him.

"I've never been good at reading you, but I know better than that." Dad moves from his perch against my bedroom door to sit next to me. "I know this is rough. I remember the first time I got... You know."

A part of me wishes he'd just say it, but I know he's trying to be sensitive. He grips my shoulder and sighs.

"I was a sophomore. Her name was Kristi—"

"I thought your first girlfriend's name was Melinda?" I interrupt, finally taking my eyes from the hole in the wall.

"Yeah." Dad nods. A tiny smirk finds its way onto his face. "I dumped her. It sounds mean right now, but I had my reasons. But Kristi, I thought she was the one when she dumped me. It took me months to get over her. But had I not, I'd never have met your mom, and you probably wouldn't be here."

"But I don't have to worry about kids," I try to joke. It falls flat, but Dad chuckles anyway. "I really like Parker... I love him."

Dad sighs and thinks about it for a moment.

"You love him?" he asks. "I'm not trying to patronize you, I promise, but are you sure it's not just a crush?"

Dad eyes me suspiciously. I can't help but smile when he grins stupidly and punches me playfully on the shoulder.

"Yeah, I love him. Not just like friends, more than that." I sigh. But does he really love me? Did he ever? Was I just a crush?

"Well, if you really love him, you'll wait," Dad says in a different tone. He swaps the sympathetic-heart-for-the-broken voice for the you-can-do-this voice. "But remember, at some point, if he doesn't come back, maybe it's not meant to be. That's hard, but don't let it bring you down."

A tear finds its way from my eye and I nod even if it's not what I want to hear. Parker will come back. I'll find a way.

"I'm proud of you, Noah." Dad hugs me, then shakes me for good measure. I find myself giggling before I realize it. He lets me go and smiles. "You're still our little boy, even if you *technically* are an adult. I hate this part of parenting. See-ing you hurt like this. But it's just how things are, it doesn't matter who you like, it's just life. Just remember, your mom and I are always here for you. Okay?"

"Okay." I bob my head, and wipe a few tears away.

Dad gets up, and at the same time my phone vibrates on my nightstand before the ringer starts blaring Black Veil Brides. Our eyes shoot to my phone in unison. I clench up when I see the name across the cracked screen, and I have to remember to breathe. Parker.

I fire my eyes at Dad.

"Good timing." He smiles and nods before excusing him-self.

I can't tear my eyes from the screen. I trace the cracks through Parker's name from when I smashed it against the steering wheel three weeks ago, but I can't get myself to an-swer. I'm horrified. How is he even getting away with calling me? I should make him wait. Make him feel what it's like to want to talk to him so bad but be unable to. Hurt him like he hurt me.

The call ends, and I feel horrible. What's wrong with me? I close my eyes and suck in a deep breath. My phone vibrates again. I open my eyes to a text from Park.

I love you more than anything. I promise I didn't mean to hurt you. I'm so sorry.

My heart shatters. I curl up on the bed and let my tears soak the sheets. It's the weirdest feeling. I'm excited. Reading that he still loves me is like giving me the world. But the oth-er part of me is still angry. All I can think of is how he wrecked me, how he ran off, how he left me in the middle of the school hallway, how my whole world crashed in on me.

But maybe it was just a moment, maybe he was just having a hard few days, maybe it's better now.

I want to call him, but I know I'll just cry the first full minute, so I wait. I want to tell him I love him too, that I want him more than anything. I lie here debating it. Do I want him back badly enough to risk letting him break my heart again? Is it worth it? What the fuck am I saying? Of course I do.

I unlock my phone and hover over the missed call. But what if he's just sorry for hurting me? I can't get the thought out of my head. What if he's not ready to be a couple again and he just wants to be friends again? What if he just feels bad? Can I deal with that?

Instead of calling him back I text Cam. I tell her that Parker tried calling, but I didn't answer. I tell her he texted me and forward his message to her. I get back a quick and blunt response that puts a grin on my face.

Call him back right this fucking minute, Noah, or I'm going to kick your gay ass the next time I see you.

I don't bother replying. I'm not going to need that ass kicking. My heart flutters at the thought that this nightmare might be over as I dial him back.

The phone rings and rings. I know it's only been a few seconds, but it feels like he's taking forever to answer.

Friday
February 23, 2019

Mom forced me to take a Pop Tart before she'd let me leave this morning. I wasn't going to eat. I don't feel like it, and I don't think I could keep it down anyway. It's sitting in the passenger seat next to me, still in its bright silver wrapping.

Parker didn't answer last night. I stayed up all night wondering what the hell was going on. Why would he call and send a message like that, but then leave me hanging when I call back?

Is he angry with *me*? Is he mad that I didn't answer when he first called? Was it my only chance, a test? I know I should have answered, but something in my head wouldn't allow it. No, maybe it's part of the counseling he's being forced into. Maybe part of it is to tear out your boyfriend's heart so you don't have to be a fucking fag anymore.

Maybe that's it. That actually would make me feel better. Then it's not just Parker, and it's not me. I might be able to deal with that.

It took me forever to get ready this morning, and as much as I tried to get out the door without speaking to my family, it didn't work. I didn't want them to see me crying and start asking questions, but it didn't happen that way. And surprise, I lied to them. I told them I was just having a hard time, and when Dad asked about the call last night I told him that Parker hung up before I could answer. I failed to mention the text.

I pull into the school parking lot and without thinking about it I scan for Parker's truck. It's second nature. He's not here yet. Good. I don't want to see him right now. No, I want to be as far away as possible.

I'm running behind today, which is so not me. If I wasn't so damn out of it, it would bother me, but I don't really care. Cam even texted me on the way here. She thought I might be sick. That would be so much better.

Finally I find a space and slide out of the car. I don't feel like it, but I quicken my pace. Mr. Beane hates it when you're late for his civil engineering class, and I'm dangerously close to it.

* * *

"I don't think he's here." Cam shrugs across the lunchroom table. "Kesey said he wasn't in second block."

"I don't care," I tell her. My voice is indifferent, *almost* cold.

I'm getting used to looking like a wreck. My hair's all out of whack, and my eyes look bloodshot from not sleeping last night. I swear the whole cafeteria watched me walk the lunch line like some brain-dead zombie. But I don't care. I don't give a flying fuck.

"Come on, Noah," she tells me. "So what happened? I know he texted you, but I never got an update. I thought things were getting better."

I look at her and cock my head to the side. I clench my jaw to keep from saying anything *too* hateful *too* quick. Like

Fuck Parker or *The prick didn't answer*. I throw my eyes to the brick ceiling and manage my breathing. Sure, he ignored me, but I need to calm down. She's right. I shouldn't think like that.

"He didn't answer," is all I say.

"Oh." Her eyes drop to the table.

I slump and force out an angry breath.

"I don't get it. He called. He texted. He even said he loved me still. But I call and what do I get? Nothing. *Nothing!*" Suddenly I'm talking fast and probably louder than I ought. "What's with that? Why would he do that? It doesn't make any sense. It's like he's trying to hurt me. As if dumping me didn't fuck with my heart enough."

"No." Camila grabs my hand and pulls it across the table. "That's not it, it can't be. The Park I know, that *we* know, wouldn't do that."

She's right. The Parker I know wouldn't, but he's been different the last few weeks. But this?

"There has to be something else, right?" she tries.

I shrug. I don't have an answer. I only have questions.

"I just want things back to normal," I tell her.

"Normal?" she huffs. "You mean back before you came out and you two were into each other but wouldn't say it? That was *normal* for all of us."

"You know what I mean," I bite.

She tips back and wobbles her head.

"Noah, I know you're hurting. I get that. But sitting here acting like you're the only one suffering isn't helping," she tells me. I scrunch my brow. This isn't what I was expecting. "You don't know what Park's going through. Neither of us does, except what he's told us, and knowing Park, he probably hasn't told us the half of it. Plus, *I'm* stuck dealing with this shit too. I'm stuck between my two best friends who are having a really, *really* hard time right now. So stop thinking you're the only one with feelings, okay?"

I fall back against my chair. I don't know what to say. *You're right* would probably be a good start, but I hate to admit it.

"Sorry," is all she gets.

She sighs and shakes her head. "We'll figure it out, Noah."

* * *

I love you more than anything. I promise I didn't mean to hurt you. I'm so sorry.

Parker's text keeps scrolling through my head, but I know he didn't mean it. At least that's what I tell myself every time I glance at his empty desk during Spanish.

But maybe Cam's right. Maybe his parents took his phone right after he messaged me. Maybe I waited too long to call him back. But what if that's not what happened? What if it was just a cruel joke? I don't want to think about it anymore. That's all I've done all day. It's like this incessant hellish loop playing over and over in my mind, and I'm powerless to stop it.

Parker dumped me. Maybe it was for the best. Maybe I should just move on. Yeah, all of that sounds great and wonderful, but I know I can't do it.

No. I want to hear his laugh. I want to see him smile. I want to watch him look at the stars and to see the stars in his eyes.

My pocket vibrates and breaks me away from my daydream, or nightmare. I roll my eyes. People really ought to realize I can't answer during school. Things are bad enough, I don't need my phone confiscated, and Ms. Anderson is extra zealous about the school's phone policy.

Could it be Parker though? No. Don't be stupid. It's not Parker.

Apparently the vibration is pretty loud because Cam looks back over her shoulder and grimaces. I shrug, and I let it go to voicemail.

Do I really want it to be Park? I huff quietly. I do. I really do. Damn, how I do.

It starts vibrating again. Really, people?

Ms. Anderson has her back to us, writing on the whiteboard, so I take a chance and slip my phone out just enough to see the screen. Mom? I *know* she knows better.

A text pops up. It's Mom again.

Call me back. Now.

It's cryptic, not to say Mom is always clear in her texts, but still. I don't have a clue, but hey, it's an excuse to get out of class and hopefully get my mind off all this bullshit. I'll take it.

I raise my hand and wait for Ms. Anderson to turn around. It takes a few seconds, but eventually she does, and I ask to be excused. She waves me out the door and says something in Spanish that I don't catch.

Cam frowns at me on my way by, and I raise my shoulders. I don't know either.

In the hallway I dial Mom back. If one of the teachers or principals finds me out here on the phone, they'll probably try to take it, but I assume that Mom telling me to call overrides them, so I've got that going for me. I think.

It rings in my ear, and she picks up before it rings twice.

"Noah." It's almost like she's asking.

"Yeah, Mom?" I ask. This is already weird.

"I need you to come home." There's an edge in her voice. The last time I heard that I had to rush to the hospital. "I need to talk to you."

"What's going on?" I straighten and tighten my grip on the phone. "Is Zach okay?"

"Just come home, okay?" she asks.

"Mom, you're scaring me." My back collides with the wall of lockers and I jump. My body tenses. "I can't just leave. School doesn't end for another hour."

"Yes, you can, I'm telling you that you can right now," she tries, but I need to know what's going on.

"No, just tell me," I demand. I can't drive home wondering like this. I'm already stressed enough.

There's a short silence on the other end. I can barely hear her breathing, and the teacher's voice from the class across the hall slips under the doorway.

"Parker..." she starts but stops. My heart thumps against my chest. Parker what? A muffled cry sifts over the line and chokes me. "Parker overdosed last night. His... Uh... His parents found him this morning."

My mind can't comprehend what she said at first, but then it hits. "But he's okay, right?" I plead.

Overdosed. That doesn't mean the worst.

Suddenly I hate every bad thing I thought about him, every spiteful thing I imagined, every doubt. "Right?"

"Noah," she emphasizes my name. My mind is racing. Why? What hospital is he at? Is he okay? "He didn't make it."

"What?" I barely get the word out.

"I'm so sorry. Come…"

Her voice drifts away as my arm goes slack and my phone smacks the floor. I fall against the lockers. The clang startles me, but I can't focus.

Parker? It can't be. No. He's okay. He can't be gone. No, that's impossible. I saw him yesterday, here at school. He called me last night. He messaged me.

The metal edge of lockers grates into my back as I slide to the floor and I can barely see through the water building in my eyes.

He's gone? No. No. No. He can't be gone. Not Park. Not my Parker.

It's as if I'm in outer space and the oxygen has been sucked from the room. I can't breathe, I'm suffocating. My mouth trembles. I hug my knees to my chest and throw my face into them and cry. I don't care if anyone hears. I don't care what they think. I don't give a damn what anyone thinks. Except Park…

A distant noise, as if from some other world, raps at my ear, but I don't look up. Parker? This can't be happening. It can't, it's impossible. I keep my face down, letting my tears soak my jeans. Then someone grabs my shoulder.

"Noah?" It's Cam. I look up for a second, but I can't hold the weight of my own head, so I let it drop back to my knees. "What's wrong?"

I try to open my mouth, but I can't do it.

"Noah?" She squeezes my shoulder.

"Parker," is all I can say.

* * *

I can't stop crying. I might never stop crying.

Camila is sitting next to me in one of the teacher conference rooms by the main office. When Ms. Anderson realized something was wrong, she brought us here for some privacy.

I didn't thank her. I should have thanked her.

Why? I keep asking myself the same question over and over again. Why would Park do it? I know it's been bad, but he had so much to live for.

No, this is all just a bad dream. It's my mind envisioning pure hell while I snore the night away. That's what it is. I just have to wake up. I have to open my eyes.

"Wake up!" I scream. "Wake up!"

Camila yelps and I scream it again.

"Stop it, Noah." She wraps her arm around me and her wet cheek presses against mine. "There's no waking up."

She struggles to say it, and even though I know she's hurting too, all I can think about is how I feel. It's like someone shoved a knife in my chest and carved out a hole, then reached in and ripped out my heart. It feels so heavy but empty. I didn't realize I could cry this much, but here I am leaning over the table with my face buried in my arms about to drown in my own tears.

He's not coming back from this. I stop sobbing long enough to take in the thought. Parker's dead. He's gone. This is my new reality. A life where Parker is not. A reality where he'll never meet me in the school parking lot again or at our spot in the country. A reality where I'll never get the chance to drive to college with him next to me and suffer through early morning classes together. A reality where I'll never get to wish him another happy birthday or kiss him. A reality where I'm stuck with only the memory of his eyes.

I can't do this. I can't.

Parker, why?

"Why?" I find Camila and beg her for an answer. "Why did he do it?"

"I… I don't know." She shakes her head.

Was his text last night the last he ever sent? Did he do it after that? My eyes widen in shock. Is that why he didn't answer? Have I been angry at him all day because of this?

Oh God, please no.

I clench my fists and squeeze my eyes shut, but I can't stop the wells at the corners of my eyes. They run too deep.

Did he mean to?

"It was an…an accident, right?" I ask.

Camila struggles to answer, but she doesn't have to, I know she doesn't know. But I have to ask.

The door creaks open. It's Mom. She runs to me and I let her wrap her arms around my neck.

"I'm sorry," she cries. "I'm so sorry."

She pulls Camila into our hug. "I'm so sorry. Let's go. We can talk on the way home."

Sunday
February 25, 2019

It's the second worst day of my life.

The last two days have been hell. I may have slept two hours since Friday, and it's Sunday evening. All I can think about when I lie down is that maybe I'll wake up in the morning and everything will be okay, but I know it's a lie. The rest of the time I just stare at the ceiling.

I tried playing a video game to get my mind off it all, but I rarely played without Parker. Even when he wasn't over, we'd play online. So that just made it worse.

Mom and Dad are worried. I think they've come to my room every half hour to check on me since Mom brought me home Friday. I know they mean well, but I'd really like to just be alone.

But we're not at the house now anyway.

I'd usually admire the pink spring blossoms along the highway, but my eyes don't move. Instead I'm fixated on the shades of puffy gray blanketing the sky. I understand them. I'm waiting to burst too. I know it, and I hate it.

I pull at the solid black tie that's squeezing at my neck. It's hard to swallow in this thing. Parker never liked them either. I remember when his Dad went through that phase where he made Park wear ties all the time. Park hated it. He was so glad when that stopped. But here I am in one, plus the white button-up shirt and black dress pants I rarely put on. All for a funeral that we shouldn't be having. Parker's funeral.

It feels so wrong to think of those words so close together. A funeral for Parker. They shouldn't be associated, shouldn't be a thought or even the faintest concept. At least not for a long time, the next seventy years or so. Or was it in sixty years that Parker said we'd actually be old? I can't remember. Dammit. Why can't I remember?

Parker was supposed to be with me forever. Forever!

My thoughts are interrupted when Dad pulls into the church parking lot and finds a spot. I lean across the seat, peering past Zach to look out the other window. I find the steeple. It's the church Parker attended, where his family goes. Is it ironic that Parker's burial place is here, or is it just me? *Stop it, Noah.* Parker wouldn't want me to think that.

I've been wondering how people are going to look at me when I walk in. The ones who know about us, at least. I haven't been in a church since that Christmas service my parents took me to two years ago, but that wasn't here. I should probably go more, but I haven't. This isn't the one I'd choose, though. I don't ever want to see this place again after today.

Dad gets out of the car first. Mom peers back and gives me a put-on smile before opening the door and rounding the car to meet Dad. Zach starts to get out but stops when I don't move. I'm not ready for this. I stare past him through the opposite window, gawking at the church doors. My chest starts to quake. I don't think I can go in there.

I still have this perfect vision of Parker. A vision I don't want to lose. I'm afraid that seeing him there, that walking through those doors, might bring that vision crashing down.

The car door clicks open.

"Noah." Dad leans in and frowns at me. He waves me out.

Zach nods at me with the same sympathetic frown and slides out with his crutches. He knows how I feel.

But I don't move. I close my eyes and focus on breathing. And all the people. There are so many people here, too many. No, there should be more. Parker deserves more.

"Noah, come on, honey." It's Mom this time.

When I don't move she dips down and sits beside me. She puts her palm on my wet cheek and taps her forehead against mine.

"I won't leave you. Come on."

I swallow and nod. She scoots back out the door and I follow. My freshly polished dress boots hit the pavement. I want to throw them back into the car, but I don't. I look up at the steeple again. I haven't prayed in a long time, but I try it anyway.

God, please take care of Parker for me. And tell him I love him.

My eyes drop to the pair of heavy wooden doors. They open and someone I don't know walks out. Mom reaches for my hand, but I shake my head. I hope she knows I'm not trying to be rude or manly. I just need to do this on my own.

The closer I get, the more I want to stop. My heart grows more leaden with each footstep. Those doors are the only thing between the Parker I know and the Parker that isn't. On this side I see a vibrant boy, cute and happy. I can hear his contagious laughter. I see his chestnut-brown eyes and that charming smile that I'd do anything for. The boy I secretly crushed on for years, the boy I loved, the boy who made me feel invincible and who broke my heart and made it whole.

He's behind those doors, but *he's* not. I don't know if I can bear seeing what's left of him, a shell, a memory of who and what he was.

We mount the last stair and Dad opens the door for Mom. She goes in first and Dad waits with the door open for Zach and me. I stop. Inside, people are milling about, talking, some are even smiling. I have to fight against the sliver of anger that rises in my chest. They don't know him like I did. They don't understand — if they did they couldn't smile. They wouldn't dare.

"Noah," Dad says.

I don't acknowledge him. Instead I close my eyes and inhale all of my fears and dreams before walking through the door. Dad wedges through a group of older men and leads us on a winding path until we enter the sanctuary.

It's nothing fancy. I've been here before. Parker invited me to come a few times for special services. It always seemed like a friendly place until now. I look around at the simple setup, but my attention gravitates to the roughly hewn wooden cross hanging on the back wall. Below it is the pulpit, and then, somewhere beyond, is Parker.

A sudden shiver threatens to bring me to my knees.

"Noah." It's a quiet, familiar voice. Cam. I find her standing to my left. Her eyes are bloodshot. She looks like she's slept about as well as me. It hits me how little I've thought about her and her grief, and I feel bad for it. She was his friend too. She *is* my friend.

"Hey." I hug her. I bury my face in her shoulder and let myself cry. I know what I'm about to see and I don't want to.

"Go on." She pulls away and nods toward the front of the

church.

I bob my head and mop the water from my cheeks. She hugs me one more time and disappears into the crowd. I glance behind me. Mom, Dad, and Zach are standing there, waiting. I turn and start toward the pulpit without them.

The first familiar face I see is Hannah, Park's sister. I always thought she looked the most like Parker, just ten years older and female. She has the same dark-brown eyes and facial features. The same squared-off jaw, the small cute nose. Her hair is almost black like his too. Joshua's standing next to her. He's the odd one out. He didn't inherit the dark complexion. Parker always said Joshua took more after his dad with his hard features and lighter skin.

Then there's Mrs. Evans; I think her first name is Connie. I always called her Mrs. Evans, though. It's easy to see that she's the one Parker and Hannah take after...or took after. She's standing in the line, shaking hands along with her children, but she keeps swiping at her face. I don't know how she's doing it, any of them. I don't think I could. I can barely move.

Standing directly beside the casket is Mr. Evans, David. I never thought of him as a mean person, except when he started treating Parker like a second-rate child. And right now as much as I want to hate him, as much as I want to lay every ounce of revulsion I feel on him, I can't do it. He looks broken.

But I still don't think I can talk to him.

My eyes stop on the casket. I freeze, my eyes glued to the cold white box. I can't do this. I can't see him like this.

I start to turn, but Dad pats my arm. I stop. My whole body quakes, and I don't even bother trying to wipe my eyes.

Finally I take a step closer, then another. The closer I get, the more I feel like I'm going to fall, like my legs are ready to give way underneath me. I know I should say something to his parents, but I'm not ready for that. I don't think I could say anything nice if I tried. So I walk past them like I'm wearing blinders and go directly to the casket.

Parker's nose is the first thing I see, his perfect, cute little nose. I slow down. Then his face comes into view, and suddenly I'm standing next to him, wondering how we both got here.

It's Parker. But it's not Parker.

He's paler. There's something unnatural about his skin. His eyes are closed. His eyes. Oh how I wish I could see them again. Just to peer one more time into their dark, warm depths and feel the rush that came every time he stared back. My legs buckle, and I almost fall, but Zach catches me and helps me back up. He pulls at me, but I don't want to leave. I want to stay here, I want to stay with Parker.

I can't leave him. I can't. He needs me, and I need him.

Dad comes up on my left and puts his hand on my shoulder.

"Come on, Noah." I don't think I've ever heard Dad's voice sound so frail.

He tugs and reluctantly I leave Parker all alone at the front of the church. We take a seat near the middle of the sanctuary, and after a few minutes everyone else is seated too, and the service starts. The man behind the pulpit is the same man Parker had to be "counseled" by, his pastor. I want to scream at him, to blame him for the casket he's praying over as if he didn't have a part. But I take a deep breath and lock my eyes on the pew in front of me. I don't hear what anyone says, it's just background noise in my head. Instead, I hear all the words Parker ever said.

I hear him telling me on the day I came out how he would always be my friend no matter what. I hear him encouraging me to tell my parents. I hear him telling me how he first realized he liked me. I hear him tell me he loved me. Then the last words, though never spoken to my ears, flash in my mind over and over again.

I'm so sorry.

It took me until this moment to realize what he meant by them. He was sorry for this. For putting me in this church to watch him eulogized, to watch all I wanted leave me behind, to say goodbye to him before I should have to. He was apologizing for *this*.

Why did you have to do it? Why couldn't you have stayed? Then you would have never had to apologize. But no. Now I'm left to live without you.

The service ends and they close the casket. I want to yell for them to stop, but I don't. Somehow I don't.

Then, as if it wasn't certain already, the deep, unsettling realization that I'll never see Parker again sets in. No. I want him back.

Against my wishes they lift the casket and somehow I follow aimlessly outside. We end up in the tiny church cemetery next to the road. The pastor says a few more words, and again I don't hear any of it. I do hear someone say *amen* and then Parker's family walks up one by one, each placing a single rose on his casket.

I wish I had a rose to give him.

They step away and the coffin begins to lower. Completely numb, I watch it disappear, and with it, all my hopes and dreams.

Wednesday
February 28, 2019

Park's desk is empty. I guess no one felt right taking it. I'm glad. I'm not sure how I would have reacted *had* someone.

No one's looking at me, though, because we're in class. Out in the hall I swear half the people I pass stare. It's not like when I came out, or even the looks they gave Parker and me when they found out we were a thing. No, it's an I'm-sorry-but-I-don't-know-you-enough-to-say-anything type of look. I wish they wouldn't. It doesn't help.

It's hard to explain, but besides the weight dragging my heart to the floor, I'm numb. I've cried so much I'm all out of tears. At least until this morning, until second period. Art. Parker loved art. While I shaded my cityscape, my mind transported back to the days I used to watch Park's hand move so effortlessly along the canvas. The way he made it look so easy, the focus in his eyes.

I couldn't handle it. I had to ask to be excused. Some *adult* I am. I ended up locking myself in a bathroom stall for ten minutes until I got control of myself. I'm getting close to that same feeling right now.

All I can think of is how Parker isn't here. No, he's under the ground. He's buried in a metal vault. He's cold and uncomfortable, cramped and secluded. He's dead. He's fucking dead.

I wrench my eyes from his old desk and focus on my worksheet. It's just words, though. Somewhere deep in my head they mean something, but they don't make any sense now. Spanish was never my strong subject anyway, but I refuse to break down while the class is practicing verb conjugation. So I look to my left.

Cam's at the desk next to me. Usually she sits ahead of me, but she asked Cooper to switch on Monday. She sees me looking and meets my distant gaze. I don't say anything. I know that she's hurting too. But I keep forgetting that, and it sends another punch into my chest. I start to tear up. How can I be so damn selfish?

I'm always so selfish. It's always about what I need, what I want. That's why Parker came out in the first place. I pushed him. I made him do it. I killed him. I fucking killed Parker.

No. You didn't kill him. It was his parents, his pastor, their stubbornness that killed him. But did I have a part? I did, didn't I?

I'm shaking. I pull my eyes from Cam and focus on my desktop. What am I doing? The pressure in my chest is building. I can't hold it back. I start to sniffle. I smack away the tears, but it's no use.

Dammit!

I throw up my hand to be dismissed, but I can't wait. I jump up and rush out without permission. In the hall I stumble, but I manage to keep moving. My cheeks are so hot, and my mind is on fire.

I want to tell Parker's dad to go fuck himself. I want to blame him for everything. I want to tell him how he made Parker do it, it *was* his pain meds that Parker used after all.

I need to let it all go, to ball up on the floor and wail. But I also need to know I didn't have a part. I don't know if I could deal with that.

I just want him back.

Monday
March 11, 2019

"I miss you, Park," I stutter.

His headstone is a slab of gray marble with his full name inscribed at the top and his birthday and…yeah.

Parker Lee Evans
February 2, 2000 to February 22, 2019

I'm not crying like I thought I'd be. I feel like I should, but I haven't cried as much lately. It feels wrong. Shouldn't it always hurt?

"I got my acceptance letter to U of I," I start up again. "I got in. I did it."

Months ago no one could have told me I wouldn't care, but I don't. I wouldn't have gone anyway. Parker and I both got into State, so I was Raleigh bound either way.

Oh, I almost forgot.

"You got into Michigan. You did it. I knew you would," I tell him. Cam told me today at lunch. Apparently Park's mom posted on Facebook that his acceptance letter came in today. She thought that's where he planned to go.

She's wrong though. She didn't know Parker like I did. We had a promise. We were going to State together.

I pause and look at the unnatural rise in the grass below Parker's headstone. Parker would have kept his promise, right? Of course he would have.

"Why, Park?" The tears start up again. I've asked him a hundred times this week. I know it's pointless, but I can't stop asking. "Why? Why didn't you say something? Was it really that hard? Wasn't I enough?"

I kick at the dirt and drop to my knees. I don't care if I stain my jeans. Fuck them, for all I care.

"Didn't you think about me? Didn't you think what this would do to me?" I plead with my hands clenched to my cheeks. "I loved you, Park. I still love you, but you took everything away. Why?!"

Thursday
March 21, 2019

It's getting dark out. I'm still trying to get over the hour we lost last week with Daylight Savings Time. I hate it. It's so useless, sort of like the grief counselor at school they finally let me stop seeing this week.

I take a seat at the kitchen table and start into my micro-waved pizza. I'd usually read a book with my snack, but I don't feel like it. Instead I stare at the wooden knobs capping the top of the dining room chair at the other end of the table. I've got homework to finish, but I'll get to it later.

A knock comes at the door. I wait for Dad to answer it. Mom's in town. I think she went out for groceries. The knock comes again. I huff, wishing they'd just go away or that Dad would hurry. It comes again, and Dad still doesn't answer it. I guess he's busy. Maybe he can't hear it. I sigh and get up.

On second thought, I'm taking the pizza with me. I shove half a slice in my mouth and make for the front door. They knock again.

Damn, they're persistent. I'd have left by now.

I get to the door and my first thought is that it better not be the Jehovah's Witnesses again. I stuff the rest of the pizza in my mouth and swallow a little quicker than I probably ought to. I open the door. Hell, I wish it *was* the Jehovah's Witnesses.

I freeze, staring into the eyes of the man I hate most in this world.

"Noah—" he starts, but I slam the door in Mr. Evans's face.

For a split second a tinge of guilt laces my chest, but it vanishes as quickly as it came. I stretch out my shoulders and turn around. I sigh when I see Dad standing in the living room staring me down. Damn.

I frown, but I refuse to face that man again. Instead, I take off down the hallway. I hear the front door open again and Dad saying something to Mr. Evans as I slam my bedroom door shut. He's probably apologizing for me right now. Apologizing to that monster.

Why is he even here? How does he have the guts to come to *my* house after all of this? I don't want to see him. He should be in the grave, not Park.

A few minutes later Dad knocks on my door.

"I'm not here!" I yell, but he comes in anyway.

"Noah," he starts. "I know you don't want to, but you've got to come out. Mr. Evans wants to talk to you."

"I don't want to talk to him," I state clearly and plant my ass on the bed, folding my arms. "He's the reason Parker's dead, Dad. It's *his* fault."

"Don't say that." Dad raises his voice just enough and shuts my door behind him. He sits next to me and puts a hand on my shoulder. "No parent wants to lose a child. No parent. I'm sure David was only doing what he thought best. It doesn't matter what we think, you can't put that on him."

"Why not?" I ask.

"Noah." Dad's sterner this time.

I lock my eyes on a pair of socks lying on the floor next to my feet and fight back the lump in my throat.

"So was it my fault?" I ask. If it wasn't Mr. Evans's fault, then it must have been mine, right? But I'm not the one who left their extra pain meds where Parker could get them. I'm not the one who made Park feel like he was less than human or that he was a second-rate son.

"Noah, stop. You have to stop this blame game. It's not healthy." Dad wraps his arm around me and hugs me. "We've talked about this. You can't do that to yourself, and you can't do it to others either. But you need to come out and talk to Mr. Evans. You know it can't have been easy for him to come here. What he has to say might surprise you."

I look at Dad. I'm confused. "What? What could *he* have to say that I want to hear?"

"Just come to the living room, okay?"

"I don't want to talk to him," I beg.

"Noah, come on. Let's go." He's not asking this time.

Dad gets up, and for a second I contemplate being stubborn and refusing to move, but I don't have the energy in me. I huff to let him know I'm not happy about it, but I follow him into the hallway anyway.

So many things run through my mind. I want to tell Mr. Evans that it's all his fault. I want to tell him that his outdated mentality killed Parker, that Parker was almost happy before coming out, and he ruined everything. But when I turn into the living room, I know I can't do it.

He's crying. Mr. Evans is crying in my living room. It's actually hard to look at him, like at the funeral. I don't ever remember him being a hard man, but it just seems wrong to see him cry. I let my eyes bore angrily into him for a fleeting second before shying away. I take a seat in the chair across the room, as far away as I can manage.

Dad nods at me, and I skew my face to show him how much I don't like this. He sighs and nods at Mr. Evans before walking away.

"I'll be in the kitchen if you need me," he says.

"But—" I try to protest, but he puts up a hand and vanishes.

I lock my eyes on the blank TV screen. Neither of us says a word, and I begin to wonder why I'm sitting here. Why is he here? Does he want to rub it in my face, lay the blame on me? What if he's right?

"I, uh... I'm sorry, Noah." These are not the words I expect to hear from his gruff voice, but it's what comes out. "I know you don't care for me, but I wanted to tell you I'm sorry."

I sidle back. I wasn't ready for this, and I'm not sure how to process it.

He reaches in his pocket and pulls out a wrinkled envelope. He fidgets with it, passing it between his hands.

"I really am, Noah." He looks away and sobs. "I don't understand what you two had. I, uh... You know I didn't agree. But...that doesn't matter now. What I'm trying to say is I shouldn't have treated you like I did. I shouldn't have treated Parker like I did. I was only doing what I thought was best, I swear. If I'd known this would happen... That he'd..."

Mr. Evans drops his face into his hand and bawls. I'm crying too now. I want to be mad at him, but I can't right now. I can't do it. No, instead, I'm crying *with* him.

"If I'd known, I would've done things differently. I was too hard. I was scared," he goes on. "I didn't know what else to do. I was scared for Parker. You know that, right?"

I refuse to answer. I don't care if he thought he was right, it wasn't. But I can't meet his question with anger, I can't even glare at him.

"Please understand, Noah, I loved Parker more than life itself." His eyes move from the envelope in his hands to me, and then back again. "I should have just loved him. And you. You too. And I'm sorry that I didn't know how to do that. I'm not saying any of this was right, but how I dealt with it wasn't right either. Would you forgive me for that, Noah?"

"I..." I can't say the words, but somehow the heat in my body is suddenly gone. Instead, I feel sorry for him. I don't think I can forgive him, though. I just can't.

"You don't have to say anything." He shakes his head. He lifts the envelope and traces every inch of it with his eyes. "Parker left two letters that day."

My eyes go wide, and I lock onto the envelope. I was told there was only one. But right in front of me, in Mr. Evans's hand, is another piece of the boy I love.

"He wrote one for us, for the world, I guess, and then one for you." A rush of fear and longing pulses through my heart when he says it.

For me?

Mr. Evans lets the letter bob in the air. "This is your letter, Noah. At first I wasn't going to give it to you. I was angry at you, I blamed you, if I'm honest, but that was wrong of me. Parker wanted you to have it."

He gets up and approaches me. I'm not sure I want it now, but at the same time it's all I want. To hold another piece of Parker, to have it, to read it. I get up. Mr. Evans holds it out for me. A moment passes and I'm paralyzed staring at the simple white paper with something scribbled on the front. Finally I take it.

The scribbling is my name in Parker's familiar script. I'm shocked when Mr. Evans leans in and hugs me. I don't fight it. When he lets go he sighs and starts to walk off, but at the door he turns around.

"I didn't open the letter. It didn't feel right to break Parker's trust like that," he tells me. His eyes fall to the floor thoughtfully, like he's weighing his next words. "Our letter was about what we did wrong. I hope yours is about what you did right."

* * *

When Mr. Evans leaves, I'm left frozen in the hallway with the envelope shaking in my hands. Another piece of Parker. But is it a piece I can deal with?

"How'd it go?" Dad comes up behind me.

I jump. I didn't hear him enter the room. Turning, I refuse to take my eyes from my name written on the envelope.

I don't know what to say. I start to open my mouth, but nothing comes out. Then I picture Mr. Evans's face again. The torment in his eyes. The lack of composure I've never seen before.

"He said he was sorry," I tell Dad. I'm numb, so it comes out without cadence. I gulp back the anxiety in my throat. "He apologized."

"And?" Dad eyes me expectantly.

"I… Uh…" Here's where I'm supposed to say I forgave him, but I didn't. I couldn't.

Dad doesn't push it. He comes over and hugs me for a

long moment. I hear him sniffle and I wonder if he's thinking about what it would be like to lose me. I wouldn't do that to him, and I wouldn't have done that to Parker either.

I bite back a seed of bitterness. But it's not right to hold onto this feeling, even if Parker's decision was selfish. I was selfish too.

When Dad lets go, I give him a blue smile and take off to my bedroom. I close the door behind me. I aim to read this letter and I don't want anyone else seeing it.

I crawl on the bed and plop down atop my pillow. The envelope is coarse under my fingertips, and for a minute I just sit and feel it, weighing it in my hands. I don't know why. I just do.

My eyes trace my name. It's been a month since he left me, almost a month to the day. I wonder if my name was the last thing he wrote. My chin trembles and I bury my face in my pillow. I let it pour.

Parker's last words to me are in this tiny envelope. The last piece of his mind, of his personality, his heart. The last unknown. All of it sealed away, waiting for me. I want desperately to know what it says, but Mr. Evans's words haunt me.

Our letter was about what we did wrong. I hope yours is about what you did right.

I pull myself together and fondle the edge of the paper. To open or not to open, that is the question, to quote Hamlet loosely. Hell, even the *Whether 'tis nobler in the mind to suffer / The slings and arrows of outrageous fortune* part rings true now, even if it might be a little out of context. Am I going to suffer even more if I open it, if I read it?

Fuck it. I rip the edge but stop short of tearing it open. I can't. I just can't do it. What if this is Park's last condemnation of me? What if it's his final breakup? What if it's about how selfish I was?

But I was. I am. Maybe I deserve it. I'm so *fucking* selfish.

Why couldn't I just be patient? Why couldn't I have given him the time and space he needed? Why couldn't I let him work it out on his own terms? I told myself it was his choice, that he was ready, but how many times did I bring it up? How many times did I tell him I wanted him to come out without actually saying it? He wasn't stupid. He knew what I meant.

Am I more to blame than his parents? No. I can't be. I didn't push him down. I didn't force him to try to be something he wasn't. I freed him, right?

Oh my God! But I put him in that situation before he was ready. My stomach drops through the bed. I feel dizzy. I throw the letter on the nightstand and bury my face in my sheets.

Let the tears come. Let the pain come. Let the weight come.

I killed him.

Friday
March 22, 2019

I've laid here staring at the ceiling for ten minutes.

I should be in the shower, but all I can think about is the letter next to my bed. I'm *going* to be late for school, but to hell with it. Mr. Beane can deal with it.

It's calling to me, like the ring that drew Frodo to the Eye of Sauron.

No, just ignore it. I get up and take a shower, hoping to get my mind off that simple but all-consuming piece of paper, but it only gives me more time to dwell on the perfect script forming my name. What does it say? Did he hate me?

I towel off and throw on the briefs I left draped over the sink. On my way back something red and blue catches my eye. It's been there for months, but somehow I'm only now seeing it. I reach down and pick up the Spider-Man suit Parker wore for Halloween. I stare at it for a long minute. He left it at my house because he knew I'd be more likely to wear it again than he would.

I'll never put it on again. Not this one.

I touch the slick fabric to my nose and inhale. I close my eyes and let the faint scent of Parker Lee Evans run through my nostrils. Musky and minty.

I start to cry.

"Why?" I throw myself to the bed and cover my face

with his suit.

Like a movie, I see our first, and only, Halloween together as a couple. I see him smiling at the front door. I see him walking into my room and twirling around to show me how the costume looked on him. He's smiling. He'll never do that again.

I blink, and my eyes are filled with the party that night. The short, awkward dance we shared. Park dancing under the orange lights like he didn't have a care in the world. I actually laugh.

Then I hear Carter call me a fag and Parker picking a fight in my defense. I see his bloodied but forever beautiful face. I feel the sensation of kissing him upside down in his truck after Cam left, because that's what Spider-Man does.

Kissing him... I want to kiss him again.

I roll onto my back. Why does everything remind me of him? This costume. Every video game I play. Every class at school. Each desk he sat in. The foods he liked best in the cafeteria. Five Guys. Every time I send an email. The painting next to my TV that even Michelangelo could never top. Everything.

I force myself to get up and lock my eyes on the painting, my birthday gift. It's the essence of everything I want to remember about us. I pick it up and imagine the stars shimmering over us and the brisk air on our skin. The way the cold dissipated when we touched and nothing else mattered, how perfect it was. That's how I have to remember him. That's my Parker. Forever.

I go back to my bed and find the letter still by my bedside. I wish it would disappear. I can't do it.

Saturday
March 23, 2019

I'm getting a late start today.

I didn't set my alarm last night. It's Saturday and I'm not scheduled at work until four. It's not like I was going to sleep that late.

I think it's eleven or something. The sun's up. A flutter of chirping outside the kitchen window announces it's spring. But my heart is still trapped in a bitter cold winter after a chilly autumn.

I take a few cookies from the plastic cookie jar and head back to my room. Breakfast of champions. Right.

I keep seeing Mr. Evans's face flash before my eyes. I can't shake the torment in his face, the anguish. I couldn't place it before, but now I know why it hit me so hard. It was like looking into a mirror, except I hated what I saw. I remember him apologizing and me just staring at him. Should I have forgiven him? But how? How could I forgive him for taking Park from me?

Because *I* took Parker from me…

I shake it away and take a seat at the foot of my bed. The plan is to play some games and then go see Cam before work, but when I switch on the PlayStation I freeze. Staring at the screen, I remember watching Parker play *Mass Effect* and *Assassin's Creed*. I remember his smile. I remember lying next to him, sure to keep my distance before he knew, and only glancing at him when I felt he wasn't paying me any attention. I memorized every line of his face that way. His nose, his cheeks, the light lines in his forehead, his deep-brown eyes, long eyelashes, the slope of his lips.

Now I wish I could get it all out of my head.

No, I don't mean that. That would be hell. Damn. To think one day I might forget any tiny detail about Park cuts at my heart. He deserves to be remembered forever.

I huff and fall back on my bed. I roll over and cradle my arms under my chest, but I freeze. Staring back on my nightstand is Parker's letter.

It's been sitting there for two nights, and every time I see it I want to open it, but I just can't do it. For what has to be the fiftieth time, I pick it up. My pulse quickens, and I can feel my face grow hot with fear. I want to know what it says, but maybe it's better to leave it alone, unopened, as a constant reminder of the love I had. *Had...*

I swipe at a tear, and put letter back. If I open it, will I lose that love? If it remains sealed I can hold on to Parker forever, but will I always question what he wanted to tell me? But what if I open it and find he didn't share my affection, that something changed? I can't lose that.

I stare at the envelope for a long minute. Every second eats at me, etching a scar on my heart until I can't bear it any longer. I curse under my breath and swipe the letter from its perch.

I pull myself to the head of the bed and sit up. The letter in my hands, I lock my gaze on it.

"Just do it already," I say and rip it open before I can think twice about it.

It's folded. I close my eyes and exhale. Mr. Evans's words play through my head again unbidden.

Our letter was about what we did wrong. I hope yours is about what you did right.

Did I do anything right? Please say I did.

I unfold the paper and open my eyes. It's handwritten.

Noah,

I'm not sure when you'll get this, but when you do it means I'm no longer here. I never wanted it to be like this. I never wanted to hurt you, ever! I mean that. It might be hard to understand, but I never wanted to hurt you. I know this letter probably won't really help, but I need to write it anyway.

I love you Noah. That didn't change. Not once.

When we broke up it wasn't because of you. I only meant for it to be temporary. I'd hoped this would all pass and I could ask you to forgive me. But things changed. They just kept getting worse.

I don't know what else to do. I'm not good enough for my family. The "therapy" is driving me crazy. Not being able to see you is killing me. No one says it, but I know my family thinks I'm worthless, an abomination, because of something I can't change. And there's that damned camp that's supposed to "fix" me. But there's nothing to fix. Is there?

Yeah, I'm broken. I know it more than most, but not like they think. I'm broken because all I want is to be loved for who I am. I want my family to understand me, but they can't. They won't.

I feel like this horrible thing, this blot on everyone's perfect little record of normality. I don't care if they say they love me. They don't. At first I didn't think it mattered. I keep telling myself that it doesn't, but it does to me.

Before I go though, I need to tell you something I don't think I ever have. I sort of lied when I told you Spider-Man was my "sexual" awakening. No, it was you. You were that crush.

I remember when I transferred into your class in middle school, I knew I "shouldn't," but I couldn't stop looking at you. You were the most gorgeous thing I'd ever seen, and you still are. It seemed really weird back then. It even scared me, but it never changed. Never.

Did you know I actually planned to play the trumpet in the school band in seventh grade? I don't think I ever told you that either. I should have when it mattered. No, I took art instead because I knew you were in art. I wanted an excuse to talk to you. You're why I love to paint.

Hell, you've been my everything since I really cared about anyone, Noah. I just couldn't tell you until recently. I wish I had sooner. I wish I was as brave as you. I wish I was stronger, but I'm not. I can't do this.

I know this isn't what you want. It's not what I want either. That probably doesn't make any sense, but it's best. This way I can't hurt you anymore, and I don't have to deal with all the shit anymore.

I'm sorry, Noah. You were everything I woke up for each morning, what I breathed for, the one thing that got me this far. I love you Noah, and I always will.

With all the love I have left,
Parker

* * *

I probably shouldn't be driving.

I rub my arm across my face to clear my vision. The tears haven't stopped since I opened the letter. The same one that's sitting in my passenger seat right now.

I'm anxious, heartbroken, scared, angry, and actually a little happy. It's the weirdest sensation. I'm everything at once, and I'm not sure how to take it all in.

Pulling into the church parking lot I take the spot closest to the little cemetery. I grip the steering wheel and inhale. I need to talk to him, but I don't know what I'm going to say. I just *need* to talk to him.

A minute passes and I'm still planted behind the steering wheel, staring at the field of headstones. He's out there, crowded between people he doesn't know and shouldn't be with, but all alone at the same time. I finally get out and start down the lawn. I wind through the markers and flowers until I find the place they buried my heart.

Parker Lee Evans.

My chin trembles, and I let the tears drain over my cheeks and soak my shirt. I drop to my knees.

"Park." It barely comes out.

Why? How? I spread my hand on the ground. How can you be down there?

"Your dad came by the house the other day." I look away, then find the headstone again. I imagine Parker's brown eyes as I talk. "He said he was sorry. He wishes he would have done things differently. I wish *I* would have done things differently."

I clamp my eyes shut and bawl. My body quakes. It hurts. It actually hurts.

"He gave me the letter." And I break down again. I don't know what to say, but finally I try.

"I don't understand, Park. If you loved me, why did you leave me? Why was *this* the answer?" I'm almost yelling. The heat rises in my cheeks, and an anger inside me rears its head. "Was I not enough? I loved you. I *love* you! And you *did* hurt me. You hurt me more than just being apart. You took *everything* from me. *Everything!*"

I ball my hands into fists and pull up a patch of grass. My heart is breaking open like a spewing volcano and its magma burns at my chest. I want to scream, to yell at him, at everything around me, to expel this pain.

Stop it, Noah. I shake my head and work to purge the anger in my chest, but it won't leave.

"I miss you so much, Park. I miss seeing you before school. I miss our nights under the stars. I miss the taste of your lips and looking into your eyes. I miss you so bad, Park.

"But I'm angry with you for leaving me. For abandoning *our* plans. For not talking to me. For not telling me what you were thinking of doing. All you had to do was say something. Anything. But you didn't."

I throw my eyes away from the headstone and peer at the crystal-clear blue sky. Why didn't you say something? I exhale and settle my eyes back on Park's name.

"I know I was selfish. I pushed you. I shouldn't have, and for that I apologize. I'll apologize until the day I die, Park, but I would have done anything to help you. Didn't you know that?"

I throw my eyes back to the sky. How can it be so bright and calm? How can it be everything I can't be? It's not fair. It's not fucking fair!

Everyone says one day I won't cry over Park, that I'll look back on him as nothing more than a memory. Fuck them. He's a mark on my soul, and I'll always remember him, I'll always be broken over him. Anything less would be wrong.

"I... I don't know if... Dammit, Parker... I don't know if I can do this without you."

Why did you have to leave me?

"I need you so much. Why couldn't you see that?"

I struggle for the words to say. I feel like there should be more, something better, something more profound, something worthier of Parker. Then a quote comes to mind. Parker always found my quotes interesting, or at least he dealt with them.

"I've never been that great with words, Park. I think you knew that. Maybe that's why I always quote others. That's not the point, though. Here's another one for you. It's from Thornton Wilder. I'm not really even sure who that is, but I think it says everything I want to. He said, and I quote, 'My only hope is that even for a moment I helped you see the world a little bit different.' I hope I helped you see the world a little bit different, Park. Even just a little bit."

I close my eyes and sniffle.

"Park, I'm going to leave now. I still don't understand, and maybe I never will, but I want you to know that I love you and I'll never forget you." I pause and get to my feet. I'm about to turn, but I stop and let my eyes roll down the headstone and over the grass that keeps us apart.

"I *need* you to know that you were loved, Park. You'll always be mine, and I'll always be yours."

Don't Give Up!

If you need someone to talk to, please contact one of the organizations below before making a decision that could bring harm to yourself. Remember you're not alone, even when it feels like it, and there is always someone who cares about you. We love you and need you to carry on your story, and be the inspiration someone else needs to keep living.

Trevor Project Lifeline
1-866-488-7386
www.trevorproject.org

National Suicide Prevention Lifeline
1-800-273-8255
www.suicidepreventionlifeline.org

Crisis Text Line
Text HOME to 741-741
www.crisistextline.org

ABOUT THE AUTHOR

Jordon Greene is the Amazon bestselling horror author of *The Reserve* & *To Watch You Bleed*. He is a full stack web developer for the nation's largest privately owned shoe retail company and a graduate of the University of North Carolina at Charlotte. Jordon spends his spare time writing, attempting to sing along with his favorite bands and playing Overwatch. He lives in Concord, NC.

Visit Jordon Online
www.JordonGreene.com

If you enjoyed this story,
please consider reviewing it online at retailers like Amazon
and recommending it to friends and family.

CPSIA information can be obtained
at www.ICGtesting.com
Printed in the USA
LVHW111453290421
685986LV00001B/117